Blue Rose Petals

John S. Hofmann

© 2017 John S. Hofmann
All rights reserved.

ISBN: 1978396589
ISBN 13: 9781978396586

Dedication

*In the final book in the series of three, I owe so much to my daughter, Michelle, and wife, Elaine. They were extremely helpful in putting together this book.
Without the hours contributed by good friends Jeri Soltis and Collette Beauchamp, I would have found it much more difficult in having this book put into print.
I wish to thank each and every one of them for sacrificing their valuable time in helping me to complete this book. Not only did all of them encourage me with it, they were there for me when I had questions concerning this manuscript.*

Table of Contents

The Unexpected	1
Adult Party	13
Decisions	28
Tinkle-Tinkle	55
The World as a Gift	62
Celebration	74
Dinner Meeting	84
Pink Sky	95
Emotionally Spent	118
Haunted by the Past	153
Secrets	185
Horrible Mistake	211
Mary	241
New Beginning	247
Blue Rose Petals	261
Written in Stone	271
Oh My God	278
Holiday Decisions	307
Christmas Program	319

The Unexpected

Amazed with the news they had just received, Henry and his wife, Kate, sat quietly in the front seat of their car outside the attorney's office. Neither one said anything, both of their heads completely filled with an array of different thoughts dancing through their minds. Any concerns they had held financially could now be taken care of easily. They disappeared like a balloon escaping a child's grasp as it sought the freedom of the open sky. Expecting Mr. Eddington, the lawyer, to give them the billing amounts for Emma's hospital stay and funeral, they instead were informed of a very large inheritance they would be receiving. It was not only unexpected, they were shocked by the very information.

At one point during their meeting Kate had offered her wedding ring to be sold to help defray the expenses they would be facing. She had gone so far as to remove it from her finger, placing it into the attorney's hand. Eric took the ring and set it down on his desk. Shortly thereafter he stopped listing the expenses and instructed Henry to return the ring to its rightful place. Henry placed the ring onto Kate's ring finger. Eric now continued reading the will, the portion concerning both of them. It was then they learned of Emma's unforeseen gift to them.

Emma was not Henry's mother, a fact that many learned for the first time at her funeral. She was the surrogate mother who offered him the love he so dearly craved. He, however, acted very much the part of her son. Emma had no family whatsoever since the loss of her husband, Paul. She was alone. There now was no one to watch over her. Henry gladly filled that void, always keeping a watchful eye out for her wellbeing. Together they thrived as a makeshift family unit, both finding comfort in one another's love.

Henry reached over and started the vehicle. As he pulled out onto the roadway in Creek Side, the small town they called home, neither one said anything to the other. At the second corner he made a left-hand turn, which led to the city park. A wide creek sat before them as he pulled the car into a parking space. He then got out and walked around the car opening the door for Kate. Together they traversed the short distance to a picnic table taking a seat, one on each side of it. Still in silence the two just sat there watching the water flowing by as it made its way downstream towards the center of town.

"Henry, what Emma gave us is truly unbelievable. I find it hard to conceive she had so much money tucked away."

"Well," Henry answered, "from what I understand her late husband was a very wise man when it came to financial matters. I don't think Emma even knew how much he had invested over the years. At least he knew she would be financially secure."

"The amount is staggering," Kate said. "When Eric said we inherited three million eight hundred thousand dollars I was totally shocked. He even said his figures were probably on the low side. Then when he informed us Emma and he set it up so the taxes wouldn't eat it all up, I was amazed."

Kate paused in her thoughts to her husband. She reached down with her right hand and rubbed her thumb across the diamond ring. Looking at Henry she smiled softly as she continued expressing her inner feelings.

"The one thing that makes me the happiest in my heart is not the money, it's that I can keep the ring Emma gave me, and I cherish as my wedding ring."

Henry smiled with Kate's comment as he thought about the fact that the money really meant very little to her. Her wedding ring was the item she loved more than anything, and what it represented. He now knew that very well. Still, it was her actions that demonstrated it most vividly to him. Offering her precious keepsake to settle bills spoke volumes to Henry's heart about the woman he loved so dearly and adored.

"Henry —"

"Yes."

"— we have to make sure this money doesn't change us in any way, how we look at life, our friends, everything. Maybe we can even keep that fact hidden... I don't know. We have to keep our lives the same no matter what. I know we should buy another house, ours is just too small, but that's not what I'm talking about. Henry, we've got to try."

Henry nodded his head in agreement. "I understand exactly what you mean. That very thought ran through my mind in the attorney's office when I heard the figure. Of course, there are some things we can indulge in."

"Like a new car?"

"And get rid of, 'old faithful,' not on your life. I've had that car for many years; she's a part of me, almost like family. I was thinking along the line of getting a new refrigerator, maybe even a stove."

Kate laughed. She knew he was on the same page as her, and that comforted her in many ways. She reached across the table as Henry made the same motion with his hand. Together they held hands as they enjoyed the tranquility surrounding them. A warm breeze kept them company. Henry was glad he had chosen this place to sit and reflect over what had just transpired in their lives together.

Henry and Kate knew their daughter was at home with the babysitter, so the passage of time was not of any concern to either one of them. They now possessed freedom from the hands on the clock's face to be together, a time to collect their thoughts. The decisions facing them now, spending of any money, had to be thought through with care and deliberation. Simple questions along that line would not be as forthcoming to them as it was in naming their daughter. That was a simple decision to make. Her full name came easily to them with her birth. Emma Elizabeth had been named after the two women each held most dearly in their hearts. Elizabeth was Kate's mother's name, while Emma represented to Henry a loving mother figure. It just seemed to dovetail with the desires of their hearts, as well as having a nice sound to it, Emma Elizabeth Morgan.

Kate and Henry always referred to their daughter in that way. They never called her Emma or simply Elizabeth, her middle name, as some people do with their children. If by chance anyone called her Emma, they were quick to correct them. Neither Kate nor Henry wanted her name to be said without the other. Whenever hearing their daughter's name spoken it brought forth cherished memories of the two women they held so closely in their daily thoughts.

"I wonder how long it will take Eric to find out anything concerning the little girl, Mary?" Kate said in a thoughtful voice. Turning her head towards Henry as she spoke, "I think Eric was a little surprised when we brought the subject up to him about her."

"With you giving birth not that long ago, I don't think anyone would conceive of the idea that we wanted another child in our lives, and especially this quickly."

Kate nodded. She then continued with her thoughts. "He said he was going to hire an investigator to track her down. That should really make a difference. They know which streets to look down, what corners to take a peek around."

"That's what they do for a living," Henry said.

"Time will tell. We'll just have to wait and see where this all ends up."

Henry looked over at Kate, her hair moving slowly back and forth in the breeze. She reached up with her hand and pulled a few strands back into place. How lucky I am to have such a wonderful person as my wife, he thought as he watched her hand make the simple movement.

Henry's attention was drawn to the creek again. Once in a while his eyes caught sight of a leaf or twig floating in the water. As they peacefully meandered by, his mind went back to the day he played Santa for the Children's Christmas Program in the church basement. The party had been put together for underprivileged children from different communities. He had been convinced to play the legendary holiday character, Santa, though he had considerable misgivings about doing so. Henry recalled how he tried to hide the large scar above his eye from the children with the hat he wore. The last thing he wanted to do was to scare the children with his ugly wound, something he had received as a youngster while protecting another student from bullies. He knew his beard and long hair would help him to disguise that fact from their eyes. It was why he grew the beard in the first place, and allowed the hair on his head to reach the length it had. In conjunction they acted as a mask to help camouflage what Henry felt was his hideous facial feature.

He recalled vividly how a little girl named Mary sat on his lap, the last in the group of children to do so. He looked down at her as his heart began to break. Her face reflected a burn, it being very evident on her cheek. Seeing it made his mind quickly reflect upon his own scar. That night Mary would come to help Henry understand one of life's questions he held hidden deeply in his soul. Many was the day he wished to have that very question answered, "Why me?" It was, however, the very same question Mary posed to Henry that turned his life around that wintery evening. As she sat on his lap Mary explained to him how she lost her family the previous Christmas. Her question to Santa was simple and to the point.

"Santa," she asked in a soft childish sounding voice, "a fire took my mommy and daddy away at Christmastime. It was the tree, and I got burned. Why did that happen to us?" To the best of his ability Henry attempted to answer her question. At one point he even placed her hand onto his scar as he lifted his hat so she could observe his own disfigurement. He explained that bad things happen to everyone, even Santa. They each found within the other the answer to their question. Bad things happen to everyone, you just have to go on.

Kate also found her mind wondering, remembering certain things that had happened in her life concerning the child. Perhaps it was the peacefulness of the surroundings that brought forth numerous thoughts to each of them as they sat at the picnic table.

Her mind revisited the evening when Henry shared with her his thoughts concerning the child. She recalled him sobbing in the pastor's office afterwards as he explained to her how the child's words comforted him through the anguish he had been suffering with for so many years. In the deepest part of Kate's heart she could see more than she had in quite some time. She understood it all. If they could find Mary, Kate was all for it. She would support him wholeheartedly in this endeavor. Yes, Kate knew he was thankful to have her at his side, as she was every bit as grateful for him. Mary, this small child relieved the pain he felt from the scar, she knew and understood that very well. That was all she needed to know. Kate's heart felt there was no question about it, they would not stop until their search was successful. It was an undertaking she recognized had to be accomplished. Together they would act as one, a team effort. Mary needed a new family, and they both wanted her to be a part of theirs.

From a short distance down the creek, the couple could hear the sound of voices laughing. They came from youngsters playing along the shoreline by a large tree. Some of its branches reached partially across a portion of the creek. A three-stranded rope had been attached to a large limb, which the kids were putting to good use. They took turns swinging out over the creek, releasing their grip and then plunging into the cool water. Some would only release their grasp at the height of the swing, attempting to flip through the air in a somersault before landing in a big splash. It was evident to both of them as they watched the kids playing, each one was trying to outdo the other. The couple smiled as they watched. They laughed at some of the various attempts the kids made in striving to be more creative than their counterparts.

The two relaxed in the atmosphere that surrounded them. Occasionally their voices turned to what future plans they had to make, perhaps contacting a real estate agent. Neither one of them was in any hurry to take that next step. That would come soon enough. They were, however, too wound up in the serenity of their surroundings to worry about such things now.

As each day turned into another, Kate frequently touched base with Melissa, her dearest childhood friend. While growing up they were almost inseparable. Sometimes the parents referred to them by the nickname, "AT," which simply meant, "always together." This simple nickname developed quickly from the parents' inquiries to each other. "Do you know where they're at?" It turned out eventually that it was easier to just say "AT" with the other set of parents just shrugging their shoulders or pointing in a certain direction. This close relationship between the two girls flourished throughout the years, getting only closer as time went by.

It wasn't always the proverbial bed of roses between them, they had their share of spats, disagreements. But those seemed to disappear quickly between them; and were soon forgotten. After all, they were typical kids growing up together. The grownups could see they were much like two magnets, drawn together as friends by unforeseen forces. Both sets of parents encouraged their friendship to blossom, feeling it would last for years. They were not disappointed in that assumption with the passage of time.

When Melissa married Greg, it was Kate who stood at her side, just as it was for Kate at her own wedding to Henry. Melissa was Kate's matron of honor as well. Both women were proud to be the loving shadow that filled the honored spot at the other's wedding. Neither would have wanted it any other way.

Kate decided to give Melissa a call since it had been a few days since they had last spoken.

"How are you doing today?" were Kate's first words to Melissa.

"I was a little nauseous this morning, but I guess that's to be expected."

"Are you sure it wasn't your cooking," Kate said in a teasing voice.

"It could be," Melissa answered, "Greg made the breakfast this morning."

"I just wanted to see how you were doing."

"Well, I expect I'll have good and bad days to look forward to," Melissa said in a matter of fact voice.

"If you need anything, anything at all you call me."

"I will."

"In fact, I was thinking of coming over this morning for a visit."

"That would be wonderful, Kate."

"You don't have any other plans then?"

"No."

"Great."

"You are bringing Emma Elizabeth; right?"

"I was planning on it."

"Good. We can have lunch together."

"Do you think your mother can make it?" Kate asked, "I would really enjoy seeing her, too."

"I'll give her a call. I know she'd love to see the baby."

"I'm looking forward to it. I'll probably leave within a few minutes. See you when I get there."

"Okay."

The three women sat at the restaurant table, Emma Elizabeth resting in her baby carrier on a chair. Her eyes were closed as she slept oblivious to her surroundings. Melissa and Susan, her mother, had exchanged the usual niceties common when women meet together with a baby being present. In this case, however, while their words were to the point, they carried a truthfulness surrounding their comments. The baby was a beautiful child who took after her mother's own good looks, something Henry was always thankful for. Many a time he commented about that fact, though Kate would dispute that concept with him.

"Does she sleep through the night now?" inquired Susan.

"Almost all the time," Kate said with pride. "If she does awaken during the night, Henry will sing a little lullaby to her and it's right back to beddy-bye."

"I love hearing your technical baby terms," Susan said as she laughed. "It's been many years since I've used a word or phrase such as that."

"If our baby wakes up in the middle of the night," Melissa said as she rubbed her stomach slightly, "Greg will be useless singing any kind of a lullaby."

"And why is that?" Kate asked.

"He's got the singing voice of a bullfrog with a sore throat."

The women laughed together as the waitress approached them for their orders. After she left, Susan looked over at Melissa and smiled.

"Ribbit-ribbit," she said.

Once again the women chuckled.

"Speaking of lullabies and such," Kate said, "I don't know if either of you know this or not, but Henry is in the process of recording a CD of various songs for children. I guess they're all lullabies, not really older children songs."

"Sounds like a good gift for someone to receive," Melissa stated as she looked in her mother's direction. Her statement was followed by a little wink.

"I guess I better remember that," Susan said nodding her head as she spoke. "Oh, by the way, Kate, did you get the invitation to the adult party?"

"I sure did, and I hope we can make it."

"I hope you can, too," Melissa said as her voice reflected a bit of disappointment in its tone. "It really wouldn't be the same without you and Henry there."

"We'll do our best," Kate said as she reached over replacing the pacifier that had slipped from Emma Elizabeth's mouth. "I haven't had a chance to talk to Henry about it. We just got the invitation, but if it's at all possible, we'll be there."

"I hope so," Melissa expressed.

"An adult baby shower, who would have ever thought of that," Kate said smiling, "with men being invited and all."

"It's not really a baby shower," Susan said, "it's just a party to celebrate Melissa's pregnancy. There aren't going to be any gifts given or expected. We did make sure of that in the invitation."

"I noticed that," Kate stated.

"The four of us parents should have done it long ago," Susan said, "it's just that we all procrastinated too long in getting it done and planned."

"And here we are," Melissa said as she rubbed her slightly swollen stomach.

"You're getting closer with every passing day," Kate stated, her voice having a small chuckle attached to it.

"Quicker than I thought, I mean, the time has just been flying by. I still have quite a ways to go, actually quite a few additional months."

"That's how it was for me," Kate relayed. "One minute it was ice cream and pickles, the next thing I was just happy it was all over with. Of course, with Emma in the hospital at the same time, Henry worried sick over his mother, there really wasn't time to think about anything else. You two will never know how much it meant to me that you were both at our home when I went into labor. With Henry not home, I appreciated all that you two did for me."

"Kate, I got the baby blanket that very morning from Robin," Melissa's excited voice proclaimed. "She's the one who made it. Her husband, Fred, brought it into work when he came in that day. Of all the days to get the blanket I had made for you, and then drive over to your home with my mom to deliver the gift... I'm just amazed how it all worked out."

Kate smiled as she reached over and pulled the blanket over onto Emma Elizabeth a little more, the very gift Melissa was alluding to.

"It was an exciting visit for all of us, I will say that," Susan declared.

"That it was," Kate said, nodding her head in agreement. "It's not like I planned on going into labor that very day, especially with the two of you there."

"It was just meant to be," Melissa said, "my mom and me visiting from out of town, things developing the way they did." Melissa took a half deep breath as she relived the events of that day.

Susan nodded her head as she offered the following words.

"I know it had to be very difficult on both of you, I mean with Emma in the hospital, you giving birth... Emma's death the same day, the funeral... I mean with everything happening essentially at the same time. The span this all took place in was unbelievable. Both of our families, Greg's as well as us, wished we could have done more for you two."

Now it was Kate who nodded her head in agreement.

"You were there when we needed you, and Henry and I are both grateful for that," Kate said.

Melissa could observe that her mother, as well as Kate seemed to drift into deep thought. Each woman's face appeared to be staring at nothing in particular. She said not a word as she played with her dessert, gently turning the whipped topping with her fork. This habit of hers was one she had done many times before. Maybe that's why she always seemed to order whipping cream on the top of her pieces of pie in the first place.

With everything that occurred within a matter of days, in Kate's mind it was one of the most emotionally charged times she had ever experienced. The recollection of that period, every moment that had transpired was burned deeply into her soul. It was the high of her daughter's birth, the deep depression with Emma's death and then funeral.

Only one other time had Kate reached this depth of inner sorrow. It was a day she would never want to live through again. That was when her mother died, and the pain she dealt with shortly thereafter with her father. Dealing with the suffering at her mother's bedside daily was one thing; her mother fighting against a foe who never seemed to go winless was yet another element to endure. It was everything in combination. The pain of the disease, her mother's passing, and the unforeseen reality of her father's reaction to it that tortured her the most. With her father walking out on her the day after the funeral, it was almost more than she could bear. Kate was completely crushed mentally by his actions. She would never forgive him for his selfishness, acting as if only he suffered through their loss. He lived in his own world of self-pity. To this day Kate didn't know whatever happened to him. It was a mystery she lived with daily.

With the mention of death and a funeral by her own words, Susan thought of her grandmother, Maria. Susan knew she most likely wouldn't favor them with many more years, if that long. That very thought alone troubled her immensely. She wished they lived closer to her. Italy seemed a million miles, however, their two weekly phone calls comforted both grandmother and granddaughter alike. They found solace in the sound of each other's voice. Even Cameo, her own mother, lived on the other side of the Country. They also shared in numerous phone calls throughout the month as well.

As Susan's mind drifted back to thoughts of Emma's death, what her own mother once told her concerning death came to light in her again. It was a memory that was clouded with years of other events covering it, but now it became clear to her consciousness.

Susan recalled how they had spoken to one another many years ago, their very own conversation involving death. Various questions concerning longevity, one's own lifespan was being asked by Susan as a youngster. What had prompted these inquiries by her was the passing of a neighbor. Cameo rationalized his death in a somewhat different manner. With Susan being a young child at the time, she thought it best to be short and to the point, a trait she always used with her daughter from that day forward. This approach worked well between them throughout the years. Her mother explained how everyone's life is like a book that is penned into daily. Each day contains a page, each month a chapter, and so on. Exactly how many pages or chapters each person's book carries is unknown. As to the length of each book, Cameo felt perhaps that part of the subject matter is better left alone. She offered no voice concerning that area.

"It might be better to change the subject matter," Melissa suggested, seeing Kate's face reflecting a sad appearance to it. Even her mother's expression was somewhat somber. The women agreed.

The rest of the meal together was spent discussing a variety of happier subjects. It was a time filled with laughter. Memories of unfortunate times were set aside, not to be brought up again.

Adult Party

Melissa laid in bed, a blanket covering her legs. Her body was propped up against the headboard with her pillow. She reached down with her right hand and placed it onto her stomach. She gently rubbed her hand back and forth across it.

"Greg, come here, the baby just kicked again."

Her husband walked the short distance to her and sat down on the edge of the bed. Melissa reached over taking his hand in hers as she put it on her stomach.

"Boy, I could feel that one this time," he chuckled. "It looks like we've got ourselves a genuine football player in there for sure. I wonder what they're paying field goal kickers these days," he joked.

Melissa smiled as she lifted Greg's hand up with hers. She placed it to her lips as she gave his fingers a small kiss. Greg gently bent over as he put his lips to hers.

"Today is the big day, we better get a move on," she said, as she looked up at him. Greg then placed his lips back onto hers giving Melissa another smaller kiss.

"I'm really looking forward to today, Honey, with the party and everything." Melissa's voice carried an excited tone to it.

"Our parents throwing us a baby shower, isn't that a little odd? I always thought women did that for women, and the guys get to stay home and watch television," chuckled Greg.

"It's not a baby shower, it's an adult baby party. There aren't going to be any gifts, it's an adult baby party, so don't call it a shower."

"So what's the difference?"

"Well, according to your mother and mine, they just wanted to do something special for us. They want to celebrate my pregnancy. That's why we're going to our own adult baby party." Melissa's voice definitely emphasized the last three words louder than the rest of them. "Your mom comes up with some good ideas, and when my mom and her get together, well, there's no stopping them."

"So we're not getting any gifts?"

"No."

"None at all?"

"No."

"But there will be food?"

"Yes."

"Do I have to get dressed up for this?"

"No."

"Good."

Once the couple had gotten dressed, a few of odd projects taken care of, Melissa reached into the refrigerator. She retrieved a dish to offer at the luncheon.

"I wonder what they'll have to eat?" inquired Greg as he looked at the large bowl in her hands.

"I don't know, my mom didn't tell me. When I asked her what I could bring, she said, 'nothing.' I just don't feel right showing up without something to offer, so I made the dip. I do know she said the food was going to be very simple and tasty."

"That sounds like my two favorite food groups, simple and tasty."

"Honey, who do you think will be there?" Melissa said as they walked in the direction of the front door. "My mom did ask me if there was anyone special we wanted to invite. I told her Kate and Henry, of course, but I don't know if they'll be able to make it. I also asked her to invite Dan and Kim."

"Well, your guess is as good as mine on who will show up," Greg said as he shrugged his shoulders slightly. "We'll just have to wait and see."

"Well, we'll know in a little while. I hope they like the dish I've made."

"By the way, what did you come up with? I know you were looking through your recipes the last few days."

"My mother said if I was to bring anything at all, to make it a finger food, or something along that line. I hope you like crab dip."

"I sure do. You certainly made a lot of it."

"I also picked up some fancy crackers to go along with it."

"What's in the little plastic bag," Greg asked, "it looks like a small sign attached to a straw or something?"

"I made a little sign with a picture of a crab on it saying it's crab dip."

"Why would you do that, they can taste it and know what it is."

"Just in case someone is allergic to it, they'll know to stay away from it."

"That's a good idea."

"I'm glad you think so."

"Actually I'm kind of looking forward to going now," Greg acknowledged, "I'm a little hungry already."

"We're not going there to eat, we're going for —"

"We're not?" he joked, pulling on her chain a little bit.

"It's an adult baby party, and I don't want to be late for our own party."

"Okay, okay, I'm coming," he said as he picked his keys up from the counter and headed in her direction by the front door.

The area outside of Melissa's mom and dad's house, Susan and Kenneth, was filled with cars. The young couple was surprised to see the amount of vehicles parked along the street, as well as in the driveway. The fact was they actually had to walk a little over a block to get to the home's entrance. As they entered through the front door Greg and Melissa were amazed to see so many individuals, even more than the clue of the parked cars led them to believe would be present. The atmosphere as they walked into the front room was warm and filled with the chatter of people's voices conversing with one another. Of course, they knew everyone there. When the individuals realized they had arrived, the sound of their voices all flew in the direction of them. They immediately began welcoming the young couple, happy to see the guests of honor had arrived.

Edith and Frank, Greg's mom and dad, attempted to get over to them. They had to, however, wait their turn as others were already doing the same thing. Melissa laughed as someone relieved her of the food dish she was carrying and headed in the direction of the kitchen. Greg stood next to her smiling as he shook hands with some guests.

"Oh, Melissa, let me give you a hug," Edith said as she reached her arms out to her.

"I see you made it," chuckled Frank as he placed his hand on Greg's shoulder.

"No one wants to miss an adult baby party," Greg whispered in his dad's direction.

"I've never been to one before," joked his father in a fairly quiet reply.

"And I bet we're not alone in that either," smiled Greg as he noticed other men standing around the room.

"You're here," was the next sound Melissa heard as her mother walked up to them, followed by her father. She gave Melissa a customary big hug and smile, as well as Greg, of course.

"You're starting to grow even more," her mother noted concerning her daughter's pregnancy. "You still have a ways to go yet though," she chuckled.

Melissa's face beamed with her mother's statement, very proud to be the expectant mother she was.

"Come in, Honey," Kenneth said as he took his hand and placed it on the back of her arm somewhat leading her into the kitchen area. "You've got to see what your mother and Edith have done preparing this party for the two of you."

Melissa could see all of the table leaves had been put into place extending its span to its optimum length. The kitchen table was filled completely with a huge variety of foods. There were hand-size sandwiches, chicken wings, Italian sausages, Swedish meatballs, and much more. On the counters additional food dishes had been placed taking care of the overage from the table. It was obvious to Melissa no one would go hungry, and if they did, they only had themselves to blame. As she admired the hard work the two women had to have put into the feast, Greg walked up behind her along with his father.

"So when do we get to attack this food?" Frank asked.

"Not for a while," came the voice of Edith from behind him. "Just remember, there are other people who want to eat, too."

"That goes without saying," Frank said as he looked over at Kenneth and gave him a little wink.

Both men chuckled to themselves with Frank's statement.

"You realize all of the leftovers stay here for me to enjoy all by myself," Kenneth said with a devilish smile on his face.

"Oh, good thing I talked to Susan already and made arrangements with her to take some food home with me," laughed Frank.

"You're a scoundrel," expressed Kenneth.

"We both are," chuckled Frank, "and maybe that's why we get along so well."

Kenneth nodded his head in agreement.

When the families got together for their usual Sunday afternoon meals, if their schedules allowed it, it was the men who enjoyed their wives' abilities around an oven or stove top the most. Both women knew how to make kitchen utensils sing out with the aroma of glorious meals and flavorful desserts.

"So where are the desserts?" asked Greg.

"Ah, now you're in for a real treat," Frank stated. "Come this way. You, too, Melissa, you've both got to see this."

The group followed Frank as they moved from the kitchen area to the dining room. In the room over the dining room table a lit European style crystal chandelier hung. Worked into the wrought iron support sections were very small branches from a little tree, some with their leaves still attached. Suspended from the light by pink and blue ribbons was a woven wicker basket, a very small blanket lying inside of it. The basket contained a small doll, which had been tucked into it. It hung just low enough for all to see its interior. Wrapped around the basket a small banner with the words, "Rock-a-bye-baby" was imprinted on it. As Melissa looked up at it she smiled, and then wiped her eyes with her fingers.

"This is so precious," were the only words she could say as she wiped her eyes again.

"Here," stated Edith, as she handed her a box of facial tissue she always seemed to have present.

"Thank you. It's just so beautiful," Melissa uttered softly.

"You know Frank and I did a lot of work on it also," Kenneth stated.

"They sure did," smiled Susan, "after all they went outside and got the small branches for us."

"And who put the final touches to it," chuckled Frank, "after all, Kenneth and I did hang it."

"Really," was all that Edith said, her head shaking back and forth.

"It's simply beautiful," Melissa said.

Edith and Susan smiled as they looked at each other. They knew their idea was met with a great deal of success.

"Thank you all so much," Melissa said as she continued to wipe her eyes with a tissue.

Greg looked down at the table, which held an abundance of fancy appearing desserts. The selection was huge and very inviting to anyone's pallet. There was everything from chocolate covered strawberries, torts, creampuffs, and much, much more.

"You ladies sure out did yourselves," Greg said as he reached for a tasty treat with his hand.

"Not now," Edith said as she gently slapped Greg's hand.

"Ah, Ma."

"I know exactly how you feel," joked Frank.

"And so do I," chimed in Kenneth.

"We'll get to it soon enough," added Susan.

Melissa turned around as she felt a hand on her shoulder.

"Kate," came the happy sound of Melissa's voice, "you and Henry made it. I'm so glad you're both here."

"We wouldn't have wanted to miss this for anything," smiled Kate.

Both women reached out to each other and hugged.

"It's a good thing you have such a large home to accommodate everyone," Henry offered.

"Especially with the piano gone," laughed Susan.

Henry smiled as his mind reminisced back to when Susan and Kenneth gave him the baby grand piano that once graced their living room. He never would have dreamed he could own such a magnificent musical gem, and here it was being presented to him by the Summers family. Henry recalled how they told him they never played it, it was going to waste in their home; that he could make much better use of it. He was thrilled by the offer and took full advantage of their gift as he played it daily in his own home. Their generosity truly touched his heart that day. He made sure they knew of that fact on more than one occasion.

It wasn't very long at all before the adult baby party went into full swing. The sound of people's voices as they visited was unbelievably loud, filling the air with various subjects. It was a mixture of laughter and tasty conversations, just as the food was when they all began to partake of it. To everyone present it was a fun filled get-together. There was good food and excellent company, a hard combination to beat.

The invited guests were all instructed strongly in the invitation that there were to be no gifts brought or offered to the couple. The two families strictly wanted a party that consisted of friends, close acquaintances, and anyone the young couple would enjoy seeing. It was meant to be exactly what it turned out to be, a celebration.

As Melissa and Greg made their rounds through the rooms visiting, they were both astonished at who was there. Doc, Kate's grandfather was in attendance along with Jean Parker. The two had been introduced at Melissa and Greg's wedding reception. Richard, Henry's partner at the restaurant was also present. Much to their surprise Terry and Robert Caldwell were also in attendance. Some of the Caldwell Advertising Company's employees were present, all wishing the couple their very best.

"We were so pleased to receive the invitation," Mrs. Caldwell said as she reached over and gave Melissa a slight hug on her shoulder. She then gave Greg a little kiss on the cheek.

"In some ways I think of you as a son," Terry stated, "with our family make up being totally females."

"I'll take that as a compliment," Greg said, a little surprised by her statement to him.

"We love both of you," Robert said. "I guess Terry and I just wanted you to know how we feel about the two of you."

Greg and Melissa were both astonished by the statement from Robert to them as well. It's not that they didn't feel close to them, it was just that they never thought Robert and Terry felt that strongly about them.

"You honor us with those words," Greg said as he smiled at them, still trying to comprehend in his mind the words that had just been spoken to them.

"Thank you," Melissa said as she placed a little kiss on Mr. Caldwell's cheek.

While working only part-time in the evenings for the Caldwell Advertising business, Greg knew they treasured his work. He enjoyed being an intricate part of the couples' company. When the business was having a hard time coming up with a solution to an ad's message, he was asked to find an answer to their dilemma. Greg relished solving the problems that would arise. Every job he undertook seemed to present a new challenge which he met head-on. Melissa would sometimes offer her views concerning the various approaches he was thinking of using. He valued her opinion strongly, and let her know that fact often.

The two families would share meals at each other's homes at different times. All four of them possessed a wonderful working relationship. Now, to hear such strong words from the Caldwells came as an unexpected revelation of sorts to both Greg and Melissa. The young couple was touched to feel they felt so close to him and his wife.

"Greg," Robert said, "when you and Melissa have the time my wife and I would like to have lunch with you and her parents as we did some years ago. When the occasion presents itself, give Terry or me a call and we can all get together."

"I know they would enjoy doing that. I'll let them know."

"Please tell your father-in-law it's our treat this time," Robert said.

"Now that, I'll be sure to mention to him," Greg said with a smile on his face.

Greg and Melissa enjoyed the party in more ways than they could have ever imagined. Over in the corner of the living room sat Fred Carpenter with his wife, Robin. His crutches stood against the corner of the couch.

"Robin, Fred, it's so nice to see you both," Greg said as he reached out to Fred, shaking his hand as the two of them smiled.

"I wouldn't want to miss out on any of the free food," joked Fred, "so we were sure to get here early."

"We did not," Robin said, "he's just joking, really, he's just joking."

"No I'm not," laughed Fred.

"Fred, really, stop acting that way."

Across Melissa's face was a large smile. Fred being Fred was what so many people loved about him, and Robin was no different. There were times when she bit her lip, with what he said, but those times weren't very often.

Fred winked at Greg.

"When people see my crutches, they offer to get me something to eat. I had three individuals running for me, each bringing back something more to eat."

"He did not," Robin said, "stop it! Melissa, Greg, he did not do that."

Greg and Melissa laughed. The one thing both of them truly enjoyed about Fred was his knack in bringing a bit of laughter into any conversation he was involved in. Though his wife never said it out loud, it was something she enjoyed about her husband as well, the humor.

Fred smiled at Greg. To him Greg represented the man who had virtually saved his family from a world of despair. When Fred lost his leg from a hit and run driver, his job as well, it threw his life into a turmoil he never would have dreamed could exist. His job and income disappeared. Fred felt the inner sorrow he suffered grow with each passing day. Bills mounted. In his heart he felt like someone trapped within a room shaped in a circle. There was no corner to hide in, no place to run to.

A few years passed as things began to get worse for him, as well as the family. It was then that Greg visited Fred with an offer that changed his life. It was a job as a part-time accountant, something Fred was not only capable of handling, he was extremely good at the profession. After a short interview with Kenneth and Susan, he filled the position. Greg even saw to it that Fred received a vehicle so he was able to transport himself back and forth to work. Eventually he became the full-time accountant for the Summers Store, and Fred knew daily in his heart who he had to thank for that opportunity.

As Greg and Melissa made their way through the party goers, not wanting to miss expressing to anyone their appreciation for them being in attendance, they stopped to talk to a couple of women Greg knew from the Caldwell business.

"The two of you must be getting excited with the approaching of the baby's birth," one woman said.

"I felt the baby kicking again this morning," Melissa said smiling.

"Sometimes it's not actually a kicking motion," Greg said in a matter of fact voice. "The baby is simply stretching its limbs."

All three women exhibited surprised looks at his words. Greg continued with his assessment.

"The baby can begin those movements anywhere from 16 to 20 weeks sometimes 25. Even a meal can trigger it, sounds, maybe even the mother's voice."

"How do you know all of this information?" inquired the woman on his left.

"When I first learned Melissa was pregnant, I began researching different things concerning her giving birth. I still do."

Melissa said not a word, her mind absorbed with the information about the baby's movements. The fact that he even possessed all of this knowledge made her chuckle, yet it was something she wouldn't put beyond Greg to do. Her heart grew a little warmer in feelings for her husband. It was something that seemed to happen quite often. Greg treated her in a very precious way, as she did to him as well.

"Do you want a boy or girl?" the woman next to her inquired.

"They must know that information already," the second woman stated as she nodded her head.

"No, we don't," Melissa said.

"Oh, doesn't that make it a little difficult when it comes to getting prepared for the baby's room, what colors to use?"

"We don't care as long as the baby is healthy. I know that's the pat statement to make, but that's how we both feel."

"I think of it in a silly way," Greg expressed. "It's like you look in the pantry and find a can where the label is missing. You don't know what's inside until you open it. It's fun to see what it contains in the end. You might have a taste for baked beans, instead you get chicken noodle soup. What it is it is. I like soup or beans," he chuckled.

"I don't like being referred to as a can," Melissa said, shaking her head back and forth as she spoke, "or for that fact, a can of beans."

The women laughed slightly at Greg's analogy. He went on with his thoughts.

"Actually Melissa is the packaging, and our surprise or gift awaits inside. Does that sound better?"

"Maybe you should wrap some ribbon around her stomach," joked one of the women.

"Don't give him any ideas," Melissa quickly stated.

At one point during the party, as Greg and Melissa were sitting in the kitchen somewhat alone, Jean and Doc walked up to them. Doc placed his hand on Jean's shoulder as he addressed the two of them.

"When Kate and Henry had their baby it was a very stressful situation with the death of Henry's mother, Emma, at the same time. I hope and pray that yours goes a little smoother than theirs."

"I hope so," Greg said.

" I'm sure it will. It's very clear to see you both have a lot of family support as you enter this juncture in your lives, but I would like to proffer a few words to both of you as I did to Kate and Henry some time ago.

Enjoy this time in your life, embrace it with all the love you have to offer each other. Your tomorrows will be here soon enough. Hang onto your precious memories tightly, but don't be afraid to step down new paths that come your way. Celebrate your dreams as one, and always hold the other's heart close to your own."

Greg and Melissa didn't expect Doc's words. Both of them, however, knew they were from his heart, and what more cherished gift was that for anyone to offer them.

As Jean listened to Doc she couldn't help but think of her own life and his, how each of them had suffered a significant tragedy in the past. Doc had lost his wife many years ago while Jean suffered the loss of her fiancé. Now they were together as a couple, something completely unforeseen by either one of them. Yes, she thought, hold each other's heart closely. She knew she would do that with Doc, just as she was sure he would with her.

"Okay you two, stop hiding in here with my Grandfather and Jean. I need you to come out into the living room," announced Kate to the small group.

"Now?" asked Greg.

"Now," Kate answered.

"But I was just going to get something to eat," Greg joked.

"Don't you think you've had enough to eat," Melissa said as she jabbed Greg in his side with her finger.

The five of them turned and went into the living room.

"Can I have your attention, please," Kate stated in a somewhat loud voice wanting to make sure she was heard. "Mrs. Summers, will you be good enough to help me out, please."

Susan left the room momentarily but soon returned carrying a large box wrapped in red paper, a large red bow on its top.

"I love the color of the paper and bow," Melissa said smiling.

"It is common knowledge to anyone who knows Melissa," Kate said, "that the color red is her very favorite. Red roses, of course, are her most cherished of flowers. But red, in general is her most beloved shade of color.

As all of you know Melissa and I have known each other for many, many years," Kate said with a smile. "We grew up together. We've been close friends since childhood. She is my dearest and most precious friend. We have been through much together... both good and bad times. There were times when I needed your shoulder to cry on, Melissa, and you were there for me."

Melissa could feel her eyes begin to get watery.

It was at this point when Kate's emotions took over her voice. The very words she was now trying to convey were filled with a quivering voice as she attempted to speak. Kate could feel her eyes begin to water as tears began to flow from them.

Melissa quickly moved the short distance to Kate as the two women embraced each other. Together they held one another as they cried, each finding comfort in the arms of the other.

"I love you," Kate said softly to Melissa.

"And I love you, too," Melissa answered.

The people smiled while some of them actually clapped their hands softly. To many it embodied a sentimental moment between the two of them. Many of the women found themselves wiping their eyes, taken by the scene playing out before them. Thick emotions filled the room. Edith passed her box of tissue around, one she always had with her being the tender- hearted person she was known to be. With her, tears were a frequent shadow that followed her wherever she went. Once the women released each other, Kate was able to find the strength to go forward.

"As everyone knows, you were instructed not to bring a gift to the party. However, I was given special permission by Susan and Edith to ignore that request. I have a gift for you, Melissa, one that I hope very much you'll enjoy and keep. Perhaps you'll even make it a part of your own family heirlooms."

With that statement having been made, Kate handed Melissa the gift. Melissa took a seat on the couch as a few people moved over giving her room to sit. She smiled as she looked around the room and then began to open the present. As she took the top off of the box, she made a happy and thrilled statement.

"Is this what I think it is?" she asked excitedly.

Kate nodded her head. "I hope it's okay with you."

"I love it, I absolutely love it," Melissa said as she removed a white baby blanket with various animals crocheted around its edge.

"Robin made this for me," Kate stated. "I've actually had it for some time now. I loved the one you gave me so much I asked her to make an exact duplicate so we both can have one. Every time I look at mine it reminds me of you. I hope this gift does the same thing for you as it does with me."

"Oh, how wonderful," Melissa said smiling, "thank you so much."

Melissa got up and walked over to Kate giving her a hug.

"When I gave you yours," Melissa said, "I thought it was so beautiful, and now I have one of my own. Oh, oh, Robin, where are you?" she said as she quickly looked around the room.

"I'm over here," came Robin's embarrassed voice as she waved her hand slightly back and forth.

"Thank you so very much. I'll love mine every bit as much as Kate does hers."

"You're welcome," beamed Robin's face.

Melissa made her way over to Robin wanting to embrace her with another thank you.

"Thank you, Robin... and thank you, Kate," Melissa said. "This is just so incredible."

"Well, your mother put me in touch with Robin," Kate said, "so she deserves a thank you, too. This has actually been quite sometime in the works. I didn't know when I'd be able to give it to you, but then we received the invitation from your mom."

"Thank you," Melissa said as she moved to her position. The mother and daughter hugged, each presenting the other with smiles.

"You're welcome, Honey."

Melissa began to unfold it for everyone to see. She held it with her arms stretched out for all to enjoy. Melissa then handed it to a woman seated on the couch so she could begin to pass it around for everyone to examine and admire.

The party went on for quite some time after that. Surprisingly none of the men pressed their wives or girlfriends to leave. Perhaps it was the friendly atmosphere, the fellowship they enjoyed together, tasty food, or numerous unknown reasons. Maybe it was all of the above.

Frank and Kenneth were sure to see to it their own food plates were kept filled. Their wives, however, were sure the two men's dishes seemed to empty quickly, faster than they should have to begin with. Neither Frank nor Kenneth had a clue as to why that happened. The answer to that question still remains unknown.

Decisions

"That was the lawyer's office," Kate said. "Eric wants us to come in tomorrow. Apparently he's got some news concerning Mary for us."

Henry looked up at Kate as he nodded his head. Those few words meant the world to him, and she knew it very well. At last they would be able to close another chapter in their lives or, perhaps, turn a new page and begin another one anew. That question would be answered hopefully with tomorrow's meeting.

"Did Mr. Eddington say what time he wanted us to meet with him?" Henry inquired.

"Eric said he has a court hearing at 9:30, but he's free for an hour before that. Basically he said to come in at our convenience. We can do it later in the day if we want to."

"Let's make it early. I don't think I can take the suspense of waiting until later in the day to get the results of his investigation."

Kate nodded her head. She knew inside there were questions to be answered, plans to be made. All in all, it was going to be an important day in both of their lives, as well as for a little girl by the name of Mary.

Nothing of consequence was said between Kate and Henry as they got dressed the next morning. Each was surrounded with their own feelings of what to expect, neither one really knowing what lay ahead of them.

As they drove towards Mr. Eddington's office, Kate reached over and held Henry's hand for a few minutes.

"I wonder what Eric has found out about Mary?" Kate stated as she turned her head and glanced out the window.

"We'll know soon enough," Henry said, his mind wondering the very same thoughts. "It's been some time now since we asked him to find her. I know he hired someone to see what he could uncover. He's must have met with some success."

"Henry, I'm a little nervous and excited all rolled into one."

"Me, too," he responded as they pulled up to a parking spot near the lawyer's office. The couple got out of the car and walked the short distance to the front door. Henry opened it, then followed Kate inside.

"Good morning, Mr. and Mrs. Morgan," the secretary cheerfully said.

Henry nodded his head as Kate replied, "Hello."

"I'll let Mr. Eddington know you're here."

"Thank you," Kate said.

Within less than a minute Mr. Eddington opened his office door. Kate and Henry followed him through the door leading into his private office.

"Have a seat, please," he said as he gestured somewhat with his hand in the direction of a couple of leather chairs.

"Thank you," Kate stated as she took the furthest seat into the room.

"So how have the two of you been?"

"Good," Henry answered.

"Good."

"So what can you tell us, Eric?" questioned Henry immediately.

"What I'm about to tell the both of you is like dealing with a two-headed dragon. First of all, the private detective I hired on your behalf has met with success. He's found the little girl, Mary. She lives in the small community of Four Pines about 40 miles from here."

Henry nodded his head gently as he listened carefully to each of Eric's words, a bit of excitement in his heart.

"The thing is, Mary has been set up for adoption. She's in that very process now."

"Wonderful," Henry said with a smile, "that means she's available to be adopted by us."

"Yes, and no, Henry. Some paperwork has been put into place. A family has been working with the court authorities for some time now. Mary had no immediate relatives, at least that anyone could find. This family, the one interested in adopting her, live in the neighborhood where Mary lived. They knew Mary's family quite well, hence the problem between you and them. Both of you are interested in adopting her from what I understand. Am I correct in that assumption?"

"Yes, you are," answered Henry.

Kate merely nodded her head in an approving manner.

"And so there's a dilemma, a wonderful one in many ways, not so wonderful in others. We have two families wanting the same child to care for and love.

Another thing of interest for both of you to consider, the family's main objective is for Mary to have as normal an upbringing as possible when it comes to her burn. They are of modest means, but nonetheless rich in morals with a wealth of love to offer her. Of course, with the large inheritance the two of you have recently come into, economically this couple cannot hope to challenge your resources."

Henry lifted his arm up and waved his hand back and forth gently informing Eric visually that that didn't mean anything to them.

"We want what's in the best interest of the child, Eric."

"I understand that, Henry, but it's still a bone of contention to be considered."

"Not by us."

"I was hoping you would say that."

Kate just smiled slightly, knowing her husband's thoughts were hers as well. Money would never be used as leverage by either of them, it just wasn't in their plans whatsoever.

"So where do we go from here?" Henry asked.

"Well, I would like to suggest something very much out of the ordinary."

" And what exactly would that be?"

"Because of the detective's research into the matter, I am privy to certain facts that one wouldn't usually possess. How he acquired this information I don't know. In fact, I don't care to know."

"We understand," acknowledged Henry.

"What would the two of you think about meeting this couple? Now, it would be done in complete confidence, I mean they wouldn't be aware of anything we've discussed today. They wouldn't know you're interested in Mary, but you could get to know them a little bit. Please keep in mind they've been working along this very line, getting Mary that is, for quite some time. They're an absolutely wonderful couple."

"Eric, you're not being completely forthright with us in this; are you? It's clear to me from what little you've said that you think Mary should be with this family; am I right?"

While Eric didn't reply at all to Henry's statement, that told Henry everything he needed to know about the family in question, as well as Eric's assessment of the situation.

"Let's get down to the core of what's going on here," Henry said, "no more beating around the bush by you."

"Henry... Henry, Kate, I've never had anything like this occur before in all of my years as a practicing attorney. When I was hired to represent you as your counselor, my loyalty, my obligation, and my responsibilities lay strictly with you, what's in my client's best interest. Now I find myself in an unforeseen quandary, and I don't know frankly how to deal with it. I guess the best thing for me to do is to just put my cards on the table and see what happens. I didn't plan on this happening, and I'm sorry for what I'm about to tell you. I believe Mary should be adopted by the Harrison family. Of course, that is not a decision of mine or yours to make; it's up to the court. Their names are Frank and Jennifer Harrison. Some of this information, of course, is in strict confidence."

Henry looked over at Kate, though neither one said a word.

Eric continued with his thoughts. "I don't pretend to know what's really in the best interest for anyone, Mary included. However, I do possess certain other bits of knowledge that I want to share with both of you.

The Harrison family had a baby girl who died of crib death. They also have a son, Josh, who unfortunately was involved in an accident when some youngsters stole a car and were speeding through their neighborhood. They stuck him when they lost control of the vehicle. He has a severe limp because of that."

"Oh my God," Kate said loudly as she placed her hands over her mouth. Her eyes bore the signs of dampness. "Why is it in some people's lives there seems to be some much suffering while others are born with a silver spoon in their mouth. It's as if nothing bad ever happens to them. I just don't understand how or why it happens that way."

Neither male answered her question. As Henry looked at Kate's expression, his wife's heart dealing with someone else's suffering came as no surprise to him. He more than anyone understood Kate carried a tender heart. It was but one of the many reasons he loved her so much.

Eric handed her a box of tissue from a table behind his desk. Kate wiped her eyes as she nodded her head back and forth slowly still comprehending what he had just told them. Eric continued as he replaced the box back on the table.

"This couple has so much pent-up love to share, to smother Mary with, as they do for their own son. I was hoping the two of you could see fit in your hearts to withdraw from —"

"Eric, I hired you to find Mary on my behalf, you've accomplished that for me. I wanted to do something for this little girl who has done so much for me. Perhaps I was acting a little selfishly in trying to find her, maybe not, I don't know. It appears to me from what you're saying you really don't want us to make her a part of our family. Am I right or wrong in my evaluation of the situation?"

"Henry, you're right. I know I was hired to find her, but now that I have and know the circumstances behind everything. Frankly I feel Mary would be better off with the Harrisons. It's not that the both of you aren't wonderful people, I just feel —"

"So that's your feelings on the subject, we should step aside, turn our interests elsewhere?"

"No, embrace the fact that two people love Mary every bit as much as you do, and want her to become an intricate piece of their family puzzle as well."

"How badly hurt was their son?" Kate asked.

"From what I understand it's possible an operation could rectify the situation, but with no insurance, and as I said, they have a modest income."

"I'm going to contact Pastor Phil," Kate stated, "he'll know the ins and outs of setting up a fundraiser for them."

"Good idea," Eric said with a smile. "I'll do whatever I can to help you out with that."

Kate smiled with his statement having been made. Already she had someone in her corner she knew would be helpful. To her it was a beginning, and that's what every new endeavor needs, a starting point.

"Henry, you've paid me for my work and for my investigator's fees. I feel obligated to give that money back to both of you. It never was my intention to go down the road this took. It's just that I couldn't in all fairness not tell you how I felt about everything."

"We understand," Kate said as she wiped her eyes.

"First of all, let's get everything into its proper order," Henry said as he slid a little closer in his seat to the desk. "We asked you to find Mary for us, that has been accomplished. Secondly, it seems you've become too involved as our lawyer in this from the other individuals' perspective. In some ways it seems like you're acting as their lawyer."

"Henry —"

"Let me finish. Also I feel your heart is very much concerned more in how Mary fits into all of this, and I commend you for that. You're looking at the big picture while I am, I'm sorry to say, paying more attention to my own feelings or desires in this whole scenario. My emotions are taking over my common sense. I'm sorry for that."

Eric nodded his head as well as Kate, both appreciating Henry's words as well as his inner feelings towards Eric, the Harrisons, and Mary.

Let's do this," Henry continued, "and please feel free to offer any alternatives you consider to be appropriate. Kate, if you don't agree with anything I say —"

"I'll let you know," she said with a little smile.

Those few words by Kate brought a chuckle to Eric.

"I know you will," Henry said nodding his head.

Now it was Eric's turn to listen and hope Henry's words went down the same path as his own desires in the matter. He could only hope they did, after all, he considered Kate and Henry good people as well as friends of his. He didn't want to jeopardize losing that relationship.

"Kate and I will step back from the whole thing, our adoption desire that is. However, if things don't work out with the Harrison family, you're to jump in with both feet and do your best to put us at the top of the list."

Eric nodded his head as his face reflected a large smile running across his lips.

"Thank you, Eric, for putting everything into perspective for us... for me especially. I know you went somewhat out on a limb expressing your feelings in this."

"Well, Eric helped you out today," Kate expressed, "and Mary did the same thing in her own way before. At least you don't have to get another haircut and shave," laughed Kate.

"Pardon me?" Eric said in confusion.

"When Henry explained to Mary that bad things happen in life, he also became well aware of that fact personally. They both came to realize her burn and his scar were simply a part of their life experiences. Shortly after that, that's when Henry had his hair cut and shaved his beard off. He told me he didn't feel he had to hide his scar anymore," Kate said smiling, "it was just a part of him."

"So that's the reason you changed so much in appearance," Eric said nodding his head slowly back and forth in disbelief. "It was Mary that caused that?"

Henry shook his head affirmatively.

"I must confess I didn't recognize you the first time I saw you after that," he chuckled.

"A lot of people didn't."

"Well, if there's nothing more, I do have a court appearance in about ten minutes or so. I better get a move on."

"There's just one more item, Eric. The money we've paid you, keep it. From what I understand now, it was well spent by us. Thank you for everything, Eric."

"No, Henry, thank you."

The men shook hands. Kate took Eric's hand in hers and shook it as well.

"Thank you," she said.

"You're welcome."

The couple turned and left the office. After getting into their car Kate shut the door. Henry started the engine.

"Turn right at the corner, Honey," Kate said in a matter of fact tone.

"Why, where do you want to go?"

"Well, I want to go see someone about a project I have in mind."

"What and who would that be?" Henry asked in a curious voice.

"Pastor Phil. I want to learn how you go about running a fundraiser."

"Why doesn't that surprise me?"

"Henry, if we do have one, would you sing at the benefit? I think that would really help to bring some money in?"

"Like you had to ask."

"Thanks, Honey."

This was a typical example concerning Henry and Kate's life together. He never could say no to her, and she knew it. No one knew that fact better than Henry, but to him it didn't matter either way. He enjoyed observing the pleasure of her smile when she got her way. Kate was sure not to take advantage of this fact, but it still was another item she carried in her arsenal of loving pleas being satisfied. Sometimes it was as simple as batting her eyes, perhaps a long drawn out please, or just giving him a soft kiss. It all worked on him, and he adored every gesture she made.

Kate would on occasion take a coin and announce, "Heads I win, tails you lose." She never fooled him with the simple coin trick. When she would flip a coin into the air as she made her choice, Henry already knew he would lose. It didn't matter at all to him. Yes, Henry loved losing to the love of his life.

The couple made their way through the church and back to the pastor's office. Henry rapped on the door as he waited for a reply. None came forth.

"It looks like we missed him," Kate said.

"You may have missed him, but will I do?" asked Pastor Phil's wife, Marsha.

"Oh, you startled me," Kate stated, "I wasn't expecting to hear a voice from behind me."

"What can I do for you two?"

"Well, Henry and I want to —"

"Henry and I," interjected Henry, "I thought this was all your idea."

"Henry and I," Kate said in a little stronger voice, "want to know what we need to do to sponsor a benefit for a family. The thing is they're not from around here, if that matters."

"Well," Marsha said, "who were you thinking about helping out?"

"The Harrison family from Four Pines. I think it's Frank and Jennifer, if I'm not mistaken."

"Oh," they've suffered quite a bit of tragedy in their lives," Marsha stated in a somber sounding voice. "We were attending a meeting of pastors and I heard all about them there. Every night they're one of the first families I pray for daily. It's obvious, even to me you must be referring to their baby and son."

"It was such a sad thing to hear," Kate said.

"Yes, it is," Marsha said shaking her head.

"I understand there's a chance, if their son receives an operation on his leg, that he could possibly regain the use of it," Kate said.

"I heard that, too, but that won't matter, the operation isn't going to happen," Marsha said.

"Pardon me?"

"I asked that same question of my friend, too. Apparently from what I understand Mr. Harrison, Frank, is a proud man who won't accept any type of charity or money the operation would cost. Unfortunately I think his wife feels the same way."

"Being proud is one thing," offered Henry, "being stupid is another."

"Henry!" Kate quickly stated in an admonishing voice.

"I wouldn't use the word, 'stupid' to describe it," Marsha stated, "it's just some people don't want to ask others for help. Everyone has their own way of dealing with life's trials or tribulations."

"Or crosses to bear," Kate added.

"I can truly understand that," Henry said as he nodded his head, thinking of the scar he carried across his own brow.

"Perhaps we're going about this all the wrong way," interjected Kate. "Let's see if we can get the approval of the Harrisons and then go from there."

"It sounds like a long shot to me," Henry stated. "I don't know if it's worth a try after what she just said."

"Well, I think Kate is right on this one, Henry," Marsha offered. "Take it one step at a time. My suggestion to both of you is to contact the family, talk it over with them keeping an eye to the fact that you're suggesting they travel down a path they won't want to hear about, let alone take. It's a fork in the road, and you'll have to convince them your direction is the right one to take. It's easier said than done. If you feel more comfortable about it, I'm sure my husband would be happy to go along with the two of you."

"I'm sure the pastor has plenty on his hands as it is, but thank you just the same," Henry said.

"Thank you, Marsha," Kate said as she gave her a small wink. "We'll keep that offer in mind."

"I'll mention this conversation to my husband just in case you want his help, that way it will come as no surprise to him."

"That's probably a good idea," Kate said. "Marsha, it's getting close to noon. Well, perhaps a later breakfast or early lunch would be a better way of describing it. What would you say to sharing a meal with us, our treat."

"You know I think I'd enjoy that. Phil has a busy afternoon and won't be back until just before dinner. Why not, I could use a little break anyway. Is it okay if I follow the two of you over to — Oh, where are we going anyway?"

"How about Richard's Steak House," Henry said jokingly, "I know one of the owner's personally."

"How long have you and Richard been partners in that business now?" Marsha asked.

"Longer than I can believe. I guess it's been a few years now. I haven't really kept track of it to tell you the truth."

"Well, I'll follow the two of you over there."

After parking their vehicles, Kate, Marsha, and Henry walked up the few steps leading into the restaurant. Henry paused for just a moment as he looked at the newly built handicap ramp Richard had installed. Richard explained to Henry his reason for doing so was really two fold. One, the law required it to be done and, two, he felt it opened a new venue of customers. Everyone should have the opportunity to enjoy Henry's voice.

As the three were seated in the establishment, Marsha looked at Henry.

"It's hard for me to believe you and Richard added onto the building so quickly after you started singing here."

"Well, once our relationship took off, and I started performing here regularly, we decided to add the additional seating space. Of course, when the bus tours added our place to their list of stops, that's when it really started to blossom. I guess you can say we're both very lucky."

"Don't under estimate yourself or Richard's hard work, and the fact that you two work so well together. I think it's a blessing for both of you."

"Richard is not only a good business partner, I consider him to be a very close friend. In my life I've been fortunate enough to have a few really close and trustworthy friends. One was a man by the name of Sam Allenby who influenced my life immensely in my youth. He taught me to speak Latin, how to play the piano. Sam was the mentor that saved me from the life I suffered from. I'll forever be grateful to him. He took the time from his own life to teach me, as well as to be my friend."

"You know, Marsha," Kate said, "Henry still has the piano Sam taught him on in our home. He left it in his will to him."

Marsha nodded her head slowly.

As Henry continued to speak to the women about Sam, the words he spoke had an almost haunting fashion to them. To Henry he was always in the room beside him, though never seen. It was easy for the women to see the deep-seated love he possessed for the man who was his counselor, and good friend. Though there was a distinct difference in age between the two, that meant nothing to them. In Henry's mind, Sam was the father figure he needed and longed to have in his life.

"Henry, your true friends are everywhere," Kate suggested.

"That's very true," Marsha added.

"Now you can't tell me Richard and Sam stand alone," Kate was quick to say.

"Of course not," Henry said.

"How about my grandfather, Doc, and you surely haven't mentioned Greg. You're also forgetting to mention Greg's wife, Melissa and her mom and dad, Susan and Kenneth. And don't forget Stella, Joe, and Jake. You and I have taken this very same walk together before. You seem to always look ahead, but not to your side to enjoy the view. Really, Henry."

"Can you see why she's so good for me, Marsha?" he said as he smiled. "She brightens even the darkest of my skies."

"Well, we don't always see the rainbow when it first comes out, it's hidden behind a few dark clouds," Marsha suggested. "Sometimes it's the sun that brings it all to life."

"So now I'm a bright sun, make a mental note of that, Honey," Kate was quick to add with a chuckle.

Marsha went on with her thoughts.

"Your life has changed in so many ways, your singing, the business, your marriage to Kate, the baby. You both have a lot to be thankful for. I would even go so far as to say the two of you have been truly blessed."

Henry understood she was right in many ways, her assessment of their situation. He knew though that even some sweet tasting fruits carry an unseen pit. There were personal items that Marsha didn't know about in his life as a child, the abuse he suffered, both physically and mentally. It was no picnic being brought up in a loveless home after being adopted.

His heart ached daily with the loss he carried for his surrogate mother, Emma. There was so much more to his life than Marsha knew about or could even have imagined.

Even the scar he bore on his brow was another stepping stone across a creek filled with rushing waters of despair. There was much he harbored within. Henry knew in his heart Marsha was right in part. There were many rays of sunshine that appeared when he least expected them. The money they inherited when Emma died, truly an unexpected gift when their thoughts were so filled with the bills for her hospital care and funeral. Henry nodded his head in agreement with Marsha's statement. Sometimes it's better to know only half of any story, he thought, and just the good parts.

"Would the two of you mind if I excused myself for a few minutes?" Henry asked.

"Of course not," Marsha said.

"I'll only be a minute or so."

Henry got up from the table and made his way over to a booth where a young couple was seated. The women watched as the young man took Henry's hand in his as they shook. It was evident to see the man was introducing the young woman he was sitting with to Henry. As Henry stood there the three of them laughed. It was very evident to Kate and Marsha that Henry and the young man were very good friends. It was written on both men's faces, and expressed in their loud laughter. Henry sat down next to the girl in the booth as the three of them continued visiting.

"That's not a good sign," Kate said.

"What do you mean?" Marsha inquired.

"Well, the fact that he sat down. Henry loses all sense of time when he's around people he hasn't seen for some time. Look at him, he's completely engrossed in a conversation with them. We may be here for a little while before he returns. It's a good thing you drove your own car," chuckled Kate.

"Oh, I've been through this many times with my own husband, it's no big deal," Marsha said, as she reached down picking up her cup. She took a long sip of coffee from it. "With me I just order a refill of coffee and patiently wait. There's no sense in worrying about it, it does no good. Take it from someone who has had to deal with this a few more years than you."

Kate nodded her head.

"Just do your best to make yourself comfortable."

As the two women turned their attention to each other, they found themselves discussing a series of different subjects. This time alone gave Kate a chance to discuss the possible fundraiser with Marsha, something she was very well versed in. The time actually passed quickly for them as they visited. It wasn't long afterwards when Henry returned to the table, though how long he had been gone escaped the women.

"Who was that couple?" Kate asked.

"Jeremy Tucker and his girlfriend, Carol Anderson, from high school. I just had to say hi to him. His father runs a Christmas tree farm south of town and does some farming as well. I haven't seen him in quite a while. One day I got a flat tire. It was pouring rain by the buckets full. Jeremy stopped to see if I needed any help. That's the type of person he is. His girlfriend and him are out on a lunch date, I guess you could call it."

"Are they serious?" Kate asked.

"I don't know, but they've been together since the ninth grade according to her."

"High school sweethearts," Marsha said, "that's wonderful."

"I guess. I will say there was a twinkle in both of their eyes when they looked at each other, at least it seemed that way to me. He comes from a hardworking family, and I'm sure she does too. I'm glad I had the opportunity to visit with them, especially Jeremy. I've always liked him and his family.

While he was attending high school, whenever I had a handyman job and needed some help, I'd give him a call. The only times he couldn't help me out was when he had band practice for football games or was just too busy. Jeremy played the drums while he was in school. I understand he is very popular in school, and even with others in some outlying school systems. He's simply one of those individuals you enjoy being around. Everyone loves him, especially Carol Anderson. Through the years I've gotten to know him really well, and his family, too. He also worked part-time for Joe along with Jake at the Second Chance Store. They loved having him around. Joe told me Jake and Jeremy are real good friends."

As the three sat eating their meals an occasional person would stop at the table, if only for a moment to say hello. Others would offer a quick wave as they walked to the cash register or out the front door. Within a short time more and more individuals stopped at the table to talk or extend their greetings. Marsha and Kate took it all in stride. If someone stayed a little longer than one would expect in a casual visit, Henry was polite. He did not rush his time with them. Henry spoke with each and everyone, always happy to see them. A large variety of subjects were covered as he conversed with them. When at last the scene at the table became quiet, only the three of them remaining, Marsha looked over at Henry.

"In a lot of ways you're very much like my own husband," Marsha stated.

"Excuse me," Henry said, a little shocked at being compared with a man of the cloth.

"He always makes time for people, just as you've done. The two of you can speak on almost every subject imaginable. With him being a pastor he's expected to do that, but you're a different shade of color, Henry, if you know what I mean. It's an attribute not everyone possesses. People feel comfortable around you, just as they do with my husband."

"Thank you, I think," Henry replied.

"You're welcome," smiled Marsha, "and I meant that as a compliment. Now, I've got to get going. Remember what I said about Phil, if you need him he's only a phone call away. Is there any timetable concerning your talk with the Harrisons?"

"Not really," Henry said, "but if I need his input, find out what he thinks, I'll be sure to give him a call."

"Henry, one suggestion. Run through your mind what you want to say to them, and then try to figure out what their answers would be to you. Sometimes it helps to take a little peek down the roadway before you take that journey. It helps to know what potholes you will be confronting in your travels, if you gather what I'm trying to say."

"I sure do, and I appreciate your help in this matter."

"As well as me," Kate added.

"Good luck. Remember Phil is available. Please let me know if there's anything else I can do for you."

"We will," Henry responded.

"Oh, and thank you both for lunch."

"It was our pleasure," Kate said. "Oh, say hello to your husband for us."

"I will," she said as she stepped in the direction of the front door.

As Marsha left the restaurant Henry reached over and took Kate's hands in his.

"Kate, do you think we've bitten off more than we can chew concerning the Harrisons' son? I don't know if I would want anyone telling me what to do concerning our own child." Henry nodded his head back and forth slightly as he waited for Kate's reply.

"No, I don't think we've bitten off too much, and I'll tell you why. Marsha said you have a knack in talking to people just as her husband does, and I think she's right. All you need to do is find the right words, put them into proper order and walla; you're all set. Honey, I have enough faith in you to know if there is any way to resolve this in the direction we're hoping it to go, you'll find it."

"I hope you're right, Kate."

Henry shook his head back and forth as he contemplated the situation now facing him. It's as simple as that, Henry thought, and walla it's done. A little smile crossed his lips with Kate's solution to it all. Walla, he thought again, if only it were that simple. To Henry it was clear. Kate had a mountain of faith that he could accomplish anything that needed to be done. However, Henry's faith was likened to someone standing by a crevasse surrounded with slippery slopes, and a strong wind at his back. Still, he thought, I'll follow Marsha's suggestion and see where it leads us.

"I know this was my idea concerning their son, and I've kind of shoved you into the spotlight," Kate stated, "but we'll work this out together, come up with a resolution. I'll get the address of the Harrisons and their phone number, then we'll take it from there. Is that a plan or what?" she said smiling.

"That sounds like a plan to me," he chuckled to himself as he listened to Kate's confident voice. He even found some strength in the sound of her words, and that comforted him.

From that point on things moved quickly, Kate saw to it. She acquired the necessary information on the family. What surprised both her and Henry was the fact that the adoption of Mary moved just as fast. This unanticipated event caught the couple by surprise as well as Eric, their lawyer.

"I knew the paperwork had been filed," Eric said, "I just didn't realize how far along they were in completing the procedure. I don't work in that area of the law, it's not really my field of expertise. For some reason the case moved much faster than I expected or anticipated it would."

He apologized to both of them. For him this error in judgment cast a shadow on his ability as a lawyer when everything went south for his clients. No one likes to look incompetent, and that fact bothered him to no end. From that point on, he would check daily on the progress of Mary's case. Some of the secretaries in the Court system would actually answer their phone with the phrase, "Nothing has happened yet," when he called precisely at eight o'clock in the morning each day. Why this case carried such an important meaning to him he never said, and they never asked. After a while the secretaries kept a keen eye on any movement the case made, their curiosity having been aroused by this time as well.

Henry sat alone at the kitchen table occasionally sipping from a cup of tea he had just made. In silence he sat in deep thought. He watched as the sun shone through the window casting a shadow upon the table from the curtains. It reminded him greatly of the many days he shared with Emma. So many wonderful memories played themselves out in his mind, sharing cups of tea together, eating fruit cake she made from her own secret recipe. Each thought brought her to life once more.

He chuckled when he recalled the day Emma invited her neighbors over to make her famous fruitcake. To everyone involved it was a party, a time to enjoy being together. Henry recalled how thrilled Kate was to share the day with the neighbors and Emma. It was from that very day the two women's relationship grew in leaps and bounds. It was evident to Henry and Kate her neighbors loved Emma deeply as well. They also watched out for her. That fact alone comforted the young couple.

Henry took another swallow from his cup as he tried to sort through the numerous impressions that had grown so deeply since the day he and Emma first met.

It was Sid, her neighbor who Henry knew loved her as much as he did. Together they held each other at her funeral, comforting one another through the suffering they were attempting to endure.

He thought of his childhood again. His youth was tragic. Henry did his best to keep his mind in an area far from its memories. Still his mind drifted to and fro.

Henry began to think of the Harrison family, their son, what to say at their meeting. He knew his words should be foremost from his heart, strong and forceful, yet tender in nature. Henry's command of the English language was extraordinary. As he drank his tea, his mind acted as a thesaurus, various words trying to fit into place to convey his simple thoughts. Perhaps it is better to keep it plain and to the point, after all, who wants to listen to somebody using words that are large and unappreciated to begin with. Henry knew he wouldn't want to listen to them either. Yes, he thought, he had better make contact with them fairly soon.

"You're up early this morning," came the voice of Kate as she walked into the kitchen, a baby blue bathrobe wrapped around her body.

"I'm just thinking to myself," he answered in a soft voice.

"About what?" inquired Kate as she walked over to the stove wanting to heat some water, only to discover it was already hot.

"Among other things I was thinking about giving the Harrisons a call today."

"So you're thinking of seeing them?"

"I was thinking about it." Different thoughts kept vacillating back and forth in his mind, what to say, how to approach it.

Kate nodded her head as she poured some hot water from an old silver colored kettle into her flowered cup. When her husband was discussing matters of importance, or at least thinking about them, she found it best to wait to see what developed. She didn't want to disrupt his train of thought, though she was always willing to add her own impressions to his when asked.

"I've kind of come to a conclusion, Kate, and I was wondering what your thinking would be on it."

"What's that, Honey?" she asked.

"It's about Mary."

"Uh-huh."

"What would you think if we simply sat back and didn't attempt to do anything about her? I mean, I don't know if we could do anything concerning her anyway."

"You mean do absolutely nothing?"

"I mean unless everything fell apart. We inasmuch told Eric that already."

"Mr. Eddington... Eric did say they are a wonderful family," Kate said as she nodded her head. "I have no problems following you either way. Whichever direction your emotions are taking you, let's simply pursue the course your heart is leading you in."

Henry nodded his head in agreement.

Kate lifted the cup to her mouth, taking a long sip from it. Her lips curled with a small smile. After a second or two she began to offer her thoughts on the subject of the fundraiser.

"There is one thing that I would like to address with you, and that's their son, I mean the fundraiser."

"As far as the son," Henry offered, "it's whatever you decide, that's fine with me, too."

Kate smiled.

"Then it's settled," Henry said with a voice that was filled with a determined solution.

"I'm going to give Eric a call and let him know what we've decided."

"And be sure to thank him for all of his help."

"I will," he said, nodding his head in a firm way.

"Oh, and mention to him we're going to talk to the Harrison family as well about a fundraiser."

"I will," Henry repeated.

It was the middle of the afternoon when Henry picked up the phone and dialed the number of the Harrisons. First he had to get a meeting set up with them, that being the first roadblock setting before him. He had done precisely what Marsha, pastor Phil's wife, had suggested he do. Henry ran his words through his mind, knowing exactly what he would say. When Jennifer Harrison answered the phone Henry introduced himself. The next few words by Jennifer took Henry aback, he didn't anticipate her reply.

"Aren't you a singer?" she asked.

"Yes, I am."

"The one from Creek Side?"

"That would probably be me," Henry said in an almost laughing response.

"It's very nice to talk to you. What can I do for you?" her friendly voice asked.

"I was wondering if I could meet and talk with you and your husband in the next day or so?"

Henry waited for her reply, which didn't readily come forth to him. The pause actually seemed to linger in the air.

"Well," the hesitant voice of Jennifer stated, "if it's okay with you, we're free tonight. Other than that it will have to wait until next week."

"Wonderful," Henry said. "Would you and your husband be free for dinner tonight, our treat? My wife and I would be more than happy to drive over and meet with you, if that's okay with the two of you, of course."

"Exactly what does this concern?" was her inevitable question.

"I have a proposition I want to address with the both of you, and I'd rather not do it over the phone if you don't mind."

"Well... okay. Of course, if my husband has other plans I'll have to let you know. He's not here right now, otherwise I could tell you for sure if it's okay."

"That's fine. Let me give you my phone number just in case."

Once the arrangements between the two of them were made, what restaurant they were going to meet at, the time, Henry bid her a good-bye. Now to inform Kate what he had found out. He was sure she would be anxious to meet with them, after all, this project was her baby to begin with.

After Henry parked the car in the restaurant area he turned to face his wife. Though he didn't say a word to her, he cocked his head slightly in a questioning fashion as he shrugged his shoulders. She knew exactly what he meant by the simple gesture. The doorway to the restaurant was not the only one they were about to walk through together, they both knew that in their hearts. As the two of them entered the diner they immediately looked around the room trying to decide who most likely were the Harrisons. A couple sitting in a booth by the window caught Henry's eye as the man raised his hand giving it a slight wave. Kate and Henry walked over to them.

"You are the Harrisons, I presume?" he asked.

"That would be us," the man replied. "This is my wife Jennifer, and my name is Frank. Of course, you already know that."

"This is my wife, Kate. It's nice to meet both of you."

Henry and Kate took a seat in the booth on the opposite side of the couple. They were much younger than either one of them thought or expected them to be. Both Henry and Kate were somewhat surprised by that fact, though neither one said anything concerning it. However, being married as long as they were now, a small facial expression to the other told each what the other was thinking, at least most of the time.

"As I told Mrs. Harrison, I had planned on —"

"It's Jennifer, please," Frank's wife was quick to say.

"This is our treat, please," Henry continued.

"Well, thank you," Frank said. "So what is so important to the both of you that you find it necessary to drive this far to visit us, and then offer us a free meal?"

"Is it okay with you if we enjoy our meal first, get to know each other a little bit before we go down that road? More importantly we're not here to sell you anything, buy anything, other than your meals, of course, or anything like that."

"Good, after all, we don't have a lot of money to begin with," Frank stated with a smile as he winked in their direction.

"You can say that again, Honey," Jennifer said as she exhibited a warm smile at Kate and Henry.

The waitress came up and handed everyone a menu. She took their drink orders and went to get their refreshments. The two couples sat exchanging small talk with Jennifer very much interested in Henry's singing at the Steak House. She explained how acquaintances of hers had attended some of the shows Henry had performed. Jennifer went on to say how impressed they were with his voice. She was curious to learn how everything started for him, the where, what, and why's. Henry explained how he had first sang a song to Kate at Richard's Steak House.

He described the fact that the employees informed Richard, the owner about him and how their relationship, like a budding flower came to blossom shortly thereafter. The story not only was enjoyable for Jennifer to listen to, she was fascinated by it.

"That's a wonderful story, Henry," she stated as he finished it.

"And the best part of the story is when he sang to me," confessed Kate as she smiled at Jennifer.

"I would think so," chuckled Jennifer. "There isn't any woman that I know of that doesn't enjoy being serenaded."

Once the meals were done, plates removed, coffee cups refreshed, Henry felt now was the time to broach the subject concerning their son's ailment, his leg difficulties. How they would react to this, "none of your business" situation weighed heavily on his mind, as well as Kate's. Both shared that very apprehension inside. Henry took a deeper breath as he began to address them.

"Sometimes when people want to discuss something that is really none of their business they stick their neck out like a turkey before a sharp ax. They don't know which direction the swing will come from, up, down, from the side, or maybe not at all. Perhaps that's not the best analogy to use, but we would like to take this opportunity to discuss something with you concerning your family."

Frank and Jennifer didn't quite understand where Henry was going with his statement. Both understood that it was about their family, and something that was none of Henry or Kate's business to begin with. However, they sat quietly waiting to see where his words were taking them.

"I do not want to make you feel uncomfortable by anything I may say, but we do have a question we'd like to address with you concerning your son, Josh. This has to do with his leg injury."

"How do you know our son's name?" Frank quickly asked, his face reflecting a shocked appearance.

"If you would please allow me to continue I'll explain everything to your satisfaction, I promise you. Please."

"Please," Kate added to Henry's plea.

Jennifer reached over and placed her hand onto Frank's arm as it rested on the table. He looked over at her, not knowing quite what to say or do. This subject matter was very far afield from what he or his wife anticipated hearing.

It was at this point when Henry put into practice what Marsha had suggested he do. Henry had run through his mind different solutions to his problem, what would be said to them, their response to any statements that could be made. He was glad for her advice, and he would be sure to follow it. But would it be the proper way of handling the situation, that was the hope in his heart. Now was the time for that question to be answered.

"You can say what you want us to hear concerning our son, but make it short and to the point. Do you understand me?" Frank stated in a serious tone of voice.

"Most definitely," Henry replied.

"Okay, just so we have that understanding."

"Kate and I would like to get your permission to conduct a fundraiser on behalf of your son. If we can raise enough money he could —"

"We don't accept charity, it's not a word in our vocabulary."

"We're not asking either one of you to accept any charity, that's not our intention in this. I can definitely assure you both of that fact."

Henry took a deep breath.

"If your son has any chance at all of having the problem with his leg rectified, he deserves that opportunity. I'm sure your son feels —"

"And who are you to tell us how our son feels?" Frank said in a tone filled with anger. "I've heard enough. Let's go, Jennifer." He began to get up from the table.

"Sit down and listen to me," came Henry's loud voice, something even he hadn't anticipated using.

Kate was startled with his statement as well as by the tone he used. A few people at other tables looked in their direction.

"Look at this scar on my face," Henry said loudly as he indicated it with his hand. "Do you think I wouldn't have gotten rid of it if I had the opportunity to do so. I know more than you could ever dream of how your son feels, and I know that because I've lived through it as well. I understand the suffering that lies ahead of him. Believe me, if there is any possibility at all he can have his leg made whole again, he warrants that chance. You need to step up and take that path together, hand-in-hand as a family.

You seem so concerned with the money issue, not accepting charity. Don't tell me you're too proud to accept anything that could help your son. You do love him, don't you?"

Henry didn't expect a reply to his question, he knew they did, but it was still part of his plan to ask that very question. Now he would turn his attention to Jennifer, harness her love for her son and use it against Frank, not as a weapon, but rather as a tool to change his thinking on the subject.

"And you, Jennifer, I know you love your son dearly, but don't allow your pride as well to discard the opportunity that's being offered to you and your boy. You need to be on your son's side in this, he deserves that much."

"Please," Kate said as she reached over placing her hand on Jennifer's hand.

Jennifer could observe Kate's eyes were a little watery as she spoke that single word to her. That fact alone convinced her of Henry and Kate's sincerity, the feelings they possessed for their son, even though they had never met him.

"What is it that brought you to us, I mean, why?" Frank asked.
"That really isn't important; is it?" Henry replied.
"I guess not," uttered Frank's submissive sounding voice.

As Henry and Kate looked across the table at the Harrisons, each could feel the couple seemed to be warming up somewhat to their proposal. That fact seemed evident to them, yet they needed to hear the word, "yes." That simple word didn't appear to be forthcoming. As they sat there Kate felt it necessary to take charge of the situation, after all, both women had children and she thought that would help her in getting their approval.

"Jennifer, if this were my own child, I'd take the chance. Josh deserves the benefit of the doubt. We can both agree on that; can't we?"
"That's very well and good, Kate," Jennifer said, "and I agree with you. But when we heard of the cost involved, it would be like trying to figure out the depth of a bottomless pool. We just can't come up with that much money. It's not that I don't want to, it's out of the question with our income. And charity is something neither one of us want to accept… or will accept."
"A fundraiser isn't charity, it's a different animal all together," interjected Henry.
"Perhaps," Jennifer said as she nodded her head.
"No, it's the same thing," Frank stated emphatically.
"What do you think Josh would have to say about it, Frank?" Henry asked.
"I don't know," Frank uttered, a puzzled look reflected on his face. "We've never asked or talked to him about it."
"Honey," Jennifer said as she looked in her husband's direction, "we've never even asked him." Jennifer began feeling somewhat guilty for at least not having taken that step with her son.

"How old is he?" Kate asked.

"He's nine."

"Old enough to know his wishes, yet not old enough to be listened to," Kate said.

Jennifer shook her head back and forth with that revelation coming to light.

"I feel very much the part of a fool," Frank stated. "If he can have the operation, no matter what the cost, he does deserve that opportunity."

"Thank you, Honey," Jennifer said. She reached over and squeezed his hand with hers.

Frank nodded his head as he tried to comprehend all that had taken place concerning their son within a matter of a few moments.

"We'll just have to make do with what we can," Frank said.

"Like we've always done," Jennifer said as she nodded her head.

"You did say, yes, to the procedure; am I right?" Kate inquired, wanting to make sure their answer was in the affirmative.

"Yes," Frank and Jennifer answered in unison.

"Good, great," she said, a very evident smile written across her face.

Now that Kate had their permission she would waste no time in making arrangements to raise the money. Kate was very much willing to invest her own time into this wonderful quest. It was Kate's prayer, her efforts, and that of others, would eventually lead them all down the path to success, or at least a chance for it.

"Oh, just so the two of you know, Henry has offered to do a benefit program on Josh's behalf."

"That's right," Henry said with a smile.

"Two of them."

"I have? Yes, I have, two of them," Henry said nodding his head.

Once again he understood the fact that he could never say no to his wife. He chuckled to himself with that thought. He had agreed to do one, now it was up to two. Still, he thought, what a wonderful reason to lose to her.

"Now, you leave everything to me," Kate said, "I'll see to it that things get moving and organized. I'll give you a call as soon as things start to fall into place. If you have any questions at all, feel free to call me."

"Kate…"

"Yes, Jennifer."

"Thank you both."

Kate never said a word, she just nodded her head with a smile softly written across her face.

Within the next few weeks Kate's personal crusade concerning Josh was moving along fairly fast. She was well organized as she proceeded forward. Half of the kitchen table was devoted to various lists, people she had called, who next to contact and so forth.

Kate got a hold of Richard who was more than happy to assist in her quest. She was even astonished by the amount of enthusiasm he presented her with. The fact that they were using Henry's talent as a fundraiser appealed to him. Being the good businessman that he was, he looked at this opportunity in two ways. One, the money raised was going for a wonderful purpose, and two, it never hurts to advertise that fact. He always believed what goes around, comes around. The only problem that was of any concern to him was being able to squeeze two additional shows into their busy schedule. He knew he would find the time no matter what… and he did.

Tinkle-Tinkle

It was a normal Monday morning with the sounds of traffic filtering through the air, people in a hurry to get to work on time. Susan and Kenneth arrived at the Summers Family Store per their customary time, early. Together they took the elevator up to the office section of the building. As was par for the course their accountant, Fred Carpenter, was already sitting behind his desk busy at work. They looked at one another and smiled. He was undoubtedly one of the best employees to ever come to work for them.

Though he used crutches to get around, having only one leg, his work ethic was unbelievable. To many who knew him he was an inspiration, not because of his disability, but simply because he could be trusted to do everything well. Fred never turned down the opportunity to help someone in need. This one fact alone held him in a position higher than he ever knew or dreamed.

Being friendly was another trait he exhibited. Possessing an uncanny sense of humor he had a knack of finding a ray of sunshine in even the dampest and darkest of days. If you were feeling down, he was the one you wanted to be sitting next to as you discussed the rainy day you were suffering through.

"So how is Melissa doing today?" Fred asked, it being the first words that came forth from his lips every day at work. It started when he first learned she was pregnant, and they expected this question not to end until she gave birth.

"She'll be in a little later," Susan stated.

"Is she feeling okay?"

"Oh, yes, she's fine. I told her to stay home, but she doesn't always listen to her mother."

"Well, she's a lot like her mother," he said, "a mind of her own, and as pretty a site as an oasis to a thirsty man."

Susan smiled as she turned and made her way towards Kenneth's office. Fred's little words, his small statements were a welcomed part of the day to everyone. People wondered how he ever came up with some of them as quickly as he did. They always seemed to fit the occasion. Halfway through the door she stopped and turned around.

"Fred, how are things going with your artificial leg, is everything moving along smoothly?"

"Like a bee in a honey factory," he joked. "I was going to tell you I'm getting another adjustment made tomorrow afternoon, if that's okay." He already knew what the response to his question would be, after all, it was Kenneth and Susan who insisted he should attempt to get an artificial leg to begin with. They worked hand-and-hand with him making sure any time off he needed would be there for him. Susan even made sure his pay wasn't docked while he was off. Fred knew that for a fact. He did the books and Susan checked his work to make sure he wasn't being cheated. Docking his pay on his own would be out of the question for her. She wouldn't stand for it.

His love for the Summers' family was almost unmatched with that of his own family. They not only treated him well, they loved his family, his wife, Robin, and their two daughters. To Fred, the Summers were an extension to his own. Greg and Melissa found him to be every bit a friend to them, as they were to Fred.

Still standing in the doorway, Susan asked him a question. "Do you remember sometime ago I said I'd like to be present when you walked without the aid of your crutches in front of your children? Do you remember me saying that to you?"

"Yes, I do, Mrs. Summers. Mrs. Summers, after tomorrow's appointment I was wondering if —"

"It's Susan!"

"I understand, Mrs. Summers, it's just I always have a little trouble calling you by your first name.

That was the one thing that bothered Susan whenever she had an occasion to speak with Fred. While he always referred to her in that manner, having the utmost respect for her, to Susan it carried the connotation of making her feel older than she was. She adored the fact he was so polite, but wished he wouldn't use that Mrs. part in addressing her. As Susan stood nodding her head, her mind came up with a quick plan to end this Mrs. Summers business once and for all. She turned and left the room without saying another word. Within a matter of a few minutes she returned, a large clear plastic canister in her hands.

"Now, Fred, in the bottom left-hand corner of the desk is some glue. Would you please hand that to me?"

Susan knew the desk contents well, after all it was her desk originally. Once Fred was hired as a part-time bookkeeper he took over her office. After six months he was hired full-time. That fact freed Susan up to work more on her various charity projects.

One Sunday Fred and his family were invited over to the Summers home along with Greg, Melissa and his parents for a meal. Kenneth and Susan surprised him and his family when they presented him with the difference from his part-time pay to his full-time pay for the previous six months he had worked for them. That day he was informed of his new full-time status. In his short tenure with them, Fred had impressed them that much.

Fred did as he was instructed and got the glue out. She unscrewed the blue top to the container. Next she put a small amount of the glue around the inside of the top. She smiled as she screwed the top securely onto the canister. Susan nodded her head in approval. Fred could see a rough looking slit had been cut into the top of the lid. It was large enough for someone to be able to place any large coins into the container or other such material. Susan then placed the container onto Fred's desk.

"That ought to do it," she said.

Fred said nothing figuring an explanation would be coming forthwith. His assumption was correct.

"Every time you call me Mrs. Summers you are to put all of the change from your pocket into this container. If by chance you don't have any change, I want you to put the smallest denomination of folding money from your wallet into it. If I were you I would be sure to carry lots of single dollar bills with you all of the time, or at least have some coins available. Now, do you have any questions?"

"No, Mrs. Summers."

Susan put her finger onto the top of the container and tapped it.

"Tinkle-tinkle," she said, "We need to hear that sound from the coins dropping into the canister."

Fred reached into his pocket. Unfortunately for him there was no change available for him to use. He looked up at Susan. Once again she tapped the top of the contained repeating her phrase to him. He opened his wallet and placed a dollar bill into the canister.

"Now, remember if you don't have any singles, you use the next smallest bill in your possession. We're both clear on that; right?"

"Yes, Mrs. Summers."

"Tinkle- tinkle."

Both of them looked at each other and smiled. He knew it would not take him long to start referring to her by her first name. Susan was confident of that fact also. She chuckled to herself as she left the room, pleased with the solution she had found. She knew if there was any amount of money in the container when they stopped using it she would turn it over to his wife anyway. It would be fun to see how long her experiment took to work.

The early afternoon was upon Fred before he knew it. The Summers family had gone and returned from the break room, their lunch time completed. It was customary for them to occasionally visit the break room and share their noon meals together with various employees. This was a ritual the employees loved as well as Kenneth and Susan. When it was possible Melissa and Greg would join in. On those days Susan was sure to pack a few extra items in the lunch bag for Kenneth. He would trade one food item of his with others attempting to steal away one of their tasty treats for a good price.

Black olives were always included in the small selection of his bargaining foods. It was his favorite thing to negotiate with. Many of the people enjoyed them as well. Unbeknownst to Kenneth, Susan overheard a couple of women refer to her husband by the name of, "Olive Tree." One woman suggested they simply refer to him as, "O.T." for short. He even has his own nickname Susan thought. She chuckled to herself. Everyone relished participating in the little game of barter. Besides, you never knew what treats you might end up with.

When the women would bring in a specialty item from home to share, especially around the holidays, everyone got a bite, that is, except Kenneth. They would make him trade for a couple of cookies, a piece of coffee cake or even for a donut. It wasn't that they were trying to be mean to him, it was simply the fact they enjoyed their boss and his bargaining prowess. If Kenneth ran out of trading items, they were sure he didn't miss out on any of the tasty goodies. The time they all spent together wasn't as boss and employee, it was friends and family.

Greg walked through the doorway into Fred's office.
"How is Melissa doing?" Fred asked.
"She's doing very well," Greg answered with a smile. He always enjoyed the relationship Melissa had with Fred, and carried between the two of them as well. He was cheerful, a joke always lingering on the edge of his lips to be told.
"Good. Greg, I was wondering if you and I could have a talk alone sometime in the near future?"
"Of course."
"Good."
"I have some time now, if you want to."
"Now is good for me," Fred said nodding his head.
"Okay."
"Would you mind if we went down to the break room. Nobody should be there now, and it will give us a little privacy."
"Or we can do it here if you'd like."
"I'd rather not have Mr. & Mrs. Summers, or Melissa privy to our conversation, I mean, they could walk in on us here. Do you mind that?"
"No, the lunchroom is fine with me."

Curiosity is the shadow that makes itself known when anyone speaks the words concerning, "alone, private conversation, or can we speak." Greg's mind was no different than anyone else's. He wondered what was so important to Fred that he wanted to reveal it only in an area where other ears would not be present.

"Well, let's go down there and talk," Greg stated.

"Okay," Fred replied as he reached for his crutches.

It always amazed Greg how well Fred moved around on one leg aided with only his crutches. If for some reason Fred had to get somewhere in the store quickly, Greg wouldn't have wanted to race him there.

Upon entering the lunchroom area, one employee stood at the counter waiting for the microwave to finish its project.

"Hi, Jason," Greg said.

"Hi, Greg," he responded, "Fred."

Fred nodded his head.

The two of them sat talking about nothing in particular, the weather, expected rain they might encounter over the coming weekend. Once the sound of the chime announced its completion in warming or cooking, it interrupted their discussion. The microwave door was opened with the item retrieved.

"See you two later, Greg... Fred."

"See ya, Jason," Fred said.

"Oh, Jason," Greg said with a smile, "I saw your new car yesterday, she's really sweet."

"Isn't she," smiled Jason.

"I love the color, too," Greg continued.

"Well, I've got to get back to work. After all, I have a car to pay for now," his voice having a chuckle attached to it as he spoke.

Greg gave a little wave as Jason walked out of the room.

"So what's so important and secretive that we need to meet in here?" Greg asked.

"First of all I'd like to keep this to ourselves," Fred started out, "and when you hear why, I think you'll understand what I'm doing, and why I'm doing it."

Greg nodded his head. There was one thing Fred knew about Greg that he admired very much about him, in fact, the whole family in general. If you asked one of them to keep something to themselves, it was locked in a safe that even Houdini couldn't open or get out of. As Greg sat listening to Fred, a smile began to take over his expression. He nodded his head in agreement.

"Fred, that's a wonderful idea," Greg stated, the smile growing broader as he spoke to him. "Thank you."

"What for?" a questioning look exhibited on Fred's face as he spoke the two words.

"For allowing me to be part and parcel of this. I feel very honored that you included me in it."

Fred nodded his head, happy inside with Greg's words having been said.

"So where and when are we doing this?" Greg inquired.

"I'll have to let you know that later. I just have to see how everything works out for me in the end. There's still a few items that need to be tied up."

Now it was Greg who nodded his head. He understood Fred's statement very well, everything now making sense to him.

"Well, what do you say we get back to work, " Fred said as he reached for his crutches.

Greg couldn't help himself as he reached over and patted Fred on the shoulder. Together the men returned to the office area, each one carrying thoughts about what they had just discussed.

This should be very interesting, Greg thought.

The World as a Gift

The candles on the table flickered giving both shadows and light to the faces of everyone seated around the table. Stella, Joe's wife always enjoyed this particular part of any special dinner she prepared involving guests. The candles brought a warmth to any conversations that were taking place. To her it was the piece de resistance of any meal, the final touch that blended everything together.

As Henry placed his cup of tea down on to the table he looked at Kate, Stella, Joe, and finally their son, Jake.

"I know it may have seemed a little awkward for you, that Kate and I invited ourselves over earlier this week for tonight's festivities, but we both wanted to share in your anniversary celebration. We hope you don't mind."

"Don't be silly, Henry," Stella said, "you and Kate are both part of our family. In fact, Henry, through the years we've always considered you a very important piece of it. To us you're Joe's younger brother, if he had one."

"Or you're like my uncle," Jake added.

"Kate," she went on, "since your marriage to Henry... well, even before that day we've loved having you around to share in our family activities. You're a very intricate part of our family as well."

Joe smiled nodding his head.

"And that goes double for me," Jake interjected with a smile.

"Thank you," Kate said.

"Well, what's for dessert, Honey?" Joe said with a gleam in his eye.

"You ought to know, Dear," Stella was quick to say, "after all, I saw you sneaking a peek this afternoon. Why don't you tell us what we're having?"

"Yeah," Jake said with a chuckle in his voice, "what are we having, Dad?"

Joe looked around as everyone turned their attention to his spot at the table.

"Well," he began, "if I'm not mistaken —"

"And you very seldom are when it comes to desserts," interjected Stella, "wrong in your guesses that is."

"It looked like a Chocolate Bavarian Torte Cake to me."

"And you're right, Honey," Stella said as she winked at him, her voice carrying a slight chuckle to it.

"Bingo," Jake exclaimed with a smile.

After Stella cut the cake and served up some more coffee and tea to everyone, she sat down and began to eat also. Everyone could hear her as she began to snicker to herself as she placed a small morsel in her mouth.

"What's so funny, mom?" Jake asked.

"I was just thinking back to the Ladies Monthly Luncheon at church a couple of weeks ago.

"And?" Jake inquired further.

"Now everyone here has to promise me you'll not repeat what I'm about to tell you."

Everyone nodded their heads in a silent agreement to keep her secret.

"Well, as I walked down the hallway towards the gym carrying my dessert offering I could hear footsteps behind me. I stopped and turned to see who it was and saw Pastor Phil. I think he was following me on purpose."

"That doesn't surprise me one iota," Joe stated. "I think he's your favorite food fan no matter what you're serving, other than me, of course."

"And me, too," Jake quickly added.

"He followed me right up to the serving tables."

"Knowing him, that sounds right," Joe said with a nod of his head.

"And then he asked me if it was okay if he sampled a little portion of my dessert before the ladies even got there."

"That sounds right," Joe said again laughingly. "You know, Honey, in all the years you've fed me, I've never had anything better than your cooking or baking, whether it was at any social events I've attended or here at home."

"Me neither, Dad."

Henry and Kate nodded their heads in agreement. Stella was a woman very much gifted in the kitchen area. To the individuals who tasted the various dishes being served at get-togethers, hers stood second to none. Kate wished she had just one dish that was truly outstanding, while Stella's were too numerous to count. At least that was Kate's comparison between the two of them. She was not jealous of her, though it was the one thing Kate envied somewhat.

"Well, anyway, as I handed Pastor Phil his dessert plate, his wife came up behind him. She told him to stop pestering me about my dessert and to leave me alone. He turned and headed towards his office, his dessert in hand, of course. Marsha watched him go and then turned to me. She placed her finger over her lips as if for me to be quiet, and then asked me in a whisper if it was all right if she had a small sample, too."

"That doesn't surprise me either," Henry said with more than a giggle in his voice. You are just such a wonderful cook and baker."

"You have no one to blame but yourself, Honey," Joe said as he placed his fork on the table. "Good cooks or bakers are hard to find these days."

"You can say that again, Dad. I can't think of a single gal at college who ever mentions cooking or baking. Well, there is this one girl I know."

"So how is college going, Jake?" asked Kate as she took a quick glance in Henry's direction.

"Well, I'm finally finishing up. Actually I can see the end of the trail," he snickered.

"It's been a long haul for him," Stella said, "and we're very proud of Jake for all the hard work he's put into it."

"Amen," Joe said.

"So you'll be all done with college and everything will completely come to a conclusion very soon?" Kate asked.

"Well, except for the bills mom and dad have, that will probably never come to a complete and final end for a very long time. As soon as I get a steady paycheck, get some money coming in, I'll pay them back."

"They really add up, don't they, the bills I mean?" Henry inquired.

"Well, it's all part of the big picture, I guess," Stella said.

"Can I have another piece of cake, Mom?"

"Of course."

"I wouldn't mind some more also," Henry added, as he held his empty plate in her direction.

"Well, we can all have a little more then," Stella stated as she reached for the silver cake server.

As everyone sat enjoying Stella's cake, each one taking a smaller second sliver, the evening sunset began to make its presence known through the front windows.

"Mom, Dad, I've got an anniversary gift for both of you. It isn't much, not a cruise or anything like that," he chuckled, "but just the same I hope you both like it. It's a little different."

"You didn't have to do anything, son, we're just happy you made it home to be with us," Joe said.

"Your father's right, Honey, we're just glad you were able to make it home."

"Well, having it fall on the weekend helped me out a lot. Anyway, I'll get it."

Jake got up and walked into his bedroom. He returned shortly with two wrapped packages in his hands. He handed a large box to his mother. The second gift, what appeared to be a book was presented to his father.

"Go ahead and open them," Jake said with a smile.

"Who should go first?" Joe inquired.

"Why don't you, Dad," Jake said.

Stella sat watching as her husband opened his package. It was a large book, a World Atlas. As Joe and Stella sat there, each could read by the other's expression that the gift was exactly as Jake had described it, a little different.

"You're next, Mom."

Stella carefully slid her fingers under the wrapping as she undid the colorful packaging. Once it was opened she reached into the box and retrieved a finely etched brass globe of the world. It was large in size, and extremely detailed. It sat on a rich mahogany stand. With her right hand, Stella gave the earth a small push sending it into a gentle smooth spin.

"These are very nice, son," Joe stated as Stella quickly agreed with him.

"We both love the gifts, Jake," Stella said as she rubbed her hand slowly across the brass globe. She could feel the smoothness of the oceans as well as the mountains reaching up from the golden metal. "It's just so real looking." Stella said as she admired it.

"These gifts look a little expensive, son," Joe stated, "especially the globe."

"The cost of a gift from the heart should never be brought into question by the gift recipient," Jake said, as he nodded his head.

"And how long did it take you to think up those words?" Joe said smiling.

"A little while. I didn't know quite what to get both of you, but this was my thinking. I know for a fact I'll be traveling around the world because I've already been offered a job, and accepted it," Jake said smiling.

"You're kidding!" Joe exclaimed in amazement.

"Oh my gosh," Stella said as she placed her hand to her mouth.

Joe got up from his seat as he stepped towards Jake giving his son a big hug.

"I miss you already," Stella stated as she got up to embrace her son as well.

"Mom, Dad, what I would like you to do is set the globe in the middle of the dining room table. The book, however, I was thinking could be placed nearby, where I'm not really sure. Every time you pass it or look at it I want both of you to know I'll have each of you in my thoughts. When I move onto a new area, you can look the location up in the book. I thought it would be a good way for the three of us to keep in touch, at least in our thoughts."

"You're always in our thoughts, son," Stella said.

"She's right, Jake, you're in our thoughts daily," Joe said.

Jake smiled.

"Your present is such a thoughtful gift, Jake. You definitely put some thought into it," Kate expressed as she got up and made her way over to Jake. She hugged him as she gave him a small kiss on his cheek.

Henry embraced Jake also as he congratulated him.

"When do you start your job?" inquired Stella.

"Well, as soon as I finish up with everything at school and get my ducks all lined up, probably a month or less."

"And where is this job taking you, do you know that or have any idea?" his father was quick to inquire.

"Well, I haven't been told that yet. When I interviewed I was told that I would be a troubleshooter of sorts, and when I get things straightened up, I would be off to the next problem area."

"Apparently the company did their homework in compiling a list of perspective candidates. They sure chose you quickly," Henry offered.

"I was told I was at the top of their list for some time, that's why they approached me right away."

"They didn't want to lose you," Stella said as she nodded her head confidently. She felt in her heart her words were very true.

"Actually, Mom, it's the kind of job I've always dreamed of. I think the thing I love most of all is there will be new challenges every day."

"And exploring the world on someone else's dime," smiled Stella.

"That was always my dream, too," Joe said. "This way I get to do it through you, Jake, while not even having to leave my front door."

"I'll send lot of cards," smiled Jake.

"I was hoping for you to help me out a little bit at the store," expressed Joe.

"Well, why don't you ask Jeremy Tucker," Jake mentioned, "he's worked with us before, and he is a good worker."

"I think I will. In fact, I know I will."

"Jeremy's a nice kid," Henry agreed. "I've known him for a few years now. He's helped me out from time to time."

"He should be getting out of high school pretty soon," Stella said.

"I'll check with him, see what he's up to," Joe said nodding his head. "After all, he's helped us out numerous times in the past like you said."

"I'm sure he'd like to make a little extra money on the side also," Stella added.

"Well, let's all sit back down and finish our coffee," Joe stated as he patted Jake on his back a couple of times as he spoke.

Once again everyone took their seats.

"Dad, you know how you and Henry always treat each other like brothers?"

"Yes," Joe said.

"If I ever had a brother, I think I'd like someone like Jeremy to be mine."

"Jake," Stella stated, "that's truly a compliment for anyone to receive."

Henry and Joe didn't say anything, but Stella's words rang true in both of their minds.

Henry looked over at Kate, she returning his glance as they sat there.

"Kate," Henry simply said.

Kate nodded her head slightly in response to him.

"Stella, Joe, Jake, Henry and I have a gift for all three of you also."

"Oh," Stella said with a surprised expression on her face.

"That wasn't necessary," Joe was quick to state, his face also exhibiting a small look of astonishment upon it.

A gift from Kate and Henry was truly unexpected by all of them.

"Did I hear you mention me also?" Jake asked, not understanding his connection to his parent's anniversary, after all, they were the ones who should be receiving any gifts, not him.

"Really, it's not necessary," Joe once again stated.

"Yes, it is," Henry said. "Kate, will you do the honors?"

Kate stood up once again and made her way over to the front door area. She retrieved her purse from off of a small wooden bench by the front door. Kate then returned, standing next to the table by Henry.

"For some time now Henry and I have both been welcomed into your home and have had the pleasure of being treated not only as a member of your family, but more importantly we've been loved by each and every one of you. It is a gift all three of you have offered to us with open arms, your love, and it is something we have learned to cherish deeply in our own hearts. No words Henry or I could offer the three of you can do justice to how we feel about all of you. We love each one of you deeply."

It wasn't the amount of words spoken by Kate that seemed to reach so deeply into the crevices of their hearts, it was the words themselves. The mood in the room became still, very thick with each person dealing with the emotions that were taking control of their senses. The words offered from Kate were not only sincere, but very much unexpected. Perhaps it was the simple genuineness of her words that touched Stella's heart so strongly, but she soon found herself reaching up and wiping her eyes. Joe and Jake simply turned their heads to the side as if trying to hide or control the inner feelings they were dealing with. All three not only appreciated what Kate had just said concerning her and Henry, but felt the deep sentiment it was given in. They understood how strong her words were, and the deep impact the words carried.

Kate reached into her purse and removed an envelope. It was approximately the size of a card. She looked at Henry and smiled. He looked up at her and winked. Kate handed the envelope to Stella, who handed it to Joe. Joe then handed it back to Stella.

"If you hand that to Jake, we're taking it back," laughed Henry.

"You open it, Joe," Stella said chuckling with Henry's statement having been made.

"Okay," he answered.

Joe took the envelope from Stella and opened it. As he did, a piece of paper fell from its interior to the floor, sliding under the table somewhat in its flight. A paperclip was attached to the paper holding two pieces together as one.

"I'll get it," Henry said.

"Thank you," Joe stated.

Henry reached down and retrieved the paper. He held it in his hand, but did not offer it to Joe. Henry wanted Joe to read the card's interior first.

The card was a typically well-versed anniversary greeting. It spoke of love shared, happy times spent together. It was not mushy, simply tender in nature. The bottom of the card was signed with love from Kate and Henry. Joe read it out loud.

"Thank you," Joe said with the completion of his reading.

"Yes, thank you both," Stella said.

He then handed the card to Stella to view.

"Thank you," Jake said, not knowing what else to do. This was, after all, his mother and dad's anniversary to celebrate, not his. He did feel, however, obliged to be polite since they had mentioned his name as well as his mother and father.

"Joe, Stella, Jake, this gift to all three of you is something Kate and I feel privileged to do. Please accept it with that understanding."

Henry then handed what appeared to be a check to Joe. Jake bent over towards his dad attempting to read it, his curiosity very much heightened by what was transpiring.

"OMG," Jake said, using initials to convey his thoughts.

"OMG," Stella said, "do you mean oh my God?"

"OMG is very fitting to say," Joe said as he stared at the check, too shocked to even say anything more about the item he held in his hand. He rubbed the attached paperclip over and over with his thumb, his mind absently doing it nervously. The numbers stared back at him.

Stella moved over closer to Joe so she could see the check in his hand. On the face of the check was scribed the amount of forty five thousand dollars. The check had the names of all three of them written on the pay to portion of it.

"Oh my God!" Stella said loudly.

Henry and Kate merely looked at each other and smiled.

"Kate and I did some checking, and we believe we're correct on what we are able to do. We were informed that a person may give a gift in the amount of ten to fifteen thousand dollars or so once a year to a relative or friend, I guess anyone. This amount can change slightly from year to year. From what we've been told, it is free and clear, no taxes being attached to it whatsoever, though you may want to check that fact out to be sure."

Joe, Stella, and Jake sat quietly trying to conceive what was going on. They all understood fifteen thousand dollars was being given as a gift to each one of them. Henry's words were more than clear on that subject. Comprehending that concept was a thing of another nature. Both Kate and Henry expected this reaction from the three of them. Henry sat quietly before taking the next step forward. He smiled at Kate, she at him.

"If I may continue," Henry expressed, not really anticipating a response to his words.

Blue Rose Petals

No one said anything, while Stella and Jake nodded their heads slightly. Joe simply sat there feeling the effects of what shock can do to one's mind.

"There is a second part to the gift for the three of you," Henry said, "it's the same and yet different."

Kate smiled as she sat quietly taking the events in. She enjoyed sitting back watching everything unfold before her. Kate felt it was like waiting for someone to open a gift where you know what the contents are, and they don't. Her insides were filled with an excitement to see their reaction, yet not wanting her eagerness to offset the thrill of the moment.

"Look at the second piece of paper," Henry instructed Joe.

"A second piece of paper, huh," he responded, his mind still swirling with what he had just gone through.

"It's under the check."

"Huh?"

"Here, Dad," Jake said as he assisted him in pulling the paper out from underneath the paperclip attached to the check.

"Thank you, son," Joe said. "My mind is running in different directions all at the same time," he uttered softly.

Jake took the sheet of paper from his father's hand and opened it. His face bore a surprised expression as he read the paper to himself. Once he finished reading it, his voice verbalized the following letters loudly.

"O...M...G," Jake said once again. This time each letter of the alphabet was stated slowly as the letters found their way from his mind to his lips.

"What is it?" Stella asked.

Joe said nothing as he sat quietly engulfed in a cloud of astonishment, not having gotten over the initial check's amount. His mind was still trying to comprehend the amount of the check, and how it came to be.

Jake sat shaking his head slowly back and forth, his brain entering into the same dimension of shock as his father. With neither men offering her an answer to her question Stella reached over and took the paper from Jake's hand. She read it slowly to herself.

"It's an I.O.U. from you to us," Stella said.

"That's right," Henry said with a smile across his lips.

"I guess," Kate said, a large smile across her face as well, "it's an OMG followed by an I.O.U."

Henry laughed at her use of the letters.

"I just don't understand," Stella said.

"One evening as Kate and I were sitting together talking about how nice it was to see Jake home over the weekend, she suggested something to me. It was such a great idea that I knew we had to... Well, we found out that it takes anywhere from eight to thirty thousand dollars a year basically to attend college. We understand that it depends on the type of college you go to, private as opposed to a state university and so forth."

All three of the family members nodded their heads as they listened to Henry's explanation of the cost of attending college. They knew all about it, and it all boiled down to money.

Kate and I had this I.O.U. drafted for the three of you. It's money that's set aside so that if something should happen to us, —"

"God forbid," Kate interjected.

"— you'll still receive a check made out to the three of you for that same amount as you have in your hand. So basically for the next three years, not counting tonight, your loan is covered. If the amount is less than the thirty figure, and Kate and I hope it is, you can keep the rest and use it as you each see fit."

Stella literally burst into tears, her eyes unable to keep the dam from holding back a single tear any longer. Within seconds, Kate joined her.

"This is a gift beyond imagination," Joe said, "but I don't know if we can really accept it. It's an awful lot of money for you two to give up."

"A hundred and eighty thousand dollars," Jake was quick to state.

"See what a college education gets you," Henry chuckled, "a mind that's quick and sharp."

"I don't know," Joe said. "You two are just starting out in life, you have a young child. I don't know quite what to say."

Henry chuckled, almost a small laugh coming from his mouth. He then offered the following solution to Joe concerning their gift to them.

"Let me repeat something that someone very close to you said concerning gifts. In fact, they're in this room as I speak." With those words having been spoken, Henry repeated the very sentence Jake had spoken not so very long ago. "The cost of a gift from the heart should never be brought into question by the gift recipient. Now, Jake, isn't that exactly how you put your gift cost into play?"

"Yes, it is," Jake said with a smile.

"Those words should also apply to us, don't you think, Joe?" Henry said.

Joe didn't know what to do. An enormous financial gift, one they could truly use, a son leaving to who knows where, and a wife demonstrating a flood of tears. It was all rolled into one mind-boggling evening.

"I don't know what to say, Henry, Kate," Joe said softly.

"How about thank you," suggested Jake.

"Thank you, Henry... Kate. This is a most generous gift. Thank you," Joe said again.

"Thank you both," Stella uttered softly, as she wiped her nose.

"Now I know why you referred to the gift with all three of our names," Jake said. "Thank you both. I know the money will be put to good use, especially with the loan payments coming due not that far down the line."

Joe, Stella, and Jake got up from their positions and hugged Henry and Kate. There was no rush in their arms to release the other from their grip. It went on for some time.

"This has really taken a burden from our shoulders," Joe said

"Helping people you love in any way possible, isn't that what it's all about," added Henry.

"And especially by family members the three of us love so much," smiled Stella.

Celebration

"Mom, Dad, I was wondering if I could treat you two and Melissa to lunch tomorrow at the Golden Rib Restaurant," Greg announced as he looked in Kenneth and Susan's direction.

"What's the special occasion?" Kenneth inquired.

"Does there have to be one?"

"No, not really."

"I'll explain why later. Oh, heck, why not now. You ever get a craving for a thick homemade tasting turkey sandwich, maybe a good steak?"

"Now you've got my attention," chuckled Kenneth.

"Well, I've had a taste for a Black Angus medium well cooked piece of top sirloin for a few days now. In fact, I can even picture an Idaho baked potato sitting next to it, smothered in butter and sour cream."

"With mushrooms?"

"Of course."

"Now I'm getting hungry," Kenneth chuckled again. He even went so far as to place his hand on his stomach while making circular motions with it.

"Is everyone up to it?" Greg inquired.

"Honey, I have a doctor's appointment tomorrow, but that's not until the later part of the afternoon, so I'm free," Melissa said smiling.

"I think I can make it," Susan said nodding her head.

"Well, I'm not going to be left out in the cold when I can get a free meal. Why not," Kenneth added. "I don't even have to look over the menu, I already know what I'm having. You can even order for me, Greg."

"I'm getting some chunky potato soup to begin with," Greg stated. "Shall I order that for you, too?"

"Now we're talking," Kenneth said as he nodded his head, his tongue wetting his lips as he spoke.

"We'll all meet here at 11:45 tomorrow morning, then we can go over there together," Greg stated. "Now that we've got the time established, I'll meet you all here then."

Looking over at Fred sitting at his desk working, Greg turned to him.

"Fred, how about joining us, it's my treat."

Fred looked up from the paperwork before him, his hand resting on a large calculator. "I might be able to make it. I still have some things I need to accomplish by Thursday."

"Let it wait," Susan stated, "it's not going to go anywhere."

"Well..."

"You can let me know tomorrow if you can make it," Greg suggested.

"That sounds good to me," Fred said nodding his head slightly.

The following day life went about as usual. Kenneth worked in his office, studying over various merchandise he was thinking of carrying in stock. Susan was on the phone talking with someone about getting donations for another charity project she had immersed herself in. Melissa would soon be arriving to complete a project she had some concerns about. Greg was visiting with different departments, checking to see if they had anything that needed to be addressed. Fred diligently worked at his desk, as was the common course for him daily.

It was precisely 11:45 the four family members gathered together in Fred's office, ready to head over to the restaurant.

"Everyone ready?" Greg asked.

"Well, I'd kind of like to finish up this paperwork before I head on over, if you don't mind, " Fred expressed.

"It can wait," Susan said as she looked over at Fred.

"It really shouldn't, "Fred expressed. "I'd like to get it into the mail by 12:30. It won't take me that long to finish."

"No, no, you come now, tomorrow will be soon enough," Susan was quick to state.

It was Susan who did the books before Fred was hired to fill her position. She understood very well what could and couldn't wait. This could wait.

"Let him be, Mom," Greg stated in a somewhat strong voice. "If he wants to finish his work, let him do it. You wouldn't want to spoil him with more time off, would you?"

Melissa, Susan, and Kenneth turned and gave Greg a nasty expression. Fred's time off, as Greg referred to as, was so he could work at getting an artificial leg fitted. Anytime he missed, Fred more than made up for with extra hours he stayed and worked. Everyone knew that. Greg could feel the sharpness their eyes carried in his direction. There were three sets of daggers, each possessing a coldness about them. It was not a good feeling at all for him to experience.

The look Susan gave Greg, he had not seen since Kate's wedding reception. He knew it meant he was in a world of trouble with her. It was the exact expression he saw the day he helped his wife give a toast for her best friend, Kate. Melissa wanted to give the toast instead of Greg who was the best man. Greg attempted to talk her out of it, but to no avail. He decided it was better to do his best to aid Melissa in her endeavor. Greg had hidden his mouth with his hand, his elbow resting on the table as Melissa spoke. No one was able to see his lips moving as Melissa uttered the words she had written down. No one could observe Greg speaking to her as he followed along with her speech. He had an exact duplicate of what Melissa held in her hand, and was now reading from it. When she began to cry, her voice very much quivering, he would instruct her to take a deep breath, tell her where she left off, and so on. All Susan could observe was a son-in-law who should have given the toast as best man, and now sat next to his wife as she stumbled through her words as she spoke. However, Melissa was still doing a credible job with her toast. As Susan watched her daughter her own heart was breaking within. Susan knew very well of Melissa's fear of public speaking. Susan's emotions started to carry bitterness towards Greg. She was very upset with his complete lack of compassion concerning his wife's emotional state. That was when Greg first observed the look she now carried on her face.

Once the toast was completed and Susan had an opportunity to speak with him, she made it abundantly clear to Greg of her feeling over what had just transpired. She expressed to him how upset she was with him for allowing it to occur, he being the one who should have given the toast in the first place. Kenneth expressed a few words to him also, but not to the extent of Susan's admonishment. Susan even went so far as to tell him she was ashamed of him. Greg was not given the opportunity to defend himself. He said very little, if anything, in reply to her words. They cutoff any attempts he made to speak.

When Melissa found out what had taken place between the three of them she asked Greg to get her a glass of water. With him not present, Melissa explained everything to her parents. How she wanted to give the toast, that Greg didn't want her to knowing how her emotions would be batted back and forth. He understood how stressful it would be for her to do it. Melissa expressed to them how Greg practiced with her giving the speech nightly. With that having been brought to light, Susan and Kenneth were beside themselves. When Greg returned Susan hugged him, her words begging for his forgiveness. As was typical with Greg, he shrugged it off knowing Susan only did it because of her love for her daughter. How wonderful is that, he said to her.

As the four of them walked the short distance to the restaurant, very little was said. All were still upset with Greg's words to Fred. They entered the restaurant, Melissa leading the way. Much to their surprise seated at a large table was Fred's wife, Robin, and her two children, Betty and Annie. Robin waved her arm to get their attention. After walking over to them, the usual greetings having been exchanged, Robin invited them to join her and the kids.

"It's so nice to see you," Susan expressed as she took a seat.

"And me, too," Melissa said. "How are you two girls doing today?"

"I'm doing okay," Annie said, "but Betty has a cold."

"No, I don't," Betty was quick to state.

"Yes, you do."

"No, I don't."

"Girls, please," Robin said.

"Yes, she does," Annie said in a whisper to Melissa as she nodded her head, agreeing with her own statement.

"I do not," came another quick response.

"Girls, please," Robin repeated.

"I wasn't expecting to see you three here," Susan said.

"Greg invited us," Robin said nodding her head slightly.

"So what's going on?" Kenneth asked.

"I asked Robin and the girls to be here as well as you, and the rest of us," Greg offered, "but my plans went awry. I wanted to surprise Fred with everyone here to celebrate his anniversary with us, when he started at the store."

He looked over at Robin and smiled, she returning a smile back in his direction.

"Fred threw a wrench into my plans when he decided to stay and work," Greg stated, "but maybe he'll still make it. We'll just have to wait and see."

"So that's what upset you so much at the office," Susan said. "What you said to him was very inappropriate. Greg, you owe him an apology. You realize that, don't you?"

"I'll talk to him as soon as I see him," Greg said.

"You better, Greg," Melissa added sternly, "and I mean it."

It was clear to everyone by the tone of her voice she was very upset over Greg's conduct, and she wanted him to definitely know that very fact. What she didn't understand was why he acted so much out of character. She would surely have a talk with him later concerning his attitude.

Susan could see by the look on Kenneth's face he wholeheartedly agreed with Melissa's statement to her husband.

The waitress came over and asked to get their drink orders. The two girls wanted to know if they could have some soda, but soon learned they would have to survive on chocolate milk instead. This seemed to appease them both.

"I'll take the bill when we're done, Miss," Greg indicated, "and just so you know, we may have another person joining our group."

She nodded her head as she turned and walked away.

As everyone sat visiting, the conversation material varied greatly in scope. Like partners at a square dance the topics moved from one partner to another quickly and sometimes back to square one again.

The children told Melissa of some of the latest adventures that had taken place in their lives. The girls expressed with a great deal of excitement the fact that they now had a new member in their family, a small black and white dog.

Susan and Melissa, along with Kenneth relived the time they had a dog of their own named Nugget, a Golden Retriever. It was a family pet they all cherished throughout its life. Melissa had a close and loving relationship with her pet. The dog was always playful, happy to see her whenever she returned from being out. Nugget's tail would demonstrate that fact to her immediately. The dog possessed a warmth that never judged Melissa, an ear always available to listen to any problem she had, and most importantly, a wet lick to demonstrate her love for Melissa.

She recalled the day they took the animal to the vet to have her put down. There was nothing more they could do for their beloved friend. She had reached the end of a fruitful life. It was now time to give her body peace from the pain she was suffering from with old age. Nugget was unable to walk without pain, her bodily functions losing control every once in a while. At times Kenneth would reach down taking her in his arms to go outside so she could relieve herself. To keep her alive was not an option available to the family, though they explored many alternatives with the vet. Melissa remembered it as one of the worst days of her life. For a young girl to bear, her furry friend's death was a horrible memory she could not erase from the chalkboard of her heart. She never wanted to have another pet after that. With the loss of her beloved Nugget, her close friend and companion, a piece of her heart also died that day.

Fortunately, for Melissa the tone of the conversation got lighter, though the subject still encompassed pets. The children went on to say they named the dog after their father, Pirate, because pirates sometimes have only one leg like their dad. The adults attempted not to chuckle after hearing the dog's name, but still felt the need to laugh a little. They just couldn't control themselves. Everyone figured Fred had something to do with the naming of the pet, after all, with his sense of humor, only he could have come up with a name like that.

Greg kept looking at the doorway to the restaurant, attempting not to look conspicuous, but still watching for Fred's arrival. At one point he excused himself from the table. He tried not to be obvious in his movements, but he needed to get to the doorway quickly. Standing at the door was Fred, his crutches supporting him as he stood there.

"There's daddy," Annie said with a smile, pointing to the front door area where Greg was heading.

"Oh, good, he made it," Melissa stated.

"Miss," Kenneth said, to the waitress as she walked by, "we will be having one more person joining us for lunch."

Robin didn't say a word. She bit down slightly on her lower lip as she took a deep breath.

Greg met Fred at the door. He smiled at Fred as he gave him a wink.

"You ready for this?"

"As much as I'll ever be," replied Fred.

Greg reached for a cane that was leaning up against the wall. He had arranged to see to it that it was placed there before Fred's arrival. Fred handed Greg his crutches as Greg gave him the cane. Fred slowly began walking towards the table where everyone sat. Robin smiled as she watched him coming in their direction. There was a definite limp present as he walked, but he moved forward with all of the determination he could muster. It was only then when Melissa, Susan, Kenneth and the two girls realized he was walking towards them on two legs.

"Daddy," screeched Betty's voice, as she jumped from her chair, little Annie already up and running to her father.

With the sound of Betty's outcry, the attention of everyone in the restaurant was immediately drawn to them. Each child moved quickly to be with their father. When they got to him, the smiles upon their faces were radiant. They seemed to light up the room. Patrons voices could be heard by Fred and Greg, but what they were saying didn't matter to them at all. Both men were absorbed in the moment as the children hugged their father.

"This is so wonderful," was all Susan could utter as she lifted her napkin and wiped her eyes.

"It sure is, Mom," Melissa smiled, her eyes very watery as well.

Kenneth said nothing, a big smile painted across his face.

When Fred got to the table, Kenneth stood up. He wrapped his arms around Fred, giving him a large hug followed by a few pats on the back. It was without a doubt a moving time for Kenneth. As the two men released their hold on each other Susan and Melissa stood up, each reaching their arms out to him.

"You promised me I would be present and able to see the kids' expressions when you walked without the aid of your crutches," Susan said, "but never in my life did I expect this today."

Susan gave Fred a large hug. Once she stopped, she again wiped her eyes. Her large smile told Fred how much this meant to her. She could also tell the same was true with him as well.

"Fred," Melissa said, "I'm so proud of you, working so hard as you had to have." She placed her hand onto his shoulder as she reached up and gave him a kiss on the cheek.

"Thank you, thank you everyone," Fred said.

"I'm sorry I said what I did about the time off remark, but I was trying to get things back in line," Greg stated.

Fred chuckled.

"I don't understand," Susan said. "What you said to him was very rude."

"Can I explain this to her?" Fred asked.

"Be my guest," Greg said, nodding his head.

"You see, Mrs. Summers, —"

"Tinkle-tinkle," Susan said as she laughed out loud a little.

Fred chuckled also.

"Just so you know, Greg knew what I wanted to do concerning my artificial leg. We even met and discussed it. I wanted to surprise the children. I also understood you wanted to be present when I walked without my crutches, and see my kids' expressions when they saw me. It seemed like the only logical thing to do was to handle it in this way. I worked closely with Greg on this."

Melissa reached over and punched Greg in the arm slightly as she smiled.

Fred went on. "Our plan was simple. We would all meet for lunch, my family, of course, would be present. I could come in later, thus everyone would be surprised as I walked without my crutches."

Robin smiled with his words.

"That certainly worked on me," Melissa said.

"And me as well," Kenneth added.

"Of course, Robin knew what was going to happen," Fred said, "after all, she worked with me when I tried to walk and so forth. When I came home from the clinic, and when the kids weren't around, she was there to help me. The problem Greg and I had was something we hadn't counted on, you being very forceful in me coming along with everyone to the restaurant."

"And that's why I said what I did," interjected Greg. "I wanted to get you all upset with me and take your minds off of Fred."

"Wait a minute," Susan said abruptly, "you told us we were celebrating Fred's anniversary date. This isn't Fred's anniversary date, when he first started with us."

"Oops, I guess I was wrong on the date," Greg chuckled. "I'm sorry. It did work as far as getting everybody here though; didn't it?"

"You ever notice something, Mom?" Melissa said thoughtfully.

"What's that, Honey?"

"That Greg seems to always be apologizing for things when we're the ones who should be apologizing to him."

"Like at Kate's wedding reception," Susan said nodding her head.

"Uh-huh, and now," Melissa said.

Betty looked up at her dad and smiled. "Daddy," since our dog was named after you, does Pirate need a new name?

"Why would he?" Fred asked.

"You said some pirates have one leg, and he was named after you. Now you have two legs, should he still have the same name?"

"Oh, now I understand, Honey. No, he can keep his name if it's okay with you and Annie."

"I like Pirate," Annie said.

"So do I," Betty offered.

"Okay girls, we'll still call him Pirate."

"Good," Annie expressed with her toothless smile.

The three families sat enjoying their lunch with many more subjects to discuss with the events that had just taken place. When their meals were completed the waitress approached Greg with the bill.

"I'll be taking that," Fred said reaching his hand out.

The waitress handed him the bill.

"No, this is my treat," Greg insisted.

"Greg," Robin said, "please let us do this, it would mean a lot to both Fred and me."

"Well... thank you."

Robin nodded her head.

"Yes, thank you," Susan stated.

"And that goes double for me as well," Kenneth added.

"Thank you both," Melissa said.

Melissa reached over and took her husband's hand in hers. Once again she was proud of him, not needing to have that "special talk" with him now. It made her smile within. She felt a tremendous relief inside. After all, he really was the man she married and loved so much. Melissa looked over at Fred sitting across the table from her, Robin at his side. Fred's fingers were interlocked with his wife's, their arms resting on the table. This would be a good day for all of them to remember, she thought. In her heart she knew everyone of them would.

Dinner Meeting

"Exactly what time are we supposed to meet the Caldwells again?" Susan asked Kenneth as she turned the handle on the front door opening it slightly.

"Greg said they wanted to meet us all at five o'clock. He said the Caldwells made the reservations, and to remember it's Robert and Terry's treat. They want to take us all out."

"In other words, don't ask for the bill, Kenneth."

"What makes you think I would," he answered.

"Because between you and Greg it's like a contest to see who can pick up the bill."

"So what's wrong with that?"

"Sometimes others like to pay it, so don't even think of asking for it."

"Okay, okay, they can pay," he chuckled.

"I remember the last time we met with them at the Golden Rib Restaurant," Susan said, her head nodding back and forth.

"So do I," Kenneth said.

She continued standing in the living room doorway as she waited for Kenneth.

"With as many meals as we seem to have at that restaurant, I ought to buy some stock in it," suggested Kenneth, a slight smirk in the sound of his voice.

"They are an awfully nice couple," Susan said. "Terry is so down to earth, and Robert, well, he's a very smart and personable man. I didn't really know what to think of them when we first met. I mean, they were nice enough and all, it's just that I thought they were trying to steal Greg from our family business." Once again Susan nodded her head as she relived that fateful day.

"When Mr. Caldwell offered Greg a job, I couldn't believe my ears," Susan continued.

"Of course, he said he just wanted Greg to work part-time, but still one thing can lead to another," agreed Kenneth. "You've got to say one thing for sure, Greg has made a great deal of money working for them. Never in my wildest dreams would I ever have thought someone could make as much as he has working evenings at home, and part-time at that."

"Don't forget Greg said Melissa helps him out," smiled Susan.

"That's true. How much she really helps him, I really don't know, but Greg does speak highly of her mental abilities. She's one smart young lady."

"Well, after all, Honey, she probably takes after her mother," Susan said in a joking manner. "Remember this, she was smart enough to marry Greg."

"Don't forget you were smart enough to marry me, too," Kenneth stated, a little devilish smile reflected across this face.

Kenneth knew in some ways that was more of a truthful statement than Susan even knew. He observed how smart Melissa was at work, being able to solve daily problems that would occasionally surface. The fact that she got along so well with everyone was a plus, in and of itself. Many a day he looked at his daughter seeing the image of his wife in her. He was proud of her, and told her so many times.

"Well, Kenneth, you did allow him and Melissa to do some of the Caldwell Advertising work at the store. Of course, that was when they were free and clear from their obligations for us. I know that freed up time for the two of them to spend more quality time at home together."

"In some ways I feel a little guilty," Kenneth said.

"Why is that?"

"I feel we should be paying him more. You know, Susan, that young man has brought a tremendous amount of business our way. The ads he came up with for us over the past few Christmas seasons were unbelievable. His ads made it sound like, if you didn't shop in our store you had no Christmas spirit in your heart."

Susan couldn't help but laugh as she nodded her head.

"The deals he's cultivated, everything in general, it amazes me. It's intriguing when you think about how everything worked out when you consider how it all started. The day I met him, I couldn't stand him."

"And you were sure to let him know of that very fact."

Kenneth nodded his head affirming that very statement. It was a fact that Kenneth was not proud of, how he treated Greg so badly when they first met.

"Then by that same evening you loved him like a son," Susan said as she stepped back into the room. She couldn't help herself as she chuckled a little out loud.

"It's all fascinating when you really think about it," Kenneth said as he stepped from the kitchen area, turning off the light as he did.

Susan simply nodded her head as she smiled.

"His parents are still on for dinner this Sunday; right?" asked Kenneth.

"Edith said she'd call and let me know. Our Sunday meals together as a family aren't as often as they once were. We have got to work on that. I love having Frank and Edith over, especially Frank when it comes to meal time."

"You just love the compliments he showers on you over your cooking," Kenneth said as he walked up to her.

"And what's wrong with that?" she asked, not really expecting an answer to her reply.

Kenneth just nodded his head as the couple left the living room area and headed towards the garage.

The Caldwells were already present at the restaurant when Susan and Kenneth arrived. Melissa and Greg arrived shortly thereafter.

"So how is everything going in the ad business?" Kenneth asked, not knowing really what else to say.

Robert chuckled slightly. "Our business, I'm happy to say, has grown in leaps and bounds. Greg has had a great deal to do with that taking place along with Melissa. I want you to realize we both understand that. To tell you the truth that's part of the reason —"

"Can I get your drink orders," the waitress asked.

Once the drink orders had been placed, Mr. Caldwell informing her he would take the bill when dinner was over, they all sat silently waiting for Robert to continue with his thoughts.

"The reason my wife, Terry, and I asked you all to be here this evening has to deal with something I never really thought I would be addressing for some time to come. Many years ago when we started our business there were numerous things we learned the hard way, while other items just seemed to fall into place. You see, I'm thinking of retiring. Terry feels it's time that we both start to take a little time to smell the roses so to speak."

"I do love roses," Melissa said with a smile.

"I've often wondered when that time would come for Susan and me," Kenneth stated as he nodded his head in agreement. "Congratulations."

"Yes, congratulations," Susan added.

"We both wish the very best for you," Greg stated.

Melissa smiled as she nodded her head in agreement with Greg.

"We still have our health, we're comfortable financially. Terry and I have talked it over extensively and we've come to the same conclusion."

Terry reached over and placed her hand on top of Robert's. He looked down as they interlocked their fingers. She squeezed them gently as he went on.

"We're worried about our employees, and the thing that concerns us the most about them is that —"

Susan couldn't help herself, she actually let the sound of a little laugh escape from her lips.

"Excuse me," Robert stated, a little irritated at the sound of her laughter, especially considering the theme of the discussion.

"Please forgive me, Mr. Caldwell... Robert, it's just that I wholeheartedly agree with your statement about concerns over your employees. People don't always discuss their inner feelings when it comes to the people who work for them every day, the people in the trenches. Yours and ours being family-owned businesses makes a world of difference. I don't mean any disrespect to you or your wife, it's just that I understand your reaction completely. You want what's best for them. That's one of the utmost items of importance you're trying to deal with. You're afraid someone would come in and clean house, give good people the boot. I admire you both for that line of thinking."

"We both do," added Kenneth.

Robert nodded his head, as well as Terry. Susan did understand their thinking on the matter, he thought, having an eye to their employees' future as well as their own.

"You have three daughters; don't you?" Susan inquired.

"Yes, we do," Terry stated.

"That's correct," Robert said.

"Well, then you really have no problems. Once you explain your feelings, what concerns you have, I'm sure they'll follow you and your wife's wishes."

"Our daughters won't be taking part in any release of the company into new hands," Terry stated. "They have their own lives to live, and besides, I don't think they could really handle it in the way it should be run. All three of them are smart women, don't misunderstand me, but there's a difference between being smart, and taking control of a thriving ad business. They're worlds apart… especially one that's in need of daily ideas to be kicked around, fresh input every day."

Kenneth shook his head in agreement. He knew that from personal experience. Many a day he was happy to know that Susan could take the controls to the business if he were ill, or something more drastic occurred. As Melissa grew older, she was given a more important role in the business operations. He had nothing to fear along those lines. Yes, either one could handle the job sufficiently if it ever came down to that. Kenneth truly understood where Robert and Terry were coming from.

"What I'm about to propose to you is something my wife and I have talked over many times," Robert stated. "It's part of a solution, but maybe not the answer to it. Terry and I would like to do the following."

Everyone waited for the next words to come from Robert's mouth, perhaps Susan and Kenneth most of all. They both felt they knew where this conversation was taking them all. Together they surmised exactly what his further words would entail. Kenneth and Susan were both sure they would carry the words to something neither one would want to deal with. However, they still needed to hear what Robert would proffer to them, to everyone of them to be sure.

"Greg, I would appreciate it if you and your lovely wife, Melissa, would take the time to think over... to talk over what Terry and I want to offer the both of you. If you decide after considering our proposal not to accept it, we'll understand. The choice... that decision is entirely yours to make. There will be no pressure from either one of us. First of all, we would like to sell our business to you and your wife."

Susan and Kenneth felt uneasy while Greg and Melissa sat in shock.

"I couldn't possibly — we couldn't even hope to buy your business," Greg was quick to say, "after all, I don't have the financial means to even consider it."

Susan placed her hand onto Kenneth's. She squeezed it very hard. Neither one said a word. This was an offer that was far afield from what they expected to be said at the dinner meeting. What both had thought from the beginning was simple. They assumed Greg would be asked to take on a much larger role in the business. The Caldwells would step into the background while he would deal with the day-to-day running of the business. Despite their inner feelings, what was being addressed was something they had no voice in. It was really none of their business. Each could offer an opinion, but that was as far as they would feel comfortable in doing. It was Greg and Melissa's voices that would say yeah or nay when all was said and done. The young couple's words carried the weight of their answer, they both understood that very well. Of course, Greg had already said he couldn't afford to buy the business in the first place, so there really wasn't anything more to worry about.

"We considered that very question also. Greg, Melissa, let us suggest something to the both of you that Terry and I have talked over extensively." Robert continued his thoughts, his wife's lips carrying a very slight curl of a smile.

"We are wondering if you two would consider the following proposal.

The business would be handed over to you, lock, stock, and barrel, no money being exchanged at all. Naturally paperwork would be drawn up and so forth, but I'm getting ahead of myself. We would receive an x-amount of money from the company, depending on how much business was done each month. This would allow you some latitude to work with. That payment would be applied to any balance the four of us decided together the firm is worth.

It's Terry's and my hope that our company would go to two people we both adore... even love. We feel it would be in good hands. When one puts their heart and soul into something they've created over the years, they want it to be taken care of. It's our baby, so to speak. We know that it would continue to stand the test of time with both of you at the helm."

These words took the whole business idea down an entirely different path. Susan and Kenneth realized that quickly. Another sentence, another item to worry about. The Summers didn't want to lose Greg, let alone their daughter. Susan started feeling an anxiety growing within her heart. What bothered her the most was the fact that she knew Kenneth and she wouldn't want to stand in the way of their daughter and son-in-law's future. They understood very well both of them could make a substantially larger income should they decide to take the opportunity offered to them. It was not only a generous act on the part of the Caldwells, it came from their hearts as well. Kenneth and Susan could see that on both Terry and Robert's faces as they spoke. They undoubtedly had deep feelings for Melissa and Greg. In expressing their feelings for the young couple, holding them so closely to their hearts, that really came as a surprise to Susan as well as Kenneth. Finding out people love your children as much as you, how precious that is to know, Susan thought.

Robert took a deeper breath before addressing the young couple further.

"There is one other thing I'd like to take the time to mention to both of you. Our employees admire you, Greg and Melissa. I know they probably don't express themselves along that line, but I know that to be a fact. What I'm telling you is very true, you're looked up to by them. We both know in our hearts they would work just as diligently for you two as they do for Terry and me. We have some wonderful employees. I know you understand that very well, Greg, you've been around them long enough to see that for yourself."

"Thank you," Greg said. "We're both pretty young."

"That's what is so wonderful about it all. Both of you are just chucked full of new ideas, fresh thoughts. You have youth, spirit, everything Terry and I had when we started out. Your youthful years are really a plus, not a detriment."

Greg nodded his head. There were many things to be considered. In his mind what intrigued him the most was Robert's approach to the financial concept. Naturally he would have to address this with Melissa. Without her input and approval, he wouldn't even consider the idea. Still, Robert's proposal was fascinating, unbelievable in nature. Greg wet his lips. Melissa looked at her husband's face, it reading like an open book to her. She could tell this proposal meant much to him. She also realized he had promised her family he would always be there for them. She would, of course, talk it over with him. They needed time alone to discuss their inner fears in doing it, and the rewards it had to offer them as a family.

"Mr. Caldwell," Kenneth interjected, "would you mind if I asked you a question?"

Robert nodded his head slightly in approval.

"I know it's none of my business, but why wouldn't you make this offer to one of your employees who's been with you for years? I mean, Greg hasn't been with your company all that long."

Robert smiled as he took a quick glance at his wife.

"First of all, the name is Robert."

"Robert, I'm sorry," Kenneth said correcting himself.

"I'll answer this one," Terry said as she looked in Greg and Kenneth's direction.

Robert reached down taking his coffee cup in hand. He would simply sit back as his wife answered the question, knowing full well what her reply would be.

"I'd like to know the answer to that question myself," Greg added.

Melissa nodded her head; she wanted to know also.

"Greg, my husband and I have a world of faith in you... the both of you. Sometimes you have to just trust your instincts. While many of the people who work for us are very good people in what they do, Greg, you're an exceptional person. We believe you would carry out our wishes on how we would want our business to continue to run. Words say a tremendous amount about people, but in your case your actions speak louder than the words you use. We've all heard an expression similar to that, and in our minds we feel it's very true with you.

At the shower I —"

"You mean the adult party," Melissa interjected.

"Yes, excuse me," Terry said.

Melissa smiled.

"At the adult party we told you we both thought of you as a son, but there's something more that needs to be said along that line... and that's to you, Melissa. Robert and I have three wonderful daughters that we love to death. I just wanted to say, if I had another one, I'd want her to be just like you."

Melissa got up from her seat and hugged Terry. Susan smiled, knowing Kenneth and she had been paid an enormous compliment by Terry as well.

"Thank you ever so much," Melissa said. "Those words honor both of us very much. Thank you."

Melissa then hugged Robert as Greg offered his hand out towards Robert. The two shook hands. Greg then moved in Terry's direction. She stood as the two embraced.

"Those words are quite a complement for both of us to receive," Greg said as he released Terry.

"And, Greg, I've worked hand-and-hand with Robert for many years. I see his traits in you when he was younger, when we first started our business.

Melissa, I've seen your fingerprints in some of your husband's ideas, the concepts he's come up with. He's even told me when an idea was yours, or you gave him a suggestion that he ran with. As far as that goes, Robert and I see ourselves in both you. It does our hearts good to see the two of you working together, each feeding off of the other's ideas, each giving the other the credit. We like observing that in both of you. It's how Robert and I have worked together for years."

"Thank you," Greg said.

"Yes, thank you for all of those very sweet words," Melissa uttered softly, her emotions holding her in its grip as she spoke.

"There is a lot to consider, we know that," Terry stated. "Neither of us wants to rush you."

"The reason we wanted you and Susan here," Robert said, "is that we didn't want to be doing anything behind your backs. I told you one time I didn't want you to feel we were trying to steal your son-in-law from you, and we don't. Now we're not only talking about Greg, your daughter is in our sights, too. I hope you both understand that one doesn't come without the other. They're a pair of young people we both love... maybe not quite as much as you, but we're sure we're in second or third place."

Kenneth and Susan didn't know what to say. Greg looked at Melissa, her eyes a little watery.

"Let's do this, since it's probably the best way of handling it," Kenneth stated as he looked around the table. "We can sit in the background along with Mr. and Mrs. — Robert and Terry."

"Thank you," Robert said.

"We'll all sit back and let the two of you talk things over. Susan and I will not... will not in any way stand between you and your final decision."

"Just as well as us," Robert said, "You two need to talk things over and come up with what's best for your family. Take your time, there's definitely no rush."

"Well, we're all done eating," Greg vocalized, "so if you don't mind I'm going to take my wife for a little walk, stop somewhere along the way and get her an ice cream cone."

"A time to talk," Robert said nodding his head.

Greg nodded his head in agreement.

"I do love ice cream," smiled Melissa. "Maybe I should take the pickle with us that's still laying on your plate," she joked.

"You'll have your answer in a week," Greg stated as he nodded his head.

"Don't you both need more time than that?" questioned Robert.

"If we don't know by then, we shouldn't have been asked to consider it in the first place."

The four adults nodded their heads as Melissa and Greg got up from the table. They all knew he was right in his thinking.

"Thank you both for the lovely meal," Melissa said.

"Yes, thank you," Greg added.

After they left Kenneth turned his attention to the Caldwells.

"Are the two of you in any hurry to leave, I mean, do you have any appointments you have to make?" he asked.

"Not that I know of," Terry said.

"Then what would you say to having a discussion on tonight's subject matter? I have a couple of ideas I'd like to address with the two of you, if that's okay."

"Of course," Terry said.

An evening of four people enjoying further cups of coffee, desserts, continued as ideas began to unfold before them. It hadn't been planned by anyone to happen that way, it just did. No one left the table until they were asked to with the closing of the restaurant. Robert and Kenneth shook hands, the women hugged. As they left through the front door, various thoughts filled both couple's minds. All that was left was for the four people to meet again in the future. As they left, each carried hopes in their hearts they could find a solution to what they all faced together. Only time would tell.

Pink Sky

The phone call not only alarmed both Susan and Kenneth, it was the timing of it that frightened them the most. The clock next to the bed read 3:30 a.m. They were both keenly aware that news at this time of morning was usually never good. Kenneth was the first to the phone, it being on his side of the bed. All Susan could do was to lie beside him hoping to glean information from this one-sided conversation. She placed her hand on his shoulder as if it would help her to comprehend what was being said on the other end of the line.

"What is it, Kenneth?" she asked.

While he didn't respond to her, the expression on his face was telling. This made Susan even more frightened inside.

"We'll be right there," he stated as he hung the phone up."

"Kenneth..."

"There's a fire at the store, it doesn't sound good."

"I'll get dressed immediately."

"Okay," was the only word that came from his mouth. Kenneth's mind was a whirlwind of thoughts running into each other and back again. The couple quickly dressed and headed to the car in the garage. As they drove towards the store few words were exchanged between them. Kenneth could see the apprehension written across Susan's face over the news. He was sure his face bore a mirrored reflection of concern as well.

"Kenneth, I hope the security guard is okay."

"Me, too."

Susan and Kenneth's eyes were drawn in the direction of the store as they made their way down the various streets. Each one of them searched the sky ahead for any signs of the building burning. Unfortunately, their scanning met with an ugly answer. For some distance ahead of them the sky gave off an eerie glow of pinkish reds. There was an occasional flickering every so often in its color. Heavy black images of smoke moved upward towards the sky in an almost ghostly fashion as they approached. As the couple's vehicle raced forward, Susan's eyes began to water. Kenneth bit down on his lower lip.

Upon arriving near the inferno, they found a parking spot and began walking hurriedly the block and a half towards the fire. A large contingency of firefighters was busy stretching additional hoses, while others directed water onto various windows and doors. Water covering the street before the building, reflected the devastation of the fire. In one area, high-pressured water sprayed from a brass fitting on the fire hydrant connection. Several heavy hoses lay on the roadway in front of the structure. Their appearance was that of very large snakes, some even laying over each other. Sparks showered down from electrical wires near a pole resembling fireworks. Its popping sounds were loud for all to hear. The smell of burning materials filled the air. Susan could feel her eyes burning from the stench it gave off. At one point they just stood there and watched. Unable to bear the sight anymore, Susan buried her head into Kenneth's shoulder as she began to sob. It was all he could do to control his own emotions as he held her tightly in his arms.

"Mr. Summers."

Kenneth turned to see a young man he recognized as a former employee from a few years earlier. He was dressed in his firefighter turnout gear, a tank on his back. The emblem on his helmet bore the name of the city fire department. Kenneth could observe the image of the fire from the clear shield that covered the upper part of his face as he looked at him.

"I just wanted to let you know Mr. Harris, your night watchman got out okay."

"Thank God," Susan stated as she squeezed Kenneth's arm.

"I'm really sorry to see your business in such a... It's really sad for me to see this as well. I overheard some firemen talking to Gordon, I mean Mr. Harris.

They think it was some type of electrical problem from what they could gather from his description of what happened. Of course, we'll have to wait to get the complete story."

"We're just so glad he's alright," Susan said as she reached up and wiped the corners of her eyes.

"Thank you for letting us know that," Kenneth said.

The firefighter nodded his head as he turned and returned quickly to his duties.

"Look at that black smoke pouring from the window up there, it almost appears like silk, " Kenneth stated. He pointed his arm in the direction of the upper section of the building as he spoke.

Susan's eyes looked upward just as the smoke turned into a red ball of flames.

"Whoa," was all Susan could say as she stepped backwards, slightly shaken by what she saw. "Kenneth, what will we ever do?"

"Well, that very thought has been running through my mind over and over. I think what we need to do is to take it a step at a time. We'll deal with things directly, and most of all try to keep a positive attitude as we sort everything out."

"What about our employees, they're like family. We just can't... we need to... "

"I know, Honey, but like I said, we'll take it one step at a time. First, when everything settles down we'll assess the damage. Next, we'll check with our insurance companies. I've got to talk to our accountant, Fred, about some financial questions I have."

"Obviously the insurance is paid up, Susan said as she nodded her head, "and as far as any financial questions you may have Kenneth —"

"Susan, you're going to be a very busy person over the next few months. Let me take charge of this. There's going to be so much for us to do. I'll need you to take care of certain things, but I'm afraid, knowing you as I do, you'll get overloaded quickly. Is that okay with you?"

"Whatever you say, Honey."

"We'll handle this together, but first we need to take a deep breath, check out our options and then take it from there."

Susan could see in the face of her husband, a determination she had not seen in quite some time. Inside she began to feel assured that everything would work out, but just what direction it would take their family next, that answer was yet to come to light.

"Oh, Kenneth, I've got to give Greg and Melissa a call, they'll want to know about the fire, and it should come from us first."

"Good idea."

"When she comes down here, and we both know she will," Kenneth stated, "we need to deal with her gently. I'm sure this is going to hit her like a ton of bricks. We need to be positive in what we say to her. She's going through an awful lot right now."

"She does have a tender heart," Susan expressed as she nodded her head.

"We can stay here and —"

"Mr. and Mrs. Summers, I don't know what to say. Maybe if I had been closer to where the fire first started I could have possibly —"

"Are you alright, Gordon?" Susan quickly asked.

"Yes," the night watchman answered.

"Thank God." Susan quickly reached out and hugged Gordon. Once she released her grip on him, she simply stepped back and looked at him.

Gordon's head was held slightly downward as he continued to speak. It was definitely clear to the Summers he felt badly about what was transpiring before them.

"Gordon, you look at me right now," Susan's strong voice said. "It's not your fault!" She then took a step forward and hugged him again.

"Thank you. I'm so sorry… I feel horrible inside. When you told me you didn't mind if I brought my dog, Ranger, in to work to keep me company at night, I never thought he'd actually spot the trouble first. As awful as it sounds, I think everything could have been a lot worse if he hadn't alerted me to begin with. I was on a different floor altogether from where the fire first started. His barking drew my attention immediately."

"And I see he's okay, too," she said as she reached down and patted the German Shepherd on his head. Susan smiled slightly as Ranger reached up and licked her hand.

"So now what happens," Gordon asked in a somber voice, "I guess that's the next logical question every one of your employees will have for you two."

"I wish I knew," Susan answered as she let out a deep breath.

While Kenneth didn't offer any reply, he merely looked at Gordon and Susan and shook his head slowly back and forth.

When Melissa and Greg arrived at the scene, the two women held each other tightly. Susan was ever so grateful for the reassurance Melissa demonstrated to her. This alone was something she had not expected from her daughter. As she listened to her words of comfort, Susan could feel the strength of Melissa's adult womanhood coming to life. It consoled her in a way she never expected or experienced before. It made her proud that her daughter showed the maturity she hoped Melissa would eventually come to possess. In the end, it was Susan who felt reassured and encouraged by her daughter.

Kenneth and Greg watched as a man walked around the scene with a grey bag hanging from his shoulder. An occasional flash emanated from the camera he held in his hand. At times he would change his position quickly, if something caught his eye.

"News is news, good or bad," Kenneth remarked.

"People always like to see a picture along with any story involving tragedy whenever they can," Greg offered.

"I suppose you're right."

"Mr. Summers, I'm Gina Johnson from the newspaper."

Kenneth turned to his left to see a young woman holding a spiral note pad in her hand, a pen in the other.

"I was wondering if you have any statement you'd like to make? I've already spoken with the Fire Chief and his initial impression is that it was some type of an electrical issue."

"Really, right now?" was all Greg could say, somewhat upset with her interference with the family during this trying time.

"It's okay, Greg," Kenneth said. "I'll be glad to answer any questions you have concerning tonight's events if you could do something for me."

"And what would that be, sir?"

"At the end of your article could you say that the Summers family will be getting together with their employees as soon as possible to discuss what steps will be taken next concerning the future of the business."

"Of course."

"And please don't indicate we're closing or anything along those lines, we just don't know how things will work themselves out."

"Okay," she replied.

"Now, what questions can I answer for you?"

"Mr. Summers, —"

"Yes," Kenneth stated in his one word sentence, as he prepared to start answering her questions.

"— I just wanted to let you know how badly I feel about what's happened."

"Thank you."

"I loved shopping here. The people were always so helpful... friendly."

Kenneth and Greg both nodded their heads with that statement by her. They both knew how true her words were.

Greg stood next to Kenneth as he answered the reporter's questions as best he could. When they finished she thanked him. She next walked over by a lone fireman standing near one of the trucks. They stood together conferring momentarily before she moved on to another area of the building to continue her interviews.

Kenneth suggested to Greg they should join the women who stood a short distance away. Before Greg could move, however, Kenneth placed his hand on his shoulder. They stopped in place as Greg turned to face Kenneth.

"Greg, let's try to keep it as light as possible around the women. I know this is very hard on their emotions, let's not add anything to their anxiety, especially Melissa."

"I understand."

Together they made their way over to them. Greg glanced back over his shoulder at the building as they walked. It appeared to him they had made some headway in fighting the flames. He turned his head back in Kenneth's direction.

"You know, Greg, there really isn't anything more we can do here tonight. Let's take the wives home and —"

"It's almost 5:30 a.m. now," Greg said as he glanced at his watch. "No one is going to go back to bed, especially now. Why don't you come over to our house, we'll get some breakfast and talk over any plans you may want to discuss."

"No, let's go to my house. I've got some paperwork in the office safe I need to check on," Kenneth said.

"Whatever you say."

"Greg, see if you can get a hold of Fred and have him come to my house as soon as possible. Tell him about the fire, he'll need to know that. Inform him not to be in too much of a hurry."

"Okay."

"I want you to be with me when I consider a few thoughts I have. I need your suggestions, your input. I think it best the two women be together, they need each other now more than ever."

Greg nodded his head.

"We can talk then," Kenneth said. He explained to the women about returning home for some breakfast, a hot cup of caffeine-laced coffee. "We'll put our minds together and see what we can come up with."

Once again Greg nodded his head in agreement. What Kenneth's ideas were, what his plans could entail would be answered soon enough. Now was the time they all needed to comfort one another. While Greg always seemed to know exactly what to say, those words were silent in his mind. An empty void seemed to take possession of his thoughts. He knew, though, he had better pull his act together. Kenneth needed him to be fresh with opinions, his brain not cluttered with the smoke and flames.

The aroma of brewing coffee being made by Susan was the first thing everyone noticed that helped to clear their nostrils of the smelly smoke that lingered in their senses. Odors from the fire, however, clung to their clothes. It was as if the stench had intentionally followed them to the house. They hadn't really noticed it until then, their minds still very much back at the scene of the fire. The smell was a stark reminder of what they had just endured. It hung in the kitchen air like a heavy anvil that needed to be removed quickly. Everyone present felt it's invisible fingers holding them in its grip. Their clothes were literally saturated with the odor of smoke.

Susan reached for the cup tree taking four from its branches. She then began filling everyone's cup with the fresh brew. The beverage would not only taste good, it would refresh them somewhat. The caffeine may even clear their minds, she thought. It would probably help to keep them awake, though that didn't seem to be needed by anyone.

"Listen up everyone, this is what I think we need to do," came Kenneth's words. "First of all you ladies are going to go upstairs and take a shower, get this grit or whatever it is off of your bodies. Thank goodness we have more than one shower in this house. We'll be using a lot of hot water this morning. Once you get some clean clothes on, we'll wash the ones you're wearing."

"Dad, I don't have anything that will fit me here," Melissa said. "I'm much bigger than I was when I lived here."

"Well, Honey," Susan said, "there's a couple pair of old slacks upstairs in your room, even a dress yet. They may still fit, I'm pretty sure of that."

"Mom, I wore a size six when I lived here."

"Well, as far as a blouse, in the laundry room I have some women's clothes I just washed. I was going to take them to the Second Chance Store. They were given to me a few days ago. I'm sure there's something in there that will fit you. Of course, if the slacks don't measure up, we'll just cut them in the back and pin them somehow. It's only until we wash yours."

"I think I'll take a look in the laundry room first before I do that," Melissa said. She knew her old slacks wouldn't do the job.

"Kenneth," Susan said, "you have clothes here, just as do I."

"What about me?" questioned Greg. "Are all of the clothes in the laundry room women's clothing? I don't really want to march around here in a polka dotted dress until I get my clothes washed."

Susan started chuckling, then Kenneth and finally Melissa. Soon they were all laughing. Each tried to imagine Greg in a dress as their laughter grew in size. It was a time they all needed, a small break in the stormy cloud that now held them in its grasp. The laughter, though not lasting long, was very contagious in nature.

"There's also some men's clothing in there. In fact, I actually washed them first. See what you can find," Susan suggested. "I'll wash yours as soon as I can."

"I probably could just run home and get some clean ones."

"That will take too long," Kenneth stated, "I want to get started as soon as possible and then we'll —"

The doorbell rang its familiar melody of Westminster Chimes. Susan went to the front door immediately.

"Fred, thanks for coming," Susan said as he entered the house.

"I don't know what to think or say," were his first words to everyone. He then shook his head, a faceless expression exhibited on it.

"Fred, I want you, Greg, and myself to retire to my home office shortly. We have a lot of work to do. Susan, as I told you earlier, I'll need you to work on some various solutions I'm thinking of. If that's agreeable with you, I'd like to handle this..." The next word tasted bitter to Kenneth's mouth as he said it out loud. "...tragedy in that way. What's your thoughts on that?"

Before Susan could reply Melissa was quick to interject her thoughts to her father.

"What's my job, where do I fit into this picture? I need something to... I need something to do. I'm still a part of this family and you're not leaving me out... out of anything. I need to be useful, be a part of... be a part of what's going to happen from here on out." Her voice seemed to ramble as she spoke, but her thoughts were clearly made.

Kenneth was surprised by her outburst, but happy to hear her feelings being communicated to him. Susan didn't say a word, her mouth too busy demonstrating a large smile. Yes, she thought to herself, Melissa's voice certainly would not be silenced. She very much wanted to help, as well as be heard. Her daughter was surely no longer the little child she had so carefully raised through the years. With Melissa's words, Susan could definitely see that developing. She was strong. Sure she was married, of course she was pregnant, but she still remained her little girl. That fact alone would always occupy a large part of

Susan's heart. This young woman would be a force to be reckoned with if she were denied having any say in what was going to happen or take place. That was made abundantly clear to Kenneth, Susan, and anyone else who heard her statements.

"Before we do anything this morning, let's all get cleaned up and then sit down and have a cup of coffee," Kenneth said. "We need to let our brains have a few minutes to rest, and then we'll start." Kenneth looked around the room seeing agreement in everyone's face.

How much could be accomplished in their meeting, remained to be seen. Kenneth understood it was better than sitting around feeling sorry for one's self. His thoughts raced in his head, and the questions were multiple in nature. What would they do, shut the store once and for all? Should they rebuild? How much actual insurance money was there to work with? There was, of course, the most pressing of all items to be addressed, what about their employees. Perhaps their lives were more affected than even the Summers family knew. They had loans to pay, rent or house payments to make. That was only the tip of the employees' iceberg, he thought. Exactly how much more of their problems were hidden beneath the water, one could only guess. How many employees could survive this catastrophe remained to be seen.

Kenneth began to realize as he quietly sat drinking his coffee how well off his family was compared to others. The house was paid for. There were no car payments. Their bank accounts were sizeable, numerous time certificates put away, stock investments doing well. Even the store was free and clear of debt. He had been a good steward of the money they made, but what of their employees' debts? It was a question that seemed like a circle, starting at one spot, running the gamut of its edge and then coming back to its starting position. That question alone was foremost in his thinking. His mind drifted in a sea of uncertainty concerning their wellbeing.

Kenneth always likened their store to a ship that brought forth a cargo of merchandise for people to buy and enjoy. Their employees loaded the vessel daily, tended to the customers like passengers, even held the ship's wheel at times. They helped to keep everything on course, a good crew doing their job well. Now, what direction would the ship take, a very large hole punctured into its hull, perhaps sinking forever. It was a tricky question to answer, one that should be studied over carefully, yet needing to be answered as quickly as possible.

He knew Susan would walk hand-in-hand with him; that was not a question that even entered his mind. Together as one they would work to save the family, each and every one of them doing their very best. Now it was a matter of finding out how they could accomplish that burden.

As Fred stood talking to Melissa, Susan walked up to Kenneth and half smiled. He looked up at her from his seated position, but said nothing. She placed her hands onto his shoulders. Reaching up he put his hands over hers. Neither said a word to the other, the touch of their mate comforting each other in silence. After a period of time it was Susan who spoke first.

"We're back to where we began many years ago," she uttered softly.

"We've been here before," Kenneth replied, "but we're stronger now, and we have experience on our side."

"And each other."

"And each other. There's nothing more important than that," Kenneth said.

"Maybe it will be easier this time around," Susan expressed.

"In what way?" he asked, surprised by her comment.

"This time we've got Melissa and Greg to help us."

"That's true," Kenneth agreed as he nodded his head slightly.

"We've got Fred, who I know will be an indispensible asset for us."

"Uh-huh, you're right again."

"And, Kenneth, I can think of one more important thing to consider."

"What's that, Honey?"

"We have the right people in place, our employees. There's no need to do any interviews if we can rebuild and stay open. That's a huge item that's already taken care of."

"You're right," he said, "we do have that. They're all wonderful people and we're very fortunate to have them all."

"Some of them go back with us many years."

Kenneth chuckled as he thought of one employee in particular.

"There's Mrs. White," he said, "she's been with us —"

"Forever," chuckled Susan.

Kenneth nodded his head in agreement.

"I can even imagine her with a hammer in her hand pounding away at something," Susan joked, "helping us to rebuild if she can."

"Funny, so can I," Kenneth agreed. "Maybe she'd even have one of those workmen aprons on."

"And a hardhat, too," chuckled Susan lightly. She rubbed her husband's shoulders gently before reaching down and placing a gentle kiss upon his lips. It was then Kenneth knew in his heart they would do whatever they could to rebuild. It was her simple encouraging words to him, her kiss, that assured him inside together they could handle anything. No matter what would be thrown at them, they would handle it together. In addition, he thought, they had Mrs. White on their side.

Once Greg returned to the kitchen, dressed in a pair of old jeans and a pullover shirt, much too big for him, he had a seat at the table.

"I was hoping you had to wear a dress," smirked Fred. "Melissa told me that was one of your options."

"That's not even funny, Fred."

"So no polka dots today," he added.

Melissa and Susan chuckled while Kenneth put his hand over his mouth attempting to hide his smirk.

Greg just shook his head, wanting the subject matter to be changed, the quicker the better.

"Well, let's get started," Kenneth stated as he handed Melissa a large pad of paper along with a pencil. "We'll go as far as we can today. I would like us to meet daily for the next little while until we have this all worked out, whenever and wherever that takes us. Agreed?"

Everyone nodded their head in agreement.

"Good."

The morning was thick with heavy questions being brought forth by one another. Some problems were simply dealt with by using a band-aid approach to it. How much damage was actually done to the building would have to be answered later. Its integrity, another item still to be resolved when it was inspected. There were more questions than answers. Melissa's list was detailed. She even wrote separate lists out for everyone to follow. They knew exactly who they would be responsible to contact. What one person didn't think of, the next one did. The group at the table were almost like spectators at a tennis match, their faces going back and forth with each volley of questions or answers being suggested by the other. Kenneth was still amazed at how much was accomplished when their meeting drew to an end.

"I wonder when we'll have some concrete answers," Melissa asked.

"Probably not for some time," Greg said.

I need to have those answers within the week," Kenneth stated. "I want to meet with our employees as soon as we can. I don't want them having to wait too long in limbo, they deserve that much from us."

"I just wish we had more answers now," Susan expressed.

"Those questions will be answered all in due time," Fred said. "When I used to ask my grandfather how long things took, he always answered me in the same way."

"What did he say?" Susan asked.

"He always said, 'You can never tell the depth of a well by the length of the handle on the pump.'"

"That's profound," she said.

"That's what we've all got to remember, questions will be answered when they can be.

Unfortunately that's not before they're ready to give their reply to us," declared Fred.

Once again everyone nodded their head in agreement.

"Well, let's all get to work, start making our calls. I would like to thank you, Fred, Greg, Melissa, for helping us out."

"It's the least anyone of us can do," Fred said nodding his head slowly.

Greg followed suit, his head also nodding a silent reply.

Melissa smiled as she nodded her head also.

Susan and Kenneth returned her smile.

"So let's meet tomorrow morning at eight o'clock," Kenneth stated.

"And I'll have breakfast ready and waiting for everyone," Susan said.

"Can I make a suggestion?" Fred asked.

"Of course," Kenneth said.

"You said you wanted to meet once a day. If we met twice a day, that gives us all an opportunity to let the others know what they've found out during the day. In addition, when we leave the second meeting, it enables us some time to comprehend what we've been informed of.

This also allows us time to help think of any solutions that could be available, but not readily in our sight at the time. Maybe it's because I have an accountant's mind, I look at things a little differently. It's like trying to find those few missing pennies in your account. The more time you spend, the better chance you have of solving it. I know that's kind of dumb to put it that way, but just the same —"

"No it's not, you're right," Susan's voice carrying a strong agreement as she spoke. "I've done the books just like Fred, I understand your thought process completely. We need to listen to him, have two meetings a day until we know where we stand."

"So it's settled," Kenneth stated as he looked around the table. "We'll see everyone back here somewhere around —"

"How about 5:30?" Susan said interrupting her husband. "Does everyone like pizza?"

Thus the first of many meetings began. Like an army they would advance towards their foe, soon to be taken on together as one. Everyone wanted what their heart desired and carried within, a return to the status quo. Kenneth would act as their commander, Susan standing next to him. The rest of them would be the soldiers carrying out their leader's commands.

The week flew by before their very eyes. Susan lived on the phone while Kenneth met with a building inspector, insurance representatives, merchandising people and others. Fred, Susan, and Kenneth had numerous meeting behind closed doors. Even Melissa and Greg weren't privy to these closed-door sessions.

Their daily routine was broken by only one consistent item. Every day at precisely noon the phone at the Summers home rang.

"I'll get it," Melissa said, knowing full well it was for her, and who was on the other end of the call.

Susan and Kenneth would take a moment from whatever they were doing to smile at the other and listen. The call would be from Kate, the same question asked every time she called. She wanted to know in no uncertain terms what the two of them could do to help them. At one point, Kate asked if she could speak to one of the parents, Susan or Kenneth.

"She wants to speak with one of you two. I guess it doesn't matter which one of you it is."

Melissa held the phone out waiting to see which one would reach for it. She tilted her head slightly, then shrugged her shoulders.

"I'll take it," Kenneth stated.

Putting the phone to his ear the two women simply waited for him to get done. What intrigued the two greatly from this one-sided conversation were the words Kenneth was using. He spoke of being economically solid, things were falling into place. There was no money problems facing them, they need not be concerned. Kenneth continually used the two-worded phrase, "Thank you," many times throughout the duration of their conversation. The last few words of their discussion were simple and to the point. "We love you, too."

"What did she have to say to you, Daddy?"

"Yes," Susan quickly added.

"Kate and Henry wanted us to know they had funds available to help us out. She said they were there for us; whatever we needed, don't be afraid to ask. The most fascinating thing about it is she mentioned giving us a few hundred thousand dollars, up to a half of a million dollars or more if we needed it."

"You're kidding me," Susan said with a shocked expression covering her face quickly.

"They must be doing really well at the restaurant and with Henry's singing," Melissa stated as she nodded her head.

Kenneth shook his head as he said, "I told you I should have bought stock in the Richard's Steak House. The most intriguing part of all is she told me it wasn't necessary that we even pay them back. It would be a simple gift from them to us. Of course, we're not going to take advantage of the gift, but it's still a staggering offer for them to make available to us."

"What goes around, comes around," Susan said.

"What do you mean, Mom?"

"We gave Henry our piano sometime ago, no strings attached. Maybe that's what they're trying to do for us," Susan expressed.

"It could be, Honey," Kenneth said, "but there's a big difference from a baby grand piano and a half a million dollars."

"A gift is a gift, and the size of it should never come into play. When Henry received the baby grand, to him I'm sure it was as big as a million dollars," Melissa said thoughtfully. It was offered without any strings attached to it, and wrapped with love. I'll even go so far as to say they would use red colored paper and a red bow."

"I think you're right," Susan uttered softly.

"I know you both are," Kenneth stated. "When did our daughter become such a philosopher anyway?"

"A long time ago," Melissa joked. "I've been hanging around both of you for a long time now, something had to brush off."

One morning while sitting around the table waiting for Fred to arrive Greg turned to Susan and Kenneth.

"Dad," Greg started out, "I got a call from the Caldwells last night. They wanted me to know there was no hurry to make any decision right now concerning their business. I think they understand better than anyone what it is we're all facing. He told me to put our family number one. Robert also expressed that if I needed a place to keep working for him or you during this period of time, his desk was available for me. He repeated to me more than once to make both of you my priority."

"And me, too," Melissa added with a smile.

"That goes without saying, Honey."

"I know, Greg, I was just kidding a little."

"Susan and I also got a call from the Caldwells," Kenneth said. "They wanted to let us know if there was anything they could do to help us, to just let them know."

"They really are a sweet couple," Susan added.

"Yes, they are," Melissa said.

After a few days, when the five of them were finally in agreement, Susan contacted a printer. She had an announcement made up to be distributed to their employees. It basically said the Summers would be addressing the workers on Saturday night at seven. The meeting place was listed along with a request for everyone to attend. The flyer informed them that all of their questions would be addressed and answered as best as they could. If they wanted to address any other concerns, there would be a question and answer period immediately following.

The sound of chatter made by the employees in the large room was significant. The meeting with the Summers was almost ready to begin. One could almost feel the thickness in the atmosphere, one filled with many unanswered questions. Not one individual was without concern to hear what the future held for all of them. It was the topic that lingered on every ones' lips as they conversed with one another. Although the fire was only a short time ago, each person felt like the wolf of despair was ready to knock on the front door. Each person in their own way tried their best to prepare for it. All knew words of impending doom are always hard to swallow, let alone hear.

On a couple of tables two large stainless steel coffee makers were at the ready for anyone desiring a cup of coffee. Cups, sugar, sweetener, and a couple of creamers sat in front of them. There was another percolator next to them offering hot water, teabags, and hot chocolate envelopes. A very large selection of donuts, croissants, and various other pastries helped to fill the rest of the table area. Off to one side was a selection of fresh fruit for anyone watching their waistline.

The hush that filled the room as Susan and Kenneth walked up to a microphone on the small stage was very pronounced. Even the slightest of murmurings quickly disappeared. Kenneth stepped in front of the microphone, a sheet of paper in his hand.

"First of all let me begin by saying this last week has been very difficult on your families as well as my own. For years you have all given us the best you had to offer. We're more than grateful to have each and every one of you as an employee, and more importantly, a part of our family."

To some sitting in the audience this was a prelude to the bad news that awaited their ears. They knew it was coming; it was obvious to all of them. The food, the coffee, everything on the tables was to help soften the words they were about to hear. How hard of a blow they would endure was only a matter of minutes away. Others sat waiting to hear what Kenneth's next sentence would reveal. Everyone's ears were glued to his every word.

"The building... the store is too far gone to be repaired. The contents, were all lost from what we observed and have been told. All that's left is basically a shell...the skeleton of what some of us called our second home, where we worked together, laughed and even shared some meals in."

As Kenneth spoke his voice quivered slightly, but he would not let it take control of his emotions. He knew he had to be positive and strong for everyone there, including his own family. Kenneth looked down at the sea of faces before him. He smiled within himself. What he observed... what he felt was the love the peoples' faces demonstrated to him and for his family. He looked to his left, Melissa, Greg, and Fred standing up against a wall. Fred's wife, Robin stood at her husband's side. He nodded slightly to them.

"I am not going to stand here and tell you everything is going to end up in a bouquet of flowers... it's not my style... and I refuse to lie to you. We are all entering a transition period in our lives together. What I will say, however, is Susan and I have taken certain steps to move on with our lives, and hopefully together with everyone here. This is the plan our family has come up with."

In Susan and Kenneth's mind they knew the employees needed a life raft to help them through this difficult period. They would do their best to help each and everyone out. Even Melissa and Greg didn't know what was about to be presented to the employees. Only Fred knew their secret, and that would soon be common knowledge to everyone present.

"Susan and I have decided to do the following. Next week, it being the usual pay period for everyone here, each one of you will receive your regular paycheck."

People looked at each other, happy to know they would be receiving at least one more paycheck. It was a single ray of sunshine, an extra week of pay that would give each of them another short breath before the waters of debt took over their lives. Some would last a bit longer, having put away some saving. Still, others would drown quickly in the bills that would engulf them.

"We understand from the contractor that it would take approximately a little over a year and a half to rebuild the store and put us back into business. The fact of the matter is that beginning within a few days, the shell of the store will be demolished. We have not been sitting on our hands the past few days, we've all been hard at work. Fortunately, there is insurance money to assist us in the demolition project, and the rebuilding. Of course, the contents were insured as well."

The word, "rebuilding," its sound alone brought forth hope to many of them. There was a chance that one day they could have their old jobs back. For others in the audience it was the words, "year and a half," that left them hollow inside. It was the timeframe that lingered in their minds. A year and a half without a job, money for bills, it all added up to the same conclusion, poverty. They would have to find another job, and soon, find some way to meet their obligations.

"I'm going to ask Fred to come up here and speak for a few minutes. Fred."

As Fred made his way up the stairs, those who hadn't seen him or heard about it were in utter amazement to observe him walking with two legs. He moved without the assistance of any aid whatsoever. Fred's gait was slow but sure. Many paid little attention to the limp that came with each step he took, too excited to see him walking. Some of the people started clapping as he made his way to the microphone. Soon the whole place was filled with the sound of their hands being brought together. He waved slightly to them, nodding his head as he moved forward. A small lump in his throat started to form.

"Thank you, Mr. and Mrs. Summers. I am here for two reasons, and two reasons only. Over the next few days, I'm going to need to meet with each one of you personally. Simply put, it's because of the fact that our records were completely destroyed in the fire. I find it necessary to have you help me fill out some forms concerning your incomes. Fortunately, Mr. and Mrs. Summers had duplicates of some of those records at home. They kept them there for such an occasion as this. They were prepared for the worse, though none of us could have foreseen this coming. I personally am very grateful for that act alone.

    At the back of the room you will find a table with a few pads on it along with some pens. Please print, and I repeat the word, 'print' your name, address, and the phone number where I can get a hold of you. You will then be getting a call from me to setup an appointment to go over the items. Please be on time as it makes my job much easier to accomplish.

Now I'd like to address the second reason why I'm up here. Your employers, Susan and Kenneth Summers have informed me of their wishes in this matter. Until the new store is completed, a grand opening being celebrated, they will do the following. Every two weeks between now and then, everyone of you will receive your regular paycheck. They understand you all possess one thing in common, bills. It is their wishes that —"

The applause was sudden, loud, and filled with love for Susan and Kenneth. The employees all realized the couple was reaching deeply into their own pockets to convey such a promise to them. People stood as they clapped, others yelling out with joy. The scene was reminiscent of a group of individuals who had just won the world's largest lottery. Many faces expressed their thanks with watery eyes. Many felt as if the wolf no longer stood banging at their front door attempting to get in. The Summers' act of generosity was overwhelming to all, let alone to comprehend.

Not knowing how else to express her feelings, one of the women began to sing a simple song. Within seconds, she was joined by everyone. The words to the song were repeated by everyone over and over again, "For they are jolly good fellows... for they are jolly good fellows... for they are jolly good fellows, and so say all of us."

The singing went on and on. Only when Kenneth and Susan walked over to the microphone stand, as he held his hand up did the group finally quiet down. Susan reached down and took Kenneth's hand in hers. She squeezed it stronger than Kenneth had ever felt her do to him before. He smiled at her, she smiling back.

"Today," Kenneth stated, "we begin anew. Together we will rise from the ashes that attempted to destroy us. We will build again, stronger, more resilient than ever before, after all, we are all family here."

Again a storm of applause filled the air. Kenneth and Susan knew they had done the right thing, and they were glad they had. It wasn't their gratitude they wanted; a simple thank you would suffice. What they truly wanted was to keep the family together; it was as simple as that. When they stepped from the platform, a line immediately formed. It was not planned, but one person followed another, each wanting to take a moment or two to personally thank the couple. Every employee, their spouses included, were in line. Tears and hugs were shared as well as joyful smiles.

At one point a woman Susan knew as Mary Claire stepped forward. She hugged Susan, and then Kenneth.

"I have no words to express what is in my heart for both of you this evening," she said. "Thank you doesn't seem enough to say." Once again she hugged both of them. Together the two women wiped their eyes as they smiled at each other. The two women once again gave each another hug. Never in Kenneth's life had he been kissed so many times on his cheek. He loved every bit of it.

Greg and Melissa stood watching as the line moved slowly forward.

"They're going to be a long, long, time," Melissa commented.

"Yes, they are, but a thank you should never be rushed."

Melissa nodded her head.

When all was said and done, everyone socialized. Susan and Kenneth were soon joined by Greg and Melissa. Fred walked up, a cup of coffee in his hand, his wife at his side.

"You've got a little chocolate on your face," Melissa joked.

"Oh," Fred said as he reached up with a napkin and wiped it away. "I do love donuts," he chuckled. "I always enjoy a dessert that's dietary in nature."

"And in what way is it dietary?" Susan asked.

"There's no calories in the hole part."

Susan and Robin merely shook their head.

"Mom, Dad, why didn't you tell us about the money issue, giving everyone their pay for a year plus?"

"We knew the two of you have enough to worry about, the baby coming, everything in general," Susan expressed. "There were a few other reasons, too."

"It's not the money and how you spend it, that's your decision entirely," Melissa stated, "it's just that we both would have liked to help out on this. We weren't even allowed to talk to the two of you about it."

"That's why we met with Fred alone," Kenneth stated. "Your mom and I wanted this to come from us. We both knew you'd ask to help us out financially."

"This is undoubtedly going to cost you a small fortune, please let us help," Melissa pleaded.

"To say the least," Fred said shaking his head back and forth.

"Fred!" was all Kenneth said.

"I'm sorry."

What this gift would eventually cost, Kenneth thought to himself, was something that only Susan, Fred, and himself needed to know.

The clock on the wall read 12:30 a.m. No one was in any hurry to leave. Kenneth remarked to Susan that his arm felt a little sore from shaking so many hands.

"I've never cried so many happy tears in all my life," she said.

"Nor have I," Kenneth stated.

Greg reached over and took the back of Melissa's arm in his hand.

"How about a donut or a piece of fruit?" he inquired of Melissa as he started leading her away from the group.

"That does sound good," she replied, realizing Greg wanted them to be elsewhere.

As the two of them walked over to the dessert table, Greg started to express an idea he had. Melissa smiled as she listened to him. She liked the idea; in fact, she loved it. The two of them would work on the plan. Together they would harvest the crop of Greg's idea; after all, working with her husband was fun. They soon would be very busy in this decidedly new endeavor.

Emotionally Spent

Edith and Frank moved as quickly as they could down the hospital hallway, their eyes darting back and forth looking for the waiting room to the maternity ward. A large wall of glass revealed to them the figures of Susan and Kenneth sitting on a couch. Greg was seated in between them. As they hurriedly entered the room it was very clear that Greg was very distraught. Susan and Kenneth's arms were both over the back of his body. Greg was bent over, his head nestled in his hands. He looked up at his parents as they came in the room, his eyes were red in color, bloodshot from crying. Edith had never seen her son so emotionally distraught. Susan and Kenneth's faces bore the same expressions.

Seeing his mom and dad he quickly stood up and embraced his mother. He buried his face into her shoulder as he began sobbing once again. Edith held him tightly. She could feel his wet tears on her neck. She knew immediately she had to be strong for her son, something she didn't know if she had the inner strength to accomplish.

Throughout Edith's life tears flowed from her eyes like leaky faucets. It was something she had no control over. Simple things caused her to tear up. Hearing any type of bad news for someone she knew was an almost impossible task to handle. Too many sad happenings in the world she'd tell her husband. Frank knew her heart was much too tender to not share in another's sorrow, Edith almost feeling the pain they were suffering. Now she needed to be there for her son. She had to muster every ounce of strength her soul possessed to help him through the tragedy he now faced. But could she do it, help him with the biggest struggle he had ever faced. She knew she had no choice but to try.

"We came as soon as Susan called," Edith said as she hugged Greg a little tighter. Susan walked over a couple of feet and embraced them both as best she could.

While Frank said nothing, knowing in his heart his son needed his mother's love more than anyone else's now, he simply turned his attention to Kenneth.

"What can you tell me?" he asked softly.

The two men made their way to a corner of the room, giving Greg, Edith, and Susan some room to console one another. Each man looked at the other. In the other's face they could not only see the genuine turmoil they each were facing, but an apprehension of what may possibly lie ahead for all of them.

"Greg called us... he was frantic. He told us he didn't want Melissa to see the fear in his face, but she needed medical attention immediately. He had already called an ambulance for her. Greg said he knew she would want us to be with her, so we were his next call. We don't really know what's transpiring, what's going on at all. We came here immediately. Greg hasn't heard anything, no doctors have come to talk to him or us. Greg is so upset, it's hard to get anything out of him. This is literally driving all of us crazy. It's the not knowing. I really don't know what to tell you and Edith.

We did get out of Greg the fact that Melissa was feeling some pressure in her chest. Greg said she told him she thought she may be having a heart attack.

Susan called you, of course, and I think she even called Kate. Frank, I'm scared to death."

"Let me talk to him," Frank suggested.

Frank reached out to Kenneth. They hugged each other trying to share their support for one another. Until they had some news, their lives lived in a void of emptiness, a vacuum filled only with a trilogy of fear, anxiety, and despair.

Seeing a nurse walking by the room, Susan was quick to get her attention.

"We need to know what's going on with our daughter, and now. Her husband is frantic, just as we all are. We need some news of what's going on... please. Please let us know something... anything."

The nurse could see the atmosphere in the room was completely panic-stricken. She had experienced this type of emotion before many times through the years. It was the not knowing of what was transpiring with their loved one that seemed to hold their emotions so tightly in its grasp.

"I'll do my best to find out what I can."

"Her name is Melissa Wilson... Melissa Wilson," Susan repeated. "We would appreciate if you would —" Susan stopped in midsentence; she had made her point well enough by the look on the nurse's face.

The nurse nodded her head as she turned and left the area.

Edith looked into Greg's eyes. Nothing had changed from when she first gazed upon his face. His expression was one of complete and utter fear.

"Greg, tell me what happened with Melissa, I need to know," Edith said softly to him.

"We were at home and — and all of a sudden Melissa turned to me and said she thought she was having a heart attack. I thought it was just something to do with her pregnancy. She told me she had chest discomfort; her throat was tight. She was in real pain. Her breath had a definite shortness to it. I didn't wait another second, I called an ambulance."

"Thank God you didn't wait. An ounce of prevention is —"

"Is worth a pound of cure, I know that, Mom. You've told me that over and over again many times."

"So what happened next when you got to the hospital?"

"They assumed the pain was from the pregnancy, but they didn't just stop there. They took her vitals and such. After some time had passed one of the doctors came over to me. The next thing I know a doctor is talking to me about some procedure they may have to perform, the use of some balloon or something. My mind was in such a fog. He said they'd have to wait and see... or something. I told him to do whatever was necessary to get my wife back in my arms where she belongs. I... I..." Greg broke down. He took a few deep breaths.

"The next thing I know they're taking her into one of the rooms for surgery. They brought me here to wait until they knew exactly what was going on with her. Since she's having a baby, I guess that's why I'm in the maternity waiting room. I just don't know."

Greg reached up and wiped his eyes.

"I can't lose one, let alone both of them. If it's her or the baby..."

"Stop that talk, and stop it right now," Edith said in a very stern voice.

"I don't know what to think; what to do, Mom."

"Well, we're going to find out, and find something out now," Edith's said loudly. "You wait here with the men, Greg, we'll be right back. Susan, come with me."

The two women left the room and headed for the nurse's station. Arriving within a matter of a few seconds, Edith made a fist and pounded it down on the counter loudly. The two nurses turned their heads quickly.

"Can I help you?" responded the closest nurse.

"It's not just me who you can help, there's five of us and we need to have some answers now. What is happening to my daughter-in-law and her daughter? Where is she, and what are they doing? We're not leaving here until we get some answers. In fact, if you can't deal with us, I'll find someone around here who will. Now, do we understand each other?"

Susan was astounded with Edith's forceful tone, but happy to see her taking command of the situation.

"What is her name?"

"Listen, Miss, I don't mean to act this way, but you people should have that information written down somewhere already. If I have to bust every door down in this hospital to get my questions answered, so be it. Should I start pounding?"

"I understand your concerns, ma'am, but —"

"You don't know the half of it, Miss. Now, what's it going to be?"

"That information can only be given to Mr. Wilson," responded the nurse.

"Well, isn't that interesting, now all of a sudden you know his name. Come on, Susan, it's time to start knocking some doors down. We'll start with the ones that say, 'No admittance' or 'Operating room.' That ought to get someone's attention around here."

"Okay, okay, okay, just give me a minute or two. I really understand your concerns, but I do have certain protocols I have to follow."

"In two seconds my protocols kick in," Edith stated firmly. "You've got that long to let us all know what's going on. If you're thinking of contacting security, be my guest. I can deal with them next, and just so you know, they don't scare me at all."

"I'll see what I can find out. Please give me a moment or two," the nurse said. "You know, I'm a mother, too, I understand. I'll get some information for you as quickly as I can."

"Thank you," Susan said. "We'll go back to the waiting room."

"For only a little while," Edith said nodding her head.

The three women turned, two heading in one direction, the other one in another.

"Edith, I've never seen you this strong willed in my life," Susan said softly as they turned towards the waiting room.

"Sometimes you just have to know when to bluff," Edith said with a small smile. "Of course, on the other hand, it may not have been a bluff at all."

Susan gave her a slight smile.

As the women entered the room, the men all looked at them with wondering expressions, wanting to know what they had learned.

"We should know something fairly quick," Susan stated.

"Good," Kenneth said.

"Thanks, Mom," Greg uttered as he looked at Susan.

"Don't thank me," Susan was quick to state, "it was Edith who put the fear of God in them."

Frank's face bore a small grin. He knew Edith had this hidden side to her, and he was thankful for it. When he had exhausted all of his remedies concerning something occurring in their lives, Edith would step up. Yes, she was very talented along that line when it became necessary.

Within a matter of a minute or two, a doctor came walking into the waiting room.

"First of all, let me apologize for taking so long in getting to you." He ignored the older adults in the room and addressed his remarks in Greg's direction. "When your wife presented herself into the emergency room our first concern was that of her pregnancy. Usually that is the cause they're suffering from, however, the more we delved into the symptoms she was exhibiting, our concerns turned down another avenue. Her problems were emanating from her heart."

"Oh God," Susan said as she placed her hands to her face. Her eyes began to water significantly as well as Edith's. Kenneth and Frank stood there silently, each man's mind trying to comprehend what this all meant to her, as well as the baby. Both fathers' eyes were moist. Greg's thoughts ran in many different directions, the safety of his wife's life and the baby. Could he lose one of them, perhaps both. Greg's cheeks remained covered with the dampness of his tears.

"Mr. Wilson, your wife had an angioplasty performed on her. All of us were handling more than just her pregnancy, therefore, I couldn't get back to you right away. I'm sorry you had to wait. Fortunately we had a cardiologist who happened to be here dealing with another patient's problems. He was able to achieve the results he wanted. In short, a tiny balloon is guided into Melissa's heart. It is inflated stretching the plaque to the side thus opening the artery. As I say, it was successfully accomplished. Everything was happening so fast. To tell you the truth, we hate it when it happens this way. Well, the blockage was eliminated and she is doing beautifully."

"Our daughter has never indicated any complaints as far as her heart goes," Kenneth stated as he shook his head slowly back and forth. His face demonstrated an almost complete disbelief in the words he was hearing.

"Has she been under a lot of stress lately? There are numerous reasons for triggering things such as this.

"Our last name is Summers, does that tell you anything."

"Oh, now I understand. She's been through an awful lot lately, you all have. With the fire, the pregnancy, who knows what else, they can all add up. The lower blood flow certainly was the final piece in the puzzle, the blockage that is. I'm sure Melissa has kept a tremendous amount of pressure hidden behind the curtain of her face."

"Wait a minute, we can talk about that later," Greg stated. "Can I see Melissa, please... please?"

"As quickly as I can get you there. Before we do that, I'd like to tell you what Dr. Field had to say. He believes your wife will soon be giving birth, within a day or so, maybe quicker. He calls them a two-fer. What he means by that is the fact that you come in for one thing, and something entirely unrelated takes place. We'll go down there now and see her. Keep it light, positive, and not very long. She does need her rest, especially with what's facing her shortly."

"Can we all go?" Edith asked.

"Me, too," Susan added.

"I'll make a deal with you," the doctor said with a slight smile indicated on his face. "Greg and the two women can go in first, then you gentlemen can go in when they're finished. Ordinarily we wouldn't do it this way, just allow Greg in, but from what I understand, we wouldn't want any of our doors damaged by one of you two women."

The men looked at each other not knowing exactly what he meant by his words.

"Now, let's go and see your wife, Greg," the doctor said.

"I know I heard you give me your name earlier, but can you give it to me again, please," Greg said.

"I'm Dr. Shore, and I'm happy everything is working out for you two."

"Thank you."

Greg reached out and shook the doctor's hand, Frank and Kenneth doing the same.

The group followed Dr. Shore as he left the waiting room in the lead. As they passed the nursing station, Edith and Susan made a point to stop and express their thanks to the nurse. The nurse gave them both a wink as they turned to catch up with the group of men.

Once they arrived just outside of the room, Dr. Shore indicated where he wanted them to stop.

"Now just wait here. Greg, you go in first, then the women can follow. If you two gentlemen would simply wait out here until it's your turn, I'd appreciate it. We only allow two in a room to visit at any one time. It's quiet now, so we'll look the other way with the additional people."

Both men nodded his head. Seeing a very small couch in an indentation in the wall, they made their way over to it and sat down.

Entering the room, Greg quickly made his way to Melissa's side. He bent down and kissed her brow. Her eyes remained closed. An oxygen mask covered her face. Greg sat down in a chair he had pulled up beside the bed. He just stared at her, watching as she appeared to be simply sleeping. Her body laid still, a clear tube running from her wrist area up to a plastic bag filled with a clear substance. As he gazed at her he reached over and placed his hand in hers. Greg began to cry lightly.

Edith started to make a movement in his direction. Susan, however, reached over and gently grabbed the back of her arm stopping her.

"Let him be," she whispered softly. "He needs to release the tension he still holds so tightly inside of him along with what he's already been through. I know he's cried many tears today, but I think it doesn't hurt him to get as many out of his system as he can. He needs some time to be alone with her now."

Edith knew she was right. She could hardly hold herself back, wanting so much to reach out and comfort him. Her son, she thought, the one she held in her arms when he suffered a simple cut or bruise was out of bounds now. She had always been there for him, and now all she could do was to watch him as he suffered within. Now, when he needed her the most, she felt guilty in doing nothing. Edith understood Susan's words well. She agreed with them. He needed time beside his wife. Her heart ached as she stood beside Susan watching.

Greg continued softly crying as he rubbed his hand over hers. At one point he stood and brushed some of her blonde hair from the top of her face. He placed a loving kiss on her brow once again. He turned in the women's direction as he wiped his eyes with a small tissue he had retrieved from a box on a table beside the bed.

 Turning his attention back to Melissa, he pulled her blanket down slightly to her waistline. He reached over on the outside of her hospital gown and put his hand onto her stomach. It was as if he was waiting for the baby to kick. He held it there for some time. It was evident to both women by his facial expression he felt the baby move. A small smile crossed his lips. They could hear a deep breath being released from his mouth. The two women thought it was a breath of relief. Greg pulled the blanket back up on to Melissa. He then sat down in the green chair near the bed.

Susan looked over at Edith and nodded her head. Edith walked the short distance to Greg and placed her hand on his shoulder. He reached up and rested his hand on her fingers. He then tilted his head in the direction of her arm resting his head against her arm. Edith bent over and kissed the top of his head.

 "Everything is going to be fine," she uttered softly to him.

 "I love her so much," he expressed as he once again wiped his eyes.

 "I know you do, Honey, and so does she."

 Greg nodded his head. The women said nothing to each other, words not needing to be said. Their feelings were expressed in silence, just as strong as if the words had been spoke out loud. No words could contribute to their feelings any better than what was transpiring between them. That was very clear to all, especially Greg.

"I think we should let the men come in now," suggested Edith.

 "I think you're right," Susan responded.

Edith once again placed a kiss on the top of his head. She was followed by Susan in her movements as she also kissed Greg. The two women turned and left the room. Turning at the doorway, Edith looked for the men. Much to her surprise not only did she see them standing beside each other talking, it was who was next to them that brought a smile to her face. It was Kate. Kate immediately went to them. After the usual hugs, Kate inquired about Melissa's condition.

"She's doing very well, although she still is recovering," Susan stated. "Kate, how did you get in here, they only allow family members in cases such as this, at least that's what I was told."

"I told them Melissa is my sister."

"She would be very proud of that assessment," Susan said.

"As I would of her," Kate smiled. "Can I go in and see them?"

"The men haven't been in yet," Susan stated, "so I guess you'll have to wait a little while."

"You go in now," Kenneth was quick to state. "We'll wait a little longer."

"Besides," Frank said, "I think it would do her a lot of good to see her sister first." Frank chuckled a little at his own humor.

"Please," Kenneth said.

"Thank you both," Kate expressed.

She turned and walked into the room. Greg stood quickly and took Kate in his arms. He hugged her very hard.

"Thank you so much for coming," Greg said, "I know she'll be really happy to see you, or at least know you were here."

"When does the patient get a hug?" Melissa said in a weak voice.

Turning quickly in Melissa's direction Greg was amazed to see her awake. Greg immediately went to her side. He reached over the bed bars and tried to kiss her, however, her mask prevented him from accomplishing that very act. He felt silly. Melissa, however, reached up with her free hand and slowly pulled the mask slightly to the side. Greg bent down and kissed her.

"I love you so much," he said.

As he reached over again to kiss her she felt tears from his cheek up against her skin.

"I love you too," she replied.

"I'll let the parents know you're awake," Kate said as she demonstrated a smile across her face.

"No, you don't," Melissa stated. "I want a hug before another second goes by."

Kate smiled as she made her way over to Melissa. They hugged gently for a very long time.

"Now you can tell them," Melissa said.

Once Kate informed them of Melissa's condition change, they all clustered in the room. Limited visitation or not, that did not stop them. They were, however, sure to keep it quiet for the sake of Melissa, as well as the fact they didn't want it discovered there were way too many people in the room. There were the expected hugs and kisses exchanged, but in addition, a deep relief in everyone's soul for her wellbeing. Words demonstrated that fact to Melissa, as well as everything else she observed about them. The tears in their eyes were a clue she could never have missed.

"We are so happy you're... we both love you," Susan said.

"We all love you," Frank added.

"Yes, we all love you," Susan was quick to correct herself, "we all do very much."

"I know," was all Melissa said nodding her head. "If it's okay with everyone, I'm still a little groggy. Can I rest for a..."

"Of course, Honey," Susan said

"You do need some time to rest," agreed Kenneth.

"Why don't I take everyone out for some breakfast and coffee, if that's agreeable with everyone," Frank suggested.

The group in general all nodded their heads, except Greg.

"I think I'd prefer to stay here with Melissa for awhile," Greg said, "a very long time."

"Kate, thank you for coming," Melissa said in a soft voice, "it means so much to me."

"Henry is home babysitting Emma Elizabeth. He told me to especially tell you that if you have any trouble falling asleep, or the baby, he'd be glad to come over here and sing a lullaby to both of you."

"Or I can," suggested Greg.

"No thank you," Melissa said.

"Ribbit," Susan chuckled.

Only Kate, Melissa, and Susan laughed.

"I don't get it," Edith said.

"I'll explain it all to you later," Susan said, "but for now, let's give these two... soon to be three a little space so Melissa can rest."

Everyone nodded their heads as they bid the young couple good-bye and turned to leave the room. Once the room had cleared, Greg had a few observations he wanted to share with his wife. He also had a few questions he wanted answered.

"The doctor informed me you're very close to delivering the baby. How are you feeling, Honey?"

"Actually I feel pretty good considering."

"He also informed me they did an angioplasty to your heart. That's really about all he said about it."

"Mr. Wilson," a nurse stated as she came into the room, "I have an extra tray of food here, if you'd like it. It's hospital food, of course, but that doesn't mean it's bad. There is some coffee. Unfortunately it's decaf, but it's better than nothing. I think there's also some toast."

"Thank you, that's very kind of you."

"As far as you eating, Mrs. Wilson, the doctor will be in to see you and then he'll let you know anything along that line. I'm sorry, that's all I can offer. He'll be in shortly I'm sure."

"Thank you," Melissa said.

"Yes, thank you for your thoughtfulness," Greg said.

"You're welcome," the nurse said as she set the tray down on Melissa's bed table. She then nodded her head slightly as she turned and left the room.

As the five adults made their way from the hospital, Kenneth stopped for a moment outside of the main entrance.

"I observed something today, and I never would have thought it could take place," Kenneth stated.

"What's that, Kenneth?" Susan inquired.

"Today I was knocked down a peg in my daughter's relationship. It was as sad for me to watch, as it was wonderful to observe."

"What are you talking about?" Susan asked again.

"It's Greg."

"Greg?" stated Edith, not at all understanding what Kenneth was referring to either.

"When I watched Greg in the hospital, his reaction to Melissa's... the problems she was facing today, everything that was happening, it all became very relevant to me, as clear as a clean window pane."

"What are you trying to say?" Susan again asked.

"I know I'm confused," Edith said.

"I never thought anyone could carry the amount of love for Melissa as Susan and I have for her, yet it was playing itself out before my very eyes. Edith, your son not only loves our daughter every bit as much as Susan and I do, but he possesses something much more precious in his feelings for her than either one of us. I can't explain it any better than that."

"Maybe it's something deep in his soul that no one can see," Kate offered. "It's like a piece of the other person's heart is held tightly in their own. That's what I think it is. It's not that you and Susan don't have it, or Frank and Edith, or even me. It's like an additional shade in the rainbow of love he possesses for her. I'm sure inside it's a very important part of him. I believe each one of us carries that same color for our own spouses, our own family members."

Kenneth nodded his head in agreement. Whether she was right or wrong didn't really matter. He was just happy his daughter had that special someone who loved her as much as Susan and he did. That was all that was really important to any of them.

Greg sat next to the bed drinking his decaffeinated coffee. Every so often he would fight off a yawn. He could tell Melissa was feeling better with every passing moment that went by. The grogginess that once possessed Melissa had now subsided. He could see it in her face, as well as hear it in her voice. As he placed the cup down on the table, Melissa's doctor walked into the room.

"So how is my patient with the broken heart doing today, better I assume?"

"The pain is gone, but I'm still tired," replied Melissa.

"That's to be expected, Melissa."

From that point on, the doctor explained to Greg and Melissa what had transpired since she first came into the hospital. Greg was grateful everything had turned out the way it had. The fact that both of their parents were there to support them meant everything to him. While Kate's arrival was a surprise to him, he would not expect anything less from her as Melissa's best friend.

"Doc, my wife is young, healthy, why did this happen? I wasn't expecting this whatsoever. In fact, this is the last thing I thought would ever happen to her."

"Women are becoming more and more prone to heart disease, especially as they grow in the workforce. She may have had this problem for some time and it just caught up with her.

Now as to your baby, Melissa, you're very close to giving birth, and that was a major concern of ours last night. None of us wanted you going into labor when we were dealing with other complications so to speak. We all want that little person inside of you to come out with a smile on his or her face. We're keeping you in here for that reason alone. Once we all feel things are on the right track, and you're up to it, we'll take the next steps necessary. That is, of course, if the little one doesn't have some other ideas of their own."

Melissa nodded her head.

"Are there any more questions I can answer for either one of you?"

"How is the procedure she just had, how will that affect her child birth," Greg asked with a concerned sound to his voice.

"Actually we believe it will be easier on her since her heart problem has been addressed. You're a young and vibrant young lady, Melissa, and we'll keep a very close eye on you just the same. Your baby and you will be our first priority. The staff here is a very good one.

By the way, one of your mothers got a little upset with our nurses. It probably was all my fault for not contacting you earlier about your wife's condition and so forth. Right after we finished up with you, another emergency came in. They needed my help on that one also. That's why I was so long getting back to you, Greg."

"What happened?" Melissa asked.

"Oh, about the mother. It seems," he chuckled, "that one of your mothers threatened to knock down some doors with her fist if she didn't get some answers concerning your health. The nurses took it in stride, but they said she was very serious in her tone and attitude."

"That had to be my mom," chuckled Melissa.

"I'm afraid it was mine," Greg said.

"Edith?"

"Uh-huh," Greg stated.

"Edith, your mother?"

"Uh-huh," he said nodding his head.

"Do you know what she looked like?" Melissa asked, still unable to believe Edith could ever consider acting that much out of character.

"I understand from the nurses both women were fairly attractive for their age, but the one nurse said her hair was brown. Does that help you out?"

Melissa started laughing slightly. "Edith, it was your mom. I can hardly believe it. She's just so meek and mild."

"Well," joked the doctor, "I'm going to keep an eye out for her if she should show up again."

"Thank you for everything you've done, we both appreciate it," Greg said as he held his hand out to the doctor giving him a handshake.

"I'll be back later to check on you again. As far as the baby goes, we'll play that by ear. Agreed?"

Greg and Melissa both nodded their heads.

"And let me see about getting you something to eat."

"Thank you," Melissa said. "I am actually getting a little hungry."

"I'll see to it right away."

"Doctor, do you think it's possible to get my husband some coffee with caffeine in it? Every time he yawns I get sleepy."

"I'll see what I can do."

"Thank you," Greg said as he let out a small yawn.

"I see what you mean," joked the doctor as he turned and left the room.

As the parents and Kate entered the restaurant they took a look around.

"Can I seat you... oh, five of you. I'm sorry, I didn't see you there, ma'am."

Frank nodded his head being the first in line.

"I liked the part where she didn't see me," Edith whispered to Susan, "my diet must be working. I never really like it when they call me, ma'am, though. It sounds like the years are catching up to me."

"That's exactly how I feel when Fred calls me Mrs. Summers."

As the group reached the table they began to take their seats.

"Coffee all around?" inquired the waitress.

Kenneth looked around the table at everyone. "Please."

"You'll never know how much it meant to Melissa for you to be here, Kate," Susan stated. You two possess an extremely close relationship. Kenneth and I are so very thankful for that."

"I'm so glad you contacted me," Kate said. "It just so happened Henry got home right before your call, so I was able to come right over. Henry makes a wonderful babysitter."

"So how are things going for you two? I would imagine you're both very busy with the child, and Henry's singing."

"It's not just that, we have some other irons in the fire that are keeping us very busy."

"Such as?" inquired Susan.

"Well, there's a family who live ten to fifteen miles from here who have been having a real hard time in their lives. They lost a baby through crib death."

"That is so tragic," Edith expressed. She shook her head back and forth slowly as she reached for her small tissue container.

Observing Edith's motions Susan's mind quickly went back to the hospital. She recalled Edith confronting the nurses at their station. What had happened there literally amazed her to watch. Never would Susan have likened Edith as acting the part of a Joan of Arc. She was sure Edith would have been flashing her sword at the nurses if she had possessed one. Edith wanted... demanded answers to her questions. She would not leave until her mind was satisfied with a response. Susan was happy that Edith possessed this other side of her, otherwise, she figured, they would still be sitting in the waiting room wondering. Her attention went back to Kate as she continued describing the family's plight.

"Their son was hit by some youngsters who stole a car. His leg needs an operation to possibly repair it. He has a significant limp. Having the operation is an unknown factor, it may or may not work." Kate let out a definite sigh.

"That's just so sad," Edith said.

"Henry and I have been conducting various benefits for the boy. We've raised quite a bit of money over the last few months with a lot of people's help. We're still short about four thousand dollars, but it will come together in the end. I never knew how hard it is trying to raise money, no matter what the cause. Don't misunderstand me, our community is very generous just the same. Thanks to Henry's singing programs, donations, it's moving faster than we ever would have anticipated or dreamed. For that alone, I'm very grateful.

Henry's partner, Richard, sponsored food nights. In other words, all the money people paid for their meals went into the fund. When people heard what the restaurant was doing, the lines were really long. Some even came and ordered their meals to go. Richard even went so far as to sponsor two more meal nights. Every drink, coffee, beer, whatever it was all went into the kitty for the boy. Even the waitresses gave up their tips. Richard has done an awful lot to help us with this project. I think the thing I got the biggest kick out of was the fact that he had donation containers placed up by the register and on each table."

Susan chuckled. "How did those work out?"

"People put money into them," Kate answered. "Whenever someone put in more than a twenty dollar bill, Henry would sing a song to the couple or individual. Usually it was done by the women at first. It didn't take long before it caught on."

"That's wonderful," Susan stated.

"When you touch people's hearts," Edith expressed, "you never know what emotions you'll stir up in them. I know that's how it is for me."

Kenneth looked at Frank, Frank returning his glance. Frank nodded his head, as Kenneth winked at him. Both wives observed this simple act between their husbands. Being married as long as the four of them had been, eye interaction told each other much of what their spouse was thinking. This day was no different. It made both women proud of what they assumed would happen next. Neither was disappointed.

"Susan do you have our..."

"I sure do."

"Edith, same question," Frank said.

"Yes, I do, dear," Edith said with a smile.

"Half and half?" inquired Frank, a sparkle in his eye.

"Sounds good to me," Kenneth said.

"Great," Frank said.

The two women reached in to their purses and retrieved their checkbooks.

"What are you doing?" questioned Kate.

"The way I see it," Edith said, "you're getting two thousand dollars from us, and two thousand dollars from Susan and Kenneth. We all want to get this young boy into the operating room. Maybe it's because we just left the hospital that makes us feel this way, I don't know, but it needs to come to an end in a successful conclusion for him. At least that's my prayer."

"You tell Henry he owes Kenneth, me, and our wives some songs," joked Frank.

"I don't think... in fact, I know they never could afford the operation," Kate said. "We were told they were of modest means, and that's to say the least. They're in the process of adopting a little girl named Mary who lost her parents in a Christmas fire. She was left with a burn on her cheek. Their hearts are filled with so much love." Kate's voice broke up a little as she spoke. "Your generous gifts will be put to good use. Thank you all so much."

"It's obvious you've met both of them before and have gotten to know them somewhat better," Susan said.

"Yes, we have. Henry and I met with them to discuss getting the boy an operation. They live in Four Pines. We've visited with them on a few other occasions."

"What else can you tell us about them?" Kenneth inquired.

"I do know this, though it's not a lot of information. They are a very loving family as I said. He's a hard worker as is his wife. They've had their share of problems. I guess we all have in our own ways. Have you ever met someone and just liked them right then and there?"

"I sure have," Kenneth acknowledged as he glanced in Susan's direction.

"Well, that's them, simple as that."

"When are you scheduled to meet with them again?" continued Kenneth.

"Well, Henry and I are going to see them the first part of next week. I guess now we'll be able to talk to them about scheduling the operation, thanks to the four of you."

"Don't kid yourself, Kate," Edith stated, "the money you two raised is the largest portion of this. You two toiled on this as well as Richard. I'd give you all an award if it were up to me."

"Well, thanks just the same. I'll let Richard and Henry know how proud of them you are."

"And you, too," Edith said.

"Say, what does he do for a living?" asked Kenneth.

"I think I know where this is headed," smiled Susan.

"So what does he do for a living," Kenneth asked again.

"I understand he's in some type of sales. He once told me the products he sells is like trying to sell ice cream to an Eskimo."

"Is he any good at it?"

"I really don't know, that's all I can say."

"Kate, are they the type of people you would want working for you?" Kenneth asked in a serious tone.

"That isn't really a fair question to ask me," she replied. "I like these people too much to give an unbiased answer to that."

"You have our home phone number, of course. Now, you inform them we're doing some hiring in the future if they would be interested. Tell them both to give us a call, and if we're not at home, leave it on our answering machine."

"I would be glad to," Kate stated.

"Good," Kenneth said.

"Oh, yes, I would," Kate stated.

"Yes you would to what?" Susan asked.

"I'd hire them for a lot of different reasons," Kate offered, "and the most important of all is they're hardworking honest individuals."

"That's all we've ever looked for in an employee," Kenneth said.

Susan nodded her head in agreement.

"Here you are," Edith said as she handed Kate her check.

"You're too fast," Susan said as she took the checkbook in her hand and began writing quickly. As soon as she finished she handed the check to Kate.

"Thank you all for the money, and I'm talking on their behalf now."

"Now that the hard decisions are made," Frank said, "let's decide what we're each having to eat. And by the way, the meal is on us."

"Frank, would you do me a favor?" Kate asked.

"Of course."

"Let me pick up the bill for this breakfast... please."

"No," he smiled, "I'll get it. Of course, if you were to grab it out of my hand, I probably wouldn't be fast enough to stop you."

"You're a good husband, Frank, but an awful liar," Edith said with a smile.

Kate also smiled at him.

"This has been one of the most wonderful breakfasts I've ever had the pleasure of sharing with anyone," Kate said. "Thank you all again."

Everyone nodded their head in agreement.

"When Melissa goes into labor..."

"We'll let you know immediately," Susan said.

"Thank you," Kate replied. "As far as your generous gifts of money..."

"Just be sure to let us know how everything works out for the boy," Edith said, "good or bad."

"I can't recall if I even told you this," Kate stated, "but his name is Josh, he's eight years old. Jennifer is his mother's name, and Frank is his father's name."

"I like him already," Frank said. "After all, with a name like that he must be almost perfect, kind of like me. I'll bet he's charming, handsome, smart..."

"We're talking about him, not you, Honey," Edith was quick to say.

"I'm just saying..."

"And that's what we're afraid of," joked Susan.

As the five of them sat eating their meals, the conversation turned back to Greg and Melissa. The young couple was very much in everyones' thoughts. Everyone possessed their own concerns and fears about what had taken place and what was yet to come. Each would live close to their phone for the next few days, or maybe even hours.

Melissa looked over at Greg slumped in a large green vinyl chair with silver armrests. His body looked very much contorted as he braced his head with one of his arms. She shook her head as she gazed at him, wondering how he could even find an ounce of rest in his cramped position. His eyes were closed. The clothing he wore was very much wrinkled. He definitely needed a shave.

"Honey, why don't you go home and get some sleep, you're acting like an old mother hen," Melissa said, shaking her head back and forth.

He looked over at her in the bed but said nothing. He got up in slow motion, almost as if he were allowing the kinks to work themselves out of his legs. Ever so slowly he moved to Melissa's side. Reaching over the silver bars to the bed he took her hand in his. Leaning forward he placed a kiss on her brow. Greg next leaned closer to her. Their lips met. Both closed their eyes as they offered this small token of love to each other.

"You really need to get some rest, Greg. We don't need you in the hospital, too."

"When I leave here it will be with you getting a ride in a wheelchair and our baby in your arms."

Melissa smiled. She wouldn't expect anything different from her husband, not now, not ever. He always watched over her, that was abundantly clear. His eyes were forever focused as to her wants, her every need, her smallest desires.

Greg's thoughts began to relive what had happened the evening before. When she first began suffering chest pains, the fear he felt within was unbelievable. This was truly an unexpected event, one he never would have conceived in his wildest imagination. It terrified him beyond belief. He would not leave her until they left together. To him there was nothing more to be said on that subject, he would stay at her side no matter what.

Within that very day, the couple became the talk of the hospital staff; Melissa with her heart problems, and expecting shortly. It was a subject with many different avenues to look down and discuss. The nurses who dealt with Greg and Melissa soon became very much attached to them, especially the older ones. One nurse started a baby pool on when and what time the birth would occur. The baby's gender was a part of it also. All were sure it would be very soon.

When there were extra food trays from patients who had gone home, they somehow made their way to Melissa's room for Greg. A footstool appeared in front of the chair Greg slept in thus allowing him to stretch out somewhat. A fresh blanket and pillow miraculously appeared on the chair when he would leave the room temporarily. A day and a half passed.

"Greg…Greg, wake up."
"What?"
"I think… will you get me a nurse? The cord to call them with is twisted and I can't get it out from underneath of me."
"I'll be just a moment," Greg stated as he quickly exited the room.
Melissa nodded her head. She knew what was about to take place, her body began telling her that in no uncertain terms.
"Okay, they're on their way," he said.
"Don't bother calling my mom and dad, or yours either. They always say these things take a long time, and there's no sense in getting them here now."
"Okay. Is there anything I can get you?"
"No. Greg, come here." She held her hand out to him as they held hands. "I love you."
"I know you do. I love you, too."
"Mr. Wilson, would you like to wait in the waiting room for now?" a nurse asked.

"No, I think I'd rather wait here for a while, at least as long as you'll let me... if it's okay."

"That will be fine for now."

"Melissa, I guess I do have to step out for just a moment. I'll be right back."

"Okay, Honey."

Greg stopped at the nurses' station momentarily to get directions to a phone. Shortly thereafter he had his mother on the line. He informed her what had just occurred. He asked her to be sure to contact Kate. With that done, he next called Susan and Kenneth. As he had with his own mother, he informed them not to hurry. In his mind he felt relieved knowing they would arrive shortly, or at least be on their way. They weren't going to sit idly by with their daughter giving birth. There was no question about that. He was positive both sets of parents would come as quickly as possible, no matter what he said. Having the parents there would be like building a bridge, he thought. The more supports there are, the easier it is to carry the load. He was happy inside that he had made the calls and not waited.

Greg returned to the room. He immediately took her hand in his as he stood beside the hospital bed. Time seemed to fly. When Melissa would let out a sound in agony, the clock's hands stopped. It was as if time lived on forever for him, and then was gone as quickly as it appeared.

"Mr. Wilson, you have family members here," stated a nurse.

"Did you call my parents?"

"Only both sets of them."

"You should have waited, Honey."

"And let them miss out on all of the fun you and I are having, you've got to be kidding me."

Melissa looked up at him and smiled slightly, before suffering another contraction.

"Somebody wants to make their way into the world," smiled one of the attending nurses as she glanced at her watch.

"Will you be going into the delivery room with her, if not, now might be a good time to see the people in the waiting room."

"I thought these things took hours?" Greg asked.

"Babies don't carry a watch, so you really never know. I've seen it many different ways. In fact, last week we had a delivery in the emergency room entrance."

Fitting Greg with a light blue gown, a cap and mask to match, he followed as Melissa was moved to the delivery room. Within a fairly short time span, Greg was presented with a daughter. After the baby was checked and cleaned, the infant was placed in Melissa's waiting arms. Greg reached over and stroked his wife's hair before placing a kiss on her brow.

"Thank you, Honey," he said as he placed another kiss on her face.

Melissa looked up at Greg as he smiled down at her. His eyes were slightly watery, but his smile helped to hide that fact.

"Thank you," he stated as he rubbed his thumb over the backside of her hand. "Now the real problem begins."

"What's that?" she whispered to him softly.

"Naming her. I haven't really thought that much about it since we didn't know if we'd have a boy or a girl."

"Well, I've thought of it a little bit."

"So what did you come up with?"

"Would you care if we copied someone we both love?"

"No, I don't care," he said, "whatever you want to do is fine with me."

"Now, it's a little different, but you know how I love roses."

"Oh," he laughed, "you want to name her, Rose. Of course, if it was a boy you probably would have used the name, Bud."

"Not exactly," Melissa said chuckling.

"Well, I'm all ears."

"If you don't like it, we can think of some other names."

"Melissa, whatever you want, Honey."

Melissa took a deep breath.

"I was thinking of Susanna Edith Rose Wilson."

"Boy that's a mouth full," laughed Greg.

"You don't like it, do you?"

"It's not that, I love it. I just wasn't expecting our daughter to have three first names is all. Well, I guess it's not really three first names."

Melissa cocked her head to one side as she shrugged her shoulders.

"So what do we call her for short?" he inquired.

"I was thinking of Rose."

"I thought so," chuckled Greg.

"Is that okay with you? I do love roses so much. In every large event in my life I've been surrounded with red roses. You gave me red roses on our first date, they filled our wedding and even the reception."

"Don't forget your wedding dress had lots of them in the material."

"You noticed that?"

"It's one of my fondest memories of our wedding, how beautiful you made the dress look that day."

"Awe," came the sound of two nurses in the room. Each took a quick look at the other, a little sign of embarrassment showing on their faces.

"Oh, we're sorry," one said.

Greg turned and smiled at them.

"That's alright," Melissa said.

"So how is my little sweetheart Rose doing," Greg asked as he reached over and kissed the baby. "What's that, Rose... you love your name. I do too. I guess I'll have to return the football. She won't be doing any field goal kicking now."

Melissa smiled.

"On the other hand, she's cute enough to be a cheerleader," he added.

"Let's not have her grow up too quickly; she hasn't even met our parents yet."

"Oh my goodness, I should let them know what's going on. You heard the one nurse say there are some family members in the waiting room. I'll go out and see them, but I'm not going to tell them what the baby's name is or sex, that's going to be your honor."

"I would really enjoy telling them," she said smiling.

Greg nodded his head. "Of course you can. Now, once you're back to your room, and everything is settled, we'll go from there."

As Greg entered the waiting room, he was surprised to see everyone there, both sets of parents along with Kate and Henry.

"How is Melissa and the baby?" were the first words out of Susan's mouth.

"Melissa is fine."

"Good," she said.

"What about the baby," Edith quickly asked.

"The baby is just fine," Greg said.

"Well, is it a boy or a girl?" Frank inquired.

"That's a secret for now," smiled Greg.

"Then just give us the name," Kenneth asked, trying to sneak an answer from Greg and discover the child's sex.

"I promised Melissa she could tell you all that information. Now, a nurse told me when the baby is brought to Melissa's room, in a little while, you can go down and see her. Then she or he will have to go back to the nursery."

"I'm so excited you two had a little boy," Edith said.

"I didn't say that."

"No, Edith, he said it was a little girl," Susan stated as she winked at Edith.

"I didn't say that either," protested Greg.

"Oh stop it now," Frank interjected. "I'll tell you what we're going to do. We'll all write down on a piece of paper what we think the baby is, boy or girl. If there's more than one winner, they can flip a coin."

"Winner, what does the winner get?" Edith asked.

"We'll all kick in twenty dollars, and the winner gets the privilege of opening the baby's college account. Of course, the winner has to pay even if they win. Fair enough?" Frank asked.

"Do I get a chance on this, I don't want to be left out?" chuckled Kate.

"Neither do I," Henry added.

"I don't see why not," Susan said.

"With six of us playing, the baby would get a hundred and twenty dollars. That's a pretty good start," Kate offered.

"I like the idea," Edith said.

"So do I," added Susan.

"Kenneth, you're in charge," Frank said as he handed him forty dollars.

"Whatever you say," Kenneth stated as he reached for his wallet.

"Let me get my purse," Kate said as she reached for it.

"Say, can I get into this, too?" inquired Greg.

"Why not, the kid could use the money," chuckled Susan.

"No you don't," Edith said, "that would be cheating."

"Do we really care?" Kenneth asked.

"No," Edith said.

"What if there's a tie?" Susan asked.

"We'll flip for a winner," Edith said nodding her head.

Greg chuckled to himself. He was going to write down girl just to mess with everyone there. Not a bad idea, he thought to himself.

Melissa sat in bed, a newborn tucked into her arms. Her smile said it all to Susan and Edith. There was really nothing to say, however, everyone wanted to find out what the results of nine months of waiting had produced.

"Ordinarily we don't allow this to happen," a nurse stated, "I mean, this many people in with the mother. Your doctor gave Melissa and Greg permission to allow it. Please make it a very short visit. Oh, and your doctor also gave us special instructions," another nurse by the name of Pam said. "He said to keep an eye out for the brunette."

Those who knew what had transpired with Edith, chuckled. Susan smiled while Edith rolled her eyes somewhat. The two fathers looked at each other while Greg just shook his head. Kate said nothing, but knew she would surely ask about the doctor's comment later. Henry knew he would ask him, too.

"Also," the nurse continued, "it just so happens the nursery is actually empty now, so you're in luck. Remember, don't be very long... please."

The sound of various voices thanking her quickly filled the room. She shook her head slightly as she left the crowded room.

It was Kate who first noticed it, but didn't say a word. The blanket the baby was wrapped in was the same one she had given to Melissa at the adult party. Melissa had done the very same act that Kate had done. They both used the gift from the other to hold their precious newborn in.

"Now, I know you're all wondering what we have," smiled Melissa, as she took a quick glance around the room. "It's a... I know you're all wondering..."

"Really, Melissa, what is the baby?" Susan stated, her curiosity burning inside of her.

"It's a little girl."

"Now that's exciting news," Kenneth said.

"Who won the bet?" Frank was quick to ask.

"Kate," Kenneth replied.

"Well, what made you say a little girl, everyone was figuring on a boy?" inquired Edith.

Kate looked over and smiled at Melissa. She took a step closer to the bed, then reached down with her hand and took Melissa's hand in hers.

"It was easy. We do everything the same. I had Emma Elizabeth, it was only natural she'd have a little girl, too."

"Isn't that cheating?" inquired Frank.

"Frank, really," Edith said.

"So what's the baby's name," Susan asked.

Melissa looked over at Greg, smiled, and then said, "I kind of took a page from you, Kate. I hope you don't mind."

"What did you do?" Kate asked.

"The baby's name is Susanna Edith Rose Wilson. If it's okay with you; that's what it's going to read on the birth certificate. Greg and I would like to call her Rose whenever we're addressing her as she grows up. Is that okay with everyone?"

"That's wonderful," Edith said. She quickly leaned over the bed and gave Melissa a kiss, and then the baby. Her next step was obvious to everyone there. She reached for her tissue container.

"I love you, Mom," Melissa said.

"I know you do, and I love you, too," Edith said as she wiped her eyes.

"Thank you," Susan said, "for making me a part of our granddaughter's name. She moved over closer to the bed and mirrored Edith's motions, giving both a kiss.

"And, Mom, I love you, too," Melissa said smiling.

"I know, Honey, and I love you very much also," Susan uttered. She reached up with the palms of her hands and wiped her eyes.

"Here you go," Edith said as she handed Susan a tissue.

"So Kenneth, are we just chopped liver or what?" Frank asked.

"You two come here now," Melissa's forceful voice demanded as she reached out for Frank with her free hand. Frank gave Melissa and the baby a quick kiss on their cheeks. He then gave a second kiss on the newborn's brow.

"You want to move over a little bit, Frank, I do think it's my turn," joked Kenneth. Kenneth duplicated Frank's actions.

"Can I give Rose a little kiss, too?" asked Henry.

" Please," Melissa said smiling.

Henry gladly complied.

"If it's okay with Greg… Henry, would you mind singing a little lullaby to Rose? I know we'd all love to hear you as well, especially Susann Edith Rose Wilson."

Henry hesitated as he looked around the room.

"I would think that honor should go strictly to Greg first," he answered.

"It's okay, Henry," Greg said with a nod. "There's something everyone here should know, and I understand it better than anyone."

"What's that, Honey?" Melissa asked.

"Ribbit-ribbit," Greg chuckled.

Everyone laughed.

"So you knew that your voice was —"

"That of a crow rather than a canary," smiled Greg, "yes, I did."

Once again there was the sound of laughter.

"So Henry, what do you say?" Greg said.

"Thank you, Greg. This is really a privilege for me, and I mean that from the bottom of my heart. If I may, Melissa."

Melissa nodded her head.

Henry gently picked up the baby cradling her ever so gently as he began to rock slowly back and forth. He quietly cleared his throat as was his custom. Henry then began to fill the room with the words to an old lullaby. As was normal for him, his voice was strong, yet tender to the ear. After a short verse, Henry walked a few feet to Greg, carefully handing Rose to him. Greg continued rocking the baby in his arms. He smiled at everyone. Henry nodded his head in Susan's direction. Greg slowly handed the newborn to Susan.

As Henry sang, a few nurses stood outside of the room watching what was occurring before them. Both smiled at each other as they silently took in the scene. Neither one had ever observed these actions before. It was something they knew they would forever hold in their memories. This very act alone was something each could hardly wait to share with the rest of the hospital staff during their upcoming break.

Henry continued singing while Rose made her way from parent to parent and then finally back to her mother's waiting arms. When Henry finished the last lullaby each woman made her way over to him, giving him a large hug. The men shook his hand and thanked him.

"I know I'll never forget what you just did for Melissa and Rose," Susan said nodding her head.

"Here you go," Edith said as she handed her a tissue.

"Thank you, Edith."

Edith nodded her head as she wiped her own eyes.

"It would have been even more memorable had I sung," joked Greg as he put his hand out to Henry. "Thank you, Henry."

"You're welcome."

"Well, it looks like everything is under control here, so I think we'll head home to our own little one," Kate said.

"Kate," Melissa said a little louder voice than one would have expected.

"Yes."

"Can we make a promise to each other today?"

"Of course. What is it you want?" Kate asked.

"Can we try and raise our two girls to be as close as we are. It would mean so much to me if we could at least give it a try."

"I would absolutely love to do that, Melissa, I really would."

"Then it's settled. We'll both work on accomplishing that together."

"What a wonderful idea," Susan said.

"It sure is," added Edith.

"And you two women are going to help us along that line," Melissa said.

"We will," Susan said.

"And we'll help as much as we can; isn't that right, Greg, Frank?" Edith said.

"Whatever you say, Mom," Greg said with a smile.

"Of course," Frank added.

"And you, too, Kenneth," Susan said nodding her head.

"Who am I to go against the grain," he said with a smile.

"So I guess it's settled," Kate said. "I'll inform Doc and Jean of all the good news when I get home."

"Thank you," Melissa uttered.

"Say, how are Doc and Jean doing these days?" Susan asked.

"I think they're getting real serious on selecting a date. She has her ring, of course, now it comes down to where and when," Kate said.

"Wouldn't it be grand if your grandfather and her got married this year," Edith said, "I mean, Jean is such a wonderful person. From what I can see they'll be heading down the aisle fairly soon."

"I hope so," Susan went on, "they're made for each other."

"Well, we better get going," Kate said.

She turned and reached over taking Melissa's hand in hers. She lifted her fingers to her mouth and gave them a small kiss. Kate then reached over repeating her actions with Rose.

"I guess today is the beginning of a new journey in our lives," Kate stated. "I do think the best part of it is that we know our babies will always have a very good friend to count on in each other."

"And we'll see to that," Susan offered with a smile.

"That we will," Melissa added.

Kate smiled.

It was only a matter of a short time before Melissa and Rose were home. Greg was overjoyed to have them both in the comfort of their abode. He pampered them in any way he could conceive of. She was not allowed to lift a finger. Being only the first day, she felt overwhelmed by his attention already. She loved it; she hated it.

In her heart she was smart enough to realize once everything settled down, life would get back to normal. Normal, she thought, what is normal? For anyone who's just had a baby, their parents' business destroyed, a heart problem, and an ad company being offered for them to purchase; what next could happen? Her thoughts flip-flopped back and forth, the more she thought of everything. Finally her mind had had enough. Still, we're a very lucky couple in many, many ways she thought. The baby was healthy, she had sort of new heart, and best of all, they were surrounded by loving people. Now it was time to get some sleep. She knew Greg had everything under control even though he had asked a million questions of the nurses. Finally, her eyelids were too heavy to be held open any longer. Her body melted into the mattress as she drifted off to sleep.

As Melissa laid in bed with her eyes closed, the scent of flowers seemed to penetrate the atmosphere of the room. She kept her eyes shut as she took a deep breath trying to capture every morsel the buds offered to her. Melissa knew Greg would get her a bouquet of her favorite flowers, red roses. She wanted to remember this moment forever, and so she took in another deep breath while being sure to keep her eyes closed. As she slowly opened her eyes, they grew larger with everything that surrounded her.

Their bedroom was filled not with just an array of various bouquets, but every imaginable spot seemed to be taken. Both of the wide windowsills held four smaller flower arrangements all by themselves. The larger of two dressers held five large plants nestled closely on top of it. Their smaller dresser had a large variety of flowered plants on its top. Melissa was simply astounded. There were plants everywhere.

Over to one side of the room was a very nice selection of terrariums. The front room coffee table had been moved into the room to help accommodate the overage. There were plants lined up against the wall. She couldn't help herself as she started counting the arrangements, both large and small. Simply unbelievable, she said to herself out loud. Aren't they just beautiful, she thought as she continued looking around the bedroom.

One flower arrangement in particular captured her eyes. It was on the center of the coffee table. A wicker baby buggy about a foot and a half long, and a foot or so high sat in its own glory. Its solid wooden wheels rested on top of the table. Large red roses along with smaller ones filled the carriage with an abundance of beauty. Baby's breath peeked out between the buds. It was an arrangement one wouldn't readily find in just any flower shop. She was sure it had to be from Greg. He and his uncle, Norm, must have ordered it sometime ago. Having an uncle who owned a floral business surely aided Greg in acquiring such an unusual container. It was perfect she thought. Melissa closed her eyes once again and took in another deep breath. How wonderful she thought to herself again.

"Hi, sleeping beauty," Greg said as he walked into the room.

"Oh, these all are so beautiful, Greg, I love them all."

Seeing nothing in his arms she quickly stated in a startled voice, "Greg, where did you leave the baby?" Melissa's voice definitely had an alarmed sound to it.

"She's in the kitchen being spoiled by her grandmother, or a more common expression would describe her as your mother." Greg chuckled.

"She's here?"

"Her, my mother, and both of our dads. We've got to get them out of here."

"Why?"

"I've only been allowed to hold Rose once. They're hogging her."

Melissa smiled.

"Where did all of these flowers come from?"

"Actually your parents hid them for me. You see, the plants and such have been coming for quite some time now. Our parents have been keeping them hidden until very early this morning. They all helped me move them into the bedroom so you could see them when you first woke up. It was the quietest I've ever seen those two women together. I was so afraid you'd wake up and your surprise would be spoiled. You needed the rest."

"Who are they all from?"

"Here, read this card first," Greg suggested as he reached for the closest bouquet. Greg handed her a white envelope, which she opened. She read it out loud.

"Congratulations, to both of you, the guys and gals in the appliance section."

"Appliance section. Greg, are all these flowers from the people in the store?"

"Why don't you read another one and we'll find out."

"Well, let's see." Melissa opened another card, which she read out loud also. "This one says, 'men's clothing, and this one is from the maintenance department. Here's one from women's wear. Oh, this is from the accounting department." Melissa smiled knowing very well who had personally sent it. Even if the card hadn't been signed, "With love, Fred and family," it held a special spot in her heart. "Here's one from the cosmetics department."

"I see that. The employees love you an awful lot, Melissa," Greg offered. "I'm sure they're so happy you're doing so well. I'll bet if you were to talk to anyone of them now, they'd tell you that immediately."

Melissa reached up with her finger and wiped the corner of her eyes.

"You know, Honey, they all love you as well," she said.

"I think it's a mutual thing for all of us. Now why don't you read a few more cards. When you read them, I can actually see their faces in my mind."

Melissa smiled.

Thus it continued, every department represented from a store that was no more than ashes a few months ago. The rebuilding was well underway. That was very evident to all who drove by the scene of the fire. The simple act of sending flowers or plants meant more to Melissa and Greg than either one had ever thought possible. Greg got up from a chair and sat on the bed beside his wife. He took her in his arms as she laid her head on his shoulder. She cried gently as he held her a little tighter. His eyes were misty.

"This means so much to me," Melissa whispered in his ear.

"Me as well," Greg said as he put his hand on the back of her head pulling it tighter into his shoulder. He could feel her head moving slightly as tear drops escaped her eyes.

"We have so much to be thankful for," Melissa softly said in a fragile voice. She began to cry a little more.

"Yes, we do… we surely do."

Haunted by the Past

"Henry," Kate said, "I just got off the phone with a Mr. Allen Parrish a little while ago. He wanted to know if your last name had previously been Lewis, that's why I'm calling you at work. I didn't feel comfortable at all in talking with him about your last name. The man told me where he worked, but I was too shaken by his question to even hear him. He gave me the phone number of where he can be reached. Did I do the right thing?"

"Of course you did," Henry said, not knowing what else to tell her. "I'll get his number when I get home for lunch."

If there were some type of problem concerning his past, the changing of his name, he would handle it. There was no need to worry Kate about anything that hadn't presented itself to them yet. Different thoughts began to fill his mind. He shook his head a little as if that would remove his questions but that, of course, did no good. With the phone number in hand, Henry thought about calling the individual.

Kate and Henry ate their lunch on the patio. Nothing more was said about the phone call. He gave Kate a kiss before going out to his vehicle. Getting into his car he headed towards the Golden Rib Restaurant. As he drove his mind was mixed with numerous thoughts playing themselves out. Before he even realized it he was in the parking lot to the restaurant. It was as if the trip there just seemed to happen. Henry got out of the car and headed into the building. Saying hello to some of the staff working there, he made his way back to Richard's office.

"Richard, can I have a piece of paper and a pen or pencil?"

"Sure," Richard responded, as he reached across his desk handing him a pen.

"Thanks."

Richard nodded his head.

"May I use your phone for a minute?"

"Of course."

"What is it, Henry, by the sound of your voice you seem somewhat concerned?"

"I wish I knew what this is all about. Some years ago I... I changed my last name from Lewis to Morgan. Morgan was the name I was born with."

"I see," Richard said, a surprised look covering his face.

"Well, there's really more to it than just that," Henry said as he nodded his head slightly.

Thoughts of his past now began being relived with every second that passed. "I was adopted by a family, if you can even call them that. They treated me like a piece of useless property. I often wondered why they even took me in. Needless to say it wasn't very long after that when I had that question answered. I was a possession to them, like a hammer, a chair, whatever piece of inanimate material you want to use. They treated me like a slave to do their bidding, whether it was painting garbage cans, fixing a broken window, washing floors, shopping. I was a dumb go-fer, as they sometimes referred to me. When I found out what my real name was, some years ago, I had it changed to reflect that fact. Of course, that was when I was out of their control and on my own. No one was going to call me Mr. Lewis if I had anything to say about it. Now somebody wants to know if I'm that person. I'm not really sure how to handle this."

"Henry, listen to me," Richard said. "If I were in your shoes trying to deal with a situation like you're facing, I'd simply give our attorney a call. Let him delve into it. You certainly have nothing to hide. Just let Eric check into it for you."

"You know, I think you're right."

"I know I am," Richard said nodding his head. "He can find out what's going on, that's why our business keeps him on a retainer. You know I'm right."

Henry looked across the desk at Richard. He knew he could trust his advice as well as Eric's. Better to give him a call and let him know what was going on. Eric would know how to handle whatever it was that may arise.

After talking with Eric, Henry felt better inside. Why anyone wanted this canister of nasty memories opened was anyone's guess. He would learn the answer to that question soon enough he thought.

"Henry, if you need anything, you let me know."

"I will, Richard, and thanks."

Richard nodded his head as Henry left the office.

The backdoor opening and closing alerted Kate that Henry was at last home. She walked the short distance from the living room to the kitchen.

"So what did you find out?" she inquired, her mind still very curious. She needed to have that question answered.

"Unfortunately, Mr. Parrish was in a meeting and couldn't be reached according to Eric." He said he'd try again tomorrow."

"So Eric is going to handle this for us?"

"Yes," Henry said, a little sigh coming from his mouth.

"Did Eric say anything about the man?"

"Well, Eric did learn that he's affiliated with some type of facility for housing the elderly. Why he would call me still remains a mystery. I'm sure we'll know more tomorrow. We'll just have to wait and see."

"If you felt it necessary to call Eric to handle this, are you really that concerned?"

"Richard suggested it since we have him retained as our business attorney anyway. Why not take advantage of that fact."

"I suppose he's right, Henry. Do you think it has anything to do with your mother, Mrs. Lewis?"

"Don't you ever call her my mother," Henry said to Kate in a very loud and stern voice.

"I'm sorry, Honey, I didn't mean to upset —"

"No, no, it's me. I'm sorry Kate, I really am. Just please don't use her name in this house, and especially the word —" Even Henry didn't want to use the word, "mother."

"You mean the word, 'mother'?"

Henry nodded his head.

"It won't happen again, Honey," Kate said. "I'm sorry, I should have known better."

"You couldn't have possibly known I would feel that strongly about that word. Please forgive me, I was way out of line for yelling at you."

"It wasn't really yelling," Kate stated, "but I sure understand now. I won't use that word again, especially if I'm talking about her."

Henry reached over putting his arm around her shoulder. He gave her a kiss on her cheek before releasing her.

"I think I'll go to bed early tonight," she stated. "I understand, you've got a lot on your mind. Give yourself a break from all of this if you can, tomorrow is another day."

"You're right. We'll see what tomorrow brings." Henry reached out to her again. He encircled his arms around her as he pulled her closer to him. She laid her head up against his chest. His arms felt strong as he held her closely. It comforted her. The small acts of love and caring he demonstrated daily to her always made her world seem so safe and secure.

"I am so sorry, really sorry for what I said to you, Kate. You shouldn't have been the brunt of my anger. I'm really sorry, Honey."

She turned her head to face him. Kate smiled slightly. Henry's mouth curled a little reflecting a small smile. Together their lips met in a tender kiss as Henry pulled her closer to him. Turning they went to the bedroom in hopes of getting a good night's sleep.

Henry didn't expect it, nor did Kate, but both started suffering the effects of a rough time trying to get to sleep. The paths their minds took almost crossed each other as they lay in bed, both filled with questions; both concerned about the same subject matter. Each of them tossed and turned, their spouse doing the same movements periodically. At one point Henry got up and went to the kitchen. He made himself a cup of tea as he took a seat at the table. The sound of Kate behind him caused him to turn his head in her direction.

"Couldn't sleep either?" she asked.

Henry nodded his head.

"Neither could I," she said.

"I don't know which is worse, Kate, the fact that I don't know what the man wants, or the awful memories of my childhood that have come back to haunt me."

Kate placed her hands on his shoulders, rubbing her thumbs back and forth slowly across them in a massaging motion. Henry tipped his head back slightly as she continued to knead them, hoping this would help him to relax.

"Henry, I know your childhood was awful, we've discussed that a little bit. I know you don't want to talk about it. I'm also aware that you changed your name not wanting me to carry the married name of Lewis. We'll get through this, whatever it is."

"If you stop and think about it, I don't know why a phone call should upset me so much. Maybe we've come into some money," he joked.

Kate started to yawn. She put her cupped hand over her mouth attempting to hide the somewhat distorted expression her face made by this physical act.

"Oh, excuse me, Honey," she said in an almost indiscernible voice. She found herself once again repeating her actions, another yawn taking possession of her face.

"You better get back to bed," suggested Henry.

"I will in a minute. We both know why this bothers both of us so much, especially you. It's a piece of your history that you want to forget. That phone call awakened hidden memories you wanted to keep suppressed. I think we all possess a room in our mind where we place certain items we'd rather not remember or recall. When anything sad or tragic occurs, something so horrible you want it hidden forever, you quickly open the door to that room, throw that memory in and slam the door shut. I would imagine some memories, especially the most terrible of them have many locks holding the door securely. It was that way with my father, the day he walked out on me. That's when I needed him the most.

Everyone of us has suffered from time to time. You're not alone in this, Henry, nor am I. If we have to open that door of yours, we'll do it together as one."

She again placed her hands on Henry's shoulders. She began rubbing her finders and thumbs on his shoulder blades. To her surprise Kate could feel a tightness in each one of them. She moved her hands to his neck, repeating her movements. Henry let out a small sigh.

"Well, I'm going to try and get some sleep. Don't stay up too late, Henry, you need to get some rest."

"I'll be there in a little while. I hate to let the rest of this cup of tea go to waste."

Kate gave him a small smile as she turned and walked towards the bedroom. After lying in bed for some time she could hear the piano in the living room being played softly. While she didn't recognize what Henry was playing, the notes from the baby grand were sweet and tender. She was sure his fingers were meandering across the keyboard with no particular destination in mind. Kate listened as the music drifted through the air, some notes lingering for some time before fading into silence.

This event happened many times before, it was not uncommon to Kate at all. When she was busy in the kitchen, Henry would occasionally walk into the living room to be alone with his thoughts. Pulling out the piano bench he would take a seat. Next Henry would gently place his hands onto the ivory keys, slightly pausing before he would begin. This hesitation was almost as though the two together, musician and instrument, were taking a small breath before beginning. Once he began depressing the keys, it was as if they became one, each trying to please the other.

As Kate laid in bed listening to Henry playing, there was no mistake about it. The delicate beckoning notes were likened to that from the score of a love song. Kate was surprised somewhat by the mellow rhythm. With what they had just spoken of earlier she would have imagined he would have been more likely to pound on the keys. Rather than that reaction, he played a peaceful and loving arrangement.

Kate got out of bed once again. Putting on her bathrobe she walked the short distance to the living room. Henry continued playing, the room almost completely dark. Kate went over to Henry and placed her hands once again on his shoulders. She looked over his right shoulder. There was no music on the stand. Kate smiled. "You're playing some of your invisible sheet less music again," she said. "From what musical score is that?" she asked.

"It's something that's lived for some time in my head. I'm just letting it find its way out through my fingers."

Kate understood him perfectly. At times Henry would sit playing with no music at all, just the melody in his mind coming to life. Kate loved listening to his non-written arrangements. At times he would hum along with the music, no lyrics accompanying the notes.

"That almost sounds as if it were a love song the way the music pulls at your heart."

"I guess you could call it that," he said softly. "One night after you had gone to bed and I was feeling depressed, Emma's death was very much on my mind. The funeral was yet to come. I actually wrote the music for this in my head that evening. When I play it, I recall Emma and the wonderful times we spent together. She was the one who really acted as my mother, not Mrs. Lewis. I hated her as much as I loved Emma."

Henry took a very deep breath before letting it out slowly. Kate released her hands from Henry as she moved to sit beside him on the bench. They sat slightly facing each other. Henry continued playing the piano. Kate reached up with her thumb and brushed away a tear that was slowly making its way down his cheek. She did the same movement with his other cheek as well. Kate knew from the first time they met that his heart was soft, and as pliable as a piece of wet clay. Though his outer appearance would never indicate that fact to anyone, she knew what his inside revealed to her, a heart that was warm and caring.

"I miss Emma greatly, too," she said. Kate said nothing more for quite some time. They sat together quietly with only Emma's song keeping them both company. At long last Kate suggested they had better get to bed, it now being almost two o'clock in the morning."

Henry nodded his head as he lifted his fingers from the keyboard.

Sitting at the kitchen table eating breakfast, Henry turned to Kate as he placed his coffee cup down.

"Should I call Eric?"

"I wouldn't," Kate said, "when he has some news for you he'll let us know.

Henry nodded his head in agreement.

"You sure slept in this morning, Honey," Kate stated, "you didn't even hear Emma Elizabeth and me when we got up."

"I was completely exhausted."

"We know, don't we, Emma Elizabeth," Kate stated as she removed a dish from in front of the young child.

Henry began playing a little peek-a-boo game with her. He knew the simple movements with his hands over his eyes would bring forth a smile and giggle from her. Henry was not disappointed. Together they played for several minutes. As she continued with her childish laughter, he took what was the next step in their small-established tradition. He started singing a lullaby to her.

"Oh no you don't, she just got up and ate," Kate quickly said. "You're not going to put her to sleep again," she joked.

"Nah," Henry said as he turned to Emma Elizabeth. "You want to play, don't you, princess. Daddy and you can play, and play, and play some more."

Henry reached over and picked Emma Elizabeth up from where she was sitting. As he held her in his arms Henry gently swayed back and forth as the father and daughter danced around the room. He began singing a love song to her as they moved in small circles. Henry dipped her every once in a while. This made the child chuckle often. It was not surprising to Kate as she observed a smile very prevalent upon the little one's face.

"Maybe someday you'll dance with her at her wedding," Kate suggested.

"Not for a very, very, very long time I hope."

As Henry was returning the child to the highchair, the phone rang.

"I better get it, Kate, it might be Eric." Henry finished up with Emma Elizabeth, giving her a quick kiss on her brow before turning his attention to the phone.

Kate turned the faucet off. She started to place a few cups into the soapy water to be washed. Her ears were very much consumed in the conversation Henry was having. Once he got off the phone, he naturally turned his attention to her.

"First of all, this does concern Mrs. Lewis. Eric talked to him this morning and he would like to know if I can meet with Mr. Parrish later this afternoon at the facility he's in charge of."

"No, you're not," Kate stated quickly. "You can meet with him, that's not the problem. You used the word, 'I' and that's not going to happen. Unless you change that word to, 'we' I don't want you going at all."

Henry smiled at Kate. He knew she wouldn't let him deal alone with whatever it was that was facing him without her at his side. She was a pillar of support when he needed her. Henry knew any meetings would include her at his side. He liked that idea.

"I'll get a hold of our babysitter and see if she's free. You know, Henry, having a retired woman watching after our toddler when we need her is really a wonderful thing to have. She's usually free at the last minute, and Emma Elizabeth loves her. We're very lucky to have Mrs. Carson readily available."

Henry nodded his head in agreement.

"Well, I'll give Eric a call back and let him know we can make it," Henry stated. "Of course, I'll have to wait until you check with Mrs. Carson to make sure she's available. I don't want to take the baby with us."

"Neither do I."

As Kate and Henry drove up to the "Golden Years Retirement Village" both were impressed with how nice the outside of the building looked. The lawn was manicured, bushes trimmed. The three-story red brick building was larger than either had anticipated it would be. Both had surmised it would be a one-story building, nothing much more than that. Getting out of the car Henry walked to the front of the vehicle where he met Kate. He held his hand out as Kate took it in hers. They entered the building not knowing what to expect.

Eric had earlier explained to Henry that Mr. Parrish would meet them in his office. When Henry questioned him about why they wanted to see him, Eric just stated it involved a Mrs. Lewis. He also informed them that Mr. Parrish wanted to know, if at all possible, that the subject matter would best be dealt with in person. Henry thought Eric should have discovered more about what he wanted, but he trusted Eric to know what he was doing. Whatever it was Mr. Parrish wanted to discuss, he would have to wait until they had an opportunity to speak with him personally. The couple walked up to a front desk area immediately to the left of the entrance.

"We're here to see a Mr. Parrish, we're Mr. and Mrs. Morgan."

"Right this way, please. He's expecting you," stated a woman behind a wooden counter. Henry and Kate followed the woman as she led them down a hallway to a door on the right-hand side. "This is his office. Apparently he must have just stepped out. Please have a seat and I'll see if I can track him down. Would either one of you like something to drink while you wait?"

"No, we're fine," Henry answered.

"Oh, you must be Mr. and Mrs. Morgan," stated an older man wearing a white shirt, tie, neatly pressed pants and shiny shoes. "I had something that needed to be addressed. I'm sorry for not being here when you arrived. I hope you didn't have to wait too long.

Oh, thank you, Mrs. Roeman, for bringing them down here. I'll take it from here."

The woman nodded her head as she turned and left the room.

"What's this all about?" was Henry's immediate question.

"Please, have a seat, both of you. Can I get either one of you something to drink?"

"No thank you," the couple answered together.

"Mr. Parrish, as I said once already, what's this all about?"

If there was anything that was going to tarnish the day for them, better get on with it now and not beat around the bush, Henry thought. After all, Henry was dealing with a subject matter he didn't feel at all comfortable with in the first place.

"I had quite a time tracking you down, Mr. Morgan," Mr. Parrish stated.

"It's Henry, if you don't mind."

"Henry, and my name is Allen."

"This is my wife Kate. Now that we've got the preliminaries out of the way, exactly what do you want to talk to me about?"

"We have your mother here in the facility and —"

"Would you mind if we just referred to her as Mrs. Lewis, I would appreciate that. The fact of the matter is I don't consider her to be my... She's Mrs. Lewis to me, nothing more, just so you understand."

"Very well," Allen nodded, "Mrs. Lewis it is."

Kate nodded her head knowing very well Henry's feelings on that very subject.

"Mrs. Lewis came to be with us some time ago. She is not a healthy woman to say the least. Not very long ago she suffered a severe stoke. Well, actually I'm getting ahead of myself.

When your — Mrs. Lewis first came to our facility she was, to put it bluntly, a real piece of work. She fought with our staff daily, threw things at them, and even spit on a few of them. Getting anyone to deal with her was a horrible chore to be faced with, believe me. I don't mean to speak badly of her, but she did test our resolve daily."

"I guess you could say she is what she is," Henry interjected.

"Over the period of time we've had her here we were hoping she would eventually fit into some sort of... she would simply fit in, adjust to her surroundings. That didn't happen, I'm sorry to say."

Kate nodded her head as she recalled the day Melissa and her met Mrs. Lewis at the home Henry grew up in. They had gone there to try and discover what Henry's name was before his adoption by them. It was Melissa who convinced

Mrs. Lewis to let them in, though it was no easy task to accomplish. Melissa had to go so far as to block the front door with her foot. After gaining entry into the house, something Kate never would have been able to do alone, she learned more than she wanted to know about Henry's youthful years. She remembered the horrible smells in the building. The house was filled with an ugly stench that seemed to cling to one's skin. There were holes in the walls as if someone had hit them, or maybe threw an item at them. The bedroom was nothing more than a pit of filth. It matched the rest of the home well. Her heart broke to think that Henry grew up in such a despicable atmosphere.

Kate was astounded as she observed Melissa's handling of this endeavor. Melissa would not be denied this information from Mrs. Lewis. The very information Melissa sought was not in any way for her own peace of mind, she did it for Henry solely. That was very obvious to see. Fortunately for the two women, they were able to obtain the information before leaving.

The most disturbing memory of that day for Kate was when Mrs. Lewis told the women Henry was actually a waste of skin. Those words alone turned a portion of Kate's heart black with hatred for her. How can someone so worthless describe Henry in that way. What tore at Kate's soul so deeply was the fact that she now despised this woman, also. She didn't like what this woman was doing to her own inner self. Never in her life could she even conceive of hating someone before. Other than the day her father walked out on her, Kate hadn't felt so pain-stricken by so few hurtful words or actions.

She nodded her head back and forth as many more thoughts of that day raced through her mind. How Henry accomplished surviving it all, she couldn't even fathom an answer to that question. Yes, she thought, Mrs. Lewis was everything and more Mr. Parrish had lightly touched on in his description of her. She had the personality of an individual who had no concept of what the word "love" meant.

"Mrs. Lewis had a severe stroke a month and some weeks ago," continued Allen. I asked Mrs. Warner from our staff to take charge of her care, supervise her, if you will. Mrs. Warner has been with us for several years now. She has more compassion for our clients than anyone can even imagine. I thought she would be the perfect individual to handle your... Mrs. Lewis. Apparently, that move turned out to be the perfect match. Still, you never know how these things will work themselves out.

Mrs. Warner dealt with her daily. Mrs. Lewis attempted to speak on some days, while completely withdrawn on others. Her face bore a blank distorted look, of course. There were times when you could barely understand her, that being most of the time. Mrs. Warner worked on her speech daily. I don't think I would, or members of our staff for that matter, have the patience or wherewithal to accomplish what she was able to do. Mrs. Lewis was somewhat able to communicate with Janice. That's Mrs. Warner's first name.

I've been told by Janice that Mrs. Lewis has completely changed in her... she is no longer the woman she was, let me put it that way. Whether it was the stroke that accomplished this or something else, I don't really know. Anyway, she informed Janice that she wanted to contact you before she died. When I heard that, I attempted to get a hold of you as soon as I could."

Henry and Kate sat quietly not demonstrating any facial expressions or offering any verbal communication whatsoever.

"It's obvious to me from your... the way this is turning out today that you are definitely at odds with her. I would not be so bold as to tell you what to do. That's not why I asked you here in the first place. My thoughts were to stand beside you at the doorway, and if you wished to walk through it, I would hold it open for you. If, on the other hand, you decided not to take that step, that's entirely your decision to make. Frankly, I was hopeful you would possibly consider speaking with her, if only for just a moment."

Kate looked at Henry, his face slowly moving back and forth as Mr. Parrish spoke. Henry's answer to the suggestion was already written on his face and in his motions. He would not darken the room she laid in, nor take the opportunity to speak with her, even to hear her last words. Too much pain held Henry in its arms to relive it all one more time. Kate felt Mr. Parrish had wasted his time in calling them in the first place.

"When you're dealing with the elderly, you get a little insight on how long someone may last with various afflictions. Of course, everyone is different. Some are feisty and surprise you, others just give up. For what it's worth, I don't believe she has much more time to share with us."

"How can you even show any compassion towards this woman, you've seen what she's like?" Henry said with an edge in his words.

Allen nodded his head understanding Henry had to have some very deep-seated experiences in his life to feel this strongly about her. Over the years he had dealt with a wide variety of people dealing with pain, emotional as well as physical suffering. He had observed individuals who withered away before his eyes. Even those who were filled with vigor and vitality one day, could be gone the next. It was a never-ending cycle that seemed to have its own place in facilities of this type. His mind tried to figure out what to say to Henry, what words would convince him to at least see her. Picking up his phone he pushed a single number on it.

"Would you please page Janice Warner and ask her to come to my office. Thank you."

"Talking to someone else isn't going to change my mind one iota," Henry said even before Allen could hang the phone up.

"I'm not trying to convince you to change your mind, I just want Janice to inform you of a few things. You're not in a hurry to leave; are you?"

Henry looked in Kate's direction. She merely shook her head slowly back and forth.

"Okay," Henry finally expressed.

"Thank you. She'll be here shortly I'm sure."

Within a minute or two, Mrs. Warner walked into the office.

"This is Mr. and Mrs. Morgan."

"It's nice to meet you," she stated as she reached her hand out to Henry and then Kate.

"Would you give them an update on Mrs. Lewis, and from the very beginning if you would, Janice."

"Of course, Mr. Parrish. Before I do that, can I ask you a quick question, Mr. Morgan?"

Henry nodded his head affirmatively.

"What is Mrs. Lewis's first name? She would never give it to us. She just said to call her Mrs. Lewis, and that was all we needed to know. Her paperwork just carries the letter, 'I' on it."

"Yes, even her paperwork states that," Allen was quick to agree.

"It's Isabella," Henry said in a stern voice. "I don't think she really liked her name for whatever reason. She slapped me across the face really hard one day when I told someone what it was. My mistake was letting her hear me. I only made that mistake one time."

"That's sad to hear, Mr. Morgan," Janice said, "but knowing her as I do, it doesn't surprise me.

Now, as far as an update, when Mrs. Lewis first came here, to say she was a handful would be an understatement. She threw things at the workers, swore at them, and that was on a good day."

Henry shook his head knowing how true her words were. He had seen that side of her many times. The fact of the matter was he had never seen her when she wasn't abusive. She had a gruff tongue and hand that carried the sting of a leather whip to it.

"The first day Mr. Parrish asked me to take her on as a care patient, I asked him if I could think it over. After some deliberation I decided to give it a try. When I explained to her I was going to be working with her she threw a plastic half filled water glass at me. I guess you could say the first shot was fired in our war."

"What did you do?" Kate quickly asked, her curiosity getting the best of her.

"I asked her what was the worst food she disliked the most. Her answer was peas. I explained that if she threw anything more at me she'd get nothing to eat for dinner but peas for a week."

"And what happened?" Kate asked.

"She threw something else at me. I think it was her tray. Suffice it to say, she got peas for dinner that very night. The first three or four days the color on the walls was spotty in her room. They were tinted in a beautiful shade of green."

Janice nodded her head slightly, a little chuckle coming from her mouth as she seemed to relive the event in her mind.

"Of course, soap and water solved that problem. She learned an important lesson that day also, she wasn't fooling around in the minor leagues anymore. Since that week, peas are my favorite vegetable. They can be a very useful tool to possess. Still, with others the food selection may change somewhat depending on the circumstances.

As time went on we had many battles together. There were some I'd let her win. After all, I wasn't out to break her. I did, however, let her know who was in charge. With someone who is nasty, abusive, and just plain mean as her, you have to keep a wary eye out, especially when you turn your back on them and walk out of the room. Fortunately, we actually came to have an unwritten understanding between us. She wouldn't throw anything more at us, and she would be fed better tasting meals.

One morning Mrs. Lewis suffered a massive stroke. Once she returned to us from the hospital we attempted to make her as comfortable as possible. I could actually sense a change in her. Communicating with her was nearly impossible. One thing I do know for sure, people's eyes can tell you more about what's going on behind them than one would ever guess. I saw in them what she needed, what she wanted, everything. It was an unbelievable thing for me to experience."

"That's what my grandfather told me one day. He works in a hospital and sees a lot of people dealing with distress every day," Kate expressed. "Grandpa told me the one expression that's very common to see in their eyes is fear."

"I know what he's talking about," Janice stated, as she nodded her head.

Henry didn't offer to add anything to their words. He sat quietly cloaked in his own thoughts about Mrs. Lewis.

"One day not so very long ago," Janice continued, "she asked for Henry. I assume that's you, Mr. Morgan."

Henry just nodded his head.

"Do you plan on seeing her?"

"No!"

"If I may say one more thing for what it's worth. Once the clock's tone is struck, there are no more hours, minutes, or even seconds, it's gone forever. It's like turning your clock ahead in the spring, you lose it, it's gone forever. Everything comes to an end here on earth. I've known many people who suffer more now because they didn't utilize those fleeting moments to put everything into its proper order with a family member. Mr. Morgan... Henry, I don't pretend to understand what it must have been like to grow up in that atmosphere, but I've had a taste of it from her. It had to be horrible to say the least. Your mother —"

Henry bit down on his lip harder than he realized with her speaking that word. The inside of his lip began to bleed slightly. He could taste the blood in his mouth.

"— is what she is, we both know that better than anyone else. I think you should see her, not for her, but for yourself. She has reached out to you, for what reason we really don't know. What you decide to do now is entirely up to you. Don't live the rest of your life wondering if you were too strong headed to not know what her final thoughts were for you. If she's the same person she was, you'll know that within a second or two. You can then say you tried. But this way you'll know what she wanted to express in possibly the last few days of her life."

When Janice's words stopped, the room fell silent. No one offered any comments, no words to follow hers. The three individuals sat quietly, each in their own thoughts. Janice merely stood by the door, quietly waiting to see what happened next.

"Henry, I don't know what you should do," Kate uttered softly. Whatever Henry decided to do, she didn't want him to make that decision based on anything she would say. She attempted to divorce herself from that choice.
"I wish I knew," he answered.
"Perhaps you need some time to think it over," offered Allen.

"No one knows what she wants to say, Henry," Kate's soft voice said, "and maybe it's best if she takes those words to her grave. I don't know. Maybe... maybe you should talk with her."

Kate shook her head slowly back and forth. She looked up at Janice and then Mr. Parrish. Finally, Kate looked over at Henry as she said, "No, no, just let her take her words to the grave with her, you've suffered enough."

Now Kate felt badly. She had offered Henry some advice, something she did not want to do whatsoever. In her thoughts she could not get over the sights and smells inside of the house Henry grew up in. What little she saw that day with Melissa was more than she could bear, so why put Henry through anymore of this. Hadn't he suffered enough at her hands. Her thoughts conflicted with each other, they kept vacillating back and forth. Kate didn't like the bitter taste of her words, but she knew they were a true representation of how she felt inside. What truly haunted Kate's feelings the most was the fact that she knew what she said wasn't really from the person she was or wanted to be. It made her feel guilty in her heart. Her emotions were heavily churning within herself. Kate's stomach began to feel a little upset.

"If I may suggest something to you," Allen stated.

Henry and Kate looked in his direction, both wondering what his next words would offer them.

"We can go down to her room. Henry, you can wait outside and just take a peek into it. You wouldn't have to go inside, but this way we can tell her you were here, we just couldn't wake her for the visit. We'll explain it was the medication that caused that, she doesn't need to know. Sometimes there are places where little white lies show themselves, and this might be such an occasion."

Now Henry didn't know what to do. In his heart he wanted to see what she looked like, see what difference the passage of time had done to her face. Curiosity is a strong foe to fight against, and inside he was losing. Finally, temptation won over his feelings, he would see her, but only from a distance.

"Henry," Kate said, "whatever you want, it's your decision."

Unbeknownst to her, he had already made up his mind. He reached over and took Kate's hand in his. He looked at Allen, then Janice. He said nothing, but nodded his head up and down slowly.

"Okay," Allen said. He glanced up at the clock on the wall. "We can go now, now is a good time. The clientele have all had their breakfast, visiting hours have commenced, and our morning social hours haven't begun yet."

"Her room is this way," Janice said as she stepped through the doorway.

Everyone stood up and began following her in the direction of the room.

"How many people do you have here?" Kate asked.

"There's probably 200 total," Janice said, "but that can vary from week to week. Most stay here with us daily. Of course, others are visiting family members over the weekend and so forth. We even have a couple that actually travels down south over the winter to live with their children for a while. They want to be close to their grandchildren. It's just a revolving door."

Stopping just outside of a door on the right side of the hallway Janice indicated they had arrived at the Lewis room.

"May I suggest that I talk to her first, see if she's awake, how she's doing today. Everyone has their good and bad days, you just never know with the elderly."

Kate and Henry nodded their heads as they stood just on the outer part of the room.

Henry noticed his breath was shorter in length, his emotions beginning to tighten up inside. Surprisingly, his body began to ache. Telltale signs of a headache began to form. His lips felt dry. The faint taste of blood still lingered in his mouth. Now he began to have second thoughts running through his mind. His body wanted to turn and run. His feet, however, felt locked to the flooring tile he was standing on. He felt almost captive, unable to move.

Janice walked into the room. There was no mistake in the tone of her voice, she was extremely cheerful, a spirit of happiness in the air surrounding her.

"So how are we doing today, Mrs. Lewis? The sun is shining, birds are singing, what a wonderful day for you and me to share together. We should both thank our lucky stars we can enjoy it all."

"Huh."

Janice peeked at the doorway every so often hoping Henry would come in and acknowledge his mother. He made no movements whatsoever. As Janice spoke she reached over and began covering Isabella with a blanket. She looked over at the doorway once again.

"Who r, aye?"

"Who are they?"

Isabella nodded her head slightly.

"Well, you know Mr. Allen, of course, and the woman is a guest visiting us today. The man behind her is her husband."

Isabella turned her head back from looking at them. She let out a little sigh.

Henry stared at his adoptive mother, contempt for her demonstrated on his face. Her blackish gray hair was combed, but thinning greatly. Across her face were deep course wrinkles. Henry thought of them as a map to a hard and anger-filled life. The skin on her arms was spotted with age marks. The coloration of it was somewhat yellowish. Dark black and blue areas were plentiful also. He had seen these before on older people. He recalled having been told they seemed to appear with elderly individuals, their bodies not able to heal as quickly. Henry hardly recognized her as the woman he had known some years ago.

Janice knew what she was considering could place her very position in jeopardy. Individuals not wanting to be recognized, were not to be introduced to the residents period. Though it was not a frequent occurrence, it did happen unfortunately from time-to-time. Henry and Kate were one such example. They were there simply to observe her, nothing more, nothing less. Interaction with her was not to be considered at all.

Some visitors, on the other hand, wanted to observe how close the shadow of death was from the bedside. In her heart, Janice detested these people. At times she would refer to them as insurance maggots. Her fellow workers understood her distaste for them, many feeling the same way as well. Insurance money, or the thoughts of profit caused many a family to surrender to temptation. Some felt, if the mind is gone, so should the body be. She had seen this play itself out many times throughout the years.

With Henry, she knew it was completely different. He was there just to observe, nothing more. Henry was not looking for an emotional healing between the two of them, but what if, she thought, what if.

"Mrs. Lewis, you have company here today," she stated.

"Oh?"

Janice held her breath momentarily.

"It's this young woman and her husband, they're someone you may or may not recognize."

"Ah," was her single word reply. She turned her head to Kate, attempting in her mind to figure out whom it was that was standing off to the side. Her failing eyesight did little to aid her in this effort.

Janice looked in Kate's direction. Not only was her face covered in an uncomfortable expression, she could see fear in her eyes. It was obvious Kate didn't have any idea of how to react to this unforeseen set of circumstances. Janice took a deep breath. Even without informing Isabella of who the couple was, she now regretted her decision. It was not her intent to place Kate in such an awkward and uncomfortable position.

Isabella lifted her hand slightly. Kate looked at it. Not knowing what to do exactly she simply stood in place. Once again Isabella raised her hand indicating for her to come closer. Kate looked at Janice, still not acknowledging her hand movement. Janice tilted her head slightly in Isabella's direction. Kate stepped a few feet forward. She didn't know why she did it, her distaste for the woman being what it was, but still she reached out and took her hand in hers.

"We know e otter?" Isabella asked.

Seeing the confusion on Kate's face, Janice quickly interpreted for her.

"She wants to know if you know each other."

"Oh," Kate said. "No, we don't know each other."

"You ook famlar to me."

Once again Janice interpreted.

"She thinks you look familiar to her," Janice stated.

"You at e house, ramber now."

"Have you been to her house?" Janice asked. "Apparently she remembers you being at her home some time ago."

"A very long time ago with a friend of mine," Kate said.

"You ont paper from ee. Wont bout Hen-ree. E here?"

"She's indicating you wanted some papers from her. Mrs. Lewis also wants to know if Henry is here."

Before Kate realized what her lips were doing she replied to her.

"Yes, he's here."

Once the words left her mouth, a chill like she had never experienced before in her life ran down the length of her back. Oh my God, she thought, what have I done. The very last thing in the world she wanted to do was to inflict more pain on her husband. Releasing Isabella's hand she turned and moved quickly to Henry. She placed her arms around his body, resting her head on his chest. She began begging for his forgiveness, her eyes somewhat watery.

"I'm so sorry, Honey, I didn't mean to say that to her. I knew you didn't want to —"

"It's okay..." Henry said nodding his head, "it's okay, Kate."

Allen and Janice stood there, neither one saying a word, after all, what could they say. Silence is golden, and both of them were now practicing that very phrase.

"Well, we came here to see what she wanted, so let's find out," Henry stated in a firm voice to the assembled people.

He walked the short distance to her bedside. Her distorted words were hard to understand or comprehend. With each word she attempted to speak, it was as if they had to be drawn out slowly from her mouth. Henry bent over to hear her better as she spoke in a broken language of its own.

"Hen-ee, it... it gud to see you. I twas hoopin... hope you come see me."

"I'm here. What did you want to say to me that was so important to you?"

"I sir-ee, soul sir-ee fur ever-thing."

Droplets of water slowly made their way down from the corner of her eyes as she labored to speak to him.

"Soul sir-ee," she said, her head moving slowly back and forth. "I shoot not treat you soul... I sir-ee, Hen-ee. I soul sir-ee."

The flow of tears grew more intense, not just from Mrs. Lewis, they came from Kate, and Janice as well. Allen stood in the doorway, not coming into the room any further. He continued leaning up against the doorframe, his body motionless against it. All he wanted to do was quietly observe the goings on. Now was not a time to intrude, enter into the atmosphere that was playing itself out between Henry and his mother.

Henry stood silently now. He demonstrated absolutely no physical or verbal response to her plea to him. His face was that of a stone statute, rigid, expressionless.

"Hen-ee, pees forth... forth give me."

Henry turned from his position by her.

"I think we can leave now," he stated as he turned from the bed area and started for the doorway.

"Henry," Kate vocalized.

Janice turned her head and watched as Henry started to leave the room. She shook her head back and forth slowly. She was understandably upset with what had just transpired, almost embarrassed by his actions. It had been her hope the two would reconcile, perhaps bury the hatchet while leaving the handle sticking out of the ground. It was not to be, and it saddened her deeply within. She had failed.

Allen moved from the doorway allowing Henry to pass by. He knew the memories were still too vivid to be simply forgotten by him. Through the years he had observed this many times between family members. Some would end in a favorable resolution, others completely opposite in nature. Getting strained parents and children together was never an easy job. Janice and Allen had talked it over many times, both coming to the same conclusions.

How some families were a tightly woven fabric, while others possessed gaping holes always amazed him. There were, of course, others very much opposite in nature, loving, caring, nurturing. The extremes were there every day to be seen by all.

He had heard bitter words being exchanged loudly between parents and siblings. Other times it was between the adult children. Who won these verbal battles in the end were of no consequence to the facility. They would be reimbursed for the care they had given. Still, it always hurt Allen inside whenever he would observe this happening. To him both armies lost on the battlefield of emotions. The flags of love they may have carried at one time were now torn to shreds. Well, he thought, we did our best. Janice should be commended for the job she had done. He would be sure to express that to her later.

Henry made his way back to Allen's office. He sat down on one of the chairs. Kate, Janice and Allen joined him within a minute or two.

"I am sorry this worked out for you the way it has," Allen stated.

"I am, too," Janice said.

Kate said nothing. She was somewhat upset with her husband for having walked out so abruptly on Isabella. The fact that he didn't say a word bothered her also. In her heart she understood why he did. How many times does one have to be bitten before you say enough is enough. Definitely he had reached the end of that trail. There were no more pathways to take or walk down. She knew that for sure now. What Henry had done, turned his back on his mother would be forever now. That was his choice, and she wasn't surprised by it at all. This decision by him would be one supported by her totally. The cover to the book was closed. There were no more pages to read, nothing more to do. The final chapter had been written between Isabella and Henry.

As they sat in the office, Allen saw to it that some coffee was brought in for everyone. They sat talking about unrelated issues. Isabella's name was not brought up whatsoever. Everyone saw to that fact. Once in a while the three of them would glance over at Henry. It appeared to all his mind was elsewhere, concentrating deeply on nothing. His stare was that of a man who was expressionless, blank in appearance. It was as if he wasn't even present in the same room with them. After about ten minutes, Henry asked if he could use the restroom. Allen gave him some quick instructions as to its direction. He stood up, informing Kate he'd only be a minute or two. Henry left the room.

"Now that Henry isn't here," Allen stated, "I'm sorry how everything turned out for him and you today."

Kate nodded her head.

"Especially me," Janice added. "It was never my intention to put you between a rock and a hard spot."

"I understand," Kate replied.

"Since you're here," Allen said, "I should take this opportunity to explain some things to you. Perhaps it would be better if I waited until Mr. Morgan... Henry gets back."

"That's quite okay. If you're speaking to me, you're talking to him as well. We address everything together as one anyhow."

"While this doesn't really concern either one of you, I just wanted to inform you that Isabella's economic picture is a positive one. She has enough money put away to handle any of her care issues. Henry is the only family we know of, we could find no others. In fact, with his name change it was very difficult for me to locate him at all. Are you aware of anyone else?"

"To my knowledge there isn't anyone else. His adoptive father is dead."

"Oh, we didn't know that. Thank you for that information. We try to keep our records up to date as much as possible. Just so I know, how did you become privy to that information?"

"Mrs. Lewis told me."

"When you say Mrs. Lewis... I thought you said you hadn't met her, or I should say you really didn't know her."

"It's kind of a long story, but I'll keep it short."

"Please."

"My best friend, Melissa, wanted to discover what Henry's real last name was. She put a plan together where we went and saw Mrs. Lewis, Isabella, at her home. Melissa convinced her we were with the courts or something. Boy was she convincing. Anyway, she obtained the information we needed. I could never in my life have done what she did for us. Henry didn't want to marry me and have people refer to me by the last name of Lewis."

"Calling you Mrs. Lewis, I can understand that," Janice said, nodding her head. What Kate said made all the sense in the world to her.

"It didn't matter to me, of course, I loved him too much to really care about that. He had his name changed to Morgan. That was his real name before he was adopted. That's why you were confused, I'm sure.

Isabella informed Melissa and me that her husband had died two years earlier than our visit to her house. I can tell you she wasn't too upset with his passing.

That's really the long and short of it."

"It sounds like you have quite a friend in Melissa," Janice offered.

"She's as close to me as any sister I could have, maybe even closer. We've been friends for as long as I can remember. I love her and her family," smiled Kate. "and they love us, too."

Janice and Allen smiled.

The three of them continued drinking their coffee. Kate inquired about the facility, what it was like for people living there. She enjoyed hearing about the activities. Janice even alluded to some noted residents who had come to live with them during different periods. The time passed by gently. It was as if the clock was enjoying listening to their conversations, its hands not in any hurry to move on. Before long a half an hour had passed.

"I wonder what's keeping Henry," Kate inquired.

"Well, let's find him," Allen offered.

"He could be looking in the dining room or over in the guest section. Sometimes people do that, they get distracted and look around a little bit,"

Janice said. "We have a card room and, of course, we run a little gift shop, though it doesn't make any money," she chuckled. "We also have a hairdresser."

"I doubt if he'd be in there," joked Kate.

"He couldn't have gotten very far," Allen suggested. "Does he smoke?"

"No," Kate said.

"Sometimes people step outside to have a cigarette."

The three of them began walking towards the dining room area. A few people were sitting at a table enjoying some beverages together.

"Hello Mrs. Perkins, Mr. Miller, Mrs. Johnson," Janice yelled out as she waved to them all.

They all waved back. It was evident to Kate they were enjoying themselves as they continued visiting.

As they turned down one hallway there was a small group of people that had gathered. A few sat in wheelchairs, others stood with canes in their hands. Some simply stood in place with their hands on the handrail that ran the length of the hallway on either side. When the three of them approached, Kate realized they were collected just outside of Isabella's room. Allen and Janice didn't know what to expect, though they had a distinct impression of what may await them. There were times when individuals met outside of others' rooms. Sometimes this would occur with a client's passing. It was their way of expressing a final farewell before the remains would be removed.

Allen and Janice picked up their pace as they headed to the room. When they were within ten or so feet from the group they stopped. Slowly they both continued to the doorway of the room to observe the goings on. What was happening in the room shocked both of them. It was truly an unexpected occurrence to observe, let alone hear. Kate stood next to them, a small sampling of a smile written across her face.

Inside the room Henry sat next to Isabella, her hand in his. He softly serenaded her with a lullaby. When he completed the song Isabella smiled, her eyes glazed in dampness.

"Oar, pees."

"More?"

"Pees."

Henry nodded his head as he began to sing another song to her. As he sang more people arrived from other areas of the building, all wanting to hear his voice and experience what was going on. The word spread quickly throughout the facility. This is something to see, Janice thought. No one entered the room, they all remained in place just outside of the doorway. The hallway slowly filled. Henry continued singing song after song.

The music that came forth from his mouth was laced with tender words, very much delicate in their sound. Some of the people present nodded their heads along with the words. The songs Henry sang were very old in nature, music that elderly people would simply enjoy hearing. Time seemed to stand still. When the speaker system announced lunch was about to be served, no one moved.

"Well, I hate to break this up," Allen said in a whisper to Janice, "but we have to get these people fed."

"Why don't we give him another song or two, it's not like our people are treated to something this wonderful every day," Janice suggested.

Allen nodded his head. A couple more songs couldn't hurt he thought. After all, he was enjoying the music himself.

When Henry finished his last song he stood up. He bent down close to Isabella and spoke to her softly. She nodded her head. Kate could see her lips moving, clearly expressing something to him. He squeezed her hand. To Kate's utter amazement Henry reached over and kissed her on the brow. Kate had no idea how to take what she just saw, her mind filled with confusing thoughts. She still harbored a strong contempt for Isabella within. Perhaps there was a healing between the two of them taking place, a mending of their hearts. She wasn't sure.

Henry walked from the room. Various people spoke quick words of thanks as he made his way by them. He nodded his head as he stepped through the gathered group. Allen, Janice and Kate followed him as he made his way down the hallway towards the office.

"I should check on the people in the dining room," Janice stated to Allen, "but I need to know what just happened."

Allen didn't reply to her, he simply nodded his head. She was not alone in her feelings, he wanted to know as well.

Kate reached over and took Henry's hand as they turned the corner in the hallway heading to Allen's office. She squeezed it tightly. Stepping inside the door Kate took a seat beside Henry.

"Mr. Morgan... Henry, what just happened?" was Allen's to-the-point question.

"When I first saw her in the room, I noticed a tremendous difference in Isabella. Within my heart I carry deep resentments for her, and for good reason. How does one forgive someone who treated you like dirt, even worse, belittled me constantly. Inside I was being torn back and forth. That's why I left the room so fast when we first went to see her. I needed to get away from her, put my thoughts in order. Once I was able to do that, I used the excuse of going to the restroom to leave here. I wanted some alone time with her. It gave me the time and space, if you will, to be with her and express to Isabella why I hated her so much."

"You actually told her you hated her?" Kate asked.

"Not only that, but other things that have hung heavily on my heart for so many years. I think it was the best thing I've ever done. I feel so free now. Isabella listened to me carefully. Of course, she had no choice, she was literally locked in her bed. She had to listen to my every word, and I made the best use of that time alone with her.

The funny thing is all she did was cry. When I would mention certain hurtful things she had done to me, she would squeeze my hand harder. Isabella's eyes were filled with more than tears. I think she saw everything through my eyes as well. Kate, I think in that short time together it healed both of our hearts."

Janice smiled. They didn't only bury the hatchet, she thought, it was flung into some distance unforeseen place to never be seen again.

Henry continued, all three of them very much interested in what he had to further say.

"I guess I came to realize that if she could change, perhaps I could, too. I didn't want to remember her in the way she was, I wanted to see her in a new and positive light. Hate is such a strong and unyielding emotion to have in ones heart. Isn't it ironic that the two strongest words we associate in our emotions each have four letters in them, hate and love."

Kate and Janice nodded their heads.

"Today my insides have been running through a maze, which way do I turn. When all was said and done, she begged me to forgive her. This I've done, I've forgiven my... mother."

The fact that Henry used the word, "mother" said everything to Kate, Janice, and Allen. The war between them was over, thought Allen. There were no losers, just two combatants stepping back from each other, a flag of surrender in both of their hands.

"Henry," asked Janice, "I saw you whisper something to Isabella. What were you two saying to each other?"

"First I told her I forgave her, and that I... I... I loved her. She said she loved me, too, and then she thanked me for forgiving her."

Janice and Kate both wiped their eyes. As they looked over at one another each carried a small smile surrounded with tears on their cheeks.

"I also told her I would be back to visit her next weekend, Sunday to be exact."

"I've learned a little about you, Henry, since I first called and talked to Kate," Allen said. "I found out you sing weekly at a business you and a friend own. You have a wonderful voice. Am I right about the business aspect of it?"

"Yes, you are."

"I also understand your business is doing pretty well by the price of your tickets. Would you consider doing something for us? Finding entertainment for our people is sometimes very hard to do. We couldn't pay you the —"

"Not only will he," interjected Kate, "there will be no fees involved whatsoever."

Henry chuckled to himself.

"Oh, that would be wonderful. Thank you, Kate," Allen said.

Once again Henry chuckled to himself, another example of never being able to say no to her. He would do a concert for them, of course, and free of charge. There was no question about it, he thought, Kate already said he would. He looked over at Kate and smiled. I'm so fortunate to have her at my side. There was no question about that.

"We do have an old piano that was donated to us some time ago, if that will do. I know for a fact it's in tune."

The memory of getting Sam's old piano immediately jumped into Henry's mind. He recalled the many hours he and Sam sat behind the keys as he learned to play it. Those were some of the most precious memories of Sam that Henry carried in the deepest recesses of his heart.

"Old pianos are my favorite instruments," he said with a wide grin on his face.

"Also we don't have any elaborate sound system or anything like that," Allen added.

"I won't need one," Henry said.

"We'll also see to it that Isabella is brought to the dining room for your ... for the residents' concert," smiled Janice.

"Thank you," Kate said.

"Yes, thank you," Henry said.

"I'll also see to it there's an announcement in our inner facility news letter," Janice added.

Henry stood up. He reached across the desk and shook Allen's hand. He shook his hand hardily, Allen definitely noticing that fact. He knew what it meant, and he appreciated it. Kate followed suit as she shook Allen's hand. Janice put her hand out to Henry.

"That won't do," he said. He put his arms around her giving her a hug.

"Thank you," he said as he released her.

"You're welcome."

Kate reached over and gave Janice a little hug, also.

"So we'll see you here next weekend," Allen asked in more of a statement than a question.

"Yes, you will," Henry said "By the way, what time would be best for all concerned?" "I would suggest 2:30 in the afternoon, if that meets with your schedule."

"That should be fine," Henry replied.

So began a small concert series by Henry that ran one Sunday a month, time permitting. When holidays arrived during the month, he would sometimes include songs to demonstrate that very fact. What was so special about these concerts for Henry was the fact that it gave him the opportunity to try new music out for his own programs.

Though Henry was not a comedian in any way imaginable, it allowed him the chance to throw in a joke or two, thus observing the group's reaction to it. Many times he was awarded by their applause with the punch line having been spoken.

Even after Isabella's death, Henry always seemed to find the time to return to perform concerts. The expressions on their faces were the only pay he ever received from them. It made him feel wealthy inside, a place in his heart where money meant nothing.

Henry could never have imagined what a phone call from Allen would lead to. It was a definite turning point in his life. The simple words, "had your last name previously been Lewis" started it all. It was a small question that carried a very large answer for all involved.

Secrets

Keeping Melissa and Greg's endeavor hidden was an almost impossible undertaking. So many irons were in the fire that it was only a matter of time before Susan and Kenneth were sure to discover what was taking place behind their very backs. Everyone was working together as one. Not one individual wanted to be the person whose tongue spilled the beans. They all guarded the scheme every bit as much as any World War II secret mission.

As each day grew closer, Greg and Melissa were on the phone more than any telemarketers. It was a wonderful problem to have as they put each and every piece into place. The response from everyone was unbelievable, but not unexpected. Never had the young couple enjoyed misleading two people they loved as much as they did, Susan and Kenneth. It almost became a running joke between them. They would laugh as Melissa would convey how she had to answer a question by Susan about her whereabouts, yet still keeping an eye to the fact they weren't going to lie to them. Each day was a new challenge, each one a new problem to be solved. Fortunately for Melissa, if she felt her mother was getting too nosey and she needed a change of subject matter, there was always Rose to the rescue. Could Susan babysit became a favorite way of hiding anything she needed time to accomplish. Susan's immediate answer was always "Yes."

At long last the day had arrived. Melissa's heart pounded inside of her in excitement. Her usual enthusiasm was extremely keen today. Greg could see it in her face, and hear it in her voice. She was simply bubbling within.

"Well, we better get going," Greg said.
"Do you think they have any idea at all about this?" Melissa asked.

Greg shrugged his shoulders.

"Your mom and dad are pretty smart. I hate to say this, but if we did pull the wool over their eyes, I'd be amazed. There's just too many people who know about it for someone not to have said something. Maybe some person they know heard about it and asked your mom and dad, who knows. We'll have to just wait and see."

"I hope you're wrong, Greg, but just the same, it should be a great day all in all."

"Well, Melissa, what they know or don't know will become quite evident one way or the other soon enough."

Melissa nodded her head; she knew they had no control over it. They'd just have to wait and see what transpired.

"We'll head right to your parent's home as soon as we drop Rose off at the babysitter's," Greg said.

Along with Rose, they got into their vehicle. After placing the baby into the baby carrier and buckling her in, they drove to the babysitter's house. Leaving the sitter's home they headed to Melissa's mother and dad's house. Neither one said anything of consequence to the other. Each didn't want to dampen the other's enthusiasm for the day's planned activities. Inside each one's emotions were churning.

After parking the car in the Summers' driveway, they got out of the vehicle. Greg looked over at his wife. Melissa's face demonstrated a look of a child carrying a secret she couldn't wait to tell. Greg hadn't expected that expression to still be filling her face. He knew she needed to put a cap on her inner feelings, otherwise they were sure to question Melissa as to why she was in such an emotionally heightened state.

"Honey, I know you're really excited, but you need to dial it down just a bit," Greg stated.

She smiled her agreement. Melissa knew he was right, but how does one shut off a large smile. Her insides were ready to burst, and all within a matter of a few seconds. Still she tried.

Entering the home,; Greg was quick to ask Susan and Kenneth if they were ready to go. He wanted their attention on him, giving Melissa a moment or two to settle down. Inside he smiled. He knew what was awaiting the Summers, just as well as his wife. He took a peek at her. She was doing much better now.

"I don't believe we've ever gone out for a buffet breakfast together; have we, Susan?" Kenneth asked.

"Not that I can recall," she answered.

"Remember, it's our treat," Greg stated, "and besides, they opened that new restaurant across town. Melissa and I have been wanting to try it out. This way we can all do it together. It will be fun."

"I'm always willing to try a breakfast buffet for a change, Kenneth expressed.

"And a buffet is the best way to gain something," Susan laughed as she reached over patting Kenneth's stomach with her hand.

Greg and Melissa chuckled.

"If it's okay with the you, I'd like to swing by the construction site," Kenneth said, "I want to see if there's anything more they've done."

"You were just there two days ago," Susan vocalized, "I'm sure there isn't any more to look at or see."

"That's not a problem, Dad," Greg interjected. "I haven't been there in quite a while myself."

"I'd like to see it, too," Melissa said.

"Well, you're driving," Susan stated, as she glanced over at Greg.

As they started towards the car Melissa took a quick look at her watch. We've got a couple of hours to kill before we need to be there, she thought. That shouldn't present too much of a problem. I wonder how long we'll be at the restaurant her mind further contemplated as she walked towards the back portion of the car. The passage of time was very much on her mind as well as Greg's. She winked at Greg as she got into the backseat of the car with her mother. Greg simply smiled his reply to her. Both knew what was on the other's mind.

The breakfast was delicious, of course. Having the choice of various food selections as opposed to a few is always fun, Greg thought. For some reason the coffee tasted especially good to him. Perhaps it had something to do with the good feelings that followed his thoughts, or maybe it was just a tasty coffee brand. He glanced down at his watch, it now reading 10:30. Seeing Greg's movement with his hand she couldn't resist herself. Melissa took a peek at her own timepiece as well.

"You in a hurry to go somewhere?" Kenneth asked, noticing both of their hand movements.

"No," Greg said. "I was just thinking about my mom and dad, the fact that we'll be getting together for dinner tomorrow. I'm supposed to give them a call later. I was just curious as to what time it was."

"Well, if you want to see the building construction," suggested Melissa, "we better get a move on."

"We have all day," Susan said slightly shaking her head.

"Oh yeah, that's right," Melissa said, feeling a little foolish for having even made the statement in the first place.

"You know, Greg, I wish we could see more of your mom and dad," Susan said as she sat her cup onto the table. "I miss not having our Sunday meals together as much as we used to. Since everything happened with the store, the baby, time just seems to slip by. Doing all of our work at home has taken a toll as well."

"That's almost an understatement," Kenneth said.

"Everybody set?" Greg asked.

"Yep," Kenneth announced. "Isn't it too bad you can't pack a to-go bag for the road from the buffet?"

"Really," Susan said.

"I think that's a great idea," agreed Greg.

Greg drove slowly by the construction site. At one point he pulled the car into a vacant parking spot. He shut the car off. The party of four sat looking at the various construction equipment assembled at the site. The frame of the new building stood high in the air before them. Different thoughts meandered through each individual's mind as they looked at it.

Greg's mind saw the flames once again, the destruction. He couldn't seem to divorce his thoughts from seeing flames forcing themselves from the windows. He thought of them as a hungry beast searching out more items to devour. The color of the reddish pink sky lived on strongly in his memories. He knew if he closed his eyes, his mind would easily relive every moment from that awful day. He shook his head slowly back and forth.

Melissa's thoughts, however, were completely different than his. Her mind encompassed the break room Henry and Kate had redone in the store for every worker to enjoy. How beautiful it was. Now all that was left of it was empty air. She couldn't believe how much that room meant to her. The Summers all shared lunches from time to time with the employees. Her father was forever trading treats with others, trying to better his deals. Her mind relived the laughter that had been shared by everyone. She smiled lightly. The laughter was as frequent as drops of rain upon a windowpane during a storm. Yes, she missed the camaraderie. While it was just one of many thoughts that came to her mind, this was a very precious one she held among others.

The framed newspaper page hanging in her office was no longer there, the treasure she would adjust if it became off center for any reason. Melissa would rub her hand gently upon the frame as she looked at it. The page was a thank you from the employees to her mom, dad, and herself as well. Under the words, "Thank You," each of their employees' names was signed. These thoughts concerning it made her feel somewhat depressed inside. She could almost visualize the signatures. While some names were written in a scribbled fashion, others were elegantly penned in a beauty all their own. This simple way of thanking the Summers meant much to them and her. How truly grateful the employees were when her parents threw the picnic for all of the employees, their family members included. While it being Greg's idea originally, her parents ran with the concept. Now all copies of the page were destroyed except for the one her father kept in his office at home. Since that date, the Summers had continued the tradition of the employee picnic until this very year. With the destruction of the store, Susan and Kenneth said they didn't have the heart to go through with it.

In Susan's mind she was most grateful that Gordon, the night watchman was safe. She smiled slightly as she recalled his dog, Ranger, licking her hand the night of the fire. Her impression was that the dog was saying everything would be okay. It was a silly thought her mind suggested to her. Nonetheless, the truth was exhibiting that very fact to her with the structure before her eyes. Perhaps Ranger was right. She hoped the heart of the building would once again be beating strongly.

Besides Gordon's safety, Susan was so thankful no one was hurt. Injury or death, those would have been the real tragedy from the infernal that early morning. It's only material things, she thought, and now they were rebuilding. Material things, she once again thought, nothing of real importance, all replaceable items. Someone's life was an altogether different subject. That was something Susan wouldn't even want to think about, or even conceive.

Kenneth looked at the structure as a whole, what was completed, what needed yet to be done. The walls and floors were all in, windows put into place. His mind was encompassed with thoughts of what would come next in their starting anew. Much had been accomplished, much was yet to come. What he found hard to believe is that the construction crew was actually ahead of the timetable that had been discussed earlier in the planning. He smiled slightly, happy in the feeling that his employees would be back to work soon, a sense of normality returning to everyone's life. That thought alone warmed him inside. Better to keep busy than to be wallowing in a life filled with meaningless idleness. Getting everyone back to work, including himself, was something to look forward to, something to strive for.

For a short time the four adults sat in the car, nothing being said. Finally, Melissa reached over and put her hand on Greg's shoulder. Greg knew immediately what she meant.

"Shall we go?" Greg asked. Not hearing any verbal response to his question he merely started the vehicle and pulled out onto the roadway. He slowly made his way around the building giving everyone an opportunity to see it in its entirety, himself included.

Greg stopped the car almost in the middle of the quiet street as his mind studied the construction over. He looked from the hidden basement of the building to its very top. His lips moved slowly. Greg's mind was definitely distracted.

"Mom, Dad, did you add another floor to the store," he asked.

"Yes, we did," Kenneth stated.

Susan merely nodded her head in agreement.

"What are you going to be selling on that floor?" Greg further inquired.

"Actually, the additional floor has been in the plans since Susan and I first looked at the blueprints. The floor plan, however, has been changed quite a bit," Kenneth announced.

"More than once or twice," chuckled Susan.

Kenneth could see a questioning look on both Melissa and Greg's faces. It was quite predominant, easily seen by both parents.

"We have a surprise for the both of you," smiled Susan.

"Another surprise?" inquired Melissa.

Susan paused and looked at Kenneth before saying anything further.

Kenneth nodded his head at her.

"Oh, wait a minute," Greg said, "I better park the car first. This sounds like something that's going to involve more than just a question or two."

Greg quickly guided the vehicle up to the curb.

"Now let's start at the beginning again," Greg said after he shut the car off. He turned in the driver's seat to better see Susan as she spoke.

"Well," Susan continued, "it really all has to do with Mr. and Mrs. Caldwell, Robert and Terry, I should say."

Kenneth said nothing, his face simply smiling. He would enjoy sitting back while Susan did the talking. This was an opportunity for him not to just listen to her words, more importantly, he could watch the expressions on the kids.

"When the two of you were offered the wonderful opportunity by them to buy their business, Kenneth and I both knew in our hearts it was too good of a deal to be passed up by either one of you. You're both smart, you need to move on. Naturally neither one of us wanted that to be too far. We want you both to remain a part of our family business. For the last little while we've been meeting secretly with Terry and Robert."

"Mom, —" Melissa said.

" Before you say anything, we want you to hear us out... Please.

Melissa nodded her head in conjunction with Greg. Each of them wondered where the next few words would lead them. Both were very curious to discover just where it would all start and end.

"With the help of the Caldwells," Susan continued, "we've come up with what we hope the two of you will agree with. The top floor will be just as it was, the offices, but newer, larger, more modern than before.

Mr. Sheppard's security office will carry a sense of authority to it, however, he's going to select the furnishings as he sees fit. Fred's office will be dealt with in the same manner. He can pick out his own furnishings, whatever he decides on. Kenneth and my office will be furnished, of course, the color selection to be decided entirely by me."

That statement by her mother made Melissa chuckle. She knew how awful her father was at putting together color schemes. Her mind went back to the time he saw a checkered suit jacket he thought was not only colorful, but that he'd look great in. He changed his mind when Susan asked him what performer he was going to be in the circus. Yes, picking out colors surely was not his forte. Everyone seemed to understand that but Kenneth.

"Exactly where is my office," Melissa asked, "and do I get to do the decorating of it myself?"

"We didn't actually allow for your office, or Greg's," Kenneth said.

"I'm still a part of this family," Melissa's voice said, a touch of sadness attached to her words. "I don't want to be left out. Mom, Dad, I want to be a part of this, too. Ever since I was a little girl I've had my own office."

Susan looked at Kenneth, both almost wanting to chuckle to themselves. In each of their own thoughts, they recalled when Melissa was young and hung

Blue Rose Petals

around the office section. At times she would be an annoyance. There were periods when she would interrupt a phone call, or play a little loudly on the couch. When Susan was working with figures, little noises became big distractions. Kenneth and Susan deliberated over a solution for quite some time. Both finally agreed to give Melissa her own, "Big Girl's Office." Melissa was thrilled. Fortunately for them, a small room between their own offices was available. Susan and Melissa even picked out the furniture together for it. Being the good mother she was, she tried as best she could to let her daughter make the decisions concerning the colors. She only suggested one change in the color scheme, an obvious clash in colors. Fortunately, Melissa went along with it.

As a youngster with her own office, it represented a large symbol of being included. She absolutely adored it. In Melissa's life it became a very important part of her childhood. Their simple solution instilled in Melissa her strong emotions of being a part of their family business. It was something she took pride in.

"Please don't leave me out, I'm still part of our family no matter where I work."

"Go on, Susan," Kenneth said, "finish up with everything they need to know."

Susan nodded her head. She looked at her daughter, a look of disappointment written across her face.

"The remainder of the top floor's design was left entirely to Terry and Robert alone. We had nothing to do with that section of the building at all. You see kids, that's going to be the new home of the Caldwell Advertising Company, if both of you agree."

"Surprise!" Kenneth's voice announced, a very large smile written across his face.

"Yes, surprise!" Susan was quick to add.

"Unbelievable," was all Greg could say.

"Oh, Mom... Dad," were the only words that Melissa could muster her voice to say. She never expected in her wildest dreams to be hearing what she did. What an idea, she thought, what an absolutely wonderful idea they came up with. In her mind she would literally be living that old expression out, having your cake and eating it too. She was truly speechless. Melissa reached over and hugged her mother.

"There's another part to this," Kenneth stated. "If the two of you agree to move the business in with us, so to speak, it will be rent free."

"Rent free would be out of the question," Greg stated.

"How do you put a price tag on love for your kids?" Kenneth added.

"You can't," Susan said in a firm voice. She nodded her head slightly as if agreeing with herself. Susan loved the look on her daughter's face, a surprised expression still lingering on Greg's. She continued with her thoughts. "That fact alone will allow you to pay any monies off to Robert and Terry in a more timely fashion."

Kenneth added, "Your mother and I have spoken to Robert and Terry concerning that very concept. With their building eventually becoming empty, they could sell it and apply any monies from the sale to what they would be owed. We both understand it is not something we should have talked about with them. We realize neither one of us have any say in this, but all-in-all, the Caldwells are so comfortable to talk to, let alone work with."

Greg nodded his head, knowing exactly how easy Robert and Terry were to deal with.

"Please forgive us if we stepped on any of your toes. I think the Caldwells, as well as us, wanted to surprise you both."

"That they did," Greg said, "as well as both of you. It looks like your mom and dad have taken any questions out of our pending decision on the business."

"We didn't mean to do that," Susan said quickly.

"I know that wasn't your intention," Greg said. "Melissa... Honey, what do you have to say?"

"Let's see," Melissa said, "number one, on the one side I can still visit my mom and dad anytime I want to while at work with you. They'll only be a few steps away."

"That's right," Greg stated.

"Here goes her numbering system again," joked Susan.

"On the other hand, number two, I can be with you at work."

"That's right." Greg nodded.

"Thirdly, I can still visit with our store employees."

"That's correct, but I still need an answer from you."

"And fourthly... yes, yes, yes, and yes," Melissa stated as she jumped slightly in her seat, much as a little child would that was filled with excitement.

Everyone laughed.

"Honey, does this mean I get my own office now?" she asked.

"Only if it's bigger than mine," Greg chuckled.

"In that case we can share mine," she responded.

"Greg, Melissa... Susan and I figured this would be the answer from the two of you. We understand this is where your hearts lie, where you both belong. We're just so happy the two of you can work together, it's like a bonus. It was for Robert and Terry, just as it is for Susan and me."

"Oh, I do have one question," Greg wanted to convey.

"And what is that?" Kenneth inquired.

"Once everything is settled and we're working, can my employees get a employee discount?" Greg said as he winked in Kenneth's direction.

"I don't see why not," Kenneth said. "In fact, if they would like to use it, they're more than welcome to share the new break room with us. After all, who knows what items they may bring with them to trade." Kenneth smirked as he rubbed his hands together in a mockingly greedy fashion.

"Melissa," Greg said, " I know you're thrilled about this turn of events, but before we say yes to this, I'd like to talk it over with my mom and dad. I just want to get their input."

"Of course," Melissa said. "Greg, can we swing by the park on the way home?"

"For what?"

"I heard they put in a new play area for kids, I'd just like to see it."

"I don't know."

"Oh, come on, Greg, we've got plenty of time," Susan stated.

"Well, okay."

Once again Greg pulled out onto the roadway, heading for the park that sat next to the river. He glanced at the clock on the dash. It was almost ten to eleven.

About two blocks from the park Melissa instructed Greg to pull over to the side of the road. As he did, Susan asked if there was a problem. Melissa smiled at her mother and dad. Greg looked at Melissa and winked. It was time for their plan to fall into place. Greg reached over to the area of the glove box and opened it. Inside he retrieved two small clear plastic containers. He handed one to Melissa while keeping one for himself.

"Here, Mom, put this on," Melissa said in a somewhat serious sounding voice.

"This one is for you," Greg stated as he handed the other plastic container to Kenneth.

Kenneth and Susan looked at what they had in their hands. As they opened them it was easy to see they each contained a small black travel mask, one used to hide the brightness of the day if you wished to sleep.

"Put them on," Melissa instructed.

"You're kidding me; aren't you," Kenneth said. "Really, is all of this necessary?"

"Father."

That word to Kenneth alone told him he should do as he was told. Whenever Melissa used that single way of addressing him, it meant whatever the circumstances were, it was very important to her. When the emotional stings to her heart were pulled the tightest, or as a child when she needed to be comforted, Melissa always called him by that single word. Yes, being called dad was one thing, father held a whole different meaning for both of them. It was his Achilles heel with her. That he understood very well.

"So how do these things go on?" Kenneth stated as he removed the mask from the packaging.

Susan already had hers on within a couple of seconds. She adjusted them with her hand so they fit perfectly.

"These really block out everything, I mean all of the extraneous light," she said.

"I know someone at work who wears a pair when they get a migraine," Greg said. "He swears by them. In fact, he told me where to get these."

Kenneth started laughing.

"What is it, Honey," Susan said.

"I feel like the blind version of the lone ranger since there aren't any eye-holes to look through."

"Are we all set now?" Melissa asked.

"In just a minute," Greg said. He lifted his hand up and moved it back and forth in front of Kenneth's face. At one point he made a sharp gesture toward his eyes. Kenneth didn't move whatsoever. Observing her husband's testing of the mask, she did the same thing to her mother's face.

"We're set," Melissa said with a smile.

"Why are we wearing these things anyway?" asked Kenneth, "I just don't understand, after all, it's only a playground area."

"It's what's beside it that —" Melissa mouth froze shut, almost giving away the surprise. "You two will just have to wait."

Greg pulled back onto the roadway as they made their way to the park. He glanced into the rearview mirror at Melissa's face. Her face bore a smile as she looked out her window, then at her mother sitting beside her. Kenneth and Susan said nothing, both wondering what was really taking place. Greg pulled up to a parking spot, a lawn chair saving a spot for him. A woman picked it up and walked to the side. Greg pulled into the parking area.

"Now just wait here for a moment," he instructed everyone in the car.

Getting out of the vehicle Greg put his hand up to his face. A single finger covered his lips, an indication to be quiet. He took a quick look around. His next movement was to let out a deep breath as he smiled.

"Now you both can get out of the car. You help your mom, Melissa, while I give your dad a hand."

Once both of the Summers were out of the vehicle, Greg and Melissa placed them side-by-side. Melissa made sure they were both facing the same direction. It was only then when Greg lifted his hand, as a conductor would, and brought it downward bringing forth an abundant of singing voices. The song they sang was one the Summers knew well. It was sung to both of them the evening they announced their plans for the rebuilding, as well as the employees' financial status with them.

Kenneth and Susan quickly removed their masks as the words to the song continued. "For they are jolly good fellows, and so say all of us." Susan put her hands to her face, overwhelmed by everything her eyes revealed to her. People were everywhere. There had to be more than 400 individuals present if not more. She was very sure of that.

Over to their right a banner was strung between two trees, it gently swaying in the breeze. It's message, "Summers' Summer Picnic, Welcome Employees and Families."

"Kenneth, our sign," Susan said as she lifted her hand pointing at it.

He smiled. As he looked around his eyes caught sight of smoking barbecues, tables containing piles of paper plates, cups, napkins and silverware. Another table held hotdog and hamburger buns along with chips. Beside them were condiments. A couple of tables behind it held a large variety of desserts. Large coolers filled with hotdogs, burgers, and cold drinks sat waiting to be used. Not far from them were big bags of charcoal. Everything was as Susan and he had done for their employees over the past several years. The only thing missing were the prizes the Summers awarded their employees following the games. Susan felt a sadness concerning the lack of the prizes. Handing them out personally to each employee meant a lot to her. She would miss that greatly.

Kenneth and Susan were so taken back by everything. It was then when they both started to look at the faces of the people before them. The immediate area was filled with a sea of smiles and happy faces. Not everyone was familiar to them since family members had always been invited to the party. However, there were still many in attendance each knew very well. There was Mrs. White, Fred and his wife, Robin, and their two girls. Ted Sheppard shook Kenneth's hand. Susan just stood there hugging one person after another, some she hadn't seen for some time. Inside she was thrilled to see them all again.

When it came to employees receiving their promised checks, it was decided by Susan to handle that task in a different manner. She saw to it they were delivered by mail no less than two days earlier. Susan surmised their family of employees didn't need to be watching their mailboxes anticipating their gift. It is always good to have money in hand when bills were sure to be on the way, she thought.

Every check that went out also included a handwritten note from her detailing the progress in the building project as well as a wish for their wellbeing. At times Susan would also personalize them should someone get sick or there was a loss in their family. This simple, but time consuming project, was well received by everyone. Many of the people would take these small messages and share them with their family and friends. The community, unbeknownst to Susan and Kenneth, placed them upon a pedestal in their feelings for the Summers family. An award for Citizen of the Year was created for that very reason. Susan and Kenneth would eventually receive the award two years in a row.

At one point Susan couldn't contain herself anymore, her emotions getting the best of her. She began to start crying. What a wonderful surprise, she thought as she wiped her eyes with her finger. When Greg saw her he quickly walked over and put his arm around her shoulders, pulling her a little tighter to him.

"Keep this up," Greg said loudly, "and we'll pack everything up and move it to your backyard. Now, where's that smile of yours we love to see so much?"

That was all she needed to hear, her smile returned to her lips. She nodded her head as she put her arm around his waist. Susan gave him a squeeze. Kenneth smiled at the two, his eyes indicating dampness to them as well.

"So when do you want to eat?" came the sound of Henry's voice. He stood before her, a large white chef's hat on his head. "You don't want to keep us culinary artists, such as myself, waiting too long, otherwise we turn from chefs into bottle washers."

"How about if you make that decision for me," Susan replied.

"Sounds great. I have my assistants ready to start at anytime." He pointed over in the direction of the barbecues. There stood Kate, Emma Elizabeth standing beside her. Next to them were Robin and Fred's two little girls. They wore much too large of aprons covering their clothes. Each also wore a chef's hat. Kate waved to them.

"They're all so adorable," Susan said smiling. "Thank you for coming, Henry, for being here for us. Please tell Kate that for me also. Oh, never mind, I'll do it myself when I get the chance."

"You're welcome."

"Henry," Kenneth said as he put his hand on his shoulder, "can we walk over to Kate's position, I want to ask a favor of you. Susan, I'll be back in just a minute or so."

Susan nodded her head. She already knew what the conversation would entail. They had talked about it many a time since the fire. She knew if it could be done, Henry was the one, together with Kate's help to fulfill their wishes.

Kenneth and Henry walked a short distance before Kenneth indicated for them to stop. It was at that juncture that Kenneth broached the subject matter to him.

The Summers wanted Henry and Kate to perform a certain job for them, and not an easy one at that. The job was to take charge of the break room's rebuilding project. How they could even improve on the job they had done originally would be a large undertaking. When finished originally the lunchroom had marble counters, oak trim everywhere along with cabinets made of the same material. How they could improve on perfection would be a mystery. They knew if anyone could do it, assuming they even had the time, of course, Kate and Henry were the ones to accomplish it. Now they would ask if it was even remotely possible. Hopefully the answer would be, yes.

Henry walked the short distance to where Kate and Emma Elizabeth were standing. Kenneth, however remained where he was standing. After observing a short discussion between them, Henry looked in the direction of Kenneth. He raised his right arm up, an okay signal indicated with his finger and thumb. Kenneth smiled at them. It's going to happen, he thought. I can hardly wait to tell Susan, Melissa, and Greg.

Kenneth returned to where Susan stood by Melissa and Greg. He bent down and whispered something in Susan's ear. She smiled broadly.

" Melissa, Greg," Kenneth stated, "we have a surprise for the both of you."

"Really," Melissa said.

"You tell them, Susan, you did all the background work on it."

"Well, it was your idea, Kenneth, you do it."

"Okay, I will." I have been talking with Kate and Henry on a little surprise for both of you. Henry and Kate have agreed to rebuild the break room to its original glory."

"Oh, Mom, Dad, I just loved that room," Melissa said. She turned giving her mother a huge hug. Next Melissa wrapped her arms around her father's neck and squeezed.

"I can hardly breath," Kenneth joked.

"What made you think of doing that?" Melissa asked, her face beaming as she spoke.

" You're not the only one who loved that room," smiled Kenneth. "I think of that area as a place where everyone can mingle together, and besides, I still have lots of trading items I need to get rid of."

"That's a wonderful thing you two are doing," Greg said.

Susan and Kenneth just smiled.

"Well, we do get some use out of it, too," Susan said.

Feeling someone's hand on her shoulder caused Susan to turn around. There was the one person she felt as close to as a sister, Greg's mother, Edith. They immediately hugged. The love they possessed for one another could only be rivaled by that of Melissa for Kate, and vice versa.

"So when do we eat?" Frank asked.

"Always the stomach questions," Edith stated.

"Just as it is for Kenneth," chuckled Susan. "I'm so glad the two of you are here.

"We would have been here sooner, but Frank thought he would like to try-out a new shortcut he heard about. You can imagine how that went."

Susan just laughed as she and Edith hugged again.

"You're still coming tomorrow?" Susan inquired.

"We wouldn't miss it," Frank stated as he rubbed his stomach.

Once again Susan laughed, while Edith just shook her head back and forth. The two of them, Frank and Edith, being there meant more to Susan than either of the Wilsons could ever have imagined. They were as much of a family member as Greg was to Susan and Kenneth.

The biggest surprise of the day came to the Summers when everyone joined in the games that were played. Some games were simple, others weren't, but all were fun to play. One could see that each contest held a tense rivalry between the participants. Every individual wanted to win badly. This was something the Summers found unusual, not expecting to see what they were observing. When the first of many contests to follow was over, the winner walked over to a table where a couple of women were sitting. The winning contestant received an envelope from one of the ladies. He held it high in the air. The people applauded loudly. He then turned, walked over to the Summers and handed the envelope to Susan.

"I wish we had a prize to award you," Susan vocalized sadly.

"Well, it doesn't matter because I have a prize for both of you," the winner announced.

The young man, who Susan recognized from the appliance section, smiled at Kenneth and Susan. He then informed her to open the envelope and read its contents out very loudly. After opening it, she smiled as she stood up and read the following.

"This entitles the Summers family to ten free hand car washes."

Once again the sound of applause was loud. So it went throughout the rest of the day. Each first, second, and third place winner received an envelope. They handed it proudly to the Summers, and awaited the prize to be announced to everyone.

The gifts they received were unusual, but something everyone would enjoy receiving. There were certificates for free dinners being brought to the home, fully cooked, ready to eat. The mixture of cuisines were surprising. There were southern dishes, southwestern, French, Chinese, Greek, Mexican, and even one from India. No one dared suggesting Italian as one of their dishes. Susan's reputation as a cook in that field was something no one wanted to compete with, or even challenge.

Everything one could imagine was listed, window washing to gutter clearing. Six women acting as one participant donated a complete spring cleaning of the Summers' home.

There were even a few holiday prizes presented to the couple. One such certificate offered a free Christmas tree being erected in their front room, fully decorated, of course. The gift included the advantage of having it taken down and ornaments returned to their appropriate containers. Ten people acting as one offered their services for a night of Christmas carols being sung for an hour outside of the Summers' home. The evening of entertainment also included hot chocolate and donuts being served by the carolers to all. Some of the names listed were unfamiliar to Susan and her husband. They surmised many of the people included on the list were relatives of store employees. This unique holiday gift from employees and strangers made Susan feel honored to receive it.

Henry and Kate added themselves in the gift giving. Both felt since they worked on the break room originally, they were certainly employees, too. The Summers enjoyed receiving their concert tickets.

A gift of a Fourth of July steak barbecue cooked and served at their home intrigued Kenneth the most. He could hardly wait.

At one point Susan read off the next prize. It was a complete Thanksgiving dinner for 20 to be served in their home. As Susan stood reading the prize, she rubbed her stomach. This act by her brought forth a large amount of laughter as well as applause. After realizing what the prize really entailed, Susan protested saying it is not fair the women be taken from their own family holiday meals to cater to them. She soon was informed that each woman was going to bring her own specialty item to be dropped off at the appropriate time. This included two large fully cooked turkeys. Susan thought this to be significant. They would also be receiving each one's very best side dish. How wonderful it would be to taste other cooks' scrumptious side dishes. Her mind ran wild with thoughts of what they would all consist of. Susan was sure there would be different flavored stuffing, vegetable dishes, and potatoes flavored in unusual ways. Who knows what dessert would entail. Perhaps a homemade pie or two she thought, or maybe something more exotic.

"How am I going to eat enough food for 20 people?" Susan expressed laughing loudly.
    "By inviting your relatives," Greg shouted out."
    The people applauded Greg's foresight.
    When Greg won one of the contests, Susan read loudly the winning gift.
    "Breakfast in bed served by your daughter and son-in-law, Greg and Melissa."
    Everyone laughed, all enjoying the couple's creativity.

There was an additional two items included with each and every contestants' prize offering. The first of two notes was written by each individual expressing their heartfelt thanks for what the Summers had done for them and their family. It was something that touched the hearts of Susan and Kenneth deeply.
    Every employees' envelope also possessed a second handwritten gift certificate indicating that for the next four years, they were willing to work a two-week period without pay. In other words, everyone was giving the Summers eight weeks of free labor over that time period. Everyone knew it was truly a hardship for Susan and Kenneth to endure by paying their employees during this crisis. They also understood where they all would have been in their own lives had the Summers not taken them under their wings.

With all of the games completed, Susan and Kenneth took a moment to sit at a picnic table to enjoy a soda.
    "What a day, Susan," he said.
    "What a day indeed," she responded.
    Kenneth nodded his head back and forth as he spoke.

"How did they know who would be doing what, I mean the job they would be assigned?"

After a minute or so Kenneth thought he knew the answer to her question.

"The envelopes all had the person's name on them," he said, "so they simply were given their own envelope back. I'll bet they were the only ones who knew what they were giving as a prize."

"So it really didn't matter if they finished first, second, or third, they just wanted to be first in line to present their gift."

"That's what I'm thinking," Kenneth said.

"Wow," was all Susan could say.

It wasn't the amount of any gift that was presented to Susan and Kenneth that mattered to them. It was the fact that each award possessed a piece of the giver's heart inside of the envelope. This spoke to each one's love for the Summers. That fact alone was what touched Susan and her husband the most.

"Our employees did a wonderful thing for us today," Kenneth verbalized as he nodded his head.

"It's just amazing, Kenneth," Susan said.

"Our family of employees really outdid themselves," he added. "We do have some tremendous people working for us. I doubt if any other businesses would have had this done for their owners. It's... it's —"

"Unbelievable, amazing, just plain wonderful," Susan suggested with a smile.

"All of the above," Kenneth said.

"I don't think any other businesses have the caliber of people we have working for us," Susan said.

Kenneth just smiled. "Before we know it we'll all be celebrating a grand opening. I can hardly wait for that to occur."

"Kenneth, we spent an awful lot of our own money seeing to it they were all taken care of. I think today they've proven to us we did the right thing. Everyone of them demonstrated their love for the both of us over and over again." Susan bit slightly down on her lip.

"Even by some who aren't even our employees," he said with a chuckle.

"You're right, Honey. How do we ever thank them for this?"

"We don't. It all comes down to this. Each one of them wanted to thank us for what we did for them. Now we sit back and enjoy the love they've showered over us by what they've done today. Just do what I'm doing."

"Exactly what is that?" she inquired.

"By soaking it all in. Susan, true love never comes with a price tag. I think the reason for that is sincerity. It's something you can never put a price tag on. However, you are right about one thing."

"What's that, Honey?"

"It did cost both of us a shinny penny over the last couple of years."

"More like a nickel," Susan chuckled.

Kenneth nodded his head.

Neither of them seemed to really care. They would move on as husband and wife, together as one, just as they always had. For many years it had been that way, none of that would change. It was now a new chapter to an old story playing itself out in their lives. They both hoped it possessed a happy ending.

The gentle honking of a horn sent Greg hurriedly in the direction of the parking lot. Melissa did her best to stay up with him, but she found that difficult.

"Thank you so much for bringing her," Greg stated as he reached over and opened the back door to the vehicle. Reaching inside he removed Rose from the car. Holding the baby carrier in one hand he closed the back door with his other.

"Would you please join us for some burgers or hotdogs, Mrs. Greene?" Greg inquired of the babysitter.

"Well, I don't know. I wouldn't want to intrude," she answered.

"Just park the car over there, it will be fine. Thank you for doing this for us, bringing Rose here."

"You're welcome," she replied. "Thank you for inviting me for lunch."

"Well, you're our babysitter, Mrs. Greene, and that makes you an employee so to speak. Please... we would both enjoy having you here."

"I do know some of the people here. It will be fun to join in with them. Thank you."

Melissa soon joined Greg at his side. She reached over unbuckling the baby from the carrier. Melissa held her in her arms. The sight of the baby drew a very large crowd of women employees immediately. As the group grew larger in size, each attempting to see the child, Greg knew it was time to leave Melissa in charge of crowd control.

"I'm going to go over and see if Henry needs any help," Greg stated. Whether she heard him or not didn't seem to matter as he watched the women gathering around Melissa. Like bears to honey, he thought as he walked in the direction of Henry. Bears to honey, he thought again nodding his head.

"Hey you two, you hogging all of this beautiful weather up for yourself?" Kate's grandfather, Doc stated.

"Do you want to buy some of it, I'll bag it up to go?" laughed Kenneth.

Standing beside Doc was Jean Parker, a woman whom Susan had grown to call a close friend. Not only was she a good employee, she possessed common sense, a trait Susan admired in her. Jean attended Melissa's wedding at Susan's request, wanting someone to represent the business at the wedding. It was at the reception where Jean met Doc. They had more in common than anyone would believe. Together they became a couple, a relationship that seemed to blossom more each day. The two fell in love; that was very clear to all who knew them. The fact that her ring finger held a symbol of that love told everyone immediately of their feelings for one another.

"I got hung up at the hospital, otherwise we would have been here sooner. From what I understand in talking with Greg and Melissa, you two were given some very unusual gifts."

"For a few years Susan and I threw this party for our employees," Kenneth said, "and we truly loved doing it. This really took both of us by surprise."

"They gave some unbelievable prizes to their employees, Doc," Jean offered. "I was personally astonished by some of them over the years. I think the days off people won really surprised them. Then with Steven Morris winning the complete week off with pay astonished everyone, me included."

"So how did this all come about," Doc inquired.

"We haven't been told," Susan said, "but to tell you the truth, we think Melissa and Greg's fingerprints are all over this."

"Everyone was sworn to secrecy, I do know that," Jean said with a smile. "To tell you the truth, I find it hard to believe you two didn't find out about it."

"So am I," confessed Kenneth.

Robert and Terry Caldwell walked up to the group.

"I am so glad to see you two," Kenneth said as he held his hand out to Robert.

"It's always good to be welcomed," Robert chuckled.

"Doc, Jean, this is Mrs. and Mrs. Caldwell."

"It's nice to meet both of you," Robert stated. "This is my better half, Terry." The four shook hands.

"Robert," Kenneth said, "we talked about moving the company with Greg and Melissa and I think it's a go."

"Wonderful," Terry said.

"Now," Kenneth added, "I understand they haven't said it was a completed deal to you two, but I'm sure they're ninety-nine percent in both of our corners."

"Great," Robert said.

As they were talking Greg and Melissa walked up. Greg was carrying one of Henry's freshly grilled hamburgers.

"Boy that looks good," Robert expressed.

"Henry has a way with burgers," acknowledged Greg. "I don't know what his secret is, but boy they taste good. Maybe he marinates the meat a head of time, I don't know."

"Then how do you explain the hotdogs?" laughed Kenneth.

The men just nodded their heads as one.

"Everyone admires Henry's skills around a hot barbecue," chuckled Kenneth.

"If one is lucky enough to burp up the taste of Henry's burgers later, it's a treasured memory to relive," Greg offered.

"Oh, don't say that," Melissa said with a grimaced look on her face.

"But it's true."

"When do I get to hold the baby?" Jean asked.

Melissa didn't answer her. She merely handed Rose to the outstretched arms of Jean. Both women carefully exchanged the little bundle.

"Greg, I understand you and Melissa have talked a little bit with Kenneth and Susan concerning our offer to the both of you on our business," Robert said.

Doc and Jean's ears perked up with that statement having been made. They both knew Greg worked for the Caldwells on the side, Melissa helping him on occasion. This, however, was something they had no knowledge of.

"We've talked it over," Greg stated.

"And?"

"To tell you the truth, we just left my mom and dad. We told them what you and your wife have offered us. Melissa and I wanted their input since neither one of them have any involvement in this to begin with. We explained about moving the business, the payments that would have to be made. My mom and dad told us they thought we were awfully young to be biting off this large of a chunk of apple at our age."

"But Greg, —" Terry interrupted.

"Yes, that's true but, —" Kenneth said quickly.

"However..." Greg said as he lifted his hand indicating for them to stop, "however, they also said they have all the faith in the world that we would do a credible job of it. The fact that Melissa would be at my side is what my mom said swayed her the most."

Everyone laughed.

"Having a good woman at my side never hurt me," Kenneth was quick to say.

"Exactly," Robert added.

"And me, too. Well, pretty soon fulltime," Doc said smiling.

"So you're accepting our offer?" Robert asked.

"Under two conditions," smiled Melissa.

"Two conditions?" Terry said.

"One, —"

"Here we go with the counting again," laughed Greg.

"What do you mean?" Terry inquired.

"Well, whenever Melissa has something important to say, she puts them all in order, one, two, three."

"That's a good idea," Terry stated.

"I'm sorry, Honey, go on," Greg said.

"One, that the name of the business remains Caldwell Advertising and, two, that both of you have got to promise to visit us all of the time. We'd enjoy having your input whenever you feel the urge hitting you."

"That we promise," Terry stated emphatically.

"Or maybe when you want us to have lunch together," smiled Greg.

"Can we come?" Kenneth asked quickly.

"Of course," Greg said.

"After all, we'll need someone to pick up the bill," laughed Robert.

Robert held his hand out to Greg as they shook hands. He immediately did the same to Melissa. Terry, however, sealed the deal in her own special way. She hugged and kissed Melissa and Greg on their cheeks.

"Congratulations, kids," Kenneth said.

"Yes, congratulations," Susan added.

"The same from us," Doc stated.

Inside Susan was truly happy. The family was all coming back together. Soon the building would be completed, employees all back in place. Their family now grew with the adding of the Caldwell employees who she would be sure to introduce herself to, at least those who hadn't attended the "Adult Party." She could also show them the break room to share, as well as inform them of the business discount they would be offered. Of course, they weren't their employees, but they would be treated as such. Any employees who walked through their doors were going to be a part of their family, like it or not.

So on a warm sunny day, not to be forgotten, many surprises were shared. All were cloaked in a wrapping of secrecy, each celebrated by people that loved and adored each other.

Horrible Mistake

The sun coming up over the horizon began shining brightly as Henry and Kate drove down the roadway towards the hospital. Henry reached up with his hand and pulled the sun visor down casting a shadow over his face. That's better, he thought to himself.

"Why is it they always schedule operations so early in the morning?" he asked.

"I'm sure if they had it their way, the operations would all take place at one o'clock in the afternoon. I don't think they do it that way just to inconvenience you." she joked.

"Having the sitter spend the night with us was a stroke of genius on your part. It was very kind of her to do that for us. I know she's a retired woman, but it sure helped us out."

"I'm a little worried about Josh and his operation," Kate said as she shook her head slowly back and forth. "It's an awful lot for a youngster to take on."

"Let alone his mom and dad," agreed Henry.

The sound of a deep breath escaping Kate's mouth brought numerous thoughts to Henry's mind. What if the operation was a failure? What if it left him with a more serious limp than he already suffered from? What if this happened, what if that occurred. Different scenarios kept playing themselves out in his thoughts.

Seeing Henry's expression Kate knew what he was thinking. It was as obvious to her as if he had spoken the words out loud.

"You're worried about the operation, too; aren't you, Honey?"

He nodded his head.

"Henry, neither one of us has any control over the results. Even the surgeon can control only so much."

"I know... I understand."

"Henry, I think we should use guarded words in anything we say today," Kate said thoughtfully.

"I don't understand what you mean," he replied.

"Maybe I'm wrong... I don't know. I don't want them to have their hopes built up too high by anything we say. Of course, on the other hand I do want them to be encouraged by anything we do have to say. They definitely need our support, and if we can —"

"Isn't that why we're going in the first place?"

"That's true. Since they don't have any family nearby, that's why I wanted to make sure we're there for them. I guess I'm talking and thinking in circles."

"I don't think so, you're just concerned like me. We each have our own reasons behind what we're hoping for, and they both deal with Josh in the end."

Henry made a few more turns before pulling into the hospital parking lot. As they walked up to the entrance, a large door automatically opened allowing them ingress. As the door slowly glided back into place behind them, they walked up to an information area. After obtaining the needed instructions on where to go, they turned down a hallway leading to an elevator section. Kate pushed the appropriate button. Within a moment or two they entered the elevator. As the door slid shut, Henry could hear Kate as she once again let out another deep breath. He reached down taking her hand in his. Kate and Henry squeezed their interlocked fingers together.

Entering into the waiting room Henry was quick to see the Harrisons sitting together. His heart almost skipped a beat. Seated between Frank and Jennifer was little Mary. Henry actually froze in place momentarily. He looked at her in an almost uncontrollable stare. Trying to divert his attention from her, he glanced to his left, then his right. Eye contact with her was something he tried to avoid.

"We're so glad you made it," Jennifer said as she stood up.

"We both wanted to be here for Josh," Kate stated.

"Thank you for coming," Frank said as he offered his hand to Henry."
"I... I... Thank you," Henry said.

Henry couldn't help himself as he tried to look at Mary without being too conspicuous. She was older now, of course, and still carried the charm she did the night he first met her. Mary's smile told him that quickly. The burn mark, he thought, was still very evident on her cheek. It broke his heart inside to look at this beautiful little girl in possession of such an ugly disfigurement. It wasn't right for her to have suffered this way. His head nodded back and forth without him even realizing it.

"Oh, forgive me," Frank said, "but this little angel is Mary. We've been very fortunate to have just adopted her, I'm happy to say."
"How wonderful it is to meet you," Kate said.
"It's nice to meet you," Mary said.
"This is my husband, Henry."

Mary looked up at Henry but said nothing. It was as if she was studying him over. He could definitely see it in her eyes, as well as feel it in his soul. He wondered if she would recognize him as being the Santa the night they met at the children's Christmas party. Henry wanted to lean down and put his arms around her, but he knew better. He just smiled.

"Do I know you?" asked Mary in an almost timid voice.
"I don't think so," he answered.

The inquisitive expression on Mary's face remained as she gazed at Henry. Frank and Jennifer, along with Kate noticed her reaction. Kate worried she may remember Henry and say something about it. She nor Henry wanted the Harrisons to know they knew her. Once they had decided to step aside in their quest for her, it was better the Harrisons know nothing of their previous intentions. That was something they both strongly agreed on.

"I remember. When I was little," Mary said softly, "I remember Santa telling me something. You look like Santa a little bit."

"What do you mean?" Jennifer inquired.

"Santa had a real beard; I saw kids pull on it."

"Uh-huh," Jennifer said smiling. "I don't think Mr. Morgan has a beard unless it's invisible," she joked.

"The scar, he has the scar," Mary stated loudly.

"Honey," Frank said quickly, "let's not talk about Mr. Morgan's scar; okay."

"He let me touch it. I remember the scar now."

Neither Jennifer nor Frank knew what to say or how to handle this embarrassing item concerning Henry's scar. They both just looked at each other with blank faces.

"Can I feel it?" Mary asked.

"Mary, please," Jennifer said loudly.

Kate looked over at Henry, he returning her look. She knew whatever actions or words that were about to take place were in his hands alone. How he would handle this was strictly up to him. She waited to see what happened, as well as everyone else. Henry knelt down slowly to be at Mary's height. He reached over much the same as he did the night of the program taking her hand in his. Henry placed her hand upon his scar. With his other hand he put it on her burn. It was as if time literally stopped between the two of them. Mary smiled at Henry. She then moved her hand down to his cheek removing a tear that was making its way down it. Jennifer and Frank stood silently as they observed it all, what was transpiring between Henry and Mary. Neither one knew what to say, let alone do.

"Santa, it is you," Mary said softly, a smile spreading across her face.

"Yes... it's me, kind of," Henry's cracked voice answered.

Mary put her arms around Henry's neck as he drew her into his arms. No one said a word. The emotions that filled the Harrisons were two-fold. They

Blue Rose Petals

wondered what was happening between Mary and Henry, two individuals who supposedly never knew each other, and what had caused it in the first place.

"Can I talk to you two alone for a minute," inquired Kate in a quiet voice.
"Definitely," Frank said.
"Yes, definitely, most definitely," Jennifer said.

Moving away from Henry and Mary somewhat, Kate quietly began to explain everything to the Harrisons. She apprized them of Henry's fear in playing Santa that night because of his scar; that he didn't want to scare the young kids. She explained further how he attempted to hide that fact from the children with his Santa hat. Kate went on to inform them of how Mary ended up on his lap, the last child to see Santa that night. As she spoke to them about how Mary changed Henry's life, the deep affect she had on him, Kate began to tear up, but did not cry. Lastly she told the couple of how Henry had wept in the pastor's office following the program.

"So Mary and Henry never knew each other before that day?" asked Frank.
"No," Kate answered.
"This is the first time he's seen her since that night?"
"Yes, it is."
"I'll be," Frank said.
"That's why she called him, Santa?" Jennifer said nodding her head back and forth in utter disbelief.
"Of course, that's why there's such a connection between the two of them. Henry explained to me later he told Mary her burn was something that just happened, it was a part of her now. He said it was true for him as well, the scar he possessed. He told her they both had to learn to move on in their lives. I think those words held true for Mary, just as they did for Henry. That's my take on the whole situation."

Frank and Jennifer looked over at Henry and Mary. He had now stood up and held Mary in a somewhat seated position in his arms. They were laughing together.

"How do I ever complete with him?" Frank said.

"It's not at all a question of competition between you and Henry. What they went through is one thing, your love for her is all together something else," Kate said. "Not every child can say their father personally knows Santa."

Frank smiled at that thought.

"I think I know how we can handle this so it works out the best for all concerned," Kate said. "Can I give it a try, I mean, if that's okay with both of you?"

Jennifer looked at Frank. After just a moment, she nodded her head. Seeing her expression and having observed her head movement, he shook his head in agreement. The three of them returned to the area of Mary and Henry.

"Mommy, Daddy," Mary excitedly said, "Santa's brother told me he came here for a special reason."

All three adults looked amazed with Mary's words.

"Santa told me…Santa's brother told me," Mary said pointing at Henry as she spoke, "that he came down here from the North Pole to tell us he had a special wish from Santa. Santa hopes Josh will be okay," smiled Mary.

The expression worn by Mary warmed everyone's heart. It was soon transferred to their own faces by the little girl's words.

"Daddy, can you hold me now?" Mary asked.

"You bet, Angel, you bet I can," Frank said as he quickly moved in her direction.

Mary reached out quickly towards Frank, almost slipping from Henry's grasp as she did.

"Whoa," Frank said as he pulled her into his waiting arms.

"Will you tell Santa I said hi?" Mary said while looking back over her shoulder.

"I sure will," Henry said.

Frank held Mary tightly as he kissed her several times on her cheek.

"I love you, Mary," he said.

"I love you, too, Daddy," she responded in her little voice.

"Kate," Jennifer whispered, "what was your plan?"

"Actually it's the one Henry used on Mary. How did he know what I was thinking?"

"Sometimes people just think along the same lines. I know it happens with Frank and me quite often," chuckled Jennifer.

"Now we can turn our attention to Josh," Kate said.

"He's never been out of my mind for a moment," Jennifer uttered.

"You did get to see him before he went into surgery this morning; didn't you?"

"We were here very early to make sure we did. I don't know if they would have taken him in without us seeing him first, but we weren't going to take the chance."

"So how is this all affecting him?" Kate asked.

"He's a brave little guy. I'm sure he saw this on TV, but when they wheeled him down the hallway towards the operating room he gave us a thumps up."

Jennifer's face broke into tears. Kate quickly put her arms around her attempting to comfort her as much as possible. The two women cried together as they held one another.

"Everything will work out just fine, I'm sure of it," Kate whispered softly into Jennifer's ear. Jennifer nodded her head. Kate could only pray her words were true.

"Oh my goodness, I almost forgot to give you something," Kate stated. Upon releasing Jennifer she walked over to her purse and retrieved a piece of paper from inside of it. Handing it to Frank, she apologized to them both for forgetting to give it to them earlier. The fact was that Kate had not forgotten to give them the paper at all, she was just waiting for the right time. After observing Jennifer crying, Kate thought it was as good a time as ever to take her mind off of her son's operation for a few minutes.

"What is this?" inquired Frank.

"You two know about the Summers's Family Store?" inquired Kate.

"They had a fire that completely destroyed it; right?" Jennifer said.

"Yes, they did. I happened to be talking to the owners one day. Their daughter is my dearest friend, she's almost like my sister to me. One day we were playing outside and this huge black dog came running over to see us. We thought it was a bear. Anyway Melissa, that's her name —"

"Kate," came Henry's voice, "the paper."
"Oh, I'm sorry."

Henry nodded his head with her words. He had seen her ask someone a question, and before the person could answer her, Kate had talked a complete circle around the subject matter and gave the answer as well. Sometimes when she was very excited she rambled. This appeared to be one such occasion. He just smiled at her.

"The people who own the Summers' Store are rebuilding it," Kate stated. "I understand they'll be doing a little hiring very soon. Would you two be interested in perhaps applying for a job there? I can tell you this from my own personal experience, they are the most generous and easy to work for people you could ever come to know. Jennifer, I know you told me you were looking for a job as well, so here's a chance at one, or maybe even two. As far as an opportunity in sales, Frank, it's made to order. What do you two say?"

"I don't know what to say," Frank said as he looked over at Jennifer.

"Neither do I," Jennifer said.

"Whose phone number is this anyway, their hiring department?" inquired Frank.

"Their home," Kate said.

"The Summers' home?" Frank's shocked voice asked.

"That's right," Kate said.

"To call them at their home," Frank said nodding his head as he spoke, "I don't know if I would feel comfortable doing that, I mean it's their home."

"We'll call them as soon as we get a chance," Jennifer said, as she reached over and took the sheet of paper from Frank's hand.

"Don't you love it when your wife does stuff like that, Frank?" joked Henry. "It happens to me all of the time."

"Me too," Frank smiled. "Thank you, Kate, we'd appreciate the chance at a couple of jobs."

"Or even one," Jennifer added.

"It never hurts to try," Kate said.

"And that's what we're doing here today with Josh, thanks to both of you," Jennifer said.

"Kate, that was very nice of you to do that for our family," Frank added. "We both really could use the... thank you. Well, I think this calls for a sip of my coffee," Frank said as he reached for his cup.

"I could use one, too," Henry said as he took a drink from his cup as well.

The two couples made themselves as comfortable as they could knowing their wait would be sometime in the making. Another hour and a half passed slowly.

Frank looked up at the clock on the wall, not really looking at the time. There was a small pendulum swinging back and forth from the lower part of it in a fairly fast pace. He wondered to himself, how many hundreds of miles it had traveled in the room going nowhere. Mary laid tucked into his shoulder sleeping. As he looked at her he thought to himself, I know Santa's brother. He chuckled.

Still holding the cup of coffee in his hand, Frank set Mary down on the couch with his free hand. He stood up and stretched trying to get the kinks out of his body. His face gave out a large yawn. Seeing the movement, Henry found himself doing the same thing. Next it was Kate's turn, as she put her hand up to her face and yawned also.

"I once heard a yawn could travel around the world if there were enough people standing in line," joked Frank.

"I'll bet you're right," Henry said.

"It's really been a while, hasn't it?" Jennifer stated as she looked up at the wall clock.

"It always seems longer when you're the one waiting. I'll bet Josh is taking a nice little nap," Henry offered.

Frank sat back down. He turned to Jennifer, but before he could utter a word, the doctor walked in. He quickly rose to his feet as well as Jennifer and Kate. The doctor had their full attention.

"Josh tolerated the procedure very well. In fact, I think he'll be running around like any normal— excuse me, I didn't mean to use that word. He'll be running around just as any other kid his age once his recovery period has taken place. We feel very confident his surgery was a complete success."

"Thank you, Dr. Gray," Frank said as he held his hand out to him, shaking it hardily.

"I'm so relieved," Jennifer stated, as she stepped forward giving the doctor a hug. "Thank you so much."

Kate and Henry said nothing, but both of their faces presented everyone with large smiles.

"I knew he would be okay," offered Mary.

"Well, I'm glad you did," the doctor said.

"He told me," she said, as Mary pointed at Henry.

"Oh," was all the doctor said. "And who is he?"

"Santa's brother," Mary said shaking her head.

"It's a long story," Frank said.

"I'm sure it is, and I'd love to hear it someday. Now, your son is going to be in the hospital for a little while. We'll see to it he begins therapy almost immediately. There will, of course, be follow-up exams."

"Thank you again," Jennifer repeated.

"There is one thing I'd like to do… or I should say, "we" would like to do. I've been operating for quite a few years now on children's legs, feet and so forth as you both know. One night over dinner my wife, Delores, suggested that I do one thing, and I've followed her advice religiously ever since then."

The doctor reached into his pocket taking out a business card from it.

"If you'll take this card to the shoe store listed on the front of it, when Josh reaches that point in his therapy, he'll receive a brand new pair of tennis shoes of his choice. Don't be concerned about the price of it. Be sure also that it's his choice, not yours. It's kind of a birthday or Christmas gift my wife and I enjoy giving our younger patients."

"A Christmas gift," smiled Mary. She then turned and looked up at Henry. He couldn't help himself as he looked over at her and chuckled to himself.

"Will you thank your wife for us, too?" Frank said.

"That I will. Now, in the next day or so we'll have everything lined up with what you need to know concerning the therapy. Any questions? Good."

The physician turned towards the doorway. Jennifer stepped forward and hugged the doctor again. He smiled as he nodded his head slightly. Turning once again he walked out of the room.

"Well," Henry said, "Kate and I are so happy for the both of you, and Josh as well."

"It was a horrible mistake on my part to not have tried to get this done for Josh in the first place," Frank stated. "I'll apologize to him when I see him, but I need to do that to both of you now. I gave both of you a hard time when we first talked… and I'm sorry for my actions."

"That isn't necessary," Henry said.

"Yes, it is. Thanks to both of you, our son has a whole new life awaiting him."

Jennifer walked over and hugged Henry, then Kate.

"I have nothing but love in my heart for what you two have done for us," she said. "Thank you both so very much."

"You're welcome, Jennifer," Kate said, "but it wasn't the two of us alone. There were many people who reached into their pockets with their own hearts and donated to this cause."

"I wish I could thank everyone of them," Jennifer acknowledged to them.

"I have an idea," Kate said. "Jennifer, if you'll get a thank you card and sign it, I'll see to it that it's place by the register in Richard's Steak House. He worked very hard on this as well. If I may be so bold, two couples donated a couple of thousand dollars each for the operation. Would you mind getting two more cards for them?"

"What are their names?" she asked.

"That isn't going to matter to them one iota."

"How can I address to them?"

"Well," Kate said as she thought for a second or two. "Just put on the front of the envelope, 'Friends of Josh.'"

"I know just what to do," Jennifer said, her voice carrying an excitement in her words. "I'll write three letters and put one in each of the envelopes. They'll all be the same. I'll wait a few days before I do it. I want to find just the right cards. I'll enclose a picture of Josh in each one and have him sign the card, too. I also want to get a card for Dr. Gray and his wife."

"That's a wonderful idea," Kate said. As I said, don't mention any amounts that were given, I mean the two thousand dollars. The amount of money that was given by whomever really shouldn't matter at all. Perhaps I shouldn't have mentioned that fact in the first place, but I wanted you to know why I wanted the two additional cards."

"I understand."

"If you'll get them to me," Kate said, "I'll see they're delivered."

"Thanks, Kate, I will."

A nurse walked into the room carrying a clipboard. "Mr. and Mrs. Harrison."

"Yes," Frank said.

"Dr. Gray said you can go into recovery now to be with your son, Josh. He also said it was all right if you took the little girl in with you."

"Thank you," both Jennifer and Frank stated.

"Well, we'll hit the road," Henry said.

Frank walked over to Henry and embraced him, slapping him on the back gently as he did. Jennifer gave Kate a hug as well. Together they nodded their heads as they turned to follow the nurse to the recovery room. Frank reached down taking Mary's hand in his.

"Good-bye Santa's brother," Mary said as she turned to go with her new parents.

"Good-bye, Honey," Henry said.

After they left the room Kate turned to Henry. She reached over and took his hand in hers.

"They're a wonderful family, Henry," she uttered softly.

"Yes, they are, all four of them." He squeezed Kate's hand gently.

"As far as the adoption and Mary, we did the right thing, Henry."

"You're right as always," smiled Henry.

Blue Rose Petals

Acting as one they left the waiting room. Their hearts were filled with more cherished memories of a day they shared together with a wonderful couple and their children.

Kate sat at the kitchen table studying over one of Stella's recipes. Beside her laid a piece of paper, a pencil in her hand. Though they never were numerous in number, it was days like this Kate loved so much in her life. The sounds of an occasion bird's voice filtered through the window screen. Kate enjoyed the peaceful silence that surrounded her. She could write down any needed ingredients, figure out what to have as side dishes, and just generally absorb some quiet time to herself. The only real sound that met with any amount of consistency at all was the periodic chimes from the grandfather's clock in the living room sounding out its chorus. Kate was so accustomed to the striking of the clock's arm, even its hourly song was seldom heard by her anymore.

At one point, Kate looked up at the clock on the wall in the kitchen. She thought to herself, better get the mail. She walked the few steps to the mailbox and opened it. Inside was a small package, some bills, a few sale flyers and a card. She tucked them under her arm as she headed towards the back door. She placed the mail on the counter, then went to check on Emma Elizabeth.

Returning to the kitchen she picked up the card and package. She placed them onto the table before her. After taking a small sip of coffee she opened the card first. It was a thank you card containing a picture of Josh and a letter. She smiled.

Taking the two-page letter in hand she began reading it to herself. The words written by Jennifer to Henry and Kate were one of the most thoughtfully worded thank you letters she had ever seen or had occasion to read. It was to the point, which Kate adored. Every word scribed by her was heartfelt and carefully written. Kate knew much thought went in to each and every word she penned. Kate wiped her eyes as she continued reading the thank you. How touching it was to read, she thought.

At the bottom of the card under its printed verse were signed the words, "With Love and Thanks in our hearts, The Harrison Family." Josh, however, had his name written on the other side of the inner part of the card. Under the words, "Thank you for everything," which were handwritten by him, was his signature. Kate rubbed her hand over Josh's photograph before returning it to the envelope along with the letter.

Kate turned her attention next to the small package. Opening it she soon discovered three envelopes. She immediately knew these contained the thank yous for the Wilsons, Summers, and Richard. Kate understood she could deliver one to Edith and Frank, and that Henry would deliver Richard's card. That was no problem for her. Still, the Summers needed to receive theirs. What a wonderful opportunity to visit with Melissa, see the baby, and give the card to her parents. The thought of visiting them made her smile.

Picking up the phone, Kate made arrangements to stop by the Wilson home. She thought to herself, why not just stop at the restaurant as well. Kate made a call to Susan and Kenneth's home. Once she had everything in order, she picked up the thank you letter and began reading it again. Kate let out a deep breath. Such a beautifully written thank you, she thought to herself again. She next put it back together and stood up. Kate placed it on Henry's place setting. She was excited to picture him reading the note, and wanted to see the expression on his face. Kate could hardly wait.

Walking around the table, Kate placed the dishes and silverware in their places. Looking over her shoulder slightly, she took a peek at the clock. Henry would soon be home, she thought. Going to the oven, she pulled the large door down. A gush of heat attempted an escape from the chamber as Kate backed away from the door feeling its warmth on her face. The aroma of a freshly cooked brisket filled the room. Taking a couple of hot pads she pulled the metal rack from its interior. In a large metal roasting pan sat the darkened meat. On its top were golden brown onions, their edges slightly burned. Kate took her cooking baster and drew some liquid from off of the side of the meat. She then drizzled it over the brisket and onions. The timer went off, confirming her assumption the meat was done. Kate had learned from her private cooking lessons with Stella that timers do not always make for a meal well cooked. She took a fork and inserted it into the meat. It gently went into the brisket. Next she checked the meat with a meat thermometer. All was well.

"Honey, I'm home," was Henry's familiar greeting as he walked into the kitchen from the back door.

"Your timing is just about perfect," she replied.

"Here, let me help you get that meat out of the roaster. It's really big. Are we having company?"

"No. I've been in the mood for a brisket and when I bought it, the size of it was determined by my stomach's craving, not my mind."

"Good, because I love brisket."

"No kidding."

Henry took a couple of large metal forks Kate had bought for just such occasions and lifted the meat onto a waiting platter. He next bent over it slightly taking in a deep breath.

"We'll let the meat rest while I make the gravy," Kate said as she reached for some flour.

"Is there anything I can do?"

"No, not really."

"Good. That gives me some time to play with Emma Elizabeth."

Henry walked from the room in the direction of the child's bedroom. Within a minute or so Kate could hear Henry and Emma Elizabeth at the piano. The child was pounding her hands upon the keys.

"She sure loves the piano," Henry yelled over the loud banging sounds.

"So when does she start with her lessons?" she joked.

As if Henry had lifted Emma Elizabeth's hands from the keyboard the non-musical sounds stopped. For a moment or two there was complete silence. Then from the living room the sound of a single note being struck drifted through the air. Once again silence filled the house. Then the same key was struck again.

"Are you giving her piano lessons?" Kate inquired, already knowing the answer to her question.

"How did you guess?"

Kate smiled as she continued making the gravy.

Sitting at the table eating his favorite meal of brisket, mashed potatoes, gravy, green beans, and who knows what dessert would bring, made Henry a very content person. Kate could see that in his face, anyone could.

"Honey," Kate started out, "I've been thinking about something."

"This isn't anything that's going to spoil my meal; is it," he said with a chuckle.

"No, Honey. I've been thinking about Mary lately."

"I have, too," he confessed.

"Do you think our thoughts are running down the same set of tracks?" she asked.

"I'm sure they are. Tell me, what have you been thinking about?"

"It's Mary's burn mark."

Henry started laughing. He wasn't very quiet about it either. He couldn't stop himself.

"Henry, it's not funny at all."

"You're right, it's not funny at all. It's just that I've been thinking the very same thing as you for quite a while now. You want to see about having her burn mark addressed in some way."

Kate didn't answer him. He knew he was right.

"Am I right?"

"Yes, you are, Mr. Morgan," she answered.

"Wonderful. Now, how do we go about raising the money?"

"I don't think I can do another fundraiser like we did for Josh. I was thinking perhaps we could... we could foot the bill ourselves. I know it would probably cost a lot of money but——"

"Money has never been the issue with us, and it never will be." Henry knocked his hand on the kitchen's wooden kitchen table for luck. "Kate, we're still doing very well. I'm making more money than I ever have from my odd jobs," he joked.

"Do you think Jennifer and Frank would accept the money from us?" inquired Kate.

"No, I don't think they would. Perhaps we should talk to Pastor Phil and get his input on this. He and his wife always have good ideas."

"Do you mind if I talk to them tomorrow about this?" Kate inquired with an inquisitive expression on her face.

"I'd love you to run with our idea. You don't need any approval from me to make any decisions in this matter. Whatever you say is golden in my book."

"Thank you, Honey. I'll stop by and see the pastor tomorrow. That's another place I've got to go to now."

"What do you mean?"

"Well, I was going to stop at the restaurant and give Richard his."

"Richard what?"

"The card. Didn't you see the card we got? I left it on your placemat."

"Oh," Henry said, "I just put it on the cabinet there."

"Well, get it," Kate said strongly. She wanted to see him read it and observe his reactions. In fact, she didn't want to wait any longer.

Picking up the envelope Henry reached in and retrieved the card, letter, and picture from its interior. He then read the card to himself. Henry looked at Josh's picture and smiled. Next he unfolded the letter and began reading it. He made no comments whatsoever as he read it, which surprised Kate immensely. She could tell he found the letter touching, his expression was obvious along those lines. Henry next folded the letter back up and returned it to the envelope along with the picture and card.

"Well..." Kate said.

Henry let out a deep breath as he looked at Emma Elizabeth sitting next to him in her chair. He then looked at Kate.

"Mary's going to have an operation, and that's it!"

Kate smiled her approval.

"No matter what the cost?" Kate stated in a jokingly sarcastic voice, knowing already it didn't matter to either one of them.

"No matter what the cost. These two wonderful people deserve that much."

"Then I'll see to it," Kate said nodding her head.

"Thank you."

"Henry, would you take Richard's thank you card to him tomorrow, that will free up some time for me."

"I sure will. I want to see the expression on his face when he reads it."

"I wish I could be there to see it."

"I'll tell you all about it."

Kate and Henry looked across the table at each other and smiled. Neither one knew what the other was thinking. Had they known that, they would have laughed. Each was thinking the exact same thing, how very proud they were of the other.

The next day Kate had her missions to take care of. She would swing by the Wilson family first and give them the thank you. Placing Emma Elizabeth in the backseat carrier, she drove the short distance to their house. Walking up the sidewalk to the home, Edith was already waiting to welcome her at the door.

"This is such a pleasant surprise to see you both," Edith said smiling. "Your phone call was a welcomed ray of sunshine yesterday."

After getting comfortable, the appropriate talk about Emma Elizabeth having concluded," Edith asked what she could do for Kate.

"I'm here because of what you and Frank did."

"Oh," Edith said.

Kate reached into her purse and pulled one of the thank you cards out leaving one still remaining. She said nothing as she handed it to Edith. Edith didn't know what to think as she took the card in her hand. This was an unexpected thing to happen to her, it confused her a little. She knew it was a card, but for what reason she was receiving it left her mind blank.

As Edith opened the card the photograph of Josh fell to the floor. She reached down and picked it up. As she glanced at the image in the photo, it really meant nothing to her. Edith didn't recognize the youngster whatsoever. She set the card and photo down on the coffee table after reading it. Her mind was a blur as it attempted to put the puzzle pieces together, the card, the picture, the unread letter. Edith next unfolded the sheets of paper. She began reading it. Kate was very much aware of its content. She wanted to see how it affected Edith. Henry said nothing, and that surprised her. Now she waited to see what Edith's reaction to it would be.

After a short time, Edith got up and went into the kitchen area. She returned shortly and sat back down on the sofa. The only difference Kate could glean differently in her reappearance was the box of tissues she carried in her hand. Edith finished the letter, stopping occasionally to wipe her eyes. When she was done Edith picked up the card and photograph. She placed all three items up to her chest. Edith held them there for some time. Kate thought this movement to be one of endearment.

"Do you know how much this letter means to me?" Edith asked, her eyes still moist.

"I think I have some idea of what you're talking about," Kate acknowledged. She knew how she felt inside when she read hers.

"Kate, whatever feelings you think this letter means to me, it's ten times that."

Kate smiled at Edith.

"This is without a doubt the most precious thank you I have ever seen or read in my entire life. It's so warm, it's…"

Edith reached again for her tissues.

"Just so you know, I have a thank you for Susan as well. Henry is giving one to Richard this morning. Henry and I also received one."

"Wonderful, just… just wonderful," Edith said.

Kate nodded her head.

"The operation was a success?"

"Yes, it was."

"Thank God."

"I would like to stay and visit a little longer, Edith, but I have several stops yet to make. Yours was the first in line today."

"I was not expecting to get any thank you for what we did, but those two words mean a lot to me in the end." Edith again wiped her eyes.

"I knew they were going to be sending the cards, I just didn't expect one for ourselves."

"Makes you feel good inside, doesn't it?"

"It sure does," Kate answered.

"Say hello to Susan for me. Oh, you are going to see her today; aren't you?"

"She's my third stop today."

"Good."

"Well, I better be on my way. Say hello to Frank for me."

"I will," Edith said. "Be sure to say hi to Henry."

"We will," Kate said, as she picked up Emma Elizabeth and made her way to the front door.

Soon the child and Kate were on their way to the next stop. One item could now be checked off on her unwritten note pad.

Knocking on the door to the pastor's office, Kate waited to hear if anyone answered.

She could hear some conversation emanating from inside the room.

"Come in, please," beckoned Pastor Phil's familiar voice.

Walking into the room, Kate was quick to notice Marsha, the pastor's wife standing behind the desk.

"Oh, you brought Emma Elizabeth with you," Marsha quickly stated. "Can I hold her, please?"

"Of course."

Marsha gently lifted the youngster up as she began to quickly cuddle Emma Elizabeth. She rocked slowly back and forth. For some unknown reason Marsha's voice changed completely within the span of a few seconds. She began speaking a language only a small child or baby could understand. Her voice began sounding very foreign in nature. Even the octave range of her words seemed to change.

"See what a child can do to my wife?" Pastor Phil stated. "First it's the cuddling, the language barrier that no one can understand, and then next comes the not wanting to release the youngster. Each act seems to follow the other instantly, and it's always the same."

"Oh, Philip," Marsha said. "she's just so adorable; aren't you, Emma Elizabeth. Yes, you are, you surely are."

Shaking his head slightly, Pastor Phil inquired of Kate what he could do for her. Kate simply handed him her own thank you note. She waited as he looked it over. Marsha moved in behind Phil's position at the desk and started reading the letter over his shoulder. As she read more, she turned and handed the child back to Kate. Marsha then quickly returned to her position behind Phil. She placed her hands on his shoulders, then bent down slightly to better see. As he set the letter down, Marsha picked it up, not quite finished with her portion of it. Pastor Phil took a deep breath before addressing Kate.

"Kate... if I could only write a sermon this delicately worded, as touching to the heart and as emotionally charged as this, I would consider myself to be an extremely gifted pastor. This thank you says so much even in the empty spaces between the words, it's unbelievable. I don't know what else to say."

"It's simply beautiful," Marsha said as she wiped her eyes with her finger. "These are really wonderful people."

"With your help, as well as a lot of others, there was a happy ending for all involved to enjoy."

Marsh nodded her head slight. "Isn't it incredible how everything worked out?"

"More importantly," Pastor Phil said, "what is it that you need from us concerning them?"

"Can I please have a glass of water?" Kate asked.

"Of course," Marsha said.

Kate took a drink from the glass. She then explained to them of Henry and her idea concerning Mary possibly getting her facial needs taken care. Kate said neither one of them knew exactly what could or could not be accomplished with the skills of a plastic surgeon, just that they wanted to try. She told them the cost would be completely paid for by them. Kate and Henry's concern was in getting the Harrisons to go along with their gift. They were, however, not to be told where the money came from. Kate made that very clear to both of them.

"Do you have any ideas on how we can handle this?" inquired Kate.

"How soon of a timetable are we talking about here," asked Pastor Phil.

"There is none."

"Good. This gives me the time I'll need to work on this. Of course, I'll want your input as usual, Marsha. She solves a lot of headaches for me, not that this is a headache, I mean —"

"She understands what you mean, Phil," Marsha said smiling.

Kate nodded her head.

"When we figure out how we'll be handling this, we'll let you know right away," Phil indicated as he looked over at his wife.

"Thank you. Now, I have another stop to make, so I better get going. I'll wait… Henry and I will wait for your call."

As Kate stood up she paused just for a moment.

"The letter I got, it really says it all; doesn't it?"

Pastor Phil nodded his head.

"It sure does," Marsha stated.

The drive through the countryside seemed more pleasant than usual. The bright sunlight striking the black and white Holsteins in the lush green fields seemed more like a painting than a real life observation. Even the white clouds appeared in a creamy fashion. Kate sang to the young child as they drove towards Susan's home. What a day to remember, she thought.

At one point Kate pulled into a roadside park. Holding Emma Elizabeth by the hand the two of them made their way down by a shallow creek and sat for a few minutes.

Kate pointed out various birds to her daughter as together they seemed to absorb the warmth the sun had to offer. Kate was sure the child understood the need for a short break, a time to refresh one's self. Soon they were once again on the road.

Parking the car in Susan's driveway, Kate and the baby were soon at the door. Before Susan even answered the door Kate's mind ran with thoughts of what Susan's reaction would be to the letter. Everyone seemed to deal with it in their own personal way, which she expected. The more she thought about it, the more she realized it didn't matter. After all, in reality it was just a thank you note. The fact that it carried more weight to it than one just signing their name at the bottom of it, should only matter to the recipient.

The door opened with Susan smiling.

"Come in, please come in, Kate. Oh, good, you brought the baby with you. Can I hold her, please?"

"Of course."

"How's my little baby-boo?" Susan said. "Did you have a good trip? You did. You're such a beautiful young lady, yes, you are."

Much to Kate's astonishment Susan began dancing around in small circles as she sang to the child. Kate also noticed the change in her voice. Just as Marsha had experienced, her voice also changed in octaves as she spoke to the youngster. At last they all made their way to the kitchen where Kate sat at the table enjoying a cold glass of lemonade.

"What did you need to see me about?" inquired Susan.

Kate did what had worked for her so well with everyone else, she just presented her with the thank you card and let it speak for itself. Susan looked at the photograph studying it over carefully. She didn't know who the child was in the picture. Unfolding the two page letter she began reading it. Once again, there were no comments made as Susan read the letter. When she was through, she folded up the letter and returned it to its envelope.

"Can I ask you a couple of questions, Kate?"

"Of course."

"This is the youngster who we donated to for the operation?"

"Yes, he is."

"And was the operation a success?"

"From what the doctor told us, yes."

"Wonderful. This thank you card and letter are from his parents?"

"Yes, it is," nodded Kate.

"They are the ones you asked about concerning a job?"

"Yes."

Susan nodded her head up and down slowly as she thought for a moment or two.

"The mother who wrote this letter has an exceptional command of the English language. In areas where she says nothing, all is said by the missing words. She implies everything through her words, and the very lack of them. I've never read anything so filled with compassion as this. I'm very much moved by the use of her simple and meaningful words. The combination of words, and how she uses them… they're just so wonderful."

"That's what I thought, too," Kate expressed.

"She has a job, where I don't know, but she's hired. This letter tells me more about her than any resume or interview could ever demonstrate. You say her husband is just like her?"

"Yes, he is," Kate said with a smile.

"Well, he's hired, too. I'll tell Kenneth not to even bother interviewing him. Maybe we'll interview them just so it looks good. From what you told me about him, and from what I see in this letter, we're getting two outstanding employees."

"I was hoping you would feel that way. Thank you," Kate said.

"No, thank you, Kate. I can hardly wait to show this thank you to Kenneth when he gets home. He hangs around the construction site watching every 2x4 that's put in. I think it does his mind well to keep busy. The fact that we're seeing our building rising again does us all good, especially him. He tells me about everything that's going on during our evening meals. His voice even carries an excitement to it.

Speaking of the building, are you and Henry still going to be able to redo the break room when it comes to that point in the construction?"

"It will be a little harder than we thought, with travel and all. Henry stayed with Greg when we worked on it the last time, and I stayed here. Of course, we have the little one now."

"Number one, and I got this numbering system of items from Melissa," chuckled Susan. "Number one, both of you are staying here, no question about it. Number two, I was a mother once, and I'm a great babysitter. Number three, you will be paid, not Henry. Now, don't discuss any payments with Henry on this. Remember how he didn't want to charge us the full rate because we were friends."

"I remember that well."

"Then we almost had to force him to take the money. Thank goodness you were there to accept the check. Now, where was I. Oh, number four, or I should say five. We love all of you just as much as family, therefore, meals are included in your stay. Any questions?"

"Stella, Henry's sort of brother's wife — wait that didn't come out right. Anyway, I've learned quite a bit about cooking and I was wondering if you'd mind if I cooked a few meals while we're here."

"You won't hear any arguments from me. Maybe I'll learn some cooking secrets from you."

"Or me from you," chuckled Kate.

"So it's all settled. You're doing the break room, you'll be staying with us. Your favorite babysitter is looking forward to it, and you'll be treating us with a meal or two."

"I guess so," Kate said smiling.

"Oh, and you and I will deal with any bills concerning the break room project between us. Is that okay?"

"Yes. There is something else, however, I should mention."

"And what's that, Kate?"

"Henry has come up with a few new ideas he wants to implement if you don't mind."

"After what you two did in that room the last time, I can hardly wait to see where this all takes us. You and Henry do whatever you want, after all, I'd love to be surprised."

"Okay."

"Now that we've gotten all of the hard stuff out of the way, let me hold Emma Elizabeth again."

Kate smiled as she handed Emma Elizabeth in the direction of Susan's waiting arm.

On the way home a thought struck Kate. It would soon be dinnertime and she really didn't feel like cooking. Why not stop at Richard's Steak House and have dinner with Henry and the child. Not only wouldn't she have to cook, it was an opportunity to see if Richard was there, thus being able to find out what he thought of his thank you letter.

Pulling into the parking lot, Kate smiled as she saw Henry's old faithful vehicle sitting in its own personal parking spot. Sometime ago, Henry and Kate had purchased a new car for her personal use. Henry didn't want to take the chance she might be caught with a vehicle that had a mind of its own when it came to starting. No wife of his would be left standing on the side of the road. Of course, when that would occasionally happen with his old faithful car, it was something they never discussed, especially by Henry.

As Kate walked in to the restaurant, it was clear to see finding a seat would be a big problem. Fortunately, when your husband is half owner in any establishment, a table magically appears. Music being played through the sound system was soft in nature. A few couples slowly moved around the dance floor. Bowls of candles lit each table in the darkened room. Kate thought it carried a romantic flavor to the scene. It wasn't very long before Henry walked up to the table. He was extremely pleased to see not only Kate, but his daughter as well.

"Henry, did you give the thank you to Richard?"

He nodded his head.

"What did he say?"

"He didn't read it. We were too busy with other paperwork that needed to be discussed and completed."

Kate shook her head back and forth, her face reflecting disappointment. Henry knew he would have to check with Richard before they left. He was sure they weren't leaving the restaurant until Kate's curiosity was satisfied.

Soon the two were enjoying one of the special entrees being offered on the menu. Henry watched Kate as she would take a bite from the meal, run it around on the inside of her mouth, chew slowly and then swallow it. Her actions reminded him of a person checking over a bottle of rare wine, smelling the cork, taking a small sip before agreeing to the selection.

"What are you doing?" he asked.

"It's something I've picked up from Stella. If you take your time to taste the food, sometimes you're able to pick out the spices that were used. She's really gifted at that. Henry, do you think some day I can come close to her level of cooking and baking?"

"You have one of the best teachers along that line that I know of. Your meals have come a long way. I don't mean they were bad... they're just different now. The flavors are more enhanced. They are different, more... not really different, I mean your meals —"

Kate started laughing. Henry had a way with words, but there were those times when they seemed to trip over each other on the way to his lips.

"I spoke with Susan about the break room."

"What did she have to say?"

Kate told Henry about Susan's desire to babysit Emma Elizabeth while they worked on the project. She alluded to the fact that they could stay with them during the construction. Kate was sure, however, not to mention anything about the cost or economics of the job. She also indicated to him that he was more than welcome to incorporate any changes his heart desired.

When Kate spoke of making a few meals at the Summers' home, her voice became extremely excited. She explained to Henry how she was going to be learning the proper way of cooking Italian dishes by Susan. Henry smiled as she talked, after all, he had tasted Susan's food offerings before, and they were simply out of this world. If she learns how to do that from Susan, he thought, nothing else concerning the job really mattered. His taste buds were in for a treat.

At one point Henry nodded to Kate indicating for her to look in a certain direction. Walking out of the hallway to the office, Richard seemed to have only one thought on his mind as he made his way directly to the sound system next to the dance floor. He reached up and turned the music off. It was then that Kate and Henry noticed he had the card in his other hand. Richard stepped in front of the microphone.

"I'll have the music back on in just a minute or two. Please bare with me for just a few minutes."

The five couples on the dance floor went to their tables. Even the waitresses stopped to see what was happening. Richard cleared his throat before he began to speak.

"Sometime ago my partner and very good friend, Henry, proposed an idea he and his wife, Kate, were working on. It was to raise money for a youngster so that he could have an operation to correct his leg ailment. I'm sure you all remember that."

There was some applause from the customers.

"Well, I'm happy to announce that his operation not only is over, it was a complete and utter success."

Now the applause was loud, a few men putting their hands to their lips and whistled loudly.

"The three of us, Kate, Henry, and myself want to thank you for your generosity. I would also like to take this opportunity to thank our waitresses and kitchen staff for pitching in. It may be of interest to all of you to know that they donated their time and tips to help see the… the… that his healing could come about."

Richard set the papers down on a stool. He began applauding the employees. Henry quickly got to his feet, Kate standing beside of him as they, too, applauded the workers. Soon everyone was standing offering their thanks to them as well. Once it had quieted down, Richard reached over and picked up the paperwork.

"Today I received a thank you card from the mother of that young boy. I haven't read it yet, but I would like to read it to everyone here... if I may. Henry... Kate... will you join me up here, please. Both of you were very instrumental in this, and such a huge and important part of it. I would like you both up here with me at my side."

As Kate reached for Emma Elizabeth a woman Kate knew from the hospital her grandfather worked at, indicated she'd keep a watchful eye over her. Kate nodded her head as she and Henry made their way up to the dance floor area.

Richard opened the card. As he did, as had happened before, the photograph of Josh fell to the floor. Henry quickly reached down and retrieved it. He handed it to Richard. Taking the photograph in his hand Richard studied it over. He then held it high in the air attempting to show it to everyone seated there. This, of course, was a futile gesture since the size of the photo was not that large for people any distance away to see.

"This must be a picture of the young man," Richard suggested to everyone with a smile.

There was a small amount of applause. Richard handed the photograph back to Henry.

"I see there's a handwritten letter in here also. I guess the logical thing to do is to read it. So let's see what she has to say to all of us."

The room became very quiet, all wanting to hear what the woman had written. A thank you is just a thank you, most individuals thought. Still, they were curious to hear what words of thanks she had to offer. Richard stepped a little closer to the microphone as he began to read the letter. Within a few sentences having been uttered by him, Richard found it difficult to continue. He reached up and wiped his eyes with his fingertips. Some women did the same thing. It was clear to all, the words carried strong emotions. The thoughts were crafted in a tenderness that reached deeply into the hearts and souls of those listening. As Richard tried to continue, he had to stop on several occasions.

At that point, Henry reached over and placed his hand on Richard's shoulder. This simple act alone made it even more difficult for Richard to go on. Though Henry had read his own copy of the thank you letter, hearing the words out loud brought a whole new dimension to his thoughts.

As Richard turned to the second page he found he could no longer speak. His throat was not dry which would hinder him in speaking, however, his eyes were much too damp to continue. At last his hand dropped to his side with the letter clutched in it. He was unable to go on. Seeing the distress on his face, Kate reached over and took the letter from his hand. She began to read where he had left off.

Many women, as well as some men wiped their own eyes as Kate spoke. Perhaps it was the fact the letter was written by a female, that the sound of a woman's voice seemed to make it even more heartfelt. Either way, her voice was bringing the words of the letter to life in a new and precious way. When she finally spoke the last sentence, she reached up and wiped her own eyes as well.

There was no applause offered, only the silence of people who understood the tragedy this woman's family had faced, and the love she offered to everyone for their help. It was all contained in this simply handwritten thank you.

After a moment or two, Richard took a few steps forward from his position by Henry and Kate. He stood there quietly for a few seconds. Kate stepped forward and placed her hand on his arm as she smiled slightly up at him.

"For those of you who would like to see this thank you," Richard said, "and the picture of young Josh, I'll place it up by the register so that it's available for you. Thank you all for your generosity."

Mary

Jennifer moved as quickly as she could to the front door of her home. The knocking had now reached six. She had been down in the basement removing clothes from the dryer. It took her sometime to get up the steps to answer the rapping on the front wooden door. Jennifer was not expecting anyone to be calling. Her hope was that it wasn't some sales person wanting her to buy something she wasn't interested in. She opened the door to find a dignified man and attractive woman standing beside him on the porch.

"Mrs. Harrison, my name is Pastor Phil, and this is my wife, Marsha. Is your husband, Frank, home?"

Jennifer nodded her head.

"We'd like to take a moment of your time to speak with you both, if we may. We're not here asking for any money, or to join our church. We'd appreciate it if you and your husband could give us a minute of your time if at all possible."

"My husband is out back. Please come in."

After calling out for her husband from the kitchen window, Jennifer invited them to have a seat and to make themselves comfortable. Frank soon joined them. The Harrisons looked at each other waiting for the silence to be broken. Pastor Phil looked at them knowing full well neither one of them had any inkling as to why he and his wife were there.

"Is your son, Josh, home?" Phil asked.

"No, he's not here right now," answered Frank.

"That's too bad, we were hoping to meet him. We heard the operation on his leg was successful. I know it's been some time now since then, but how is he doing?"

"In the time it's been since the operation," Frank said, "his leg has improved beyond belief. He's talking about trying out for a baseball team."

"I think that's because he works so hard at his exercises," offered Jennifer. "He's a gutsy little guy, I will say that."

Frank nodded his head in a definite affirming fashion to his wife's comments.

As Jennifer spoke, a young girl walked into the room. She wore a pair of jeans along with a flowered blouse. Her hair reflected a couple of braids in the back. Her tennis shoes were somewhat worn, as though they had traveled many miles in fun-filled quests. She looked like any typical child for her age. The only thing different about her was a burn mark that marred her cheek. Pastor Phil was somewhat surprised by its size. That fact alone brought a small smile to his lips. He thought it would have been much larger by the description he had received from Henry. Perhaps in Henry's mind it was bigger. He imagined that was due to Henry's own scar. Pastor Phil surmised a disfigurement of any kind on the owner's face or body would appear much larger to them. Perhaps scars on other individuals would naturally look that way to them.

"This is our daughter, Mary," Jennifer was quick to say.

"It's so nice to meet you," Marsha stated.

"Me, too," Mary answered.

"If you wouldn't mind, Mr. and Mrs. Harrison, I was wondering if we could speak privately," Phil said. "I do apologize for showing up at your front door unannounced. Our discussion won't take too long. I know you don't know why we're here, but you'll both understand in a minute or two."

"Why don't you go outside and play in the backyard, Mary. We'll be having dinner in a little while. I'll call you when we're ready," Jennifer said.

"Okay, Mommy."

Mary turned and went through the kitchen, and then out the door leading to the back yard.

Pastor Phil looked at Marsha, then back at the Harrisons. He then began to address Frank and Jennifer concerning their daughter. Taking a little deeper breath than he usually did before discussing matters with various people, he began expressing the opportunity being offered to them and their daughter. He explained how he found it best when dealing with individuals to just take the straightest route forward to any subject matter that was being dealt with. This had worked for him many times in the past. Pastor Phil spoke of funds being made available to them for an operation to, perhaps, repair her cheek. He went on to inform them that if they would agree to it, a consultation with a plastic surgeon could be arranged. It was their hope that they could possibly explore various options together. At least this way they would have some idea what possibilities were even available.

At one point, Marsha expressed to the Harrisons that there would be no cost to them whatsoever. She explained monies were ample to pay for the procedure. Marsha repeated that to them on more than one occasion. It was her hope that that fact alone would help persuade them in this proposition.

Frank said nothing as he listened, his wife sitting at his side. She reached over and took his hand in hers. The silence in the room was very evident to all four of them. Still, the Harrisons said nothing as they ran his offer through their minds.

"It's Pastor Phil; right?" inquired Frank.

"Yes, it is."

"Where are you two from, if I may ask?"

"We're from Creek Side, a little drive from here, but a pretty one to take."

Frank looked over at Jennifer. He could see in her eyes and facial expression, she was thinking the same thoughts he had running through his own.

"Exactly who is the person or persons offering this gift to us?"

"Well," Phil said, "I'd rather not say. They would prefer to remain anonymous."

"Is it a group of individuals; you did say they?"

"Well, no. I guess I can tell you that much."

"You did say you were from Creek Side?" Frank asked again as if confirming something in his mind.

"Yes, we are," nodded Pastor Phil.

As Frank asked the questions, he could feel the grip on his hand by Jennifer becoming tighter with every reply the pastor made. He turned and looked at his wife. She had a small but very evident smile across her lips. She nodded slightly at him. Frank returned her smile as he nodded his head as well.

"Pastor," Frank began, "first I'd like to thank you and your wife for coming here today with this truly unbelievable gift for our family, especially Mary." He looked at Jennifer once again, her head still nodding slowly up and down. "I almost once made the fatal mistake of not holding my hand out, accepting money, and the chance to make my son's leg whole. When you consider where he is today, I was wrong. I was a stubborn fool then. Thank God I was cured of that. We listened to some very kind and understanding people who changed my thinking on —"

"Our thinking," interrupted Jennifer.

"Our thoughts along that line," continued Frank. "If the funds are available, as you say they are, we would be happy to give Mary the opportunity to have her cheek mended, if at all possible."

"What can be done is a mystery right now," Phil said, "but we'll know better once we cross that bridge."

"Thank you both so much for... for everything," Jennifer said.

"My wife and your wife can get together," Phil was quick to say. "If it's okay with you, they can make any arrangements. I've always found when it comes to details, women are better left in charge. I'm sure they will be able to work very well together."

"Before we offer you some refreshments," Frank said, "I do want to make sure you do something for us, if you wouldn't mind doing that, of course. I apologize in the way I said that, it was kind of on the blunt side."

"That's all right," Phil said.

"Will you thank Henry and Kate for this?"

"Pardon me?" Phil said.

"Our son needed an operation. It was Henry and Kate that saw to it the money was raised to have that accomplished. They even sat next to us as the procedure was taking place.

When Mary first saw Henry at the hospital she thought he was Santa. Apparently he played Santa in some Christmas party your church sponsored for children. My wife and I couldn't help but see the love he possessed for her. I think... I know Mary and I are growing closer every day in our love for each other. Maybe Henry helped that day, I don't know. Still, I'd like to think that he helped me out in that area, as well as Kate and others.

Kate even addressed some issues we had concerning money problems. We were... are very appreciative for her concerns, let alone helping us out along that line.

So when you said you're from Creek Side, you may as well have said the money was from Henry and Kate. They're the only ones we know from that town. In every way they've touched our lives; it's been unbelievable. You tell them we're more than happy to see to it Mary has the operation. In fact, I'll call them myself as soon as you leave."

"Please don't do that," Phil said in a strong sounding voice.

"No, no, no, don't do that," Marsha said at almost the same time, her voice almost frantic.

"The last thing either one of them want to hear are words of thanks," Phil said. "If they had wanted that, I'm sure I would have come here with other words concerning the paying of any operation. Accept it graciously in the manner it is intended to be given. When I convey to them you're willing to have Mary see a plastic surgeon, that will be thanks enough. I'm very sure of that in my heart."

Marsha shook her head slowly up and down.

Jennifer and Frank also nodded their heads in agreement with his words. After all, Jennifer thought, pastors are supposed to know about such things as a thank you and so forth.

Time was not wasted between the two women as they made arrangements for Mary's appointment. Numerous phone calls were exchanged as well as a few appointments being made and kept. This undertaking was more than either Marsha or Phil realized when they first spoke with the Harrison family. They both not only became attached to the parents and Mary, but Josh soon played a large part in their hearts also. The one thing that bothered the women so much was due to the fact that this was not going to be a one-time operation. There would be a few more possible procedures that would have to be endured not only by Mary, but by the family as a whole. It was a difficult time for all to go through.

As time passed, the remnants of the burn began to fade away. It would never be gone completely, they all understood that very well. The surgeon was pleased with his work. Ninety- five to ninety-eight percent corrected is always a good number to express. However, what a difference her face revealed with each month that came and went. While Henry and Kate stayed away from it all, Pastor Phil and his wife were sure to see that photos of the family were shared with them. Marsha would also take a few candid close-up photographs of Mary. Henry and Kate loved seeing them. While the expense of their gift was never discussed by anyone, the Morgans thought it to be a good use of their resources. In their minds, money was the means to bring forth smiles where there once were tears.

New Beginning

It was the beginning of a new day for everyone. This day was much like any other for most people. It was another week of trying to make a living. While individuals dressed, ate breakfast, in general prepared for a normal day at work, for others it held a totally different meaning for them. This was the special day they all looked forward to. The employees would be opening the store to a long awaited grand opening. The front page of the newspaper declared that loudly with a photograph of the building and long article. The Summers Family Store would soon be back in business.

When the date for the grand opening had first been announced, many store workers circled it on their calendars. It was a day to be celebrated, a time to be cherished. This lone Monday morning, among many others, was one none of the employees would ever forget. The same was true on the night of the fire. Now, new memories would be cultivated, the sad ones could be let go. Like smoke in a strong breeze on a day long gone, the ugly recollections they had lived through were now fleeting memories.

No one knew that better than Susan and Kenneth. They were up and dressed well over an hour before their alarm clocks would sound loudly begging to be heard. Sitting in the kitchen drinking their coffee, they would chuckle, then laugh. Susan's voice would giggle like a youngster awaiting an expected gift. She was excited beyond belief. Though Kenneth was subdued with his inner feelings, Susan knew he was just as thrilled as her.

It had been a long, hard, and expensive struggle for them to endure. There were happy days when the sound of laughter was near to everyone's ears. Still, occasionally a sigh of depression could be heard from the other. They did their best to keep their words positive at all times, even cheerful. Sorrow doesn't like to share company with a smiling face, they both understood that strongly. When delays struck, materials not arriving on time, they learned to live with their disappointment. Eventually everything worked itself out. Those days were now gone. They would be remembered, but released from their memories as soon as possible. Now, was the time to enjoy the new building with their family members close by. It was, after all, a new beginning for all to embrace. This wasn't a day of work the employees were going to, it was a true celebration with their fellow workers, the family together once again.

Standing outside of the back entrance to the store, employees gathered waiting to go inside. They all looked forward to beginning their various jobs once again. Susan and Kenneth stood together on a porch. Soon more and more employees formed a large group. Over top of the door a sign had been erected, or at least what appeared to be one. It was covered with a large plastic tarp. At one corner a rope had been attached.

    Susan shouted out as loud as she could to everyone. "I need a count down from every one of you." She yelled out again with all of her might. "Ten, nine, eight..." The sound of the crowd was loud to hear as they all joined her. With the final number being declared, Susan yanked the rope as hard as she could. Nothing happened. Oh no, she thought. Someone in the back of the group yelled out, "Ten, nine, eight..." Everyone joined in again counting as they laughed. Once again Susan grasped the rope even tighter and pulled it with all of her strength. Nothing happened again. The crowd began cheering, having fun with what was occurring. Others felt sorry for Susan at the same time. Very frustrated Susan bent down and grabbed the end of the long rope. She began wadding up the rope into a ball.

As it grew in size, Kenneth chuckled to himself. He had not seen his wife this embarrassed or determined in his whole life. Finally, it was about the size of a volleyball. With all of her might, she threw it up at the sign trying to get even with it. She missed it completely. As the rope came down in a small jerk, the tarp was released and fluttered to the ground. The crowd went nuts as they read what had been hidden behind the covering. In large block letters were the words, "Welcome Home."

Not one employee entered the store that day without thanking the Summers personally with a quick hug or a handshake. Two people spent a little more time thanking Susan and Kenneth than the rest. They were Frank and Jennifer Harrison. Both were grateful to have new jobs. Now they would have two incomes that were reliable. They could move forward knowing financially there was stability as part of their lives. It was a heavy burden lifted from their shoulders, thanks to the Summers and Kate.

After the last employee passed by, Susan shook her head and said in a disgusted voice, "Dumb rope." Kenneth laughed as he put his arm around her. "You'll laugh about this someday," he said smiling as they entered the store together.
    "You'll be sure to remind me of it, I'm very sure of that," she said.
    "Maybe once or twice a day," he chuckled.

The fiasco with the rope was only one of many memories that awaited everyone inside that day. At each cash register was a large bouquet of long stem red roses. Baby's breath was tucked in between the fresh flowers. A huge red bow was wrapped around the container. The card on each one indicated the same thoughts, "Best wishes on your reopening." They were all sent from Robert and Terry Caldwell. Terry knew of Melissa's love for red roses, something she heard about and observed many times over. Terry, who loved roses as well wanted them to be included in this special day for Melissa and the employees.

Melissa and Greg found her mother and dad as they walked around the first floor. When they were close enough, each wrapped their arms around the other. Kenneth and Greg smiled.
    "Your long wait is over," Greg said.
    Kenneth looked slowly around the room observing the large amount of customers in the store. "I think this day will forever be etched in my mind," Kenneth said nodding his head ever so slowly.

"Did you two happen to see Henry, Kate and Emma Elizabeth by the main entrance?" Melissa inquired.

"Oh, they're here?" Susan's surprised voice said.

"Come with me, you've got to see this," Melissa said. Everyone followed her as she led the way in a somewhat hurried fashion. Approximately twenty feet from the outer entrance, they all stopped. They could see the Morgans welcoming everyone as they entered the store. Every adult woman was handed an article by them. Looking a little closer each could observe what it was, a CD. They knew immediately what was transpiring. The three of them were giving a welcoming gift to each woman that entered the store. It was a collection of love songs Henry had recorded sometime earlier.

"We shouldn't disturb them now," Susan said as she looked at Greg and Melissa, "but don't you dare let them leave without talking to us first."

"We won't, Mom."

"Now I have something special I want to show the both of you," smiled Kenneth. "It's this way. He turned and started towards the elevators. Because of the added floor and their dealings with Fred, the Summers had additional elevators added in the construction process. Altogether, there were three. They were in different sections of the store allowing the customers easy access to their shopping desires. A few escalators were also put into place.

Pushing a button sent the elevator up two floors. Getting off at the third floor, Kenneth instructed Greg and Melissa to follow them. Susan led the way as they walked through the maze of customers shopping. Reaching a single door a sign declared, "Private, Employees Only," in black letters on a chrome piece of metal. The Summers stopped.

"Now, you two don't know what's behind this door," Susan said smiling. "We've kept this a secret from you for a reason. Walk in and take a look around." Susan stepped to the side as Melissa reached for the handle. Turning it, she walked into the room followed by Greg. Melissa put her hands to her face, completely astonished by what she saw. It was the new break room. The room was much larger than the other one. Her eyes slowly walked around the room not wanting to miss anything.

Over on a wall was the exact duplicate of the picture she had picked out years before. It was a large photograph of a black baby grand piano with a single rose laying across the ivory keys. Red rose petals were scattered about. The photo alone brought back the memories of Henry playing a baby grand at the Christmas program the night she first met him. The flower represented the roses Greg gave her on their first date the following morning. How precious it was for her to see it hanging on the wall in the new break room. On the other walls, various pictures had been selected by Susan to give the room a relaxing atmosphere.

One particular photograph was that of a lone tree standing on a small hill. It stood tall and proud. There was a sunset behind the branches and trunk bringing the tree's beauty forth to enjoy. In the bottom right-hand side on the glass, a small drawing was etched. It was a little twig consisting of six leaves. Lapping over and around the leaves were three black olives. Just below the olives were the initials, "O.T." Susan wondered how long it would take her husband to realize what the picture really meant. To Susan it represented her husband's trading skills, using black olives as his main tool of barter. The letters were to represent Kenneth's nickname, "Olive Tree."

Melissa continued looking around the room, not daring to move deeper into it. She just stood there motionless, not wanting to miss even the smallest item. There were many things much the same from the last one, others completely different. The oak cabinets, rich marble counter tops, sink faucets; all were very much the same. The crown molding was white, not oak as before. The tables and chairs, of course, were new as well as the appliances. Yet, somehow it was richer in appearance.

Looking up Melissa realized it was the ceiling that decorated the room. It was not flat at all; it was totally different. Henry and Kate had completely done the ceiling in a tray effect. It almost appeared as a single step downward within a few feet from the walls. From the edge of the ceiling indentation, recessed lights gave a soft glow to the room's interior. Other lights were available to be turned on should more light be needed. It was inviting, it was comforting, it was captivating to the eye.

In the middle of the room, inlayed into the floor in a circular fashion were the words, "Together We Are Family." Within the circle of words were four red hearts representing Susan and Kenneth, along with Melissa and Greg.

As Melissa slowly walked into the room, she noticed at the far end, a wall exhibiting a large empty space. It seemed to need something to fill the bareness of the area.

"Why isn't there anything in that space," Melissa inquired, "it looks like it needs something to be hung there."

"That's where the sign that says, "Welcome Home" is going to be put up shortly," Kenneth said.

"I hope they don't use that dumb rope to hang it," Susan said, shaking her head in disgust.

"No, they won't, Honey," Kenneth stated as he chuckled to himself.

"Now, we're all going to move onto another area not everyone has seen," Susan said. "Follow me."

Once again the three individuals followed behind Susan as she led them to the elevator once more. Melissa had a great desire to ask her mother where they were going, but she also loved a surprise. She kept her mouth silent as they got off at the top floor to the building. A fairly large receptionist area was the first thing they observed. There were a few chairs along with a coffee table in the middle of them. A door on the left side of the room read, "Caldwell Advertising." On the other side of the secretary, another door depicted the words, "Summers' Family Store."

"We have a receptionist now?" Melissa said.

"Actually she'll handle both businesses for now," Susan stated.

"Hello, my name is Ellen," said the woman in her middle to late forties. "Mr. Wilson, this must be your wife, Melissa, and her parents, I'm sure."

"You're absolute right," Greg said. "How is your first day of work going?"

"Very well," she answered.

Greg smiled as he opened the door leading into the Caldwell section of the upper floor. They followed him as Melissa pointed out a few different things they had helped with. It was, however, the Caldwells who did the majority of the layout for the business. With their years of knowledge, Greg and Melissa realized it was the right thing to do. This was undoubtedly one decision neither one of them would regret.

As they entered Greg and Melissa's private office area, Susan and Kenneth chuckled seeing two desks abutting each other. The view out the window was spectacular to behold. The trees were lush in color, the river twisting and turning. Off some distance away the beginning of small mountains could be observed. It was a beautiful view.
"It's very nice," Susan said as she walked up to the window and gazed out.
"Thanks, Mom," Melissa said as she looked at her.
"It's a little different of a layout than I would have expected with two desks in the room, but it is very nice as your mother said," Kenneth added.
"Thanks, Dad."

The one thing Greg liked so much with Robert and Terry's layout was that each office had a good view to enjoy. Some of the ad employees marveled at how the new working area was made to order. Having a large conference room, there was plenty of space to spread out and be comfortable in during their weekly scheduled meetings. Every employee was assigned their own private office now; it was perfect. Greg could see where the Caldwell fingerprints were all over the design of the offices. He knew he couldn't have done a better job in setting it up. Robert and Terry took advantage of every space available, putting it to its very best use and more.

After a short tour of the offices, Greg being sure to introduce everyone as they went by, Susan made a short announcement to all of them.
"Be sure to take advantage of your family discount in the store, and remember this, the break room is always available for your use as well."

"Don't forget to bring any trading items you may have with you, too," added Kenneth.

The employees knew full well what Kenneth's statement referred to. They were informed by Greg, along with Melissa, of that very fact on more than one occasion.

"I would like to take a look at the roof now," smiled Susan.

What those words meant was very important to Melissa and Greg. They could see the finished product Susan and Kenneth had so carefully worked on with the construction crew. On the roof was a covered section, which resembled an outdoor restaurant of sorts. There were tables of various sizes with large umbrellas protecting them. One could easily imagine sitting there on warm summer days eating their lunch. If rain threatened, a covered area hindered anyone from getting wet.

When fireworks would fill the sky on holidays, the roof would afford a spectacular viewing point. A railing with metal netting protected anyone from possibly getting too close to the edge. It was an ideal protection should a child be accompanying anyone who took advantage of the area.

The one thing Susan and her husband wanted included was a private stairway. The fact for that was simple. Any employee could get to the roof without disturbing the receptionist.

"What's that?" Greg asked.

"Oh, that came from the Caldwells," Susan said.

Over by the railing was a matching set of high-powered binoculars. In front of each sat a small metal stand so if a child wanted to use them, their shorter height would be easily accommodated. The binoculars faced the park area of the city. Both could, however, be moved in almost any direction. It would be an ideal spot to enjoy looking around the countryside. Greg could visualize the Caldwells, along with their grandchildren, making use of this area. He enjoyed that thought very much as he visualized it in his mind.

It now became obvious that the next step was to see the Summers' portion of the new construction. A brass plate with the words, "Mr. Sheppard, Store

Security," led them through the door to see Ted. He immediately stood up welcoming them. The office was very much in keeping with the theme of his title. A large leather sofa was up against one of the walls. Matching leather chairs sat before his large ornate walnut desk. A few photographs and awards hung above a large matching walnut cabinet. On top of it were many more awards along with plaques for various achievements. However, it was very cluttered with too many items.

"I love the furniture you picked out," Susan was quick to state. "However, I do have a problem. You have too many awards and plaques. You can expect someone from maintenance to be contacting you shortly to hang the other plaques. Also, I want you to pick out some additional shelving for all of these wonderful items. They need to be exhibited with the honor they deserve, and for everyone who comes in here to see. They deserve that... as well as you."

"Thank you, I will," smiled Ted.

"Well, it's onto Fred's office now," Susan said.

Fred's office was completely different in its appearance. It was more modern and had a taste of its own. Melissa loved it and was quick to tell him so. Bright colors were everywhere. Fred explained his daughters and wife helped him to pick out the room's decor. They had selected much the same furniture as Ted had, a couch, desk and chairs. There was also a cabinet adjacent to the wall. Fred said the bright colors were something his kids liked. Inside himself he liked the fact they were bright, like the days that lay ahead of them.

Leaning up against the wooden cabinet were his old crutches. On top of the cabinet was a small package covered in a blue clothe. A sign was taped to its front. The words, "Do Not Touch!" were evident to read.

"Why are your crutches here?" inquired Greg. "I thought you would have thrown them away quite some time ago."

Fred took a deep breath. "They're a reminder to me to never take anything for granted."

No one said anything; they just absorbed his words as they looked at them.

"Well, Fred, what you just alluded to very much fits in with your gift from me," Susan said smiling.

"What gift?" he asked.

255

Susan walked over to the cabinet. She took the little sign off of the covering as she placed her hand underneath the cloth. Susan then carried it over to Fred.

"I hope this will help remind you of what you just said," Susan stated. "I know this item did that for me when I first looked at it." Susan placed it on his desk.

Fred carefully removed the covering. He stood there silently as he nodded his head slowly up and down comprehending what lay before him on the desktop.

"Thank you very much, Susan," he said softly. She smiled as she reached out to him. He placed his arms around her as she returned his hug.

Kenneth, Melissa, and Greg attempted to see what was on the desk behind them. Viewing it made no sense to them whatsoever. The object was only about an inch tall by three to four inches in width. It was completely distorted in shape. There was a bluish black color to a small part of its top. It appeared to have been burned by extreme heat. What it was couldn't readily be identified by anyone else.

"What is it, Mom?" asked Melissa.

"Sometime ago this was given to me by one of the construction workers when they started tearing down the building. It's a piece of history between Fred and me," she chuckled. "This is what remains of a container Fred had in his office that he put money into when he called me Mrs. Summers. It's melted now, deformed beyond imagination. This is all that remains of it. If you look at it you can even see the coins that are melted together. Those coins were put in there every time he called me Mrs. Summers."

"Unbelievable," Kenneth said.

Fred smiled as he said, "Thank you again, Mrs. Summers... Susan."

"Tinkle-tinkle," she laughed.

Once again they reached out to each other and hugged.

"There's still other things we have to look over," Kenneth stated. "We'll talk to you a little later, Fred."

Fred nodded his head.

"Oh, Susan," Fred was quick to say, "if you don't mind, I'd like to put this... this distorted wonderful memory on the cabinet next to my crutches. It's kind of an honored area for me in this office, if you know what I mean."

"Of course," Susan said.

The group of four now moved to the other area of the Summers' offices. On the outside of one of the doors, taped to the area describing whose office it was, was a piece of cardboard. Written with a black felt marker in all caps were the words, "BIG GIRL'S ROOM."

"What's this all about?" Melissa asked.

"Honey," Susan started out, "you're always saying you're a part of our family. No one knows that better than Kenneth and me. You have and will always be that in our hearts. Kenneth and I understand you'll be at the ad portion of the floor very often, we know that very well. But when you have an occasion to be here, you'll need your own office. This is that room. Of course, it's very bare inside, no furniture in it whatsoever. You'll have to pick that out yourself. We wanted to keep this a secret from you. Now, do you want to remove the cardboard?"

Melissa smiled as she reached up and pulled the cardboard covering off revealing the words, "Melissa Wilson, Vice President." Susan and Kenneth waited for her to make some sort of expression or reaction to it. She said nothing as she simply wiped her eyes with her hands. That was all they needed to see. They had done well. Melissa reached over and hugged her parents.

"Now, why don't you take a look at your new empty office," joked Susan.

Melissa reached over and turned the handle, then walked into the room. Inside the room was as bare as her mother had just indicated.

As Melissa continued her very slow perusal, her heart almost stopped momentarily. On one section of a wall a framed item immediately caught her eyes. Without even realizing what she was doing Melissa walked slowly towards it. It was the framed back page thank you she had lost in the fire. Now she possessed another one, a most treasured gift to be sure. She smiled as she turned and looked at Greg, then her mother and dad. Melissa was simply thrilled.

Surrounding the framed thank you were hand painted small green branches. There were many red roses reaching out from them. Some were in full bloom and others just buds. Melissa couldn't help herself as she reached over and touched a few flowers. In her mind, they were almost alive. Oil brush strokes seemed to almost reach out from the wall. The workmanship displayed was magnificent. Her words were filled with many questions wrapped into one sentence.

"How, where, when, who?" she stated as she looked at the three of them. Susan looked at Kenneth, his smile very large upon his face.

"I was able… your mother and I were able to get this," Kenneth stated, "another few copies from the newspaper. We knew you would want one, if at all possible."

"Thank you Mom," Melissa said as she grabbed her quickly hugging her. "Thank you too, Daddy. It's just so wonderful." She reached over and hugged her father. It was a moment all three would remember from this day of surprises.

"Mom, Dad, who did the extraordinary artwork, it's unbelievable."

"Kenneth, why don't you tell her what happened," Susan said.

He simply nodded his head. Kenneth took a deeper breath as he conveyed to Melissa and Greg how they had heard of a couple in need of work. He explained how they had the occasion to meet with them in the couple's home to interview them concerning their employment. This was a charade on the part of the Summers. They both already knew they were going to employ them, that having been established by Susan even before their arrival.

While visiting, Susan happened to notice some small oil paintings done by the woman. They were almost lifelike in appearance. There were trees, landscapes, a large variety of subject matter. The human form, however, was not part of her repertoire. Still, one could almost feel a breeze in the paintings of the sky and trees. Susan asked the woman if she would consider doing a project she had in mind, a painting for her daughter. Kenneth explained how Susan was sure to get her approval, a price worked out in advance of hiring the two individuals. Neither one of them wanted the woman to feel obligated in doing the painting had she been hired first. That wouldn't set well with both of the Summers. Susan made the necessary arrangements to get her into the building and so forth. She even insisted in paying for any expenses the woman could incur in travel and meals. Susan left nothing to chance as she even gave her the payment in full before they left for home.

The remainder of the day was very much what Kenneth and Susan expected it to be. They made the rounds greeting every one of their employees, saying hello to customers. As was expected also, the atmosphere was festive for everyone. It was good to be back to work, their workers' faces reflecting that strongly.

When the Summers came around a corner, they chuckled. Sitting in a chair sat Gordon Harris, the night watchman. Next to him was his dog, Ranger. The dog sat quietly taking in everything around him. Little children were lined up to pet the dog. A small homemade sign hung from the dog's neck. "Will work for doggy treats." Susan and Kenneth both chuckled as they waved to him. Gordon smiled as he waved back. They knew this simple act by him was his way of adding to the grand opening festivities. Both loved his endeavor to touch the lives of even small children.

At one point, the Summers ran into the Morgan family. Kenneth was quick to thank them for passing out CDs as gifts to the customers. When he offered to pay for them, he was quickly thwarted by Henry. He argued that it was good advertisement, though Kenneth didn't believe that to be the case. Kenneth knew they just wanted to be a part of the welcoming of customers into the store. For that he was grateful.

Susan addressed the break room project with Kate alone. They worked out a plan on when she could pay Kate for the work they had done. The only words about the break room job that Susan mentioned to Henry concerned the beautiful job done by the couple. Susan did mention the photograph and how much Melissa loved it. Both Kate and Henry were happy their hard work was appreciated. They were, however, very proud of it themselves.

The one thing Kate was sure to mention to Susan was the fact that she ran into the husband and wife combination of Frank and Jennifer Harrison. Seeing them at work in the store made Kate very happy within. She mentioned it several times to Susan in their short conversation.

To say the opening was grand in nature would be equivalent to saying a drop of water is wet. It was clear to see. At one point Kenneth placed his hand on Susan's shoulder as they looked down from a balcony at the people below them. Gone was the turmoil they had lived through and endured. It was washed away by the numerous smiles that radiated from the faces that surrounded them from below.

Blue Rose Petals

The sweet taste of an early spring was gone as the warmth of summer days came to call. With its appearance, picnics could be planned, barbecues lit and various other summer attractions welcomed and appreciated by all. It was a time in the small community of Creek Side when people actually stopped and smelled the roses a little more. There was the cardboard regatta to look forward to, the homemade kite flying contest to enter and, of course, the annual pig roast and barbecue contests. The town grew immediately in size if only for a few days with each event that took place. The community enjoyed the visitors that came bringing an economic richness to their town. Still they were glad when they all left and their lives once again returned to an environment of less crowded streets, restaurant seating available once again, and a peaceful quietness of an occasional horn being blown.

It wasn't very long afterwards when the chill of an Autumn day made itself known to everyone. The transition between the seasons seemed to move faster with each passing year. This was Henry's favorite time. His arms would harvest the beauty of leaves falling from trees, or simply enjoy a bush showing off its colors proudly. Lush and full, they were awesome to view. He would take long walks with Kate and their child trying to absorb it all before the season ended. Even the burning of leaves discarded from the trees had an odor that filled the crisp air for blocks. It was a glorious time of year for him. There was Thanksgiving to look forward to, and Christmas hiding just around the corner on the calendar. Excitement was everywhere to be seen and heard.

Henry walked the short distance down the hallway leading to the main part of the restaurant. A few people sitting at various tables waved to him as he made his way to the front door. Henry acknowledged them as he opened and walked out of the front door. Getting into his, "old faithful car," he drove down the street towards his home. The sound of his stomach let out an unfamiliar groan as he made a turn into the driveway to their home. I sure can go for Kate's cooking tonight, he thought, as he opened the door and got out of the vehicle. He entered the back door giving the handle a turn as he walked in.

"I'm glad you weren't too long," Kate stated as she headed in the direction of the oven to remove the meal.

"So what's for dinner?" he asked as he walked over to her.

"Nothing too exciting, a pork roast and potatoes. I also made up some of your favorite vegetables."

"Sounds great," Henry said as he gave Kate a small kiss.

"What did Richard want you for?"

"He likes me to go over the bills with him once in awhile. I think he wants us to know we're making money. "

"Good."

"It sure smells good in here."

Kate turned her head from the oven and smiled at Henry.

"Thank you, dear. By the way, Henry, I got a call from Tom Tucker this morning."

"Oh," was all he said.

"I bet you know what he wanted to talk to you about."

"You're probably right."

Kate nodded her head as she reached into the oven to retrieve a covered metal dish from its hot interior.

"I don't know why he feels he has to do this every year, but it's really nice of him to offer." As Henry spoke his head dipped downward as it began moving slowly back and forth in thought. He began to replay in his mind the circumstances of that summer day some years ago. In his mind, it was as vivid a memory as though it had just happened.

It was warm, a refreshing breeze finding its way through the tree branches. Even the air seemed to carry the aroma of growing flowers. It truly was a day

Blue Rose Petals

to remember, he had thought, the beauty of another midsummer day. Henry had stopped by to see his good friend, Joe, at his place of business, the Second Chance Used Store.

As Henry made his way to the back of the store, he yelled out a customary joking comment, "Say, Joe, you alive back there or just sleeping as usual?" Joe always returned his inquiry in a joking fashion. Today Henry's comment was met with a deafening silence. Henry walked to the office portion of the building wondering if he was there. Sitting at his desk, Joe stared blankly at the wall across the room. His cheeks were resting in his hands, his elbows on the desk. Henry could see by his facial expression something was definitely awry. Joe's eyes carried a very distinct dampness to them, his face very flush.

"What is it, Joe?" Henry was quick to ask. "Is this about Jake?"

"I just found out the Tucker family has... has learned their son, Jeremy, was killed in action not very long ago." Joe started weeping once again.

Henry slumped into a nearby chair. "Oh God, no," was all he could say as he placed his head in his hands. He began sobbing uncontrollably.

Kate's voice brought Henry back to reality.

"It's because of what you did for the Tucker family, I'm sure that's why he offers us a free Christmas tree every year since his son's death. I believe it helps him to keep the memory of Jeremy alive and close to his heart. Maybe that's why he wants you to get the pick of the litter, so to speak. It's his way of thanking you for what you did.

When you sang twice at the funeral, and then spoke so eloquently about Jeremy, no one could hold back their tears. I've never attended such a moving ceremony in all my life, other than your mother Emma's, of course, and my own mother's as well.

Honey, the songs you sang that day were beautiful. I will say the one you did in the church, the first song was very unusual. It's not one I would expect to hear at a funeral for anyone, and yet it was very touching, heart-rendering to hear. Maybe for a military funeral it was very appropriate, now that I think about it. It brought out the emotions of everyone there."

"One day when Jeremy was home on leave," Henry said, I ran into him and his girlfriend, Carol Anderson. She was bubbling over with excitement. Jeremy had just given her an engagement ring. Their lives would soon be united as one. I was thrilled for both of them."

Kate nodded her head as she recalled Henry telling her of seeing Jeremy and the engagement ring being spoken of.

"I asked him when he'd be home for good. His reply to me was when his tour was over, or there was peace. He told me every soldier wishes for peace to come, but few ever see it happen. It just never seems to last that long. There's always one more battle to be fought somewhere in the world. He went on to say it's a soldier's favorite word to hear. Jeremy told me that was his one true wish above all… that everyone could share in its meaning. Kate, he used the word 'peace' more than once when I spoke with him. That's why I sang the song, 'Let there be peace on earth.'"

Nodding her head slowly back and forth, she uttered very softly, "That explains everything to me. His wish... the song... everything."

"I spoke with his family about singing the song and why I wanted to use it. It was something I felt I needed their permission before doing so. They understood my feeling on the subject. I explained how it all came about for me, the very words Jeremy said to me. They thought it over and then agreed with me. It was probably one of the hardest things I've ever had to do. When Emma died and I had to sing at her funeral, it carried a great deal of pain for me as well. This, however, was an agony I had to endure for a completely different reason."

"Oh, Honey," was all Kate could utter.

"That was the last day I saw him alive, I'm sorry to say."

"And how sad is that," Kate said, as she shook her head slowly back and forth. "Our town suffered greatly with his death. I think the fact that we're such a small community makes the river of pain run even deeper when we endure such a loss. We all feel it, each and every one of us."

"Anytime a young man or woman is lost in the service of their country, it's a sad set of circumstances we have to live with," Henry said thoughtfully. "It's hard on everyone, no matter how large or small the community is they come from. I guess it goes without saying it's the family members that carry the biggest burden of all."

"The things I remember mostly from the funeral," Kate said, "and there's a number of them, is you singing, and the eulogy you gave. Your words were the most touching I've heard anyone speak concerning the death of another person. If anyone hadn't known Jeremy before that day, what you said about him actually seemed to bring his life alive once again. They were uplifting, and heartbreaking words at the same time. Henry, I was so proud of you that day. I never would have been able to do what you did for his family... never.

The parade of mourners that walked through town from the church to the cemetery at the other end of town was so heart-wrenching to watch. I've never seen so many people lining the street as they did on that day. I know there were many people I never recognized standing along the route.

The flags... it was a sea of flags everywhere. In fact, I've never seen so many flags of different sizes being held on display from kids to adults alike. The noise of nylon flags flapping in the wind... just unbelievable."

Kate took a deep breath before going on. Henry could see his wife was getting very emotional as she spoke of that day. Her gentle words went on recalling everything that pulled so strongly on her emotions, and his as well.

"But the one thing... the single item I recall so vividly even now was the sound of the drummers from Jeremy's high school band. I understand he played the drums when he attended there. You couldn't help but notice there were other high school drummers represented from the outlying area schools. Their uniforms demonstrated that fact alone. I watched as they marched slowly in four lines, their drumsticks vibrating across the snare drums they carried sending out a continuous rhythm of sound... and then ending it with two loud bangs on their drum edges. It literally sent chills down my spine as they passed by. Everyone could literally hear them for blocks as the sound of the drums echoed off the buildings. Even as we entered the cemetery, the sound of them playing vibrated throughout the area.

To tell you the truth, when we finally got to the cemetery I was actually thankful in my heart it was almost over with. The emotions I dealt with that day were horrible to live through."

Henry nodded his head in agreement, his eyes continuing to water as he sat silently.

"I'll forever remember the men and women from the various military organizations as they walked together carrying their flags, it was just... Henry, did you happen to see where some of them were carrying baskets full of rose petals? Each basket was wrapped in a different color of cloth, some red, some white... and some in blue."

Henry once again nodded his head, but said nothing as he relived the day with her touching description of it. He couldn't speak, his throat was too tightly wrapped with emotion. For Kate to express her feelings about that day, he knew was good therapy for her. It didn't hurt his soul either to listen to her words being spoken. He could feel his heart healing a little inside as he sat there with glazed eyes.

"I heard Greg's Uncle Norm and his wife, Marylou, from their florist shop stayed up throughout the night removing petals from roses. They then dyed many of them in the color blue. To see red, white and blue rose petals being dropped in front of the hearse carrying Jeremy's remains, as his family followed behind was almost more than I could bear. To me it was a procession of sadness I hope never to witness again."

Henry merely nodded his head once again agreeing with her words. He took a deep breath. His words to Kate were slowly spoken, immersed in the pain he felt so deeply inside.

"I heard..." Henry stopped with those two words being spoken. He didn't know if he should go any further with the subject matter that was lingering within him. There was a pronounced silence for quite some time as Henry sat at the table. His hands were clutched together tightly, the fingers intertwined with one another. Observing him, Kate decided she should not say anything, simply wait until her husband felt comfortable enough to share the thoughts he so carefully hid inside. Henry lifted his head slightly and stared at the window. He swallowed a couple of times as tears ran down his face.

Kate felt she needed to do something. She walked the short distance to his position, bent down and placed her arms around him. Kate rested her head upon his shoulder. This very action by her brought forth a flood of tears from Henry. Kate could feel his body trembling as he sobbed. While she said nothing to him, her actions conveyed everything he needed to know.

After some time had passed, neither one of them moving from their position, Henry was finally able to take control of his emotions.

"Henry... Honey, I know Jeremy meant an awful lot to you, but is there something more to this you're not telling me?"

Henry nodded his head slowly.

"Why don't you tell me what it is. We all know it's always better to get any turmoil out and let it see the light of day, than to keep it penned up inside. We can talk it over, maybe that will help."

After taking a deep breath Henry reached over taking Kate's hand in his. She immediately sat in the chair next to him. The two of them reached out taking each other's hands. It was only then that Henry felt comfortable enough to express to her what tormented him so much inside.

"I heard, and it was later confirmed to me, that Carol —"

"Carol?" questioned Kate.

"Carol Anderson, Jeremy's fiancée, apparently, she suffered a complete emotional breakdown when she heard the news about Jeremy. Her family actually had to take her to the hospital at one point. I understand they had to medicate her heavily." Henry nodded his head back and forth as he spoke. "Her depression was so great she wasn't even able to make it to the showing at the funeral home. I did see her in the church with her family, and at the funeral itself. Her father and brother had to hold Carol's arms as they walked on both sides of her. She was very unstable in her gait. It's just so sad to even think about it. Two people's lives destroyed, and for what?"

"How long had they been together?"

"Since the ninth grade."

Kate pulled Henry's hands towards her. She lifted one at a time as she placed a kiss on each of them.

"There's just too much sadness in the world at times," Kate expressed. "I've heard Greg's mother say those very words many times."

"Yes, there is," agreed Henry. "I think that's why I love autumn so much. The leaves take your thoughts and surround them with the beauty they possess. It gives my mind a chance to be distracted by them."

"Yes, they do," Kate said.

"Kate, we've got to do something. I don't have any idea what can be done, but nonetheless, something is going to be done."

"Just be sure that whatever you come up with includes me."

"Oh, it will," Henry said as he nodded his head in a very affirmative fashion.

Having a mind that was able to capture and hold tightly onto anything with ease had always been a large part of Henry's life. He was able to hear a musical score but once, and could then play it from memory with nary a mistake. Hearing the words to a song being sung for the first time could be repeated word-for-word, whether it was within the span of a few minutes, or even years later.

This gift, as he thought of it as, was a blessing as well as a curse. It allowed him the opportunity to be successful in many ways, though at times Henry thought it wrapped him tightly in a blanket of torment.

Good times could be lived over and over again as if they had just taken place. They were brought back to life as quickly as the blinking of an eye. The memories of Emma, his surrogate mother, the many cups of tea they shared together, good times; wonderful ones. The first kiss Kate and Henry had shared so long ago. They were numerous in nature, all written on the chalkboard of his mind that could never be erased.

There was, of course, the other side to the coin. He could easily recall the misery he had to suffer through as a youngster. There was the agony from the brick that caused the scar over his eye. Every single injury he had endured, they were all there as if written on a stone tablet.

Still, he was grateful in the end for this unasked-for gift, one he very seldom shared with others. Henry thought it best to keep it a secret from everyone. Over the years that was what seemed to work the best for him.

Henry's thoughts drifted back once again to the day of the funeral and the many memories it held for him.

"I saw Greg, Melissa and their parents along the route," Henry said. "Greg wore his old uniform in honor of Jeremy."

"That doesn't surprise me one bit," Kate said. "I'll bet they helped Norm and Marylou out with the flowers the night before. They probably were the ones who covered the baskets with material as well."

"I'm sure they all did."

"Henry, there had to be numerous individuals from the outlining communities in attendance to fill the area with so many people along the route. I was told some of them came from as far away as a hundred miles, some even further. To me it was simply unbelievable, the showing of love and support the people offered to the Tucker family."

Henry once again nodded his head in agreement as he recalled the events again in silence. Kate's description of the day was keen in every detail. It was evident to him it was very much recorded deeply in her memory.

"When the guns fired their salute," Kate went on, "I not only jumped, it made my heart race."

"It was the same for me, too," Henry said.

"I know I was a sea of tears when the honor guard took the American flag from the top of the casket, folded it and... and then presented it to Mr. & Mrs. Tucker. I felt so sorry for them."

Kate walked over to the counter. She took a couple of tissue from a box. With her right hand she wiped away some tears. She turned and carried the box over to Henry's position. He removed a couple of tissue from the container as he wiped the corners of his eyes.

"I think, Kate," Henry uttered in a very soft voice, "the most heart-wrenching part of the day for me was when taps were being played at the cemetery. The fact that the bugler was hidden behind a small knoll made the moment even more heartbreaking for me. The slight vibrato of the bugler's notes as they drifted through the air touched my heart... almost breaking it. It was as if the music came from the cemetery itself. Whoever played the taps did an amazing job."

"They sure did," Kate said.

Once again Henry nodded his head in agreement.

Written in Stone

Henry and Kate sat patiently waiting for the appropriate time slot in the town hall meeting to put forth their proposal. Not only was he eager to have his idea addressed, Kate knew he was determined to accomplish his goal. No matter how unusual it may sound to some of the audience in attendance, he was adamant in his thinking. She understood well that Henry had an excellent command of the English language and would be able to convey his thoughts without any problem. She also appreciated the fact that he could do it in an easy and thoughtful way. Finally with the old news having been taken care of, various discussions being held, the suggestion was made to move on to new business. With the question offered to the floor by the chairman, Henry stood up. The chairman immediately recognized Henry. Kate looked up at Henry's face. She was proud of him and excited to hear his presentation.

"Our community is no more nor less than the fabric it's made up of, our people, our history, the memories we carry so close to our hearts. As a small town we have much to brag about to those who pass through or come to visit us. We gather together at times along the picturesque creek that meanders through our community in various areas of it. There's the sight of children walking in the water along its edge while others swing from the tree rope into their favorite swimming hole. Others simply cast a line and bobber along its edge. It's yet another treasure we all possess, a gift from Mother Nature for all of us to enjoy.

The white church steeple up on the hill at Miller's Road that can be seen for a few miles from town, it reaches out across the miles beckoning us home. It is, after all, the first sign many of us observe as it welcomes us from our travels.

On the east side of town, nestled at the top of a large hill is our famous 'Sunset View Park.' Almost nightly young people, as well as some individuals not so filled with youthful years, find themselves enjoying the beauty of a sunset. Many an evening picnic has been shared between friends there. There were nights when I've personally observed individuals on blankets sitting and watching as the sun descended slowly over the hills. They all are there hoping to share in the beauty of a majestic sunset. Once the sun is tucked safely into the evening we are able to gaze down at twinkling lights glowing from our town below.

Some of our most beloved and cherished items stand in the form of war memorials down in the park at the creek. They are the very symbols of why we can enjoy our lives every day. These are but a few beloved treasures we enjoy every day. They are jewels for all of us to share, riches we all possess, each and every one of them.

The reason I bring these comparisons up is really quite simple in nature. If I may, I would like to address one in particular that is beginning to show wear and tear from many years of faithful service. What I am referring to is the old stone bridge on the west side of town that crosses the creek there. The bridge was built some seventy-five to eighty years ago. It has accomplished its job well.

We've all heard people speaking from time to time about tearing it down and replacing it with some type of new steel span. It is because of that talk that my wife and I are here this evening. My wife, Kate, once crossed that bridge with Emma Greene, a wonderful woman who for many years I proudly referred to as my mother. As many of you now know, we were never related, but she cared for me just as if I were her son. It is but one of many things about her that I shall forever be grateful for.

Kate informed me that Emma expressed to her that the bridge brought back many wonderful memories of when she was a very young girl. She indicated to Kate that a very similar bridge to ours was built when she was a young girl. Emma recalled still hearing the voices of the workers in her mind as she would cross it from time to time. It is our hope and dream that this old stone bridge be revitalized, brought back to its original splendor for everyone to continue to enjoy. We all could benefit from its —"

"Henry, please excuse me for interrupting you, but —"

"Yes, Mr. Mayor."

"Henry, please call me Carl, just as you do outside of this building."

"Thank you."

"Henry, I would be the first to join in with you when we speak of the old bridge and how much of a landmark it is to all of us. However, when it comes to the community purse strings we all have to keep a wary eye on what we spend them on.

If I may first say something not concerning the subject of the old bridge. Henry, there isn't a single person gathered here tonight that doesn't appreciate all of the things you've done for this town. You and your partner, Richard, have brought in a lot of business with your singing, the bus tours, everything. It goes without saying that not one of us here wants to turn your idea down, however, we're probably talking in the neighborhood of a few hundred thousand dollars. It could be even more than that. It's not something that can be done cheaply. I'm sorry, Henry. I do have some idea what these things can cost in having dealt with other projects such as this in the past. Granted they didn't deal with a stone bridge, however, I hope you understand my concerns."

Henry nodded his head slightly affirming what Carl had just said. He looked down at Kate as she gave him a slight wink of her eye.

"Carl, may I give up the floor to Mr. Eddington at this time?"

"Of course, you may, Henry."

"Thank you. Eric, you're up."

"Thank you, Henry," Mr. Eddington stated, as he stood up. "I have the distinct privilege tonight of requesting something on behalf of Mr. and Mrs. Henry Morgan, or Henry and Kate as we like to call them." He smiled at both Kate and Henry as Henry retook his seat. One could see it gave Eric great pleasure in speaking to the group of assembled town folks, as well as the elected officials.

"On behalf of Henry and Kate, in my hand I now hold a note of guarantee to the community of Creek Side to pay in full for the complete restoration of what we refer to as our beloved, 'Old Stone Bridge.'"

Everyone was simply stunned.

"As most of you know, I'm a practicing attorney here in town. This document by them basically states the project will be free and clear of any debt when completed with no, and I repeat the word, 'no' cost whatsoever to the town of Creek Side."

It was unmistakable to hear the murmuring of various voices throughout the room.

"There is, however, some conditions the Morgan family, Kate and Henry, wish to have made as part and parcel of this project.

Concerning the bridge, on each walkway a brass plaque with both of the Greene's names would be placed, Emma and Paul Greene. The exact wording on it will be worked out at a later time. The cost of these nameplates is included in the restoration project. The plaques would basically say the Greenes saw to the restoration of the bridge as a gift to this community.

Now, are there any questions you may have up to this point?"

"I do."

"What is it, Carl?"

"This is a very significant and generous offer to our community, to be sure. I don't mean to be a prude, but just the same I have to ask it as part of my job. Before any work would be commenced, let alone talked about, I need to ask you a question or two. What if the cost is more than what they have set aside to accomplish this task?"

Some members of the audience nodded their heads in agreement with those words coming to light.

"We knew this question would most likely be asked," Eric stated, "in fact, we expected it. After the estimate is acquired, an additional $100,000 over and above that amount would be placed in a trust should any unforeseen circumstances arise concerning this project. Of course, any amount of monies not required for the project would be returned to the Morgan family.

In addition, over the top middle span of the bridge for all to see would be a metal sign denoting it as the 'Freedom Fighters Bridge.' On each side of the bridge, at the corners, a 4x6 nylon American flag will be flown 24 hours a day. Lights would be put into place for nighttime illumination. The flags will fly as a reminder to everyone who sees them that somewhere in our world our flag is waving in the sunlight. Kate and Henry have even accounted for the monies to replace the flags as they become worn. In other words, this bridge is to represent all of the men and women who served our country from the Revolutionary War to today's date and beyond."

Kate looked over at Henry and smiled. The name of the bridge was her idea. When she mentioned it to her husband, Henry agreed quickly.

"We'll always remember Jeremy when we cross the bridge," Kate whispered, as she nodded her head.

"And his family, as well as all the others who have served our country," Henry said softly.

Now the room grew a little louder in sound with Eric's statement having been made. People looked at each other smiling. It was evident to the individuals there, that if they didn't know of some distant relative who served in the service, they at least knew of someone who was serving now. That thought alone surfaced quickly in everyone's mind. The audience included some vets who were excited about the project. It was easy to observe that all of those present liked the idea. This brought a smile to Kate, Henry, and Eric as well.

Some individuals present looked at each other wondering how the Morgans came to have this much money to offer their town. Many felt that Henry and Richard had to be doing very well in their business venture together. Richard's Steak House always had an abundance of cars parked in the large lot. Henry's CDs were selling well; everyone knew that. The buses visited regularly for his shows. Still those in attendance felt this was an awful lot of money to be offered to their community.

"I would like to inform everyone here," Eric said, "and especially you, Carl, because of your well-founded questions concerning this. We would like to inform you of a couple of additional items.

We have already done a fair amount of preliminary research into this project trying to anticipate questions the council might have for us. I am happy to say a few contractors have looked over the bridge. They both came to the same conclusion. One, it's not in as bad of condition as one would expect by just looking at it and, two, the costs of it actually turned out to be less than we expected it to carry. I would be more than happy to give you the paperwork concerning their findings. If, however, the council decides to have an independent estimate conducted, the Morgans have also agreed to foot the cost of that item.

Now, if I may, I'd like to turn the floor back over to Henry."

"Of course," Carl said nodding his head.

Never in his wildest dreams did Carl expect to hear what he did at this usual scheduled town meeting. Inside he felt excited to be dealing with something that wasn't going to cost the towns' people any money whatsoever. Unknown to anyone but himself, he also loved the old stone bridge. As a kid he loved riding his bike across it. He'd stop midway over it to look down in the water for fish, an occasional turtle. Frogs, of course, were everywhere. These were strong memories of his own to be cherished. The opportunity to save it thrilled him.

Henry stood up once again as Kate released his hand. He rested both of his hands on the back of the chair in front of him as he began to speak.

"I really don't have much more to say concerning this project. It is our hope that the powers to be approve our proposal. This is another piece of this town's history needing to be saved, restored to its original glory. Once a landmark is gone, a small piece of our history forever dies with it. With those comments of mine being made, I'll simply have a seat and await your decision. Thank you for your consideration in this matter."

As the three of them sat drinking their refreshments in the restaurant, Mom's Country Kitchen, Eric smiled at the couple seated at the table with him.

"Henry, Kate," Eric stated with a light smile on his face, "I was very proud to be a part of tonight's meeting, even though I was just a small cog in the project."

"Don't kid yourself, Eric, you were one of the components to our proposal, a very important one." Henry went on. "You did so much leg work for us, contacting people, meeting with them. We needed your participation in this and you were there for us. Thank you."

Eric smiled at Henry.

"Their approval came awfully quick I thought," Kate said. "I was expecting it to take a month or so, discussions, more hearings."

"It probably would have from what I've heard of these things," Henry vocalized, "but with Carl having everything staring them in the face, written proposals, a check already made out, what could he or any of them say."

"They really had nothing to lose, it was all put into place for them," chuckled Eric. "If you really look at it from their standpoint, they all were winners. They didn't have to jump through all of the hoops, piles of paperwork it entailed with trying to get the bridge torn down and replaced. The need was there, of course, the bridge is in need of repair. Next the money was offered to them for nothing. When the people hear it's not costing the taxpayers anything at all, it will make all of them look like geniuses to the community."

"And that's not all bad," Henry said. "We get what we want, they get what they need."

"Exactly," Eric stated, "and you've got to remember one thing though. If they would have handled this problem on their own, the old stone bridge would be gone. We, on the other hand, would be stuck with some new ugly looking metal bridge."

"I never thought of it in that way," Henry said.

"It's what helps to make our town quaint, why people enjoy coming here," Eric said. "Say you two, how does a covered wooden bridge with the name 'Morgans' Crossing' sound to you?"

Kate and Henry laughed as well as Eric.

"Well," Kate offered, as she lifted her soda glass in the air, "to Paul and Emma, and their bridge restoration."

"And to the people it represents as well," Henry said smiling as he lifted his teacup.

"To us as well," Eric added, as he placed his coffee cup next to theirs.

They clinked them gently together as they smiled at each other.

Oh My God

"Oh my God!" were the only words she could express as Kate stood in the doorway to their home. Her face demonstrated a complete and utter astonishment. An older thin man approximately six feet tall or so stood before her. The ends to his grayish black hair swayed slightly back and forth from a light breeze. His attire was that of a somewhat wrinkled black suit. The grayish white shirt he wore had seen a better day. An older tie hung from his neck. It was tied with a somewhat sloppy knot. Black heavily worn dress shoes covered his feet finishing off his apparel.

Kate didn't know what to do, invite him in or slam the door quickly in his face. As she pondered her response he took a small step in her direction. Kate quickly retreated back a foot or so, still suffering the effects of what her eyes were beholding.

"Doc told me where you lived."

"You've talked to him?"

"Yesterday. Your grandfather suggested that I should think long and hard over what I was about to do, that is, contact you… attempt to talk to you."

Kate's eyes began to water as she looked at him. Her mind darted from thought to thought as she stood staring at him. What a difference his appearance now held from when she had last seen him. Kate tried to think of what to say, but could only come up with one word.

"Why," was all she could mutter as she shook her head back and forth.

"Honey, —"

"Please don't call me that."

"Kate, what I did to you was unforgivable, leaving you as I did when you needed me the most. Can I come in so we can talk?"

"I don't know, Dad... I just don't know."

"I understand. It's been a few years... actually many now since your mother's death and me leaving you all alone. Look, let me give you some time to comprehend the fact that I'm here. I'm staying at the Evening Rest Motel at the edge of town. I've taken a room there for a couple of days. If you feel you can somehow find it in your heart to let me sit down and talk with you, you can reach me there. I wouldn't blame you if you decided not to, but if you can just please take —"

Kate reached up and wiped her eyes with the inside of her fingers.

"Well, you know where I am, the decision is entirely up to you. If you decide not to meet, as I said, I'll understand. Please Kate... give me a second chance to —" Looking at her flush face, he stopped in midsentence once again. "It was nice to see you just the same."

Her father stepped from the entrance area and turned towards the paver walkway. He looked back over his shoulder for a moment as he began walking down the pathway from the house. Kate reached for the handle to the door. She slowly closed it after taking a few seconds to watch him as he walked away. With the sound of the door handle clicking into place, she turned her back to the heavy wooden door. She let out a deep breath. Her back gently found its way to the door as she put both of her hands to her face. She began to weep. Kate slowly slid downward to the floor, her legs buckling as they reached out from her body. She continued sobbing as she buried her head deeper into her hands. Kate sat there for some time as she contemplated her next move. Her thoughts were cluttered with memories of her father, the death of her mother. The tears upon her face caused her make up to run, leaving dark trails down her cheeks. Her dampened eyes blackened even more from the eye shadow she wore.

It had been some time now since her mother had passed. Seeing her father awakened every memory of her mother's death as if it were only yesterday. Like a dam breaking it flooded her thoughts of how it once had been, and how abruptly it had all changed. It all took place within the span of a few months. She relived the long hours in the hospital room holding her mother's hand as her body withered away. Kate took another deep breath as she attempted to remember the many precious good times they had shared together before the diagnosis of cancer came from the doctor's lips. The torment of observing her mother's pain was all she could bear as her mother dwindled from the vibrant woman she once was. Though her father was at her side then, and after the funeral, he was but a wisp of smoke quickly gone in the wind of his own despair. Her father's abrupt departure left her to deal with her suffering alone. If not for the fact that Doc, her grandfather, had insisted that she come and live with him, she didn't know what she would have done. This trauma she endured in her life caused Kate to mature quickly for her young age. She had to.

Returning to the living room she sat down in a beautiful oak rocker, a housewarming gift from her grandfather some years before. She began rocking slowly, attempting to gather her thoughts. Seeing her father once again, were the only thoughts her mind now had room for. The frequency of questions she held for him were furiously dancing back and forth. What do I do, how should I handle this, why did he return? Soon her husband, Henry, would be home. He would know what to do. More importantly, he would deal with this unforeseen set of circumstances in a way that would bring comfort to her soul in the end. She was sure of that.

    Kate began to hum softly an old song her mother used to sing to her when she was a young child. Why that simple tune found its way from her memory to her lips, she had no idea. Still, it warmed her heart with thoughts of her mother. It's been such a long time now, she said to herself as she continued to rock slowly to and fro.

Hearing the back door open and close announced Henry's arrival home. It was no surprise to Kate when her husband walked into the room that the first words out of his mouth were, "Are you okay?" He hurried to her side as he knelt down on one knee next to her. Kate nodded her head slowly up and down. He placed his hand gently under her chin and lifted it. He understood that Kate was not suffering from any ill effects, however, her face told him her emotions were very much strained.

"Is Emma Elizabeth alright?"

Kate nodded her head. "She's in school. No one's hurt, just me, my inner feelings."

Henry nodded his head. What had caused this misery to begin with was the next immediate question in his mind. He waited patiently for her to speak first. In his heart he knew she did not need to be bombarded with questions now. He would wait, no matter how trying it was on him. She needed some time to settle down and catch her breath. That was all too evident to him.

"When you feel up to it, we'll talk," he said.

She smiled slightly at him as she nodded her head.

"Thank you, Honey, just not now. I'll be okay. I just need some quiet time to myself."

He slowly nodded his head in agreement. Though questions continually raced through his mind, he knew his wife well enough to give her space when she needed it. This was obviously one of those times. Henry stood momentarily beside her and then walked over to another chair in the front room beside a black baby grand piano. He picked up a white blanket lying across a partial wicker-backed chair and returned to Kate's side. Handing her the large baby blanket, a gift from her closest childhood friend, Melissa, she laid it across her legs.

"Henry... Sweetheart, I know you want to know what happened but, please, I would like to be by myself for a little while. I'll explain everything to you in just a bit."

"Whenever you're ready," he answered.

Kate watched as Henry turned and went into the kitchen area. She got up and walked the short distance to the couch. She threw a small pillow up against the armrest and then unfolded the blanket. Spreading it over her body, she laid down. The softness of the white blanket comforted her. In her mind it was as if the two women, Melissa and her mother, were there with her, consoling her, attempting to alleviate her pain. Kate pulled the baby blanket up to her neck while wrapping the remainder of it around her body. She soon drifted off to sleep.

Henry pondered what to do next. The fact that his wife's emotions were being pulled on heavily concerned him to no end. Whatever it took to straighten out the dilemma or problem Kate was facing would be dealt with quickly, he would see to that. What caused it; that was what was most perplexing to him. He'd know soon enough, he thought. The movement of the hands on the kitchen clock was not moving fast enough for him. He sat drinking cups of coffee, waiting for Kate to awaken. Henry walked over to her position. She laid cloaked in the warmth of a baby's blanket, not needing to be disturbed. That he knew very well. He returned to the kitchen and drank some more coffee.

Hearing Kate stirring slightly, Henry quietly stood up and walked the short distance to her side. Kate's eyes remained closed. She didn't move whatsoever now. Taking a corner of the blanket, he put it over her upper body and shoulder. As he looked down at her, even with the dark makeup on her cheeks, he thought of how beautiful she was. What a treasure I possess in her. She was all any man could dream of or hope for in a wife. Her heart was tender. She had a mind that was quick to offer solutions to problems when needed. Henry found himself standing above her for some time now. He simply stood there watching her in silence. At one point, he reached down and gently rubbed the side of her face with his thumb.

Why, he didn't know, but he remembered the joke an old man once told him. It happened after a program he did at the retirement village. It related to a woman sleeping.

"A woman is never as attractive as when she's sleeping," the gentleman offered. "For one thing, her eyes are closed and she can't see what you're up to. The second reason, her mouth is shut and she's not yelling at you." Henry just nodded his head back and forth as he chuckled slightly. What a dumb joke, he thought to himself. Many a day he had heard various silly and simple jokes from the elderly he was entertaining. While a few were clever, most were outdated with the passage of many years. He filed them away in a little drawer in his mind. Perhaps they would be repeated by him someday, perhaps not.

Kate laid before him surrounded by the quietness of the empty house. He wished with every part of his mind she would awaken now. Henry needed to know what upset her so much. It was driving him nuts inside. Turning away from her, he once again walked into the kitchen. Now is not the time to disturb her, he thought. His questions could wait a little longer, even if he couldn't.

It had been an hour and a half now since Henry first walked through the kitchen door. He contemplated waking Kate again. If she sleeps too long now, she'll be up half the night. That was something he didn't want to envision. Having his wife upset was one thing, her sitting in a darkened room unable to sleep with only the thoughts of what had just occurred was something else. He decided to wake her up. Gently rubbing his hand on her shoulder, he quietly called out her name. She slowly began to stir.

"Are you really alright?" he asked.

She nodded her head slowly back and forth, indicating she was not. Kate was unable to let the words in her soul find a voice to express her thoughts as she looked up at him. She began to cry softly again. Tears from her eyes ran slowly down her cheeks in a small current of sorrow. Henry pulled her closely to his body. He cradled her in his arms. She laid her head on his shoulder seeking an emotional sanctuary to comfort herself in. He could feel the weakness in her body as he pulled her closer. She was clearly exhausted by the whole ordeal. He kissed her on the top of her head, then again on her brow. No words were offered by him. Henry let the closeness of his body speak for him, the support he held for her. For some time they held each other, their bodies almost melting into one. Neither one offered to release the other from their grip. Both were thankful for one another.

At long last, Henry slowly released Kate from his arms. He reached down and took her hands in his. Saying nothing he began to rub his thumbs on the outer part of each hand. He looked down at them as he did. It was his wish that she would speak to him first, thus allowing the door to be opened to whatever it was that needed to be addressed. Inside he knew she was still very fragile. Henry had never seen his wife in this state of emotions. When he would finally be able to speak with her, he understood his words, whatever they would be, would have to be thoughtfully put into any responses he would make.

As they sat on the couch Kate finally began to explain what had occurred earlier with her father. The last thing she expected was to face him at their own front door. Kate went on to express her hatred over what he had done to her. How much she needed him with the loss of her mother, only to have him turn away and leave. Kate told Henry everything, she couldn't help herself. The words flowed from her mouth like a torrent, each sentence filled with pain and disgust for his weakness.

Henry sat quietly listening to her. Not once did he stop to ask her a question or even make a thoughtful comment. Let the words empty themselves from her mind, he thought, let her release it all now. He would be nothing more than a set of ears to be spoken to, at least for now.

As she spoke her face would fill with tears. Kate would lean down onto Henry's shoulder and bury her head into it every so often. He continued to say nothing to her as he held her gently in his arms. Nothing she said, other than the fact her father had resurfaced, was anything new to him. Throughout their marriage he had gleaned different items concerning her dad and his disappearance. Even Doc had spoken to him in confidence on occasion concerning Kate's father. While Henry never outright asked about him, the pieces of the puzzle were there to be seen and put into place.

Henry glanced at the grandfather clock up against the wall. Emma Elizabeth would not be home from school for some time yet to come. That eased his heart somewhat. She didn't need to deal with what was happening with her mother now. While Kate had spoken to her daughter about what had transpired concerning her grandfather, it was always a vague amount of words used to describe it. That seemed to be enough for Emma Elizabeth, as she never carried the subject matter any further than that.

"Henry, what do I do? How should I handle this? Do I see him?" The questions came quickly, one followed by another. Finally he could take it no longer. He put his finger up to her face. Next he pressed it gently against her lips. She immediately became silent. Henry pulled her once again to him.

"We'll take it one step at a time once we get everything in order," he whispered to her. Kate simply nodded her head. The simple sound of his voice reassured her. She would follow his advice; that was clear to her. Henry had much more experience in his life when it came to dealing with unforeseen problems or tragedies. Kate understood very well any advice he offered her would be cloaked with love, a keen eye to protecting her if necessary.

"Kate, let's move to the kitchen table so we can sit and talk this all over. I'll get you a cup of coffee or tea, if you'd like."

She nodded her head.

Together they moved to the kitchen table. Neither one said a word as they took their seats. Henry didn't make any movement to make the coffee as he sat in his chair. It appeared to her he was wrapped in thoughts of his own. Finally Kate offered to make them some coffee. Henry declined having already consumed five to six cups. His fingers began to tremble a little from the effects of the caffeine he had consumed. Henry rubbed his fingers together, though it didn't seem to alleviate his condition.

As Kate sipped her coffee she simply looked at Henry, waiting for him to speak, wanting him to. What he would suggest to her, she had no idea. It was now Kate who wondered what thoughts he held inside of him. She waited patiently for him to express himself.

"Honey," he started out, "I think we should handle this a little differently. By that, I mean we should get some input on how to deal with your father's... his return into your life. I really don't know enough about what transpired or happened when your mother... when she passed. I don't know what words transpired between the two of you. The people who really know that are four in number from what I can gather. Kenneth, Susan, and Melissa were there when this all took place some years ago. The other one, of course, is your grandfather, Doc. If I was in your shoes, and this is only a suggestion, I would talk to them. See what they have to say, get their ideas and input. All of them went through this with you in one way or another. Granted, they didn't reach the depth you did, but what can it hurt to talk to them."

Hearing the silver pot's whistle sounding from the top of the stove, Kate got up and walked over to it. She fixed herself a cup of tea in her favorite flowered cup. Kate next blew gently over its top in a somewhat cooling fashion. Placing it to her lips she took a lingering drink from it. Henry could tell she was deep in thought. He waited to hear what her next words would be to him.

"He said he would only be here a couple of days," Kate stated as she slowly nodded her head. Why should that matter, she thought. If she never saw him again, what difference would that make to her anyway? What if he came back to tell me he is dying? Could he want money from us? "Henry, I think I will ask for everyone's input in this. I need to hear some other people's ideas."

"Good. Concerning your father, let me make the arrangements if it comes to that," suggested Henry. "If you decide to see him, I'll see that he's... you two get together. I'll be right beside you; you can be assured of that.

I'm going to make some calls and see what can and cannot be accomplished as far as meeting with the people. Is that okay with you, Honey?"

Kate nodded her head in agreement.

"You sit down and drink your tea. I'll use the phone in the bedroom, if you don't mind."

Once again Kate nodded her head.

Henry made his way into the bedroom. He didn't come back for perhaps a half an hour. Kate was surprised at the length of his absence, and yet she wasn't, the more she thought about it. After all, this was a subject matter foreign to her as well as the people Henry was talking to. She took another drink from her cup, it almost empty now. What plans he was making, she'd just have to wait and see. Her heart trusted him without question. That was all she really needed to know.

Henry returned to the kitchen and took a seat at the table. He inquired of Kate something she very much didn't expect of him. He asked her what was the hardest dish she ever prepared for an evening meal. She looked at him with a slightly shocked expression. Kate thought for a little while and then described her choice to him. When he asked her what made it so difficult she explained each measurement had to be precise. It was very time consuming to prepare. Even in the oven you had to check on it quite often.

Next Henry asked her what she would prepare as secondary dishes to accompany her meal offering. Once again Kate thought for some time before relaying her answer. Henry nodded his head as he smiled slightly. Much to her surprise he continued on with his line of thinking. This time, however, it concerned desserts. Going through the same routine of questions Henry asked how much time was involved and so forth. Finally he explained to her his thinking.

"Tomorrow evening you will be having six dinner guests not counting us, of course. There will be Susan and Kenneth Summers, Melissa and Greg, your grandfather Doc and Jean. Emma Elizabeth will not be here for dinner. I've made arrangements for her to be out of the house at dinnertime. In fact, she'll be spending the night at a friend's home. The reason they will be coming is really two-fold. We are going to address the issue of your father's presence in town. Also you will be so busy tomorrow shopping and preparing a gourmet meal for everyone, you'll have no time to think about what happened today. Honey, that's my plan, it's as simple as that. If for some reason you don't think you can handle my idea, we'll use one of the back rooms at the restaurant. The choice is entirely up to you."

Kate nodded her head back and forth with a thoughtful expression on her face. "I guess I'll be doing a lot of cooking tomorrow. With everything I'll be preparing, I really won't have much time to think about anything else. You know what, Sweetheart, I think I'll ask Stella to come over and visit while I'm getting everything put together."

"Should we ask Joe and Stella to come for dinner, too?" he inquired.

"I don't know. Yes, we probably should, it's the right way to handle it."

"Well, you'll have to give her a call. It's awfully short notice though." Henry continued on. "Everyone I called said their plans would be changed no matter what so they can be here. I think they all realize how important this is to you."

"I'll call Stella. You know, Henry, they're both as much a part of our family as everyone else."

"So they'll both be here for dinner also?"

"Yes."

Henry nodded his head. The only thing left to do now was to check and see how long her father would be in town for sure. That was something he didn't really want to address. Perhaps he could stop at the motel and get that question resolved in the morning. Maybe he'd be lucky and not have to deal with him at all. Time would answer that question soon enough.

The next morning after dressing, Henry told Kate he was off to the restaurant. He knew, however, his first stop would be the motel on the edge of town where her father was staying. What he would say or do remained a large question in his mind. Kate said she would be shopping for a large portion of the morning needing to go to various stores to pick up the items she needed for her impromptu meal. Henry and Kate gave each other a light hug and kiss as they each headed down their different paths for the day.

Pulling up to the motel, Henry found a vacant parking spot near the front door and parked his old faithful vehicle. Walking in to the office he moved to the main desk area. After explaining to the manager who he was looking for, the clerk pointed in the direction of a man sitting on a new picnic table over by some children's play equipment.

"That's him over there," he said.

"Did he say how long he was staying?" inquired Henry.

"To tell you the truth, I figured he'd be leaving today. He told me it would be day-to-day on the room. You'd really have to ask him."

Nodding his head, Henry thanked the man for his time.

Henry knew he had to find out how long Kate's dad would be staying there. If she didn't want to see him, that was fine with him, no problem. If, on the other hand, she decided to talk to him, he needed to know if he would be there long enough for that to occur. Henry decided to talk to her father, though he wished there was another option. Walking over to Kate's father he questioned in his mind what to say.

"Hello, young fellow," Kate's dad stated as Henry walked up. "That's a pretty nice car you have there. It's kind of vintage like me," he said with a small smile. "How long have you had it?"

"For many years," Henry answered as he took a seat beside him at the table.

"I had one similar to it quite some time ago. I sure loved it."

"As I do mine. It was the first car I could afford, so it's kind of like my baby."

"Baby," the man replied as he nodded his head back and forth. "I was hoping to see my baby girl today. I haven't heard from her, so I guess that's going to be out of the question. Well, she's not really a baby, she's a young woman. Actually a beautiful young lady." Kate's dad slowly nodded his head back and forth as he spoke of her. Henry knew memories were running through the man's mind, just as it would be for him if the circumstances were different.

After a delayed amount of time he continued on. "From what I've learned from her grandfather she's got a child of her own now. I wasn't even there for that... or her marriage for that matter. From the looks of her house, I understand they're doing all right. Her home is very nice from the outside."

Henry said nothing to Kate's father. He sat there quietly listening as he spoke.

"Oh, my name is Christopher," Kate's dad said, as he held his hand out to Henry.

"I'm Henry. So how long are you going to be around? It sounds as if you've given up on seeing your daughter."

"I don't know," was all he replied. "Tomorrow there's a bus leaving for... well, it's heading west from here. They always say, 'Go west young man.' The only thing wrong with that scenario is I'm not young anymore, but west is the direction the bus will be taking me. I suppose if I waited another day or two after that, I'd have more choices to pick from."

Henry looked at Christopher's face. He could see his wife's face in his eyes. When he spoke, his lips seemed to reflect her expressions as well. For a man of his age, he seemed to carry himself well. His clothes were of a simple attire, an older pair of dark slacks, a light blue shirt and some worn black dress shoes.

"Why don't you wait a few days, maybe she just needs time to take it all in. After all, what's a day or so if it's really that important for you to see her."

With those few words being said, it was as if a door seemed to be opened to Christopher's memories. He began speaking of the life he once cherished with his wonderful wife and child. He spoke of how deeply he loved both of them. Kate's father referred to the family's best friends, Susan and Kenneth, and their daughter, Melissa. Christopher smiled slightly as he related to Henry how they took trips together, the deep friendship that had spawned between the two young girls. He chuckled slightly as he told Henry about the phrase, "AT" and the meaning of the initials, always together.

After a short time Christopher addressed the tragedy of Elizabeth, the death of his soul mate. He explained to Henry how utterly disillusioned he became. His faith no longer seemed to matter to him. The cords that once held and supported him were nothing more than pieces of frayed material. He would look occasionally at Henry as he expressed his thoughts. Christopher would take deep breaths every so often. It was definitely clear to Henry his words came straight from his heart.

"I couldn't take it anymore," he said. "With Elizabeth's death, the final straw had been placed upon the camel's back. It broke me. Henry, she was a beautiful woman both inside and out. My wife deserved better than what she got. I watched her dying, pain encompassing her every waking moment. I became very bitter within the blink of an eye. Worst of all, I began to suffer from a deep and ugly self-pity that grew from within. It was almost like the cancer that consumed my Elizabeth. It just grew stronger with every passing day."

As Henry sat next to him, he could see his every facial movement. He had been down that dirty dusty road himself, and he could appreciate every word that was spoken. One can only take so much, he thought. It's your desire for survival that keeps you going.

Christopher put his elbows upon his knees as he rested his head into his hands. Almost in a whisper he asked Henry a simple question. "Have you ever contemplated suicide?"

"No, I haven't, " uttered Henry as he shook his head back and forth.

Christopher nodded his head. It was then that he spoke to Henry of his desire to do that very thing. However, he knew the last thing he wanted was to have Kate find him afterwards. It was best, he thought, to just leave. Go as far away from everything as he could. Perhaps he could make it look like some type of an accident, and his daughter would be none the wiser. He explained to Henry his mind was not thinking clearly at all during that period.

After being away for quite some time he thought he could return to be with Kate and ask for her forgiveness. He learned she lived with her grandfather, his wife's own father. Kate's dad conveyed to Henry, with that knowledge he knew she would be well taken care of. He expressed it was better that way. Being with a grandfather that loves her, instead of a father who found solace in a bottle of whiskey was better for all involved. "I never drank a lot, but on occasion I used its contents to comfort me. Stupid, isn't it," he muttered.

As Henry listened to Kate's father he began to feel sorry for him. In his own heart he could begin to understand what had taken place in Christopher's life. Still, there were items that pulled heavily in his own questioning thoughts. Henry felt much could have been worked out differently had the opportunity presented itself. However, one has to walk in the other's shoes to truly feel how comfortable they are, or how much they tightly pinch your toes.

"So what are you going to do about it?" asked Henry.

Christopher didn't answer Henry; he merely sat quietly thinking. "You from around here, Henry?"

"Yes, I am."

"I saw you pull up to the motel office, I didn't know if you were getting a room or what, that's why I asked."

"I live here in town," Henry said. " I just had to ask the owner a question."

"Can you wait here for a second?" Christopher asked.

Henry nodded his head.

Christopher got up and began walking in the direction of the rooms. He opened a door and disappeared momentarily. Returning to Henry's position, he handed him a 12x8 inch leather satchel. It had two small straps that held it closed. As Henry took possession of it, he was surprised at how thick and heavy it was. It was as if the straps were doing all they could to keep the contents within it safe.

"You seem like a pretty honest guy, Henry. I wonder if you could find it in your heart to do something for me," Christopher asked.

"What is it?"

"Could you see to it that this gets to Doc McDonald? He's a local —"

"I know who he is."

"Well," Christopher continued, "if you could see that he gets this — It's for Kate's eyes alone. Would you explain that to him?"

"Of course."

"So you'll do that for me?"

"I'd be glad to."

"Thank you, Henry, I'd appreciate that."

The two of them sat at the table for a little longer. Henry finally stated he had some things he had to take care of. He stood and shook Christopher's hand. Henry tucked the satchel under his arm as he walked to his car. After opening the door, he turned and looked in Christopher's direction. They both waved good-bye.

The dining room table was set and ready for use. Candles were placed a third of the way down from each end of it. Kate learned that very quickly from Stella. It was one of her first lessons in cooking. Presentation, presentation, presentation, Stella stated more than once to her. The light the candles presented could never be forgotten as an essential part of any important gathering of guests to one's home. They help to draw out good conversation, as well as give the atmosphere a warm feeling. Candleholders were one of the first things Kate purchased after her first cooking lesson.

Everyone was gathered in the living room. They visited, exchanged small talk, and in general simply shared smiles. No one actually knew why they were there other than the fact they were asked to attend. They did understand, however, it was very important to Kate that they be there. Henry was sure to explain that much to them. What Kate and Henry needed or wanted of them remained a secret to everyone.

Together Stella and Kate had cooked a meal that would rival any gourmet chef's offering. Having taken a small sample of it, Henry and Joe were sure no one could compete with its excellence. Kate invited everyone to take their seats as the sound of the grandfather's clock struck six o'clock. Greg sat beside Melissa, her mother and father next to her. On the opposite side of the table Doc and Jean, took their seats. Next to them Stella and Kate sat. At each end of the table, the seating positions were filled by Henry and Joe. This was the most honored and treasured spot at the table in Henry's mind. Whenever Joe was in their home, Henry saw to it that Joe always possessed one of these important sitting areas. It was a simple item in seating, but one Joe always felt proud to possess.

Kate was sure to see to it that everything, and everyone was taken care of. Stella assisted in this endeavor, which Kate was very grateful for. During the day as the two women worked preparing the meal, Stella not once asked her why Kate needed her assistance. The fact that she asked her for help was all that really mattered to her. Kate, on the other hand, was so thankful to have her around. Stella's words to Kate kept her mind occupied, and that alone was what she had hoped for. It was a joy for Kate to have her there, and Stella could tell that easily. Kate expressed that to her on numerous occasions.

With the meal finished, two different desserts having been served and almost demolished by the men, it was time to sit back and enjoy an after-meal cup of coffee or tea. This also was the opportunity for Kate to open the subject matter they all had been invited for. Kate took a deep breath before she started out.

"I have had something happen recently in my life that has to be dealt with in one way or another," she stated. These few words captured everyone's attention immediately.

Doc sat a little taller in his chair, knowing in his mind what was about to be presented to the group of individuals. He had talked to her father; he knew Christopher was in town. Most likely, he thought, she had seen and spoken to him as well.

"Not very long ago my father came to our front door. He wanted to talk to me. Frankly, I didn't know what to do. He's been gone more than a few years now. To say I was surprised would be an understatement. I was in shock to be honest with you. He was the last one I would have ever imagined to be standing on the other side of our front door."

Everyone was in awe with her few words, except Doc. It was as if all present knew the ramifications of her words. The only exceptions were Greg, Stella and Joe. None of them knew or understood what had transpired between Kate and her father. Doc had spoke of the circumstances at one time to Jean, but he had been vague about it all. Jean was sure the whole story would soon be presented by Kate to all present. She was right in her assumption.

Kate went on to explain her deep heartache with seeing him standing before her. She described to them how when she needed him the most with her mother's death, he disappeared. Kate spoke of his selfishness, of her anguish. Her words were filled with a harsh contempt for him. In essence, she felt he betrayed the very love she had once held so strongly for him.

"What do you think he wanted?" Melissa asked.

"I think he wanted me to forgive him," Kate said as she shook her head from side to side.

The room was silent as everyone had a variety of different thoughts running through their minds. Melissa asked if it was all right with her father and Greg if she told Kate how rocky a start Kenneth and Greg had when they first met.

"I would rather you not," Kenneth said. I think I would like to do that myself."

Melissa smiled. Greg squeezed Melissa's hand.

"Kate," Kenneth stated, "what do you think of Greg and my relationship with him?"

"It's absolutely wonderful, just like Doc and Henry. In fact, it's as strong as Henry and Joe."

"It wasn't always that way," Kenneth said. Susan reached over with her hand and placed it on Kenneth's. Kenneth looked around the room before he started. He spoke of how Melissa had brought Greg to their home to meet her parents. Kenneth told them of literally kicking Greg out of their house, telling him never to return again. With his words he painted a complete picture of that horrible day and how he had treated Greg, let alone his own child. He spoke of almost losing his daughter that evening. "Forgiveness is never an easy route to take. It's a pit with edges that are lined with items hoping to trip you up, suspicions everywhere. Greg was kind enough to forgive me that day, something I will forever be grateful for."

Kenneth pushed his chair back slightly as he stood up and walked the few feet to Greg's position. Greg stood up. The two men hugged. Melissa wiped her eyes with her napkin. Susan simply smiled with watery eyes.

"You know, Honey, I know something about forgiveness, too," added Henry. Much to everyone's surprise, Henry conveyed the story of his mother, Isabella, and the circumstances surrounding her. He told them how much he hated her, and the fact that he was given the opportunity to tell her that before she died. His words were to the point, direct in nature. "We made up. I never would have thought that possible when I was growing up. You were there, Kate. You probably understand that more than anyone here. You saw what and how that all occurred."

Kate nodded her head.

"Grandpa, how did my father know where I lived? My name is changed and everything. How do you think he got that information?"

Doc looked around the table before he spoke. "He, of course, knew where I lived. The fact of the matter is... Kate, I've been in touch with him off and on through the years. Very seldom could I write him, but he would send me a letter periodically. A couple of times I even received a call, usually when I least expected it. From what I could gather, I think... I believe he feels deeply sorry for what took place between the two of you."

"Really!" Kate said, her voice a little tough sounding.

"I wanted him to decide how everything should be handled between you two. I guess him showing up at my house, and then yours were his first steps in that direction. I think he's holding out an olive branch. He hopes for your forgiveness. I guess it's as simple as that."

The room became very silent. Some individuals reached for their coffee cups and took a drink, others just waited to see what happened next.

"I guess it's my turn," Melissa said as she squeezed her napkin with her hand. "There was a day when I needed to be forgiven for the insensitive and cruel words I spoke to you, Kate." Melissa smiled slightly. "Kate, you forgave me. I didn't have any idea if you would or wouldn't. I'm so thankful you welcomed me back into your life as your best friend."

Kate nodded her head as she recalled the day Melissa came to her grandfather's home and begged to be forgiven for what she had said concerning Henry. Her earlier words hurt Kate greatly. Melissa had expressed to her that Henry wasn't good enough for her. He didn't reach Kate's status in life, and should be discarded. Her words broke Kate's heart inside. Then to have Melissa come back a few days later and apologize, it was simply unbelievable. Kate had never heard Melissa ask for anyone's forgiveness. It made the words even more precious for her to hear. Neither Kate nor Melissa ever talked to anyone concerning their conversation. What was said concerning Henry that day would never be heard by him, let alone anyone else. It would remain a deep secret between the two of them, as it had always been.

"Can I ask a question?" Greg said.

"Of course," Kate answered.

"Do you still love your father?"

"Of course she does," Melissa interjected.

"Not necessarily," Greg stated.

Kate didn't say a word. The question hung heavily in the air. Melissa looked at Greg thinking he may be right with his assumption.

"I'm not really sure anymore," Kate said. "At one time there was no question concerning my love for him, but now I just don't know."

"I'd like to say something, if I may," Stella stated. "Kate, you're almost like a daughter to me —"

"Get in line," Susan said quickly.

Everyone laughed.

"We both love you very much," Stella said with a smile as she looked in Susan's direction and winked. "I can't tell you what or what not to do, none of us here can."

The group seemed to nod their heads in unison with her words.

"What I can tell you, however, is think this through very carefully. He is your father, if nothing else. He will forever be that person in your life, like it or not. You obviously haven't made your mind up on what to do, otherwise we all wouldn't be sitting here making suggestions. The decision you're about to make is one of the most serious things you'll ever contemplate or consider. Take your time. It's too important of an item to rush yourself. Consider this one thing, love always takes the time to listen, no matter how minute that love is.

Kate, you're very lucky in one respect. You have Henry with you. Lean on him. Get his opinion, but trust your instincts. Most importantly, live with your decision. Don't second-guess yourself. That can do more harm than the question itself.

Remember a few weeks ago when we were making that elaborate chocolate cake, and we couldn't remember if we included one of the ingredients?"

"You threw the whole mix away and we started over," Kate said nodding her head.

"That's what you need to do, make sure every ingredient is accounted for in your decision. Do that, and you'll come up with the right answer. I think everyone of us here can agree on that."

"Thank you," Kate said, "each and every one of you for your help."

"Now I'm hungry for chocolate cake again," joked Kenneth.

They all laughed as the women started clearing the table. The men, of course, agreed to have another piece of dessert along with some more coffee.

The sound of water spraying onto dishes in the washer could be heard faintly in the living room. Henry and Kate sat on the couch, her body cuddled up under his arm. Her legs were pulled up tightly to her body. Henry's hand rubbed her shoulder and arm gently in an up and down motion. His head laid against hers. Both of them had their eyes closed, enjoying the quietness that surrounded them. The company had left some time ago. Now was a time to simply give themselves a few moments of restfulness.

"Honey, I wish I could make up my mind. I feel like one of those ships you see in a stormy picture. I'm being thrown one way by the waves, and then back again the other way."

Henry bent down kissing her on the top of her head. He really had no idea what words of comfort to offer her. For all practical purposes, he had nothing new to say.

"I wonder how long my dad will be in town?" Kate stated in a matter of fact sounding voice rather than a question.

Henry took a deep breath. He squeezed Kate's arm slightly. "He'll be gone tomorrow."

Kate pushed away from him, shock expressed on her face. "How do you know that?"

Henry began explaining the circumstances of meeting with her father. He told her it was because of that fact alone, how long he would be in town that he spoke with him in the first place. If she wanted to talk to him, he needed to have that information available for her. After his explanation, she simply nodded her head.

Blue Rose Petals

Henry stood up from his position beside her and walked into their bedroom. He returned carrying the leather satchel he received from her father. Taking his seat again, he reached over and turned on a light beside the couch.

"This was given to me today by your father. I was supposed to give it to Doc, and instruct him to see to it that you got it. Your dad has no idea who I am. I didn't offer to inform him of that fact either. What's in it, what it contains, I have no idea. That's all I can tell you about it." Henry handed the satchel to Kate. "I'll give you a little time to yourself. If you need me, just call."

As Kate took the leather package she reached out and grabbed Henry's arm. It was evident to him she wanted him to stay with her. He would, of course, comply.

The weight of the item was the first thing that drew her quick attention. She did not expect it to be as heavy as it was. Kate undid the first strap. She took a deep breath as she began undoing the second one. The top large flap remained over the contents of the satchel. Kate took her hand and rubbed it across its top. She looked at Henry, but said nothing. Finally Kate lifted the top of the flap up to discover what its interior possessed. Inside were a huge amount of envelopes. They were jammed tightly into the satchel. Kate had to literally pull very hard with her hand to release even one of the envelopes. Finally she pulled with all her might. Like a spring loaded device the contents flew slightly into the air from her lap and across the carpeting of the room. Henry chuckled slightly with the movement of Kate's hand as the various envelopes almost jumped out of the old case. He helped her pick them up. As he did, he noticed something peculiar about each envelope. On the outside of each one, a day and date was scribbled across the front. He lifted one up and pointed that fact out to Kate. Her face looked puzzled by it, just as Henry's had earlier. Together they started putting them into order by date. Some were written within a week of one another, while others showed gaps of a few months or even more. By this time both of them were sitting on the floor, the couch to their backs as a backrest.

Once they were all placed in order Kate took the first one and opened it. She removed the sheet of lined paper and began reading it. Henry watched Kate as she read one after another. Her lips demonstrated the movement one is accustomed to seeing when someone reads to themselves. Henry sat beside her quietly. He didn't pick up or read any of the letters she had finished reading. This was between her and her father. He was there for support, nothing more. If she wanted him to read anything, he was sure she would point that fact out to him.

As the evening wore on the amount of letters Kate consumed with her eyes grew. Henry got up from his position and made her a cup of coffee. Bringing it to her he simply placed it beside her. Her eyes glanced over at it. She nodded her head in what he took as a thank you, and then immediately went back to the letter in her hand.

Henry returned to the kitchen once again. He picked up the phone and called a friend of Emma Elizabeth's. Henry wanted to make sure all was well in her overnight stay. Since he hadn't heard anything from when she left school, he wanted to check on her just the same. As was expected, all was well.

The hands on the clock told Henry Kate had been at her task much longer than he had anticipated. He looked down at the pile sitting before her. It was still considerable in size. While some letters were a single page in duration, others were as long as five or six. Another thing that caught his eye was the fact that some were written on both sides of the sheet.

When Henry suggested she should put the pile down and go to bed, it was as if she didn't even hear him. When he repeated himself she simply nodded her head, too engrossed in what the letters were telling her. Henry was tempted to reach down and pick up one of the recently read pages. As his hand made a movement towards it, he caught himself and stopped. Henry bent down and kissed Kate on the top of her head. She barely moved. He nodded his head slightly before he turned and headed to the bedroom.

With morning having arrived Henry got out of bed and made his way to the kitchen. He figured Kate would have breakfast ready, or at the very least have the coffee perking. What he found was his wife's upper body lying across the kitchen table sound asleep. Various letters lay strewn around her on the table. Her left hand still had a letter crumpled in its grasp. Unbelievable, he thought to himself. Leading from her position at the kitchen table, Henry could see a line of letters taking his eyes back to the edge of the couch. He shook his head slowly back and forth. Henry couldn't see Kate's face from his position. As he walked over to her, he observed her eyes appeared to have a darkened look surrounding them. He knew at once what they told him. She had been crying. Bending down over her, he placed his hand onto her shoulder. He whispered her name as he gently rubbed her slowly with his hand. Finally she began to awaken. She looked up at him as he placed a small kiss upon her cheek. Her mouth demonstrated a little smile. The more she awoke, the realization of what was sitting before her, the letters, took over her thoughts once again.

"Henry, all of these letters were written to me by my father. Some of them end halfway through; others go on and on. Each one of them carries the same premise. They all have exactly the same theme. He tries to explain what my mother's death meant to him. As I read each one, I could hear his voice in my head. Henry, every single one of these letters contains an apology to me... every one of them. In one he simply wrote my name and the words, 'I'm sorry.'" Kate wiped her eyes once again.

"My father speaks of drinking, and how he fought daily with the liquid devil, as he called it. He mentions it quite often. As I read through them, it was also very evident to see he was getting better. Even the way he writes, the words he says. His hand movements in putting down the words, it's smoother as time went on. You can actually see a difference. It's as if his hands and words are fitting back into place. They're finding their way to his normal clarity. For a man, my father always had beautiful penmanship." Kate reached over and pulled one of the letters to her. "Look at the way the words are written." Kate handed Henry the letter. Henry nodded in agreement as he looked at them. Not only were Kate's words true, she had picked up on even the smallest of indications by his writings what was going on within himself, what he was dealing with.

"Honey, he stated in these letters that he... he even mentioned having thoughts of ending his life." Kate's voice became broken as she spoke. "It's just so tragic." Her face quickly broke into tears. "I never imagined, never suspected he took her death so hard. My father loved her every bit as much as I did, maybe even more." As Kate wept Henry put his arms around her trying to comfort her. While Henry didn't know how much it comforted her, in her heart Kate welcomed his strength. It was the love and understanding she needed, and he was there for her.

After a short time, Henry walked to the counter and retrieved a box of tissue. She pulled some out and began wiping her eyes.

"I love you, Henry."

"Just as I love you," Henry said as he gently rubbed her face below her eyes with his thumb.

Kate took a deep breath as she reached over and took another letter from her left side. She picked it up as if to point something out in it. "In this one," she indicated with her hand, "he talks about his battle to quit drinking. My dad never drank before my mother's death. I know that for a fact. It's not just in this one, he writes about it several times. Look through them, you'll see." Kate's words were more of a statement than a command. Henry understood what she meant. He did what he knew needed to be done by him. Henry simply listened, nodded his head in approval with her words.

"Where does this all take us to concerning your father?" he asked.

"I want to see him," Kate said, as she nodded her head.

"You sure read a lot of letters last night," Henry stated as he looked around.

"I never went to bed. The last thing I remember was the clock chiming out five times. I'm really exhausted. My body feels completely dead inside."

"The table top is not a very soft pillow. You go to bed, sleep for a few hours and then we'll deal with everything." Kate nodded her head as she got up and headed in the direction of the bedroom. Henry bent over and started picking up the envelopes. He took care to make sure each one was in line with the date on the outside of it. Once that was accomplished, he walked over to a drawer by the sink and opened it. He retrieved a couple of very large rubber bands and wrapped them around each group of letters. Placing them down on the table he went to the leather satchel still laying on the floor in the living room. He placed it beside the letters. Henry wondered how many letters had been written by Christopher. He imagined it was somewhere between two and three hundred. How many there were exactly didn't really matter. Henry paused for a moment. His thoughts were simple. Every one of these tells a story of how he lived through his missing years from Kate. Henry was glad he had stopped and talked to him at the motel. Getting the satchel from him, being there when she opened it, it was all very important to him. Now she can rest, her mind free from the years of not knowing the answer to endless questions she possessed. While not all things were completely answered, the rest of them would eventually fall into place. Now she could move on and he would be there to help her. Henry thought to himself as he looked down at the letters on the table, it's the start of a new day in more than one way.

"Honey... Kate, would you like some breakfast?"

Kate's blurry eyes looked up to see Henry holding a wooden tray. There was a plate with eggs and a couple pieces of toast on it. To one side were pieces of bacon. The silverware looked as if it had been polished slightly. Her favorite cup held steaming coffee. A six-inch tall, slender vase held a single flower. She smiled right after she yawned. How thoughtful he is.

"Henry, you said my dad was leaving tomorrow?"

"Yes, but tomorrow is now today," he replied.

"What time is it?"

"About 10:30 or so."

"We're going to miss him," came her frantic voice.

"So you still do want to see him?"

"Yes," she replied in a somewhat excited voice.

"Okay. You get dressed and we'll leave as soon as we can."

Kate jumped up from the bed. Henry sat the tray down beside the bed as he watched Kate quickly heading for the dresser and then closet.

"What about your breakfast?"

"I'll eat it when I get home."

Fat chance of that, he thought. Who wants cold eggs and soggy bread. An old piece of bacon sounded good to him though. A cup of coffee, even cold was something he could deal with, but not Kate. He went to get his keys.

As Henry and Kate made their way to the bus stop, Henry tried to remember everything Christopher said about leaving. He recalled him saying he was going west, though he never did say when the bus was leaving. We'll just have to wait and see, he thought. As they pulled up to the bus stop the area was vacant. No one was there waiting for the out-of-town bus to arrive.

"It looks like we've missed him," Henry said. He could hear his wife sniffling softly at his side. Henry looked at Kate, her head was slightly tilted downward. He got out of the car and headed to the motel. After conferring for a little while he returned to the vehicle. "The bus left 45 minutes ago." Kate didn't reply, though she nodded her head in disappointment. Henry started the car up and began driving down the road. Kate reached in her purse and pulled out a couple of tissue as she wiped her nose. She became lost in her own thoughts. Kate paid no attention as to their direction or the amount of time they had driven. Without even realizing it, Kate soon fell asleep with the rhythm of the road slowly rocking her back and forth.

The sound of the vehicle slowing down caused Kate to stir somewhat. She yawned frequently as she adjusted herself on the car's seat. Looking up she was amazed to realize she didn't know where she was. The city seemed fairly large in size as she glanced around. She looked over at Henry only to realize his attention was strictly on the roadway. He made a turn or two as they made their way through the traffic. Still trying to adjust to her sleepless night, she gave off a large yawn again as she nodded her head back and forth.

"Where are we, Henry?"

"You'll see soon enough."

After making a few more turns Henry eventually pulled into a vacant parking spot. He turned his body to face her. "I don't know if we're here on time or not, but this is the first stop in the bus route from home. If your father is here, this is our best shot at finding him. Kate, if he's not here we'll go on." Henry nodded his head as he spoke. "We'll find him." Kate smiled gently at him.

"Let's see if he's here," Henry said.

Kate nodded her head in agreement as they got out of the vehicle.

The two of them began their search of the bus depot. Within a minute or so Kate suggested they split up to enhance their abilities of meeting with success. Kate headed in one direction, Henry in another. As Henry walked down one hallway he noticed what appeared to be her dad coming out of a washroom, a suitcase in his hand. Henry walked over to him.

"What in God's name are you doing here, Henry?" Christopher asked.

"I think you forgot something back in town," Henry answered. "Come with me, it's over in this area to the left." Kate's father followed Henry, though he had no idea whatsoever of what he was speaking of. Perhaps he had left something in the motel room, he thought. As they turned the corner, there stood Kate. Both father and daughter froze in place. Neither one made any movement towards the other. They stared at one another.

"Here, give me that suitcase," Henry said trying to break the ice between them. Those simple words were all it took. Kate rushed the few feet and grabbed her father putting both of her arms around his neck. He, in turn, did the same to his daughter, wrapping his arms around her body. They hugged for what seemed like a long time to Henry. What a wonderful use of time, he thought to himself. Together they cried. Kate buried her head into her father's chest, he squeezing her long and hard with his arms. People walking by smiled. Reunions at airports or bus depots are quite common in nature, but this one appeared different to the onlookers. Perhaps it was the amount of tears shed, or the fact that they looked so much the part of a father and his daughter welcoming each other home.

As Henry observed them, he formed a plan in his mind. Christopher would move in with them, no question about it. Emma Elizabeth would meet and learn to love her grandfather. If he wanted to work, that was entirely up to him.

Henry could find him a job somewhere… anywhere. He would not push that issue, it didn't really matter to him.

When Kate finally released her father, her eyes were very red, even milky. Christopher's were damp as well. It was at this point that Henry asked Christopher if he could see his bus ticket. Kate's father reached into his pocket and handed it to him to look at. Henry, however, placed it into his own pocket. "You're coming home to live with us, therefore, your ticket is useless. I'll hold onto it as a souvenir of a new beginning commencing today."

"Live with you?" came Christopher's shocked voice.

"He's my husband," smiled Kate.

Christopher's face reflected a complete and utter disbelief. Kate moved over to Henry's position. She reached up and gave him a kiss on his cheek. "My dad will be living with us, that's so wonderful."

"We have the room," Henry said.

"More than enough," she answered.

"I would want to earn my keep," Christopher said.

"How about tutoring our daughter," Kate said. "After all, it was because of you I got such good grades in school."

"Or maybe you were such a smart young daughter," Kate's dad said.

Henry turned to Christopher. He held his hand out to him. The two men smiled as they shook hands. "Welcome home, Dad," Henry said.

"Home is where the heart is," Kate said as she took her father's hand in hers.

"So I've heard," smiled Christopher.

Together the three of them turned and headed towards the entrance. Kate, standing between the two men wrapped her arms around each of the men's waists as they exited the building. The daughter and father were now united, their bond soon to be strengthened with the love each still carried for the other.

Holiday Decisions

As Henry walked into Richard's Steak House, he made his way back to the office. Richard looked up from a pile of paperwork setting before him on the desk. He placed a few sheets down on the desktop that he had been looking through.

"How you doing, Henry?" Richard asked as he rolled his chair back slightly from the desk.

"Better than can be expected for this time of year," he answered.

"I thought this was your favorite time of year with Thanksgiving and Christmas just around the corner?" Richard put his elbow down on the desktop, then rested his chin on his hand.

"It most definitely is, but it sure can be busy with shopping and everything. It's hard not to love this time of year with all the wonderment of the season. I think it has to do with the different colors that light the town, the homes, just everything in general. That's not even mentioning the snowmen and lighted yard fixtures. And when there's fresh snow on the ground, or covering bushes, it's so beautiful."

"One of my favorites is when the bulbs on bushes melt the snow slightly, and then the snow actually turns the color of the bulbs a little bit," agreed Richard.

Henry nodded his head as he visualized it in his mind.

"So what did you need me for? Kate told me you called and wanted to talk to me."

"It's our annual Christmas Show. Can you believe we have five weeks to go and we've been sold out for two weeks already?"

"That's good to hear," Henry said, a somewhat surprised expression showing across his face.

"Henry, I never mentioned this to you, but I actually got calls inquiring about tickets for the program as early as last February."

Henry nodded his head back and forth, his face reflecting a smile.

"I also got a call from our buddy, John Steward, again."

"Oh."

For the last few years Richard would talk to Henry concerning John, Richard's old friend and music producer about an idea John wanted to do. He was relentless in his goal, calling Richard many times during this period. Henry would listen patiently to Richard as he would explain everything to him. Then Henry would once again say, no. As much as Richard tried to convince Henry it was a good idea, Henry's mind was set.

"Look, you're not going to change my mind on this," Henry said.

"Henry, you once told me you thought of me as a very close friend, which is how I feel about you as well. We're more than just partners in a business. Please let me do this with John. I promise you I'll never ask another thing of you." As Richard spoke, he lifted his hand up to show Henry his fingers were crossed.

"Isn't that a way of saying you might not be telling the complete truth?" chuckled Henry.

Richard nodded his head in agreement.

"Alright. Let's go through with John's idea and yours," Henry said.

To both men's surprise, John came walking through the office door.

"Is this a setup or what," questioned Henry.

"What are you talking about?" John inquired.

"You didn't set this up between you and Richard?"

"I don't understand," John said.

"Believe me, Henry, it's not what you think at all," Richard said.

"I just happen to say I'll do the show while you film it, and then all of a sudden you walk in the door," Henry said nodding his head slowly back and forth in disbelief.

"It wasn't a setup, Henry," Richard stated.

If there was one thing Henry knew about Richard more than anything else, it was that he didn't lie. Neither man would ever consider doing that to the other.

"So you're going to let us film the show, wonderful," John said.

Now, explain it slowly to me so I'm sure I understand every aspect of it," Henry said.

It was now the opportunity Richard and John had hoped for. John explained to Henry how cameras would be brought in for the Christmas program. Some additional lighting would have to be put into place, but it would not be obtrusive. They would only be taping the program, not televising it in any way, shape, or form. The program could then be edited as they saw fit. The bottom line was simple; they would have a copy of the Christmas program that could be sold, if it reached the standards of the three men.

Unbeknownst to Richard and Henry, John had already contacted a few television networks to see if they would be at all interested in showing the final product. If not now, maybe some future date, after they viewed it. John had all of the faith in the world that Henry's program would be everything he could ever hope for. This was not the first Christmas program he had seen Henry perform. He had, in fact, taken in many of Henry's holiday programs. John loved the fact that you never knew what to expect in them, and that's what made them so special and unique. When they're spontaneous, John thought, it gives the program a real life feel you just can't plan. The quality was always first rate, he had no worries along that line. Whether he could compete with shows of this nature was no concern to him either. After all, this was Henry we're talking about.

"And one last thing, Henry," John said, "we will need to have a copy of your scheduled songs and so forth. We'll need to know what to expect for camera angles and so forth."

"That will be fine as long as it doesn't get passed around. I want some things to be just available to me should I change my mind and go in a different direction. It's just how I've done things, I suppose I always will."

Richard nodded his head in agreement.

"Okay, I'm on board with you two," Henry said reluctantly.

"Great," John said. "Well, I've got a lot to do now. Thank you, Henry. After years of asking you, I'm finally going to get this done."

"You're welcome."

"I'm going to get started right away. I'll be in touch with you shortly, Richard."

Richard nodded his head as John left the room with a large smile beaming from his face.

Richard started chuckling to himself, and then just loud enough for Henry to hear.

"Okay, what is it?" Henry asked, his curiosity getting the best of him.

"I was just thinking back to when we first got together. You sang to your then girlfriend, Kate, from a corner of the dance floor, my employees telling me all about it. Now look at where we've come since that day."

"What's it been now, Richard, at least eight years?"

"Much more than that, ten to twelve, maybe even fifteen."

"The date really means nothing to me," Henry said, "when we started that is. What's really important to me is the friendship we share; it means everything to me. Our business has surely grown together."

"I know when we added on the addition to the back section for more seating, that was really a big step for me."

"Me, too," Henry added quickly.

"When we expanded the theater section a second time last summer by adding the three hundred plus seats, I will say the big muscle in my chest started tightening up a bit."

"And it was your idea to do it to begin with, remember that fact, Richard," Henry said, his head nodding back and forth slowly as he spoke.

"I can't argue that point with you."

"There is one thing I know many of our customers really enjoy."

"What's that, Henry?"

"When we bought the land for the extra parking. Some of the bus drivers even mentioned that fact to me."

"Me, too," Richard agreed. "Henry, why haven't you moved on with your career? The brass ring only lasts for so long, you realize that?"

"For a couple of reasons. When we first started out in business I made you a promise we'd do it together. I wasn't about to have you spend all of your money, and now mine as well with the addition, and then what, walk out on you. I'm cut from the same piece of cloth as you are. We're both men of our word. Besides, Richard, it's more fun to be a big fish in a small pond, if you know what I mean."

"You could have had the world with your talent."

"There's something to be said about small town life, we both know that. We're very lucky, the people come to us, it's not the other way around. This is where I want my family to live, my daughter to flourish in. I couldn't really ask for anything more."

"I must confess I always have the same problem with you, Kate, and Emma Elizabeth every year."

"What's that?"

"It's when you take your vacations with Melissa, Greg and their little— well, not so little one now, Rose. It just seems so dead around here when you're gone. We all miss you."

"We actually miss being away from here as well," Henry said.

"The two girls have really grown. What are you feeding them anyway?" joked Richard.

"For the last couple of years Greg's mom and dad, as well as Melissa's parents have gone along with us on trips, what have you. I never would have imagined Emma Elizabeth having two sets of grandparents, so to speak. The Summers and Wilsons treat her like their own."

"That's wonderful," Richard said, "and why wouldn't they, they're both great kids. I remember the day you brought every one of them in here for dinner. Those two girls were like two peas in a pod. It was nice for me to see everyone that night."

"When Rose was born, Melissa asked Kate to make her a promise. Simply put, they would see to it the girls' friendship would be as close as their very own. Kate and Melissa work hard at it. They both make the drive back and forth whenever they can to help cement the kid's relationship. I think the one thing that touches me so closely is that not only has that been accomplished by them, but I've seen the two women grow closer as well."

"Say, how is the ad business and store doing, anyway?" Richard asked.

"Great, both are doing very well," Henry nodding his head as he spoke. "I think Greg and Melissa own the advertising company outright now. I'm sure it's been that way for some time though. I would never ask them that, it's none of my business. We're both very happy for them.

Oh, Kate and I went to one of the Summers famous picnics again this year. I love doing the cooking. It seems larger every year, and every year it seems better."

Richard simply smiled.

"Henry, we better get to what I wanted you here for in the first place, or I'll forget what it was. The reason I wanted to talk to you is simple. I need to know if there's anything you're going to require for this year's program. Over the past few years you've always come up with something unique, and I'm sure this one won't be any different, but just the same, is there anything in addition you desire?"

Henry pondered Richard's request for a moment and then nodded his head back and forth. "The only thing I'm curious about, or even gave any thought to was the decorations. Every year you outdo yourself along that line. You really have a knack in making the smallest items come to life."

"My mom and dad always took great pride in making our home warm, inviting and filled with the holiday spirit. As kids we used to even make homemade items, Christmas trinkets we called them. Anyway, I think that's where it all stems from. I guess they're the ones I have to blame for that."

"Or thank."

"That, too," Richard said, nodding his head affirmatively.

"So it sounds like we're basically all set then."

"I'll have everything ready for you but, of course, you still have some of your regular shows to perform in the meantime. I think I'll start adding the stage decorations within a week or two. I've always enjoyed the colors of the Christmas season, no reason it should be any different this year."

"Whatever you think, and if you need any help just let me know."

"Sounds good."

"Well, I've got some odds and ends to do, and my stomach is telling me Kate's dinner is waiting, so I'll see you later."

"Say hello to Kate and Emma Elizabeth for me."

"I will."

As Henry left the room Richard glanced at the desktop. He then reached down and picked up the papers he had laid down earlier and began to study them over again.

Henry walked the short distance down the hallway leading to the main part of the restaurant. A few people sitting at various tables waved to him as he made his way to the front door. Henry acknowledged them as he opened it and walked out the door. Getting into his car, he drove down the street towards his home. The sound of his stomach let out an unfamiliar groan as he made a turn into the driveway of their home. I sure can go for Kate's cooking today he thought as he opened the door and got out of the vehicle. He entered the back door, giving the handle a half turn as he walked in.

"I'm glad you weren't too long," Kate stated as she headed in the direction of the oven to remove the meal.

"So what's for dinner?" he asked as he walked over to her.

"Nothing too exciting, a pork roast and potatoes. I also made up some of your favorite vegetables."

"Sounds great," Henry said, as he gave Kate a small kiss.

"What did Richard want you for?"

"He was wondering about the Christmas program."

"Oh."

"Would you believe we're sold out already?"

"No kidding."

"So, Kate, have you given any more thought about the Christmas program and my idea concerning it?"

"Some."

"And?"

"I just don't know. It's a wonderful idea, but I just don't know."

"Well, it's something we can work on together, but it's not just my decision to make. Think it over, we still have plenty of time."

"Henry, I wish there was something more we could do for the Tucker family. This has got to be an awful time of year for them. People always say the holidays are the hardest times to go through when you've lost someone. The Tuckers deserve better. They're such a wonderful family."

Henry looked at Kate wishing for an answer to her thoughts.

"I've got it, Honey," she was quick to state, her voice excited as she spoke. "Let's send the family tickets to the Christmas program. It's a small gesture but still —"

"Great idea."

Now Kate was silent, but Henry could see in her face her mind was busy with activity.

"I think there's eight of them counting the grandparents. Can you come up with that many extra tickets?"

"I'll make sure we do. I think I'll add something to the program, perhaps a song to honor our service people, maybe just a few words to let them know they're not forgotten by their families and friends wherever they're serving."

"Just like you did some years ago at the church Christmas program."

Henry nodded his head.

"You've given me another great idea, Honey, but I'll still have to check it out with Richard."

"What idea is that?" Kate asked, her face showing a bit of confusion written across it.

"How about adding a matinee along with our evening performance? It's more work, but then we know we'll have the tickets for sure. If we don't sell all the tickets, I'll just entertain whoever is there."

"That would be a first, half a room full of people for you."

"What's your thoughts," Henry said, "yea or nay?" his voice exhibiting excitement as he spoke.

"Let's go for it," she answered, "yes, let's do it," she said in a happy voice.

"I'm sure Richard will go along with your idea, Kate."

"My idea?"

"You always have the best ones, why should this be any different," laughed Henry. "I'll give him a call when we're done eating."

"Good."

"By the way, where's Emma Elizabeth?"

"Visiting with friends this evening."

"When will she be home?"

"Tomorrow, she's at a sleep over with some school friends."

"I'm sure they're having fun. She's a very popular girl, after all, she has her mother's good looks."

"And her dad's outgoing personality."

Henry chuckled. Kate just nodded her head as she placed a piece of pork on her plate with her fork. She began cutting it with a knife.

"And where's your dad?"

"He's over having dinner with Doc and Jean."

Henry simply smiled to himself.

"Kate, how long have Doc and Jean been married now?"

With that simple question being asked of Kate, her mind quickly went back to the day of the wedding. She smiled as she recalled the garden wedding taking place in Doc's backyard. It was a beautiful day filled with an abundance of wonderful memories. Kate smiled as she recalled being in the wedding party with Melissa as bridesmaids. Greg and Henry were the groomsmen. One of her most precious recollections of that day was the fact that Susan was the Matron of Honor. It was Kenneth who felt very proud as he walked Jean down the aisle to be given in matrimony. He felt very honored to be included in this memorable moment in their lives.

Once the ceremony was completed, the parties retired to Richard's Steak House for the reception. It was a day filled with laughter, celebration and most of all love.

When Kate didn't answer him right away, Henry realized she was deep in thought. He didn't say anything more as he spent his time enjoying the meal she had prepared for him.

"This is really another good meal you've made," Henry said as he placed another piece of pork into his mouth."

"I'm learning what seasoning can do to awaken the flavor in different foods. Stella has taught me so much about cooking. She's been an absolutely wonderful teacher. Between her and Susan, I feel the kitchen has become a very comfortable place to be in.

Kate's mind once again drifted back to one late afternoon cooking session at Stella's home. That day Joe came home from work a little early. While standing at the counter, he reached in behind Stella and took a small morsel from a plate sitting before her. This was not an uncommon thing for him to do, loving his wife's cooking as much as he did. When he commented on how tasty it was, Stella told him that it was Kate who actually made the meal. Joe laughed as he informed Stella he now possessed a backup cook if she ever got the flu, and was sick in bed. He told them it was his secret plan all the time, though neither woman held any credence in his story.

"Well, I'm going to give Richard a quick call and see what he thinks about giving two performances."

"Tell him I said, 'hi,' Kate interjected. "Henry, what would you think if the tree we use to decorate the stage for the Christmas program comes from the Tuckers? We could have a little sign or something made for it."

"That's another good idea. I think they would like seeing it on the stage being used."

"It will be as if a piece of their son, Jeremy, is there to enjoy it as well."

Henry nodded his head. What an idea, he thought.

As Kate picked up the table and put the dishes on the counter, Henry made his way over to the phone. Shortly thereafter, Kate couldn't help but overhear the two as they spoke about the Christmas program. From what she could hear of Henry's words, Richard thought the ideas were good ones.

When Henry hung the phone up, he walked over to the kitchen table and took a seat. Hearing the coffee percolator rumbling to a finish, Kate opened a cabinet and retrieved two cups from the second shelf. Placing them down on the counter, she filled them with the freshly brewed coffee. Kate carried them over to Henry as she took a seat next to him. She placed one in front of him.

"Thank you, Honey," Henry said as he picked the cup up and took a sip from it.

"I gather Richard approves of the ideas," Kate stated.

"You aren't going to believe this, but Richard had the same thought running through his mind as well. He said he just didn't feel comfortable asking me to do an additional program."

"Doesn't that beat all," Kate smiled as she took a sip of her coffee.

"Great minds work as one sometimes," Henry said, "yours and Richards."

"So it's all set, one day, two programs."

"Yes. I've never done two before in a row, but to tell you the truth, I think it will be fun to do. The only thing I'll have to worry about is not to forget one song from the earlier program and vice versa.

Richard said he's going to contact the printers first thing tomorrow and get it all rolling, tickets, advertising, everything. This is when I'm happy he's in charge of stuff like that. He does an awesome job, and that fact alone takes a lot of pressure off of me."

"You two make a good team."

"Just like we do," Henry said as he gave her a little wink.

"So you have everything set for the performance now. You know which songs you're going to sing and in what order?"

"Other than addressing a few odd issues and your final decision that I've been waiting for, yes."

"I know you want it to happen, I just have a few reservations. We both know it's a big step forward."

"I understand," Henry said. "Well, there is something you don't know about." Henry bit down slightly on his lower lip. "John, Richard's friend wants to film the program. I suppose they'll do both of them since they can learn from the first one concerning camera angles, where to place things, that sort of stuff."

"Film it?"

"Yes, just so we have a copy we can keep. It's really no big deal." Henry's words almost stuck in his throat with that very statement. He had objected to it over and over again. Now, it was no big deal. Even his own mind suffered a little quake with his statement.

"I don't know, Henry."

He knew he had said enough on the subject, it was now time to let her contemplate her final decision. Any large decisions were always discussed between the two of them, yet this matter bore a different texture to it. They both understood that all too well.

"Well, if it comes down to a tie, I can always flip a coin and see who wins," chuckled Henry.

"Or I can flip a coin," Kate said with a smile on her lips.

"Now there's a thought," Henry said as he shook his head slightly.

"I'll have an answer pretty soon for you."

"That's all I ask of you."

Kate smiled.

As Henry took another sip from his cup, he looked across the table at Kate. She is truly a beautiful woman, he thought. He could see Kate's beauty very much exhibited in their daughter as well. Both possessed a complexion smooth, creamy, and soft to one's eye. Each one possessed high cheekbones. Even for Emma Elizabeth's young age she was stunning. Yes, he thought, thank God she took after her mother. That thought had entered his mind many times, especially when he looked in the mirror at his own image. It was hard for his eyes not to go immediately to his ugly scar. It was that way for him every time he gazed at his reflection. That would probably happen for the rest of his life, he thought. What made him smile inside with those thoughts was one important thing. In Kate's mind, his scar didn't matter to her at all. How extraordinary a woman and wife she was to him. I'm so lucky he said to himself.

Christmas Program

Christmas music from a sound system played softly in the background as people filed into the auditorium and began taking their seats for the matinee program. The atmosphere was not only festive in nature, there was a joyfulness very much present surrounding those in attendance. The room's decorations not only inspired their holiday spirits, it brought forth an enchanted feeling of happiness and contentment. Everywhere smiles were prevalent. One only had to gaze around the large room to observe the excitement that was anticipated and looked forward to by everyone.

A portion of the stage held a huge Colorado blue spruce tree lit by an over abundant amount of tiny colored lights which beckoned to be enjoyed. The branches were decorated with a very odd assortment of ornaments. There were no round shiny modern bulbs; no plastic ones whatsoever someone would expect to find hanging from the tree, or perhaps other such adornments. The beautiful pine tree, however, had popcorn strung on its branches which wrapped around it. In many spots it was tucked into the greenery filling even the smallest of areas. The popcorn led ones' eyes up and down as it made its way around the tree.

That, however, was not the only garnishment which presented itself for the audience to enjoy. A very large assortment of antique hand-blown bulbs also helped to fill many of the branches. Present also were numerous handmade ornaments that were hanging from each bough adding to its glory. Silver tinsel dangled from it everywhere, reflecting brightly the colors of the lights as well as that of the bulbs.

To anyone who was somewhat older in age, the tree took them quickly back to their childhood years. Their minds were able to rekindle once again a forgotten era of their youthful years. It was something they could all enjoy again. The tree was truly magnificent to view. Its form was perfect in every way.

At the very peak of the huge tree was a large silver star. It was not something that anyone could purchase, let alone find in any store. One could imagine finding it within a forgotten trunk in the corner of an attic. It was handmade out of aluminum foil, something a child would fashion with their own hands. The crinkling of the foil gave its shape a very aged appearance. This crumpled affect allowed it to capture even the smallest light's glow, giving the star a personality of its own. It was the finishing accessory that brought the heart of the tree to life.

Beneath it, a large assortment of gifts had been placed. They were wrapped in the traditional color schemes of Christmas greens, silvers, and golds. Huge bows with wide ribbons adorned many of them. The gifts called out to be opened, their treasures to be discovered from within. There was, however, one present that begged to be admired over the rest. It was somewhat larger than the others. One could not help but notice its beauty. It was the only present that bore the color red. Wrapped in shiny red paper, a white-flaked gold ribbon surrounded it. It stood out from the rest. On the front of the package in silver letters for all to see were the words, "Donated by the Jeremy Tucker Family."

Sitting off on each side of the stage were large beautiful plants. There were a total of twelve colorful poinsettias, which sat in large containers. Huge bows and holiday wrapping helped to draw attention to them. Some possessed as many as five to six flowered plants. The various colors of them were very much eye-catching. Richard had decided to use twelve, one plant for each day in the song, "The Twelve Days of Christmas."

On the right-hand side of the stage an old brown piano sat, its bench pulled out somewhat at an angle away from it. It appeared to be waiting patiently to be brought to life. Across the full length on its top was a simple but elegant floral arrangement. It was very much in keeping with the holiday atmosphere that surrounded it.

As individuals found their way to their seats, attached to the back cushion of each one was an envelope. It contained a Christmas card signed by both Henry and Richard wishing them a Merry Christmas, and thanking them for attending.

Henry and Kate peeked through an opening in the curtain, hidden from anyone's view, They watched as individuals picked up the envelopes and opened them. This idea was Kate's alone. From what the couple could see, her suggestion was met with many smiles as people read the cards.

Kate recalled the three of them working on the project. As the two men sat together at Henry's kitchen table signing cards they drank coffee and enjoyed an occasional holiday treat. When they would complain to Kate they were suffering the effects of writer's cramp, she would get them another tasty treat. This seemed to distract them from their aching fingers. It also helped them to make it through the next pile of cards that awaited them. She was sure to see to it that the next batch of cards was always ready and waiting for them, as well as a different selection of delectable treats. The three of them laughed, made little jokes, savoring very much their time together. It wasn't work, it was enjoyable, that is, until the word "matinee" found its way into the conversation. Kate told them not to worry, she had plenty of cards to cover that performance as well. The men grumbled a little bit but continued on with their writing. A few more yummy treats quickly found their way to the kitchen table.

Richard spoke of his childhood, his brother and sisters, his parents. Henry said nothing about his own childhood. He sat absorbing every memory Richard had to tell them, wishing inside he had a happy holiday story he could convey to him. There were none that he could offer. His Christmas memories were of a stocking that never existed, and even if it had, it would be as empty as a moonless night.

Henry always took great care to celebrate this holiday with his family. It was not a time to be taken lightly; after all, it still was his favorite time of year. Perhaps the reason for that alone was because of the loneliness that seemed to grip him inside. He observed the smiles on other's faces as he grew up. No family of his would suffer the way he did. Theirs would be a sky filled with stars, songs sung together around the piano, and most importantly, love to be shared. That was his only wish when it came to a Christmas gift. He smiled slightly to himself as he thought, what better gift could anyone possess.

At one point in the evening, Kate could not resist her temptation to ask Richard a question that had for so long lingered in her mind. She needed her question answered, and for some reason she felt now was the time to get it resolved.

"Richard, can I ask you a personal question?" Kate said. "Now, if you don't feel comfortable answering it, that's quite okay."

"What is it?" Richard replied as he put his pen down on the table.

"Some years ago when we all worked so hard to raise the money to have Josh's leg operated on, you not only bent over backwards in helping us, you did everything possible and more to accomplish our goal. You were a very intricate part of the success we were able to obtain. Before I ask you my question, I just want to thank you again for helping Henry and me out."

"Yes, thank you," Henry was quick to say.

"You're both welcome," Richard said, a gentle smile showing on his face.

Kate nodded her head. She then continued on with her question.

"When you attempted to read the thank you letter in the restaurant to everyone, I could see the difficulty you were having in dealing with it. I also felt the strong emotions that surrounded you. Would you mind telling me why this affected you so much?"

Richard looked over at Kate. She could see he was biting down somewhat on his lower lip with his teeth.

Without saying a word, Richard stood up and walked over to the counter. He filled his coffee cup once again as he leaned his back against the counter. He took a drink from his cup and then looked at Kate.

"It all has to do with Michael," Richard began. "I loved him with all my heart. He suffered from a birth defect, one of his legs being somewhat shorter than the other. Perhaps that fact is why I so deeply understood what this young person was dealing with in his own life, along with his family. In Michael's case, there was nothing that could be done to correct his... his problem. We, however, had the ability to do something to assist Josh. I was very happy to have had an opportunity to help him in any way that I could.

Michael was truly a joy to be around. His heart was filled with so much love. He demonstrated that daily to everyone. Michael never asked for anyone to pity him. He simply loved life. Unfortunately, he was taken from us at much too young of an age. The passage of time has done little to erase the memories I still hold for him so close to my heart."

Richard's voice quivered as he spoke, his eyes becoming watery. He took a very deep breath before he continued on.

"When I heard the circumstances behind what this young boy endured, knowing how his family suffered... just as mine had; I knew in my soul I had to do something to help them. I did it in memory of Michael...my little brother. Michael is in my thoughts every day, and always will be."

Henry and Kate understood his last sentence easily. Thoughts of Kate's mother lived daily in her heart, just as Henry's soul held the same level of memories for Emma and Sam.

"Perhaps now you can understand," Richard said, "why Josh's fundraiser touched my heart so deeply in so many ways."

Richard reached up with his right hand and wiped his eyes.

Kate moved quickly to Richard's side and gave him a hug. Together they shared tears.

Henry didn't find it necessary to say anything in response to Richard's explanation to Kate's question. In Henry's mind, his business partner and good friend took an even higher position on the pedestal he had placed him on in his heart.

"If I may say one more thing to both of you," Richard said as he continued to wipe his eyes with the palm of his hand.

"Of course," Kate said.

Henry nodded his head.

"Henry, through the years I have come to love you and your family very much. In numerous ways I feel a deep kinship between us has grown stronger with each passing day. When I look at you, or when we occasionally sit and talk, I see my kid brother, Michael, very much alive in you. Perhaps that's why I feel so strongly drawn to you. Our relationship is one of the highlights of my life, just as it is with my own family."

Henry walked the few steps to Richard's side. They stood looking at each other for a moment or two. Each of them exhibited a small but distinct smile on their faces. No words were exchanged between the two men on the subject, they just embraced, each one comforting the other. It was a moment in time neither one of them would ever forget.

As Henry and Kate continued watching the audience, she turned to him and smiled.

"Doesn't the stage look simply beautiful," Kate stated as she nodded her head.

"It does. Richard told me a few days ago he had been making homemade ornaments for a few weeks now, that is, when he had the time. As you can see, some of his handiwork is really quite elaborate. Richard mentioned again how it took him back to his childhood memories of his brother and sisters, especially his mom and dad. They all used to make them together each year, and by the looks of these, they had lots of practice doing it. He had to have made the star on the top of the tree."

Kate nodded her head. "Look at the hand blown bulbs, where did he get those? They look just like the ones Emma used to give out."

"Richard told me he spoke to Sid and his wife, Jackie, asking them if he could borrow some ornaments for the tree. Apparently, Sid said he could under the condition the two of them be allowed to help in doing the decorating along with him. I don't know if Sid was worried one might get broken or what." Henry chuckled with that thought. "Anyway, Richard told me he set the time up with Sid, and when he and Jackie showed up, they brought the whole neighborhood along. He went on to say as they were decorating it, he put some Christmas background music on. Apparently, everyone sang along with each song that played. Richard even went so far as to treat them all to a meal when they were done. I heard they all had an absolutely wonderful time together."

"Kind of like what you did some years ago at Emma's," Kate said, "everyone singing together as they decorated her tree."

"Yes, it was."

"Those cameras take up more area than I thought they would," Kate said shaking her head.

"I guess that's to be expected. Oh, by the way, both Christmas programs are sold out. I couldn't believe it when Richard told me that this morning."

"That's wonderful, Henry." Kate looked up at him as she let out a small sigh. Henry knew immediately what she was thinking. "You're really sure about this; aren't you?" Kate inquired again.

"With all my heart. The voice is ready," he answered with a nod of his head.

"Actually, Honey, I'm excited about doing this."

"So am I," he said. We've worked on this for quite some time now. It's time that it come to fruition, and we move on from here."

"Henry," Kate's excited voice exclaimed, "over in the middle... the fourth row back, it's the Tucker family. They all made it."

Henry replied with only one word, "Great."

"Oh, and look to their left," Kate's voice proclaimed again, "it's Greg, Melissa, their daughter and both sets of parents. My dad is sitting next to Doc, and on the other side of them is Jean. Henry, doesn't Jean have a beautiful outfit on?" Kate said pointing with her finger as she spoke. "Oh my goodness, Joe, Stella, and Jake are here, too. I'm so glad Jake made it home for Christmas this year." Kate's smile grew larger as Henry placed his hand upon her shoulder.

"Richard made sure they all got free tickets. I don't know where they're sitting, but he also saw to it that Sid and his wife, Jackie, received tickets for every neighbor who helped decorate the tree."

Henry looked down at Kate's face, her eyes sparkling in the subdued light. He pulled her to him as he reached down gently kissing her on the lips. Kate placed her hand around his neck as she gave it a light squeeze.

"Tonight we take another step forward in our lives," Henry said as he nodded his head.

"Henry, I still have some fears that are surrounding me. I guess I just can't help myself."

"What's your heart telling you?"

"Everything is going to be fine," she said, "and I'm just being foolish."

"Well, I'll be there. To tell you the truth, I'm actually looking forward to this. In fact, I can hardly believe how excited I am to be doing this together."

"Good luck, Honey."

"To both of us," he replied. Henry simply shook his head slightly. He lifted his hand from Kate's shoulder after giving it a gentle squeeze, his face bearing a small smile.

Kate nodded her head. She thought she'd wait for a few moments more to observe her husband as he was introduced.

"Ladies and gentlemen," came the announcement from Richard, "it is with a great deal of pleasure that I introduce to you a man who not only possesses a singing voice from heaven above, but I'm proud to say is a very dear and wonderful friend of mine. So without further ado I proudly present to you, Mr. Henry Paul Morgan."

To say the applause was loud would be an understatement to anyone who was fortunate enough to attend the program. It not only reverberated throughout the large room, it was long and heartfelt by his many fans. As much as Henry tried to quiet the crowd they would not be silenced, they went on for quite some time. Kate watched in awe from behind the curtain she had slightly pulled back as she witnessed her husband enduring the love being demonstrated for him by those in attendance. Henry held his hand up numerous times attempting to quiet them, a microphone clutched in his other hand.

"Thank you so much," he stated over and over, his voice actually quivering as he spoke. "Never in my life have I been so honored by this many people. I am truly taken aback by all of this. Thank you," he again uttered.

Henry never expected this strong of a reaction from the people in attendance. This simple act by the audience was because of what Henry represented to them. He was a man they loved and held in high esteem. Though Henry and Kate never realized it, the two of them were well known throughout the state and beyond.

Henry reached up and wiped his eye with a couple of his fingers. This only brought forth a second stanza of appreciation for him. He was truly overwhelmed. All he could do was to stand there and absorb it. He knew this day would forever be etched deeply into his memory, as well as his heart.

Once everything eventually settled down, Henry began with an older seasonal song, "The Most Wonderful Time Of The Year." As he sang a medley of holiday songs, he could not help but observe just about everyone present was lip-singing along with him. Some of the people in the audience swayed their heads back and forth as they listened to the words.

It was less than a quarter of the way through the program when Henry announced he wanted to take the opportunity to regale everyone with his favorite Christmas carol. Stepping behind the two-stacked electric pianos, he started to play the introduction to the song, "White Christmas." He began to sing. At one point during the song a female's voice began to accompany Henry from behind a curtain in the back of the room. From then on they sang the rest of the musical score as a duet. The unseen voice was full and rich with each and every word that came forth from her lips. The gallery of people was transfixed, as if mesmerized by the sweet nectar of each word that hung gently in the air. It was impressive, striking to listen to. With the end of the song, Henry continued playing softly the melody to the crowd.

"So what do you think of the voice?" Henry asked.

The applause answered his question quickly, they approved.

"Would you like to meet her," was his next question, "and learn a little more about her?"

Again the audience applauded.

As Henry continued playing the song slowly, using it as a background for his inquires; he smiled as he looked around at the various individuals seated before him.

"Would you please join me on stage so we can sing the song once again together. Let everyone present enjoy your beautiful voice in person, as well as your charming personality."

Henry began to sing the song softly again. A small softly lit spotlight brightened the back area where Kate and Henry had stood behind the curtain. A young girl wearing a silver sequin blouse and dark dress slacks, very much appropriate for the holiday season, stood in the spotlight. She slowly stepped forward from the drapes heading in the direction of Henry. Her blouse sparkled with her every step as she walked towards him. Even the sequins on her shoes glittered with her arrival. She was a vision of beauty, and very much younger than her voice led people to believe her to be. Some speculated her to be no more than ten or twelve years old. The crowd began to murmur with the sight of her. All were very much surprised at what their senses told them to expect, and what their eyes revealed to them to be the truth. As she walked towards the stage she once again joined in with Henry as they harmonized together as one. When the song came to an end Henry continued playing the music even though it was drowned out by the audience's applause. Once it quieted down enough, the girl put the microphone again to her mouth.

"This is definitely his favorite Christmas song, but I know in my heart it's the same for many of you here tonight. Would you please join us as we all sing it together. Come on, you all know the words."

As the assembly of people began singing along the young girl walked among the crowd. She periodically held her microphone out to different individuals inviting them to sing into it. This simple act alone made everyone present feel a part of the afternoon program. While the song itself was not long in duration, Henry continued it as long as he could. The verse was repeated over and over again. No one seemed to notice or care. At long last the song came to an end, though the ovation seemed to go on forever.

"We both thank you so much for your applause," Henry expressed, "but more importantly for your help in singing my favorite holiday song. Ladies and gentlemen," Henry continued with a smile, "I would like to take this opportunity to introduce to you the young lady standing next to me, and to thank her once again for helping me in singing, 'White Christmas.' Some of you may already know her, but for those of you who don't, this is my lovely daughter, Emma Elizabeth."

Another sampling of applause was offered to both of them.

"When our daughter was born she was named after my wife's wonderful mother, Elizabeth, and someone who treated me very much with all the love she possessed, Emma, my own mother. While both women passed sometime ago, each of them loved the same Christmas carol. I'm sure they're both looking down at tonight's festivities with smiles on their faces. So with your permission, I would like to have Emma Elizabeth sing that very song to both of them."

It was at this point something very unusual would take place, something that had even been kept a secret from Kate. Henry would accompany his daughter on the piano at home almost daily as they rehearsed her song, as well as various others. Unbeknownst to Kate, the father and daughter team would sneak out of town to accomplish their planned surprise. Going to the recording studio where Henry recorded his own CD's, the secret was put into place. Now they would implement it, and hope that Kate and the audience would enjoy the young girl's efforts.

Henry turned and walked over to the piano and sat down. He placed his hands upon the keys but never struck a note. Looking at Emma Elizabeth, he waited for her to nod her head indicating she was ready. Henry simply nodded his head in return. From the speaker system came the music of a symphony orchestra as it played the introduction to the chosen song. Emma Elizabeth slowly lifted the microphone to her lips as she began to sing "Silent Night."

Kate peeked from beside the curtain she had partially pulled to one side as her daughter sang. Her face bore a look of surprise, not expecting Emma Elizabeth to be accompanied by a complete symphony orchestra.

As his daughter sang, Henry couldn't help himself as he gazed down at the spectators in the darkened crowd. He wondered how they were enjoying the evening, how they liked his daughter's voice. After a short look around he smiled inwardly to himself. He knew the answer to that simple question; individual expressions answered that question for him. He could see the joy that was written on their faces. Inside, his heart sang with joy.

Emma Elizabeth's voice was strong, carrying the words to the song with ease and deeply felt tenderness. Much like a virtuoso playing a violin her notes were likened to its sound. It was similar to a rosined bow being drawn slowly across the instrument's strings by the musician, the fingers gently vibrating. Thus it was with her own voice. It was true and pure, a small amount of vibrato lingering with certain notes.

Halfway through the arrangement, a second voice from the CD joined the young girl. It was the recorded voice of Emma Elizabeth herself. Together their voices melted as one. Emma Elizabeth would sing the higher notes, her voice reaching ever so gently to the heavens effortlessly. As the audience sat listening to the solo, some felt her voice had an angelic flavor to it.

    Then something occurred that was unforeseen, except to Henry and his daughter. Emma Elizabeth began singing in Italian as her counterpart continuing on in English. It was clear to everyone her solo was not only presented in a different way, but filled with loving emotion for the two women the song was dedicated to.

Done in an extremely slow fashion, the room lights began to fade from their illumination. Very few people in the audience even noticed the transition as it took place. The spotlight on Emma Elizabeth grew softer, but not enough to hide her from view. The only two things lit were her and the crinkled star that rested on the tree's top. The rest of the room was blanketed in darkness. As the final word to the song hung in the ears of the audience, it slowly drifted into infinity. It was then when something Henry didn't expect occurred. Not only did the audience give her a showering of praise with their hands, they presented her with a standing ovation. The lump Henry felt in his throat was the size of a baseball.

With the conclusion of the song Kate smiled happily as tears ran down her cheeks. She was so proud of her daughter. Her husband was right, she thought, the voice was ready.

The remainder of the program went very much as it had been planned from the very beginning. There was an abundance of festive holiday songs by Henry, of course, and a few solos by Emma Elizabeth as well. Father and daughter sprinkled duets in Italian throughout the program much to everyone's delight. Some Christmas arrangements had never been heard before by anyone other than Kate and her father in their home. Henry had composed the music and words to these pieces, especially with Emma Elizabeth in mind. They were written to best put forth the range of the four octaves his young daughter possessed. Her voice was truly extraordinary. Whenever she finished a solo, one could easily tell the audience had literally fallen in love with her.

As Richard watched from the back of the room, he felt a hand on his shoulder. Turning he observed his long-time friend, John, standing slightly behind him. Leaning over to Richard, John whispered in his ear. "This program is pure gold. It has everything anyone could wish for. It's like those old variety shows they used to carry on television during the holidays. Thank you and Henry for allowing me to record this program. It's filled with surprises, and talent beyond belief. It will be interesting to see where this takes all of us."

While Richard didn't say anything in reply to John's words, he simply nodded his head as his face bore a distinctive smile.

"I'd like to have a little fun this afternoon, if I may," Henry said with a chuckle. He walked over to the old piano and sat on its bench. "Some years ago my wife,

Kate, then my girlfriend asked me to play a holiday piece for her on this very piano. When I asked her what she would like to hear, she replied, 'Musician's choice.'"

As Henry spoke, Emma Elizabeth made her way over to the electronic pianos. Most of the audience didn't seem to take notice of her movement, being too indulged with Henry's story.

"This old instrument holds a world full of memories for me. It is what I was taught to play the piano on. A wonderful man by the name of Sam Allenby took the time from his own life to teach me. Some of you may even recall him. He was not just a wonderful man, he was a gentleman, something all men should strive to be."

Henry reached up slightly and placed his hand on the top portion of the old piano. It was very obvious as he slid his hand slowly across it, he relived memories of Sam and their precious time spent together. Without saying a further word, he reached down putting his right hand upon the keys dragging them from the lower case keys to the upper. He smiled. "It still sounds just as good as it did then. So with your permission, I would like to play that very holiday piece for you today, and dedicate it to my lovely wife, Kate."

Most members of the audience applauded, while others waited to hear what song he had selected to play for his wife. Once the room was quiet, Henry placed his hands upon the keys bringing the old piano to life as he began playing. The song, however, was presented in a completely different fashion than anyone expected. Henry played four crisp notes, each one the same. Emma Elizabeth answered him with the next four notes to the song from her position at the electric pianos. Her notes were all in the same pitch, though lower in sound. Henry then played four more quick notes, soon followed by his daughter again. From that point, on the two musicians blended their instruments together in harmony as they continued to entertain everyone with the upbeat musical score to "Sleigh Ride." Henry smiled as he looked at Emma Elizabeth, she returning one in his direction. The tandem was literally having fun together.

At the appropriate time in the music, she would make the electronic piano give off the sound of a whip's crack. He could tell by her smile this was her favorite part of the musical arrangement. As they continued playing the holiday piece, each one would take over portions of the score. It was as if the instruments were frolicking back and forth in a cheerful expression of a "Sleigh Ride." When they finished playing, not one note was out of place, dropped, or awry in anyway by either one of them. It was undeniable to everyone Emma Elizabeth was a gifted musician, as well as her father. The audience recognized their performance with a very large amount of applause. Emma Elizabeth and Henry looked at each other smiling. Henry nodded his head slightly as he gave his daughter a wink.

What appealed to the crowd the most, however, were the duets by the father and daughter. It was clear it was the one thing everyone seemed to cherish the most. Henry found it necessary to include her in more parts of the program than he had anticipated, something he truly relished in doing. Their program was lengthened by this very fact, but did either one of them seem to care... not one bit.

As everything finally drew to a conclusion, Henry took the microphone in his hand and made a simple statement to everyone.

"The first time I ever had an occasion to sing in public I sang the song 'I'll Be Home For Christmas.' The words to the song are printed on the back of your Christmas cards. That night a young soldier was reunited with his family. It is a precious memory I hold deeply in a very special spot within my heart. As we go through another holiday season, let us all offer a silent prayer for our service men and women's wellbeing. Let each and every one of us remember how much they give so that we may enjoy this day together... and let us never forget those who gave their all. Tonight, I would like to end this program with that very song. If I may, I wish to dedicate it to the Tucker family in Jeremy's memory, someone many of us knew and loved deeply."

As the orchestra arrangement from the CD played the background to the song, Henry walked the few feet over to Emma Elizabeth's position. He reached down taking her hand in his. They both lifted their microphones as they began singing together as one. After the first verse had been sung, Emma Elizabeth released her hand from her father's grip. She then stepped slightly forward as she beckoned gently with her free hand to the audience inviting them to join in. Within a few moments, the room was filled with the voices of everyone present. The atmosphere was thick and loving. Many couples interlocked their fingers as they held hands, or simply put their arms on their loved one's shoulder or around their waist. A few people had tears in their eyes. Upon the conclusion of the song, Henry and Emma Elizabeth made a simple statement that summed the program up.

"Merry Christmas," his daughter smiled, her hand waving slightly back and forth to the crowd.

"Merry Christmas," Henry said, "and may God bless each and every one of you."

The End

Made in the USA
Monee, IL
22 October 2022